PUFFIN CANADA

THE PRINCE OF TWO TRIBES

Comedian SEÁN CULLEN's many stage and screen credits include the CBC's *Seán Cullen Show* and *Seán Cullen's Home for Christmas Special*, *The Tonight Show* with Jay Leno, the Showcase series *Slings and Arrows*, and the Toronto stage production of *The Producers*. He is the winner of three Gemini Awards. Seán is also a member of the Stratford Shakespeare Festival Acting Company.

THE PRINCE OF
TWO TRIBES

SEÁN CULLEN

P
C

PUFFIN CANADA

Published by the Penguin Group

Penguin Group (Canada), 90 Eglinton Avenue East, Suite 700,
Toronto, Ontario, Canada M4P 2Y3 (a division of Pearson Canada Inc.)

Penguin Group (USA) Inc., 375 Hudson Street, New York, New York 10014, U.S.A.
Penguin Books Ltd, 80 Strand, London WC2R 0RL, England
Penguin Ireland, 25 St Stephen's Green, Dublin 2, Ireland
(a division of Penguin Books Ltd)
Penguin Group (Australia), 250 Camberwell Road, Camberwell,
Victoria 3124, Australia (a division of Pearson Australia Group Pty Ltd)
Penguin Books India Pvt Ltd, 11 Community Centre, Panchsheel Park,
New Delhi – 110 017, India
Penguin Group (NZ), 67 Apollo Drive, Rosedale, North Shore 0745,
Auckland, New Zealand (a division of Pearson New Zealand Ltd)
Penguin Books (South Africa) (Pty) Ltd, 24 Sturdee Avenue, Rosebank,
Johannesburg 2196, South Africa

Penguin Books Ltd, Registered Offices: 80 Strand, London WC2R 0RL, England

First published 2010

1 2 3 4 5 6 7 8 9 10 (WEB)

LIBRARY AND ARCHIVES CANADA CATALOGUING IN PUBLICATION

Cullen, Seán, 1965-
The prince of two tribes / Seán Cullen.

ISBN 978-0-14-317122-5

I. Title.

PS8605.U4255P753 2010   jC813'.6   C2010-905121-1

Visit the Penguin Group (Canada) website at **www.penguin.ca**

Special and corporate bulk purchase rates available; please see
www.penguin.ca/corporatesales or call 1-800-810-3104, ext. 477 or 474

All that I do—books, stories, performances—is
dedicated to my wife, Kimberley.
She is constantly writing the story
of my life without the benefit
of an editor, spell checker, or proofreader,
but she always gets it exactly right.

An Introductory Note
from the Narrator

Hello again, and welcome to the second instalment of The Chronicles of the Misplaced Prince. I'm so pleased that you've decided to read this book. I hope you *can* read; otherwise, this experience will be frustrating for you. If you've read the previous book in the series, you will be aware that Brendan has decided to stay with his Human family despite discovering that he's really a Faerie.[1] Most people would be happy with just one life, but Brendan is determined to have two.

Pretending to be someone you're not is very difficult. For three years I pretended to be the Dalai Lama. No one was convinced, mainly because I didn't look like the Dalai Lama. Nor did it help that the Dalai Lama took out ads in major newspapers warning people that I was trying to be him. I finally gave up. I still haven't forgiven the Dalai Lama.[2]

Pretending not to be someone you actually are can also be very challenging. In the weeks following the adventure detailed in *The Prince of Neither Here Nor There*,[3] Brendan

---

[1] See Book One of The Chronicles of the Misplaced Prince.
[2] Although, annoyingly, the Dalai Lama has forgiven me. Just another reason to be disappointed in him.
[3] See Book One of The Chronicles of the Misplaced Prince.

has been carrying on with his training in the Arts while trying to maintain a normal home life with his Human family. The most difficult part is being unable to share his troubles with his friends. Having erased Harold's and Dmitri's memories of the quest for his amulet, he is now utterly alone in the world.[4]

Fine. I keep having to reference the first book, hoping that you've read it. Why you wouldn't have read it is beyond me. It's a wonderful story and a brilliantly narrated tale. If it were up to me, I'd just soldier on with the second book. However, my editor has insisted that I take this opportunity to tell you what happened in the first. She has no faith in your powers of memory. She also believes that some of you may be determined not to read the first book and start on the second instead. These types of readers should be discouraged, in my opinion, but you know editors: they try to winkle every last penny out of the reading public and are unwilling to leave any eye uncatered to. So, against my better judgment and wishes, I'll provide a brief synopsis[5] of the first book, *The Prince of Neither Here Nor There*.

---

[4]   See Book One of … oh bother! I suppose I have to recap some of the action in Book One. Otherwise, I'll be writing the same footnote over and over again.

[5]   A synopsis is a brief summary of a larger body of work. By its very definition, a synopsis is brief, but I added the word *brief* before *synopsis*. Why this lack of economy with words? I'm paid on a word-by-word basis. So, in a way, I should be glad of the opportunity to pad my wallet with an unnecessary summary of the first book. And I am, now that I've thought it through.

Brendan Clair, a fourteen-year-old student of Robertson Davies Academy in Toronto, is a typical adolescent: pimply, clumsy, and awkward. At school, he spends his time with his little cohort of similarly nerdy friends: Harold Chiu, an artistically talented, overweight boy; Dmitri Krosnow, a Polish immigrant who's trying to master English; and Kim, a sporty tomboy who has hooked up with the group for no apparent reason, given that she's super-cute (just don't try to tell her that or she'll brain you with her field hockey stick). Together, the friends try to negotiate the dangerous waters of the ninth grade while avoiding the attentions of the school bully, Chester Dallaire.

The arrival of a substitute teacher, the mysterious Mr. Greenleaf, sparks off a weird reaction in Brendan. He begins to see and hear things that no one else can. He believes he is going mad. Everything comes to a head when he has a vivid dream in which he is informed by the imposing and terrifying Deirdre D'Anaan that he's not Human but rather a Faerie who was adopted by a Human family. On waking from the dream, Brendan confronts his parents. They confirm that he is adopted, but they themselves are unaware of the Faerie angle. They believe he is a normal boy whom they rescued from an orphanage as a baby. Brendan's sister is furious that Brendan is special and becomes even more annoyed with him than usual. For his part, Brendan wishes he wasn't anything but a normal Human kid.

The next day, on his way to school, Brendan has a series of bizarre experiences: he hears a rock snoring, he talks to a tiny man who claims to be a lord of squirrels, and finally he is accosted by Orcadia Morn, a powerful Sorceress who claims to be his father's sister, his closest Faerie relative. She wishes him to join her in a war against the Humans. But Kim, who it turns out isn't a regular teenage girl but rather a Faerie assigned to protect him, engineers their escape. They race through the subways and sewers of Toronto, encountering magical beings along the way, and end up on the Island of the Ward at the Faerie Refuge of the Swan of Liir. The Swan, and indeed the entire island, is a meeting place for the Faerie Folk of Toronto.

Terribly exciting, don't you think? Take a moment if you need it.

At the Swan, Brendan meets other members of his family and learns the stunning truth: that his Faerie mother died in childbirth and, in a fit of grief, his father, the dark and dangerous Briach Morn, suppressed baby Brendan's true Faerie nature and hid him in a Human orphanage before exiling himself to the Other Side.[6] Are you keeping up?

Brendan also learns that before he can be fully fledged in the Faerie world, he must find the amulet that was stolen from him at birth. With no one else to turn to, he enlists Harold and Dmitri to help. Further developments reveal (what,

---

[6] The Other Side is a netherworld where Faeries live apart, able to watch our world but not participate in it. A Faerie may return from the Other Side rarely, and only for a brief time.

did you think I was going to recite every last detail?) that the amulet is in the possession of a homeless man named Finbar, who's been a fixture on Brendan's walk to school and, it turns out, is an Exiled Faerie, no less. Stay with me. After Brendan promises to help him regain his full Faerie status, Finbar leads the boys to the orphanage where Brendan was left all those years ago. That's when Brendan uses his Faerie powers to erase his friends' memories of recent events and send them to safety before going in to meet his fate.

Finbar lives in the basement of the now-condemned building, and it is there that Brendan receives his amulet, but not before Orcadia makes a last attempt to destroy him by holding his sister, Delia, hostage. This prompts Brendan to unleash his powers—powers he didn't even know he had. Finally, Brendan's estranged father, Briach Morn, breaks through from the Other Side, pulls Orcadia out of the world, gives Brendan his secret name, and initiates him before returning to the Other Side forever. Phew!

So that, in a nutshell, is what any dumdum should need to get on with the rest of the story. I want you all to know that I wrote the above under protest and will be submitting an official complaint to the Narrators' Grievance Committee. So there, Editor! Eat that!

As I said before, Brendan is now quite alone in the world. He has Compelled Harold and Dmitri to forget everything that happened. His sister's memory of events has been similarly expunged.[7] Now he must face the challenges of his training alone.

Another fly in the ointment,[8] as if one were needed, is that Brendan has developed some kind of block with respect to his Faerie abilities. He can't connect with the energy of the universe. Something is holding him back. He is increasingly convinced that the problem is a mental block rather than a physical one.

Mental blocks are the most difficult to overcome. They are problems we create for ourselves out of our own fears and hidden desires. I myself have experienced many different forms of mental blocks. Of course, as a narrator, I have experienced Writer's Block. Most writers refuse to even mention Writer's Block for fear of contracting the condition. I'm not one of those superstitious types. I have no fear of Writer's Block. I can say it any number of times and know that it's not like some kind of virus that will affect my mind, taking away my ability to write. Writer's Block. See? Still writing! Writer's Block. Writer's Block. Writer's ...

...

...

Sweet, blazing fish dumplings! I'm back. Certainly it's unapparent to you that for the last four months I've been going through the most horrendous writing dry spell of my

---

[7] Could have said *erased*. Said *expunged*. Deal with it.
[8] I've often wondered why flies are so attracted to ointment. Very little research is available on the subject.

long career. I've been sitting looking at the blank page for days on end, weeping in frustration. After intensive therapy I'm finally able to put pen to paper and continue with this story. From now on, I beg you not to mention Writer's ... You-Know-What. Not even in casual conversation. If you have to mention ... "it" ... do so a good distance away from the book and in a very low voice, preferably with a foreign accent that's difficult to understand without listening carefully. I will never mention ... "the thing" ... again. From now on, let's have a code word for that "thing." If we must mention it, I will refer to it as "my cousin Dave," and you'll know that what I really mean is Writer's Block ...

...

...

...

That bout was worse than the last. I almost missed the publishing deadline. Please. Please. Please. Don't mention "my cousin Dave" again or you'll never find out what happens in *The Prince of Two Tribes.*

Enough about "my cousin Dave"! Let's get underway. Many readers have been writing me with questions. "What's the Pact?" "Are there Faeries in other countries?" "How do Faerie powers work?" "Is a platypus a mammal or a reptile?" All good questions, but only three are relevant to our story. I hope the book will answer them. But I thought the Pact might deserve a little explanation of its own. Therefore, I've decided to write a prologue for you, which I have pithily entitled ...

Prologue

The battle was over.

Black, oily smoke rose, drawn into long, dark ribbons against the leaden sky. In the west the sun hung low on the horizon, staining the blanket of clouds a bloody red. The wind swirled around the hilltop, whipping cyclones of snow around the silent figures who surveyed the battlefield.[9]

The war was at an end, with great loss to both sides. The Alliance of Free Humans and Fair Folk had defeated the Dark Ones and their army of Human slaves. Now the victors stood on the hill, waiting to decide the terms of peace. Their faces, still begrimed with blood and soot, were grim. Many Humans had been killed and many Fair Folk sent on the final voyage to the Far Lands.[10]

They stood in the centre of a ring of ancient stones, their black surfaces etched with intricate symbols. Each stone stood higher than a tall man's head, and together formed a rough crown for the hilltop. In the centre stood a single stone, twice as tall as the others but of the same dark rock.

---

[9] The location of this battlefield is the topic of some debate among Faerie scholars. Some place it in western Europe. Some insist that the battle took place in the steppe country of what is now called Russia. Still others suggest that it took place on the site of a shopping mall in New Jersey. We may never know for sure.

[10] The Far Lands are the Fair Folk's equivalent of heaven.

Around this solitary stone, the victors were gathered. Pennants attached to long spears snapped in the breeze.

"A woeful day, my Lords," said Merddyn, the most senior of the Faeries and leader of the Fair Folk. He appeared to the Humans as an elderly man, though still tall and sound of limb and bright of eye. A long white beard, matted with mud and filth from the battle, hung down the front of his simple black armour. His sinewy arms were bare and patterned with tattoos. "Much is lost, but we have gained an important victory. Our rebellious brothers and sisters have been brought to heel. Now perhaps there will finally be peace between our peoples."

"Aye, peace," said the Human King, scowling through his thick beard, black and streaked with grey. His face was smudged with soot and blood, a patch covering the scarred socket where his left eye had once been. "Peace. But for how long? What's to keep your folk from rising against us once more in times to come?"

"You have no right to insult us in this manner," one of Merddyn's commanders said disdainfully. "We have fought by your side to bring the rebels down. We have even slain brothers and sisters! Such a sacrifice, turning against our own … "

Merddyn laid a hand on the Faerie's shoulder.

"Forgive Ariel." Merddyn smiled sadly. "The war has been hard on him, especially raising arms against his own brother. To question his sincerity is unkind."

"I spoke rashly and thoughtlessly. I apologize, Lord Ariel." The Human King bowed his head slightly. Ariel grudgingly returned the gesture. The King continued. "You have been true to your word, but the fact remains …

Your folk live long. I will pass away, and so will my children and their children. How can we ensure that in the future Humans will be safe?"

"The generations of the People of Metal[11] may pass quickly compared to ours, but remember this: though your time upon this Earth is shorter, you are also more fertile. You will soon greatly outnumber us. That, in essence, is what sparked the conflict between our peoples.

"The time has come for us to go our separate ways. We separate until Faeries and Humans learn to live together in peace, without jealousy and fear. While we wait for that day, we will come to an agreement. We will mark out the boundaries of our future."

The Human King nodded grimly. "So be it. We shall have a Pact."

"First, some unfinished business. We must deal with the prisoners." Merddyn raised a pale hand and beckoned to a knot of people waiting at the bottom of the hill. The Human and Faerie warriors moved forward, forcing a group of shackled figures ahead of them. The Humans carried heavy swords forged of dull black iron, their armour a hodgepodge of leather and metal plates. They were heavily bearded and scarred, and they were all male. The Faerie warriors also wore armour, crafted of thin pieces of glimmering crystal. In their hands they carried weapons made of the same ghostly material, fancifully carved and decorated but

---

[11] *The People of Metal* is the Faerie term for Humans. They call us this because of our propensity to mine for ore and craft things from it and because of their physical aversion to iron, which causes a bad reaction on contact with Faerie skin, ranging from rashes to toxic shock and death.

deadly nonetheless.[12] The Faerie troops were made up of both male and female warriors, long-limbed, lean, and dangerous. Some bore tattoos that wound in intricate patterns of leaves, stylized animals, and flames over their entire bodies. Shimmering colours tinted their skin and hair.

Marching together, the warriors of the two races prodded their shackled prisoners up the path until they arrived before the Human King and Merddyn.

The prisoners were weighed down by iron collars that hung from their necks, bound by lengths of chain to fetters on their hands and feet. As they came to a halt, they fell to their knees under the weight of the iron that was already burning painful welts on their skin. All save one.

The leader of the vanquished Faeries strained to remain upright despite his pain. He clenched his teeth as he raised his face to look at his captors. The Humans, including their battle-hardened King, took an involuntary step backwards as they saw the naked rage and hatred that twisted the otherwise handsome face. Merddyn didn't flinch. He met the fierce gaze with a stony glare of his own.

"Taín Mab Dubh." Merddyn's voice cut easily through the howl of the cold wind. "Taín, Son of Darkness: this is the name you chose for yourself. You defied the will of our rightful Council and took up arms against family and friends. You declared yourself above and outside our Law." Merddyn's voice commanded the attention of all. "You are finished. You and your followers have lost the battle and the war."

---

[12] This crystal material is somehow spiritually linked to its owner. When the owner dies, the armour melts away, returning to the Earth. This is the main reason Faerie artifacts are rarely found. They're biodegradable. Always thinking, those Faeries.

Taín laughed. "Wise Old Merddyn. Selfless Merddyn." The Dark Faerie Lord sneered and spat at Merddyn's feet. "Merddyn the Fool. With you by my side we could have crushed the People of Metal. Now you would have us living as outcasts on the edges of the world, left to haunt the dark and lonely places. Ghosts! Worse than ghosts, for are we not flesh and blood?"

"Taín, you are wrong." Merddyn shook his head sadly. "To fight the Humans is futile. One might as well take up arms against the tides of the seas or the winds or the air. They will outnumber us ere long. An honourable peace is what we must have to ensure that we survive."

"Pah! Peace? Slavery! The People of the Moon were born to rule. You have doomed them with your cowardice. You are all cowards!"

Ariel lunged forward, too quick to be restrained, and struck the prisoner across the face with the back of his mailed hand. The crack of the contact echoed on the hillside. Taín staggered and fell onto his face.

"Keep your idle taunts to yourself, dog! Merddyn fears no one, least of all you!"

Taín forced himself up onto his knees. He grinned, bright blood drooling from his split lip. "All slights will be remembered, *Brother* Ariel! Lapdog Ariel! Your treachery will be remembered and *avenged*," the Dark Faerie hissed. He lunged against his chains but succeeded only in pitching himself forward onto his knees.

A Faerie in exquisite armour inlaid with pearls reached out and restrained Ariel. "We all have reason to be bitter," the Faerie said, his grey eyes full of pain. "We must learn to forgive."

"Never." Ariel's voice broke. "He killed my sister. Let me go, Greenleaf." Ariel was weeping now. "Let me go."

"Enough!" cried Merddyn. "The time has come for judgment." Merddyn raised his hands above his head. Silence reigned on the hilltop. Even the wind seemed to pause. "Taín Mab Dubh, you have broken our Law. Now that Law will judge you. You shall be bound and imprisoned by our strongest Ward. The term of your confinement shall be the term of this world's existence. Your prison shall be within the Bone of the Earth itself." Merddyn drew back his arm to indicate the standing stone that occupied the centre of the circle. A ring of Faeries stood around the stone. As Merddyn nodded, they began to chant an eerie melody that made the hackles on the necks of the Humans rise.

Slowly more Faeries joined in. The chant grew stronger, filling the very air with a shiver of power like the resounding of an invisible bell. The stones in the outer circle shimmered, steaming gently as the water on their surfaces evaporated, boiled off by a mystical inner heat.

"What is this? What Ward is this?" A tremor in Taín's voice betrayed his growing fear.

"A Ward devised especially to contain you and your fellows," Merddyn replied. He raised his arms with a shout. The voices of the Faeries rose to an ear-shattering shriek.

The stone at the centre of the circle erupted into white-hot flames blazing with tightly leashed energy. The Faeries, too, radiated power, their hair standing out, crackling with blue sparks.

"No! NO!" Taín struggled against his chains. His enemies watched with horror as their leader was dragged by unseen forces toward the glowing stone. Taín clawed the turf, desperate to stop his progress.

"You cannot hold me!" the Dark Faerie Lord shrieked. He was almost at the foot of the stone. "You have not defeated me!"

Taín was drawn into the blazing stone, sinking into the shining surface like a rock into a pool of glowing oil. A clap of thunder rolled out across the battlefield. The light died, leaving the rock standing still, cold and black.

Merddyn turned to the other prisoners. "You have seen what will happen to those who continue to rebel. If you agree to accept the Pact with the People of Metal and live by its articles, you shall be freed. But … " Merddyn's eyes hardened. "Should you break the Pact, you will face the same dire punishment. What say you?"

The Dark Faeries were silent. The lesser among them turned to those who'd been the lieutenants of Lord Taín. There were three of them: a brother and sister, Orcadia and Briach Mac Morn. They were pale of skin, beautiful to behold even in defeat. They sneered defiance. The third was tall, with dark brown skin. His long chestnut hair hung in curls around his face. His mouth curled in a crooked smile, his honey-brown eyes crinkling with humour.

"Well, now! Very generous terms, I should think." He chuckled. "One would be a fool not to accept."

"I'm glad you see it that way, Pûkh," Merddyn replied. "I would not wish to continue this conflict. We have all suffered enough."

"I agree." Pûkh grinned, showing bright, even teeth. "Besides, there is plenty of world for all of us to share.

I don't expect I'll ever be completely at ease around Humans, not the way you are, but I will find a little patch for myself and those who wish to come with me."

Merddyn didn't respond. He turned to the Human King. "Strike off their chains."

"And then?" the King growled.

"Then we have a Pact to strike."

"There are still fugitives," the King said. "Not all surrendered and not all lie dead below."

"They shall be hunted down and given the same option," Merddyn said.

"And if they refuse?"

"There are many more stones like those in this circle," the Ancient Faerie said with great weariness. "Come, there is much to discuss."

Greenleaf went to a Faerie who knelt in the mud, her armour spattered with blood and grime. Her golden hair hung in muddy tangles. As he approached she looked up and smiled.

"Brother," she said. "I have missed you."

"And I you, Deirdre," Greenleaf replied with a sad smile. He reached out an elegant hand and helped her to her feet. "Let us go home."

Later, in the darkness, Merddyn made his way back to the circle of stones. The talks had gone late into the night, but the Pact was in place. After long negotiations, the Humans and Faeries had agreed on three basic rules. First, Faeries could continue to live among Humans as long as they submitted to Human rule. Second, Faeries were forbidden to interfere in Human affairs. Third, any of the Fair Folk who refused to accept the Pact were to be exiled to the

Other Side.[13] Or, they could choose to live in one of a few Sanctuaries established by the more powerful Fair Folk. These Sanctuaries were forbidden to Humans and would be hidden from the world by powerful glamours. Pûkh was already gathering supporters to join him in a kingdom he planned to call "Tír na nÓg," or "the Everlasting Lands."

Merddyn simply wanted peace. The Pact was difficult to accept, even for him. Essentially, it made Fair Folk dependent on the goodwill of Humans for their continued survival. He imagined a future in which Faeries would fade from Human memory, existing only in legend, as tales to frighten children around hearth fires.

Merddyn had one more task before he could rest. He wearily entered the circle of stones, lit up by the moon's silver light. The stones now contained imprisoned Faeries, those who'd refused to accept the terms of the Pact. With the Faerie glamours, no one would recognize the rocks as the prisons they were.

Merddyn closed his eyes and let the energy gather in him. He reached out with his mind, raising his arms, palms upward. Beads of sweat instantly popped out on his forehead.

With a grinding sound, the stones rose from the ground, trailing clods of black earth. The massive rocks hovered for a moment, then began to circle Merddyn. Faster and faster they sped. The roar as they passed through the air was like the scream of a hurricane.

Suddenly Merddyn dropped his arms. The stones shot off in all directions, catapulting high into the atmosphere.

---

[13] The Other Side is the netherworld that exists in the space between the physical world and the Afterlife. Faeries who grow weary of life sometimes choose to enter the Other Side.

The speed of their passage ignited the air. Like shooting stars in reverse, they flew higher and higher. The central stone lanced upwards like a rocket and disappeared into the dark sky.

Merddyn fell to his knees, exhausted. His limbs quivered as he gasped for breath.

"That was a pretty piece of work, Merddyn."

He looked up to see Pûkh standing across from him on the now-empty hilltop. Behind him stood two Faeries, a tall man with silver hair and a dour face, and a tiny woman with wide grey eyes and a vague, dreamy smile.

Merddyn rose shakily to his feet. "The stones are hidden now by glamours and distance. Not even I know where they will fall. They will never be found."

"Never is a long time, Merddyn." Pûkh chuckled. His pale brown eyes twinkled. "A long time."

With that, Pûkh turned and melted into the shadows, his two companions close behind.

PART 1

Feet in Both Worlds

SCHOOL

"I'm outta here!" Brendan announced, cramming the last of his books into his backpack. "It's Friday and I'm gonna go straight home. I might sit in my room and listen to music. I might lie on the couch and watch TV. I might just stare at the walls, drooling. I don't care! It's Friday and I'm going home."

Harold looked annoyed. "We still haven't gotten any work done on our presentation for social studies. No, let me rephrase that: *you* haven't gotten any work done on our presentation for social studies."

"We only have until next Friday, Brendan," Dmitri agreed. "We'd better get on the bowl."

"Ball," Brendan laughed. "Not bowl, Dmitri."

They were standing in front of Robertson Davies Academy's main entrance. Students streamed past them down the stone steps, eager to start the weekend. Only one week remained before the Christmas break, and the mood was high. Exams would follow the two-week layoff, but no one worried about that now. All thoughts were on freedom.

"Can't we just put in a couple of hours now?" Harold pleaded. "I'm serious. I don't like leaving things until the last minute."

Brendan swung his bag over his shoulder, shaking his head. "Sorry, guys. I just want some time to myself. I've been really busy lately."

"Oh? We hadn't noticed," Harold said sarcastically.

"What have you been up to, Brendan?" Dmitri asked in a gentler tone. "You've been very reoccupied."

"Preoccupied. And it's just stuff. Family stuff," Brendan said vaguely. He was telling the truth. Most of his time outside of school was being eaten up by "family" activities. His Faerie relatives were keeping him busy training him to harness his new abilities. He spent every extra minute with Kim, Greenleaf, and other Faerie tutors working on his new perceptive skills. When he wasn't doing that, he was being thrashed in sparring sessions with Saskia, the Warp Warrior who tended the bar at the Swan of Liir on the Ward's Island. So far, his schoolwork hadn't suffered too badly, but his friendship with Harold and Dmitri had. He hardly saw them outside of class. As he looked into their faces, he saw that they were unhappy. He had to make a gesture of some kind.

"Listen," he said. "Why don't we get together on the weekend and do the work then? You guys can come to my house and we'll get the presentation into shape."

"I guess," Harold said reluctantly.

"My mum will probably be baking this weekend."

Harold's face visibly brightened. The chubby boy was a fan of Brendan's mum's cookies. "Okay. When should we come over?"

"Tomorrow," Brendan decided. "Let's say, two o'clock."

"Okay." Dmitri smiled.

"See you then," Brendan said. He waved and set off toward the park and home.

Dmitri and Harold watched him go.

"I wonder what kind of family business he's got that keeps him busy every night of the week," Harold pondered.

"Who knows?" Dmitri shrugged. "My family keeps me busy, I guess. My babka hasn't been feeling well."

"I'm sorry to hear that," Harold said. "Tell her I say hello."

"Really?" Dmitri asked, confused. "Okay. But you've never met her before."

"Haven't I? I thought I had once."

"I don't think so."

"I could have sworn I had." Harold's eyebrows scrunched together as he tried to dredge his memory. "I could have sworn."[14]

"Don't worry about it." Dmitri clapped him on the back. "Are you taking the streetcar?"

"Yeah," Harold said. "Let's ride."

As Brendan waited at the crosswalk for the light to change, he saw Chester Dallaire on the other side of the street. They hadn't spoken since he'd released Chester from the Compulsion in the hospital room weeks ago. Chester had only just returned to school after a long psychiatric evaluation.

He was no longer the same hulking bully who'd terrorized their little group every day. He was quieter. He kept pretty much to himself, having discarded the cadre of rough friends he'd once run with. He'd lost weight and cut his hair.

Brendan felt a pang of guilt. These changes were the result of his actions. He had unwittingly used his powers on Chester, powers he'd been unaware he even possessed. Chester had been bullying Brendan and Kim

---

[14] Of course, Harold *has* met Dmitri's babka, but that day was erased from their memories. Again, read the first book. If you haven't yet, why are you reading this one, you strange, strange person?

when Brendan had said simply, "Get lost!" He'd learned the hard way that he had to be careful what he said to Humans. A Faerie can Compel people to do things with words alone, and the stronger the will behind the words, the stronger the Compulsion. Brendan's command had sent Chester fleeing across the country in a desperate, mindless effort to lose himself. The police finally found him and sent him to the hospital until Brendan released him from the Compulsion. Brendan remembered that moment and the grateful reaction of Chester's mother with a great deal of shame. He hoped that Chester was okay and had suffered no lasting damage. When they passed each other in the halls, Chester never spoke to him but just nodded in acknowledgment. At times, however, when Brendan was in the cafeteria or standing talking with his friends, he'd catch Chester staring at him. Brendan wondered how much of his ordeal Chester recalled and if he knew of Brendan's involvement.

Chester was trudging north to the subway entrance. He must have sensed Brendan's eyes on him because he looked up directly at him. He stared for an uncomfortable moment and then nodded his head once. Brendan lamely waved a hand and looked away, walking across the street into the park.

The high-pitched buzz of a small engine approached. Kim coasted up on her scooter, her silver crash helmet flashing in the weak December sunlight. Her real name was Ki-Mata, but she allowed Brendan to call her by the name she used in Human company, Kim.

"Is that a new scooter?" Brendan asked.

"Yep! Og totally freaked when I told him how the other one got trashed. I had to beg and plead and generally grovel, but he agreed to build me a new one." Og was Brendan's Faerie uncle. A rough and hearty fellow, he hardly seemed the type to be good with his hands. Og was an Artificer, however, the Faerie equivalent of an engineer.[15] He had built a scooter for Kim, which she'd trashed during the headlong escape from the mad and dangerous Orcadia. "He wasn't happy, but in the end, he couldn't say no."

"I'll bet." Brendan laughed. He couldn't imagine many people, Faerie or Human, who'd stand in Kim's way if she really wanted something. In spite of her toughness, she was what most of the boys at RDA would call a hottie. But should any of them call her that within earshot, she'd likely brain them with the field hockey stick that perpetually jutted out from her backpack. Brendan supposed that was part of the reason she was so appealing. She was pretty and kind of terrifying at the same time.

"What's your problem?" Kim asked suddenly.

Brendan realized he'd been staring at her. He tried to look nonchalant. "Nothing."

"How have your training sessions been going?" Kim asked.

"Brutal. I can't seem to get anything right. I've lost whatever connection I had to my abilities."

"Sorry, Brendan. You've got to get up to speed. You have to practise."

---

[15] Artificers use their Faerie powers and skill at working with their hands to create functional works of art. They harness spirits to build motors. They place extraordinary power within ordinary objects. They also reproduce Human technologies in forms that Fair Folk can use. Faeries adore Human gadgets: cellphones, MP3 players, DVDs, and computers are all fascinating to them. Sadly, because of the Faeries' strong magical affinity, most Human technology won't work for them. That's where Artificers like Og come in. They build items that function just like the Humans' versions but run on the natural ambient energy of the Earth.

"Why? What's the big rush? Faeries live a really long time, right? I have years to practise. Decades! Centuries!" They crossed the street into Queen's Park. The trees were stark and bare now. No snow had fallen yet, but Brendan could sense the winter in the rawness of the wind as it rattled the dead leaves around their feet. One of the benefits of being a Faerie was the way his senses were heightened and tuned to nature in a way he'd never imagined before the glamours that concealed them had been lifted.

"See ya 'round. Get some sleep tonight. Or better yet, work on your meditation!" She gunned the motor and took off across the park.

"Oi! I'm trying to get some shut-eye here!" a little voice cried. Brendan unzipped his jacket to reveal BLT stretching her tiny arms as she stood in his inner pocket. Ever since his uncle Og had gifted the Lesser Faerie's services to Brendan on his Quest for the missing amulet, she'd been his constant companion. She had a taste for sweets that bordered on addiction. Blinking, she looked up at Brendan and flapped her gauzy wings.[16] "What's the racket?"

"You shouldn't sleep so much in the day," Brendan scolded. "You end up being awake all night."

---

[16] Faeries are only one of many different types of what Humans might call Magical Races. The Faerie world is divided into two major types of Faerie: Greater and Lesser. Greater Faeries are of normal Human size and possess various kinds of powers. Lesser Faeries, or, if one is more politically correct, Diminutives, are small enough to sit in the palm of one's hand. They come in a vast array of physical forms. Some resemble birds. Some are mammalian. Some look like insects. Many but not all varieties of Diminutives can fly. Some even live in and breathe water. BLT's real name is Basra La Tir, but Brendan calls her BLT because he found her hidden in a sandwich.

"What can I say? I'm a night person." She yawned and burped.[17]

"Well, I'm a sleep person. And I want to get some. So try to shift your schedule."

BLT scowled. "What am I supposed to do all day while you're in that idiotic Human school?"

"What did you do before you were assigned to me?"

"Sleep."

"Oh brother," Brendan groaned.

"Who are you talking to?"

Brendan nearly jumped out of his skin. He spun around to find a girl standing on the path. Thin and pale, she wore an oversized black leather motorcycle jacket over a Weezer T-shirt and tattered black jeans. Her black hair was gelled up into a spiky mohawk. On her hands, she wore black woollen gloves with the fingers cut off, revealing black painted nails.

"Sorry." She laughed. "I didn't mean to scare you."

"You didn't," Brendan said quickly. "I just didn't see you there."

"Of course you didn't." She smiled. "Nobody sees me unless I want them to." Her blue eyes sparkled. They were a blue that Brendan had never seen on any person before: sapphire shimmering with deeper shades of violet. He realized then that she was a Faerie like him.

His heart raced. He'd been told by Ariel, Greenleaf, and Kim to be wary of any Fair Folk who approached him

---

[17] Greater Faeries, unlike Humans, require very little sleep. They replace sleep with short periods of silent, trance-like meditation. Lesser Faeries, however, are like Humans in their need for sleep. No one knows why. One theory is that they burn more energy, like birds. Another is that they're too high-strung to meditate. Yet another is that Lesser Faeries are just too lazy to learn how to meditate. I'd subscribe to the last theory.

without a proper introduction. After his experience with Orcadia, that seemed like sound advice.

The girl stepped closer and held out a hand. "I'm Charles." She pronounced it "Sharles." "My friends call me Charlie. You can, too, if you like." She spoke with a soft accent. She sounded French or maybe Quebecois.

Brendan stared at the hand but didn't reach for it. "Charles? That's a boy's name."

"Real smooth." BLT had crawled out of her hiding place to sit on Brendan's shoulder.

"Shut up, you little pest," Brendan said.

The girl dropped her hand and shrugged. "It's my name. I'm a girl. That makes it a girl's name, doesn't it? Don't I look like a girl to you?"

"Uh, yeah. I guess so," Brendan said dumbly. She was a little punk for his taste. Still, he could see that under the makeup, hair, and shredded clothes, there might be a pretty cute girl. He pushed the thought away. He had to concentrate. This could be a potentially dangerous situation.

He looked around for Kim but she was long gone on her scooter. He had to deal with this on his own.

"What's the matter?" Charlie pressed. "Am I scaring you?" She laughed, crinkling up her nose. He felt sure she was mocking him. "You look a little worried."

"I'm fine." Brendan didn't know what to do. He knew other Faeries lived in the city. He saw lots of them in the Swan and sometimes on the street, going about their business like ordinary citizens. He sensed them. More accurately, he felt they were different, like him. They never approached him, however. They nodded or smiled and went on their way. Ariel had laid down the rules where Brendan was concerned, and the Fair Folk in Toronto followed them. He was not to be approached, and his Human family was off limits.

In spite of the rules, here was this Faerie stopping him on his way home from school. He didn't know what to do.

"I've got to be going," he said and started walking away.

She trotted after him and matched his stride. "You don't want to meet me?"

"No thanks."

"You're very rude." She pouted.

"Just leave me alone, okay?" Brendan said, trying to walk faster.

She matched his pace easily. "Don't you like girls?"

Brendan stopped and faced her. "I'm not supposed to talk to strangers." As soon as he said it, he felt like an idiot. "Just leave me alone, all right?"

"He's right! He's not supposed to talk to you!" BLT confirmed. Somehow, a tiny person sticking up for him made the situation seem even more childish and humiliating.

"Lose the big idiot and spend a little time with Lord Chitter, yer ladyship!" came a voice from below. "I can certainly appreciate a pretty girl." They looked down to see a tiny man dressed in what appeared to be the fur of a grey squirrel. He held a minute spear in his hand. He blinked his glossy black eyes and grinned. Chitter bowed low, sweeping off his little cap. Brendan had made Chitter's acquaintance only a few short weeks before on the fateful day he'd spent running from Orcadia. The Lesser Faerie ran with the squirrels of Queen's Park, pilfering picnic baskets and generally making a nuisance of himself.

"*You're* the idiot," Brendan shot back. "And you're only five inches tall."

"You're the idiot," Chitter retorted, "'cause you ain't interested in her."

BLT fluttered into the air, pushing up her sleeves. "Don't you call Brendan an idiot!"

"Or what?" Chitter stuck out his tiny chin.

"Or I'll thrash you, you furry little creep!"

"He's an idiot and that's the truth."

BLT snarled. "All right. You called down the thunder!"

"Hold on, there!" Brendan quickly grabbed BLT before she could launch herself at Lord Chitter and stuffed her into his jacket pocket. BLT shrieked and struggled but Brendan zipped up his pocket, trapping her safely inside.

"Now look what you've done!" he snapped at the strange girl. "Just leave me alone." Brendan turned on his heel and marched away.

The girl caught up with him as he reached the far end of the park. "I don't want to cause you any trouble. I just want us to get to know each other."

Brendan whirled on her. "I'm not interested, all right? I can barely keep the friends I have. I don't need any new ones."

"I want to help you," she said. "I know the training is hard for you."

"And you're making it harder. If you really want to help, just leave me alone." His voice rose to a shout. A couple walking by stared. Embarrassed, he simply turned and walked away.

Charlie didn't follow. When he ventured a look over his shoulder, he saw her standing at the edge of the park, watching him. She gave him a cheeky little wave. Brendan sneered and turned toward home.

INSTRUCTION

"Concentrate!" Mr. Greenleaf's crisp command rang in Brendan's ears.

"I'm trying," Brendan grumbled, his breath steaming in the cold, clear morning air. "It isn't easy, you know. And I'm *tired*," Brendan said pointedly. Greenleaf had called him at 6 A.M. and demanded a training session that morning, despite the fact that it was Saturday. Brendan had made his way grudgingly to the ravine Greenleaf had specified, an out-of-the-way spot in High Park where they could train without anyone about.

"Don't bother answering me! If you're talking, you aren't concentrating," Greenleaf chided.

Brendan bit off a reply. He was losing his cool with his teacher and with himself. Greenleaf was wrong. He'd been concentrating so hard for the past hour that he felt the beginnings of a headache blossoming in his skull. He had to make a conscious effort to unclamp his jaws. No matter how hard he tried, he couldn't maintain his focus for long. Greenleaf had been uncharacteristically stern when Brendan had arrived at the training session. Usually, the dapper Faerie was mild-mannered and affable. He had a seemingly inexhaustible reserve of patience. Today, he was harsh in his criticism and testy in his comments. Brendan had never seen him behave this way.

I imagine I'd be sick of teaching me after a few weeks, too, he thought to himself.

Brendan tried to calm his mind, once again bending his will upon his current test subject.

The brown chickadee hopped about the clearing oblivious to Brendan's efforts, following the desires of its tiny brain and ignoring Brendan's attempts to influence it. Brendan could sense the staccato thoughts of the jittery bird just at the edge of his perception, but he couldn't read them clearly or manipulate them in the slightest. It was like trying to read the pages of a book through a pane of frosted glass while riding on a train. What he'd done effortlessly while fleeing from Orcadia, communicating with the birds, using them to help him escape, now seemed completely impossible. The failure was both exhausting and infuriating. After another moment of futile mental strain, Brendan threw up his hands in frustration and disgust.

"It's hopeless."

"Nothing is hopeless. You're just lazy, that is all." Greenleaf leaned against the thick trunk of an oak tree at the edge of the clearing, his arms neatly crossed, a picture of composure. As always, he was impeccably dressed. Today he was wearing an exquisitely tailored three-piece suit[18] of sage green fabric that showed off his lean frame to perfection. Over his suit, he wore a three-quarter-length grey topcoat that hung open. Though the early winter morning was crisp,

---

[18] The three-piece suit has become a mainstay in men's tailoring: pants, jacket, and vest. It's much more classy than the one-piece suit (also known as overalls) and less unwieldy than the eight-piece suit (basically a three-piece suit with two scarves, a hood, one glove, and pantyhose).

he was unaffected by the cold. He scuffed the dry leaves with his foot in a show of impatience. "You must concentrate and stop wasting my time."

Brendan and Greenleaf were in an isolated clearing in High Park, the vast forest in Toronto's West End. In mid-December, few members of the public were taking advantage of the park. After training almost exclusively on the Ward's Island in the Swan of Liir or thereabouts, Greenleaf had thought that getting away from prying eyes and the spectators that Brendan tended to attract might be a welcome change and give him a different perspective. "A change is as good as a rest," the dapper teacher declared.

"A rest is also as good as a rest," Brendan grumbled. Greenleaf merely laughed and ignored his student's griping. Which annoyed Brendan even more.

He'd wanted nothing more than to relax at home the night before, but his mother had other ideas. She recruited him as an escort and baggage handler on her trip to the mall. Christmas was great. Brendan wasn't one of those people who hated the holiday, but fighting through the crowds at the mall to get that special gift at that special price wasn't his idea of a good time. He wished he could turn on his Faerie speed and whip through the job in a minute or two.

Unfortunately, not only would his mother have seen him for what he really was, but he was also completely unable to conjure up his Faerie abilities whenever he wanted to. For some unknown reason, he was having trouble connecting with his gifts and practising the Arts with the ease other Faeries could manage. There were many theories about why. Greenleaf and Kim believed he was having a mental block because his Faerie nature had been suppressed by his father's magic for so long.[19] Briach Morn had woven powerful glamours to hide his son in the Human world. Perhaps they had stunted his abilities. Og thought that his skull might be a little too thick and offered to drill a hole in Brendan's forehead to let the energies escape more easily. Brendan graciously declined that offer. Whatever the real reason, Brendan had to endure endless training sessions, which was why he was here, in the damp, misty park at ten on a Saturday morning instead of wrapped up in his bed, sleeping in like a normal teenager.

Still, it was a novelty to be out in the open air. He and Greenleaf were all alone, with no distractions. Maybe that was a good thing after all.

The clearing they occupied was in a ravine, away from the path. To make sure they wouldn't be observed, Greenleaf wove glamours all about the clearing to deter casual observers who might wander through. Though they were out in the fresh air, Brendan felt oppressed by his own failure. Greenleaf pushed him hard, and the pressure was starting to take a toll. They'd been working all morning and Brendan was exhausted, with no progress to show for his efforts. On top of that, it was a Saturday, a day for goofing off, not for trying to practise mind control on birds.

For what seemed like the fiftieth time, Greenleaf demanded, "Concentrate!"

"Yeah! Concentrate!" BLT echoed. She sat on a branch above, chewing a slice of pineapple with a desultory sneer on her face. Brendan had been trying to get the little

---

[19] Please do not mention "my cousin Dave."

Faerie to eat fruit instead of junk food to get her sugar fix, but BLT wasn't enjoying the switch. Beside BLT sat Titi, the Diminutive Faerie who was Greenleaf's companion. Titi was altogether more refined than BLT. She sat primly, watching the proceedings with mild interest. Where BLT was rough and ready, her clothes slightly dishevelled and stained, Titi was a proper little fashion plate, fastidiously coiffed and carefully clothed in the finest mini, ultra-fashionable designer wear. How she got such tiny clothes, Brendan couldn't guess. Perhaps she stole them off Barbie dolls in the super-chic shops of Yorkville.[20]

"You can do it, Brendan!" BLT called. "Concentrate!"

"I'm trying to concentrate! How am I supposed to concentrate with you saying concentrate every five seconds?" Brendan snapped, kicking the tree trunk in frustration. The chickadee, startled by the sudden movement, flitted to a higher branch.

"That tree never did you any harm," Greenleaf said dryly.

"Never did me any good, either," Brendan retorted.

"Oh, but it does do you good. It is part of a massive interconnected system that provides you with the air you breathe and the food you drink," Greenleaf said, stroking the bark of the huge tree lovingly. "You are a part of this tree. We all are. Kicking it is like kicking yourself."

---

[20] Yorkville is a part of Toronto where rich people buy expensive things. They aren't necessarily nice things, but if they are expensive, rich people feel obliged to buy them to prove that they are rich. It's a sad, endless cycle of spending. I wish I had that problem.

"If I could kick myself, I would,"[21] Brendan said, slumping to the ground. "I just can't seem to do anything," he groaned. "I can feel the bird's thoughts like an itch in my brain, but I can't get inside them."

Greenleaf studied him for a long moment, a thoughtful expression on his face. He pushed himself away from the tree trunk and stood in front of Brendan. "You lack motivation, that's all," Greenleaf said. "You were under duress, fearing for your life at the time. The terror focused your mind. You have to learn to do these things without any threat."

"Maybe it was a fluke. Maybe I haven't got any power of Compulsion. Maybe whatever gift I had got burned up or something ... or worn out. Have you ever thought of that?"

"Interesting theory. Very interesting indeed." The tutor pushed away from the tree and stood erect. The corner of his mouth turned up into a sneer. "That would mean you are utterly defenceless ..." His pale grey eyes narrowed.

Brendan took a step backwards. The look on Greenleaf's face was one he'd never seen before. It was dark and predatory. Greenleaf took a step toward Brendan. Brendan backed away, bumping into the tree stump with the back of his legs. "I ... I guess so."

"And no one knows you're here," Greenleaf hissed. "What a foolish, trusting child you are, Breandan! You let me lead you out here into the woods alone where no one

---

[21] People often use the expression "I could have kicked myself ... " I don't think it's possible. I was part of a scientific research group that attempted to study the act of kicking oneself. Despite extensive trials and the waste of a lot of government grant money, only one of us managed to kick himself, and that was after his leg was severed in an automobile accident.

could help you. Not even that annoying Ki-Mata can save you now."

"What?" Brendan was confused. For the first time, he realized how strange it was that Kim hadn't come along. She usually didn't let Brendan out of her sight for long. When Brendan had questioned her absence at the beginning of the session, Greenleaf had said she was busy, and he'd taken that for granted. "What are you talking about, Greenleaf?"

"Now you will pay for what you did to me!" As Brendan watched in horror, Greenleaf's face flowed and swam until the handsome features were transformed into the leering face of Orcadia Morn.

"Whoa!" BLT cried. "You get away!" The Lesser Faerie reared back and hurled the remainder of her pineapple slice, hitting Orcadia in the side of the face. Orcadia snarled and sent a lancet of purple energy at BLT, striking her from her perch. She fell motionless into a drift of leaves.

"BLT!" Brendan cried, stricken.

Titi rose from the branch, transforming before Brendan's eyes into a spiky little bat creature with a wet, snuffling muzzle and talons for hands. She fluttered to Orcadia's shoulder and perched there, watching Brendan with glassy black eyes.

"She's gone! Worry about yourself," cackled Orcadia.

"No! No! This isn't real," Brendan stammered. "You've gone to the Other Side. My father sent you there."

"Fool." She waved an arm and the whole of her body was transformed. She was Orcadia Morn, beautiful and terrible. Her wild white-blond hair crackled and snapped with energy. She raised her hands, holding them slightly apart. Brendan watched, mouth agape, as a ball of energy gathered between her palms. "This time you won't escape."

"This can't be happening … " Brendan gasped. "Green-leaf … "

"That simpering dandy was no match for me. I took his place, concealed by glamours. Now I will have my revenge." She leapt forward. "You followed me to your doom, like a lamb to the slaughter."

She was right: no one knew where he was. He couldn't even cry for Human help, concealed as he was within the glamour surrounding the ravine. Kim didn't know where he and Greenleaf had gone. He was utterly alone. If he was going to survive, he had to do it without any outside help.

Brendan scrambled backwards, falling over the stump to escape her attack. The air rushed out of his lungs as he slammed onto his back on the hard ground. Gasping for breath, he scrabbled through the carpet of dead leaves as Orcadia came on, igniting the dry grass where she stepped.

"I will!" she cackled. "There won't be enough of you left to sing a song over!" Orcadia raised her hands. Between her palms, a fierce light collected as she drew energy from the surrounding air. He watched in fascination with his acute Faerie Sight as tiny motes of light swirled into a ball. He smelled ozone and felt his hair begin to stand on end from the static electricity. "Breandan Morn! Prepare to DIE!"

TALENT

Brendan's mind flooded with panic. His heart was racing. He couldn't get enough air into his lungs. *Do something!* his mind screamed.

"You can't escape," Orcadia cackled. "And no one can help you. It's just you and me!"

Brendan's back came up against the rough bark of the tree trunk. He could flee no farther without turning his back to the threat. His chest heaving, he pressed himself into the tree, wishing he could disappear. His eyes searched for a way out, and he almost failed to see the crackling orb sailing at his head. He ducked and rolled, coming to his feet as the tree erupted in flames.

How had Orcadia managed to fool everyone? How had she escaped from the Other Side? His father had said she couldn't come back!

"You can't be here!" he said suddenly. "This isn't real."

"It's real, weakling." Orcadia raised her arms and purple fire erupted above her. The flames fanned outward and ignited the dry, dead branches of the winter trees. Instantly, the forest above Brendan was ablaze.

"Stop it!" Brendan cried. He was terrified, not only for himself, but for the Humans who might see the flames and come to investigate. He knew Orcadia had no compunction about revealing herself to Humans and wouldn't hesitate to harm any who came near.

Brendan pushed himself up onto his toes in a fighting stance as ash and cinders began to rain down. Sparks ignited tiny fires in the dry leaves on the ground around him. "Go back to the Other Side, Orcadia. You can't do this here."

"Why don't you cry for your Human mother, weakling?" Orcadia laughed. "Don't worry! She won't survive long after you're gone. Neither will your father or your sister."

Brendan gritted his teeth. The thought of his Human family in danger awakened something within him. "You will not touch them," he said coldly.

"Or else what?" Orcadia sneered.

"GO!" he shouted as powerfully as he could, putting all his anger and fear behind that one word.

Orcadia shuddered. Battling against the Compulsion, she clawed the air for purchase. Brendan's heart soared.

"I did it!" he crowed. "I did it! I Compelled you!"

His elation died as he saw Orcadia's features grow calm and her shuddering cease. She shook herself like a dog climbing out of a pond and then stood still, a vicious smile blooming on her lips. "Nice try. Is that the best you can do?"

Brendan didn't answer. He merely closed his eyes and stretched out his thoughts.

The sensation was like flinging a door open in the back of his mind. Suddenly, he could feel everything: the jittery minds of the birds in the trees flickering like strobe lights, the buzzing slumber of young raccoons curled in their dens, nestled against their mothers. He even heard the cold, alien pinpoints of thought that marked the passage of ants, worms, and insects as they burrowed in the soil underfoot and in the tree bark, seeking refuge from the winter's chill. He reached out with his mind, looking for help …

That's when the park warden ran into the clearing.

Obviously, the warden had seen the flames and was coming to investigate. Seeing Orcadia, she stopped short and stared, her face a mask of shock. She was perhaps twenty years old, looking pathetically defenceless in a green parka with the city parks logo on the sleeve.

"What's going on here?" the warden asked, her eyes taking in the bizarre scene.

Brendan lost his concentration immediately. *How had the warden gotten through the glamours protecting the clearing? Maybe Orcadia isn't worried about maintaining them anymore?* In desperation, he cried, "RUN!"

The woman hesitated for an instant, and that was enough time for Orcadia to act. As the warden turned to flee, Orcadia let loose a crackling ball of power that sizzled after her, striking the girl directly in the back, turning her into a staggering mass of flame. The warden screamed, ran on for a few ragged steps as if trying to escape the agony, and fell to the ground, her synthetic jacket blazing.

Brendan couldn't believe his eyes. He stood rooted to the spot, unable to shift his gaze from what seconds before had been the park warden. At last, he turned to see a look of crazed, gloating satisfaction on Orcadia's face.

"What's the matter, nephew?" she smirked. "She was only a Human girl. They're a dime a dozen. They breed like lice, Humans."

"I'll kill you," Brendan said through gritted teeth.

"Ah! The creature has some claws after all. Let's see if he can scratch!" She flung another crackling orb of power, aiming squarely for Brendan's chest.

Without thinking, driven by rage, Brendan warped into motion, tapping into the bizarre energy that made him a Warp Warrior. He felt the world around him slow down. Even in the throes of his fury, Brendan loved this feeling. Though he always had trouble reaching a warp state, once he was there, he never wanted to let go. To him, it seemed as though he were moving at normal speed while the whole of creation moved in slow motion. He saw the dry leaves on the trees slowly crisping as they smouldered in the cold wind. He could almost see the air moving the branches, the charred particles streaming past. Overhead, the clouds had ceased to trail across the face of the sun, arrested in their passage across the sky. Brendan, despite the threat facing him, grinned with delight.

Turning his attention back to Orcadia, he watched the sizzling ball approach, fire boiling up and dying down like solar flares on the surface of a tiny sun. Brendan almost laughed out loud. "This is too easy!" He stepped to one side as the ball of energy drifted harmlessly past. He turned to face Orcadia.

"Time to slap you down again," Brendan said grimly. "Don't you ever learn?" He dashed to the side with the intention of going around behind his adversary. His plan was good, but it didn't survive his running into the tree trunk. Where there had been open space before, a solid oak now stood. He crashed into the rough bark of the thick trunk and staggered, falling onto his back in the carpet of musty leaves.

His nose felt as if it had been whacked with a hammer. Spots swarmed before his eyes. He tasted blood in the back of his throat. He tried to sit up, but Orcadia's foot slammed him back to the ground. His vision cleared. Orcadia leaned over him, her head blotting out the weak early-winter sun. The branches of the hoary old oak tree waved.

"Well," she snarled. "That was too easy! I made you think the path was clear and you ran straight into a tree. Fool! A child could have seen through that trick! But then again, you are a child and a fool both!" The bat creature on her shoulder chittered with laughter.

Her tone twisted in Brendan's heart like a knife. Her disdain ignited something in his soul. He would not be beaten. He cast his mind about, searching for some contact. *Birds? No. Not powerful enough. Bugs? Not enough of them in the cold weather. Raccoons and squirrels? Maybe ...*[22]

Then he felt it. A slumbering yet powerful presence, so ancient and deep that it formed an underlying hum of life, slower and more ponderous than the animals and birds and insects. He reached out to it with all the strength his soul could muster. He felt the presence stir.

"Well?" Orcadia barked. She pushed her foot harder into his chest, her slim heel gouging his ribs. Brendan ignored the pain. He concentrated as hard as he could. He felt the thing stir. His mind was filled with a huge and powerful voice ... The thing was speaking to him, but it wasn't really a voice. More like an intention, a question.

Help me! Brendan shouted with all his might.

He got through. There was a ripping, popping sound of something tearing loose from the ground. Orcadia yelped in surprise as a tree root as thick as a man's arm coiled around her ankles and yanked her from her feet. Brendan

---

[22] Never count on a squirel or a raccoon to have your back. Anybody with a peanut or a crust of bread can distract them.

gasped for breath, hauling himself erect. He watched in wonder as the scene unfolded before him.

The oak tree was moving. The root circling Orcadia's feet wound tighter and moved higher to grip her waist. As Brendan watched in amazement, one gnarled limb of the ancient oak bent down and entwined Orcadia's arms, pinning her to the earth. The tips of the branches dug deep into the dead leaves and into the soil, completely immobilizing the flailing Faerie Sorceress. She struggled mightily but to no effect. The oak's limbs were filled with strength, the wood unbreakable. The grinding and popping of the woody sinews was like a series of gunshots in the crisp winter air.

Brendan couldn't believe what had happened. "Did I do that?" he whispered.

"The tree did it," came Greenleaf's voice, obviously in some discomfort. Even stranger, the teacher's voice was coming from Orcadia's mouth. "You asked it to help you and it did."

Suddenly, the flames that had been blazing all around were extinguished. In fact, no sign remained that there had been any fire at all. The clearing was restored to how it had looked before Orcadia had wrought ruin upon it.

To Brendan's astonishment, BLT leapt up from the leaves and flew to his shoulder. "Nice one, boss!" she cheered, pumping her fist.

"BLT! You're okay!"

Brendan looked down and was shocked again to see that Orcadia was melting away. In her place lay Greenleaf, trapped beneath the tree's limbs, his clothes rumpled and smeared with dirt. Titi melted back into her normal shape, flitting down to rest on Greenleaf's chest, dusting leaves from his jacket with fastidious flicks of her wings. Despite his situation, he smiled up at Brendan.

"We played a little trick on you, I'm afraid," Greenleaf chuckled. "A glamour to make me appear as Orcadia. I had to frighten you into using your powers. Obviously, you haven't lost them. You just need to have a little incentive."

"But the girl?" Brendan sought out the place where the park warden had fallen and saw only a raccoon waddling away.

"An improvisation on my part," Greenleaf said. "I made you see a girl in place of the raccoon."

Brendan shook his head in disbelief. Then another thought struck him. "Wait a minute. I *talked* to a *tree*!"

"Ah, indeed." Greenleaf nodded. "That actually *did* happen. It's quite amazing. Ki-Mata will be very excited to hear about this. Apparently, you also have a latent Talent for manipulating the green world. Remarkable!"

Brendan tried to absorb this news. "I can talk to birds. I am a Warp Warrior. I can Compel people, and now I can talk to trees!"

Mr. Greenleaf grunted. "And I think it would be an excellent idea if you would talk to this tree again and tell him to let me go."

"Oh, yeah. Okay." Brendan closed his eyes and thought hard. He reached for the mind of the tree. He could still sense it, but somehow it was slightly out of his reach.

"Uh-oh … " Brendan scratched his head. "I'm not sure I can."

"Of course you can. Just try."

Brendan closed his eyes and tried to shut out everything but the sound of the tree. He concentrated for a minute. Then another. Finally, he threw up his hands.

"I can't do it! I can feel the tree's mind, but I can't seem to get through."

"Oh dear," Mr. Greenleaf frowned. "I don't relish lying out here for the next few days."

Brendan snapped his fingers. "I know." He reached into his pocket and drew out the small block of smooth wood that was his Faerie cellphone. Og, his Artificer uncle, had fashioned it for him to replace the one that was fried during his last adventure. All his old electronic devices had suffered a similar fate. In the end, Og had made him a new watch and an MP3 player out of Faerie-friendly materials. The watch served as a sort of glamour projector, as well as a timepiece. He had trouble maintaining a reliable Human disguise but was getting better all the time. The watch was a useful backup for when he dropped his concentration.

Tapping the centre of the block, he waited for the faint glow of the keyboard to appear and started to dial. "I'll call Kim. She's a pro with vegetation, isn't she?"

"No!" said Greenleaf with uncharacteristic desperation creeping into his voice. "Not Ki-Mata! I'll never hear the end of it!" Greenleaf and Ki-Mata had a rather adversarial relationship. Though both were participating in Brendan's Faerie education, they often had differing opinions about what form that education should take. Ki-Mata would revel in Greenleaf's predicament.

"I'd say you haven't got much choice." Brendan kicked one of the thick roots imprisoning Greenleaf. It didn't budge.

"Very well," Greenleaf sighed. "Call the she-devil."

"Ho! Ho! Ho!" BLT crowed. "This is going to be good!"

Titi sneered.

THE HOT POT

Brendan glumly took in the view out the window of Roncesvalles Avenue below. Pedestrians, shoulders hunched and umbrellas clenched, leaned into the wind that had blown up on the way to the café from the park.

Until a few weeks ago, Brendan would have been just as uncomfortable in the cold and wind as those unfortunate Humans. Since his initiation into the Faerie world, he found that the weather didn't bother him anymore. His Faerie heritage was proof against most extremes of cold and heat. He found, instead, that he relished the coming of winter in a way he never had before. His senses were awakened to the subtlety of the natural world. He could smell the rain. He could hear the approach of the winter. He felt the ground settling and steeling itself against the encroaching frost. Brendan marvelled at the newfound depth of his perception. He found it confusing and exhilarating at the same time.

One hazardous element of the change was that he had to be on guard at all times around his family and friends. Already, he had slipped up on a couple of occasions, walking out the door wearing only a T-shirt on sub-zero mornings or making comments on the voice of the wind or the minute cries of dying leaves to Dmitri and Harold. The way he could hear these things was often quite distracting.

He was learning to filter them out when need be. They became like a background hum or white noise most of the time. If he did get lost in the world's secret sounds, Kim was usually quick to kick him on the shin under the table or glare a warning at him. Brendan was aware, though, that he wouldn't always have her there to catch him when he slipped up.

Thinking about Harold and Dmitri depressed Brendan. He missed the easy friendship they'd shared before he found out about his Faerie nature. Only a few short months ago, Brendan, Harold, and Dmitri had found one another on their first day at Robertson Davies Academy. As they skulked together through initiation week, hiding from the worst of the hazing, they formed a bond. They were the nerdiest of the nerds. Harold, overweight and sensitive, was a brilliant artist, rarely seen without a sketchpad under his arm and charcoal smudges on his fingers. Dmitri, small and cheery, was the object of many a bully's attentions, with his strange accent and trusting nature. But together, they covered each other's backs.

That's what they used to be like. Now their relationship was strained. Brendan no longer had to wear braces or glasses, and his acne was largely gone.[23] He was no longer clumsy, thanks to heightened Faerie awareness of the world around him. And along with the physical changes had come a change in their relationship. Brendan had to maintain a safe distance from his friends in order to keep his secret. Having a secret was lonely, and Brendan's loneliness was even deeper because they had shared an adventure that Harold and Dmitri could no longer recall. Dmitri and

---

[23] One good thing about being a Faerie was that Brendan could alter his Human guise. It was better than Clearasil!

especially Harold were wary of him in a way they'd never been before. Brendan had no idea what to do to alleviate the problem. He hoped their friendship would survive the strain.

Brendan felt himself sinking into self-pity. To distract himself, he looked around the café. Though he'd had weeks to get used to the idea, he was still shocked at how the Faerie world existed in the cracks of the Human world. The café they sat in was a good example. Before his awakening to his Faerie side, he'd walked by this corner many times. Where Roncesvalles split with Dundas Street West stood a bank building that was now occupied by a coffee chain. Brendan had shared a hot chocolate with his father a couple of months ago and never suspected that a café catering to Fair Folk existed on the same spot.

Kim had arrived at the park in good humour to find Greenleaf trapped in his wooden prison. After a few minutes spent savouring his predicament, she'd made the roots of the tree narrow slightly so that Greenleaf could wriggle out. Mission accomplished, the three of them had walked over to the café for a hot drink. But instead of stopping at the coffee bar, Kim and Greenleaf continued through to the hallway that led to the washrooms. Brendan was puzzled.

"Aren't we going to have a drink?" Brendan asked.

"Yeah," Kim said. She jerked a thumb at the ceiling. "Upstairs."

"Upstairs?" Brendan hadn't noticed any upper floor. He followed Greenleaf and Kim into the hallway. Brendan expected his friends to go to one of the restroom doors or the employees' entrance. Instead, they walked directly into a blank wall between some stacked boxes of paper cups and vanished through the solid surface. Brendan stopped short.

"Hey!" The wall looked completely solid to him.

A young woman in a green apron came out of a door marked EMPLOYEES ONLY and found Brendan staring at the wall. "You looking for something?"

"Uh," Brendan stammered. "I, uh … " How could he explain? *My friends just disappeared through a wall.*

Suddenly Kim's head popped out of the solid surface. Waves spread out from her like ripples in a pool. "You coming?" Seeing the young woman, Kim smiled. "Hey, Cassie. What's up?"

"Not much," Cassie replied. She smiled at Brendan. "You must be Brendan."

"Yeah." He nodded, still a little confused. "You're … one of us?"

Cassie winked and grinned. For an instant, Brendan glimpsed her true appearance, her dark hair sparkling with silver streaks and her golden eyes. The moment passed and Cassie returned to her glamour as a mousy-brown-haired Human woman. "First time at the Pot?"

"I guess so," Brendan answered.

"Have the hot chocolate," Cassie suggested. "And good luck with the Proving Challenges. I'm sure you'll be awesome!"

Cassie turned before Brendan could answer and went back through the employees' entrance. Brendan stood looking at the door. "Proving Challenges?" Brendan didn't like the sound of that. "What's she talking about? Proving what?"

Kim ignored his question. Grabbing his elbow, she pulled him through the wall.

He found himself at the bottom of a stairwell. Golden light shone down from above as he mounted the stairs.

Lively conversation, laughter, and the hissing squeak of a milk steamer greeted his ears as he rose into a warm, airy room.

Brendan stood at the top of the stairs and looked around. Tall windows lined the walls, looking out over the street. Rain pattered on the skylights above, mixing with the mutter of conversation to create a pleasant buzz. Small, round tables were filled with Faerie patrons of every description. Here and there, Lesser Faeries flitted in the air, some delivering drinks or pastries, others merely visiting with friends. Behind the counter, its wood polished to a golden lustre, a male and a female Faerie worked swiftly, steaming milk, drawing espresso, plating delicious-looking cakes and pastries.

"Brendan!"

Kim and Greenleaf had found a table by the window and were waving him over. He wended his way through the small forest of tables. He was so distracted, gawking around the room, that he bumped into an old man.

"Excuse me," the old man said. For an instant, Brendan's eyes were gripped in the bluest, most intense gaze he'd ever encountered. The old man smiled.

"Forgive me, lad. I'm awfully clumsy."

"No problem," Brendan mumbled. He was about to apologize himself, but the man moved on. Brendan turned and watched him go to the stairs and disappear. He was struck by the sudden realization that he'd never seen an old Faerie before. He was about to go after the old man when Kim called again.

"Brendan? Come on!"

Brendan shook his head and went to the table.

"What's the matter?" Greenleaf asked.

"Nothing." Brendan shrugged. He was about to tell them about the old man, but something made him reluctant to mention him. He sat down, his mind's eye still full of that blue stare that seemed to come from a million miles inside the old man's head.

"Hey!" BLT's head popped out of his breast pocket. She had taken shelter from the rain on the walk over and now looked about eagerly. "The Hot Pot? They have the best pastries here." The Diminutive Faerie began to climb out of her perch.

"No way!" Brendan said. "You aren't allowed any sugar."

"Come on," BLT pleaded. "Just a little bit. I need a pick-me-up."

"Uh-uh! It's for your own good. We'll see if they have any fruit."

BLT mimed barfing and dropped onto the tabletop. She began hunting for stray crumbs or grains of sugar.

Kim stood up. "What'll ya have? My treat."

"Café au lait," Greenleaf said.

"Uh … " Brendan shrugged. "Hot chocolate, I guess."

"With plenty of whipped cream," BLT chimed in.

Kim nodded and went to the counter to order.

"Sorry, Greenleaf," Brendan said for the fortieth time since the incident at the park. "I didn't mean to cause you any trouble. I guess I didn't really have control."

Greenleaf waved away Brendan's apology with an elegant hand as he removed his gloves. "Think nothing of it. I was trying to provoke a reaction from you and I did. You acted instinctively. I want you to remember how you felt in that moment because that is the place inside you that you need to tap into when using your new abilities."

"Yeah, right!" Brendan snorted. "I don't want trees crushing people all the time." *Besides, I don't want to be angry or afraid all the time.*

"Don't worry. Control comes with practice. I doubt that trees will attack very often." Greenleaf laughed. "Seriously, though, I want you to try to access that place when you're not in a stressful situation. You didn't hurt me, but when your power comes from a place of strong emotion, you tend to lose control."

Kim returned to the table and sat down. "Drinks will be here in a minute." She smiled sweetly at Greenleaf. "You're lucky I could bail you out." Kim's sardonic comment broke into Brendan's reverie. She grinned and winked at Brendan. "I may not be there next time you get into trouble."

"I'm eternally grateful, Ki-Mata. You, however, took your sweet time." Greenleaf sniffed and plucked a dead leaf from his rumpled jacket, crinkling his nose. "This will never do." He ran a hand over his jacket and the wrinkles disappeared completely, as though his palm were a steam iron.

"Please forgive me." Kim grinned. "I got here as quickly as I could." She started to giggle. "I'm just glad I got to witness the great Greenleaf in such a compromising position."

"Very amusing it was, I'm sure."

"Oh, it was. It truly was."

"I'm so glad. However, I believe there is another aspect of this incident that is far more intriguing. Our plan to push Brendan out of his comfort zone has yielded some interesting results, more interesting than we could have imagined. It would seem that our Brendan has another Talent."

"Yeah." Kim raised an eyebrow. "Looks like you've got the same gift as me. Welcome to the Green Art Club, Brendan!" She punched him in the arm.

"Ow," Brendan grunted. "That hurt." Kim may have looked thin, but her willowy frame was strong as steel.

"Sorry." Kim laughed. "You're such a little girl!" Brendan immediately tried to return the punch but Kim swivelled her shoulders, making him swing wide. His arm followed through and swept BLT from the table.

"Waaaaa!" the tiny Faerie cried as she tumbled backwards, flapping her wings furiously. Titi sat primly on Greenleaf's shoulder, casting her eyes heavenward as she took in BLT's antics.

"If I may interrupt your playtime, children," Greenleaf said, shaking his head, "I don't think what Brendan has manifested is the Green Art. From what he described feeling, I believe we may be seeing a different kind of Art altogether."

"What do you mean?" Kim's face became serious. She swung her brown eyes onto Brendan and looked at him with interest.

"Drinks coming through! Hot stuff!" a squeaky voice cried, breaking into the conversation. A fluttering gang of Lesser Faeries struggled to keep a tray of foamy beverages aloft and upright. Kim quickly reached up and grabbed the tray just as the tiny waiters were about to lose their grip. She lowered the tray to the tabletop, depositing the drinks in front of her friends. The Faeries waited for the empty tray and then streaked off across the room, back to the counter.

"Well?" Kim asked, sitting down and turning her attention to Brendan once again.

"Tell her what you told me, Brendan."

"Yes! But first," Kim said, smiling, "try the hot chocolate."

Brendan took a sip to give himself a moment to collect his thoughts. He'd had hot chocolate before, but this was something else. Rich, creamy chocolate flooded his mouth, filling him with warmth, sending a rush of pleasure exploding through him and tingling down his throat. An instant later, his mind was filled with the most wonderful, comfortable contentment. His eyes went wide. The chocolate was satisfying not just to his taste buds but to his mood as well. He felt safe, happy, and secure. A gentle smile spread across his face.

"It's awesome, eh?" Kim smiled back. "No one does hot drinks like the Hot Pot."

"Can we get back to the subject at hand?" Greenleaf suggested. "Tell Kim what you experienced, Brendan."

Brendan tried to settle his thoughts, feeling tempted to take another sip but resisting. Finally, he said, "I dunno. It's hard to put into words. I was kind of desperate. I thought Greenleaf was Orcadia and I was gonna get fried, so I reached out with my mind for help. There weren't any animals or birds close, none that I thought were big enough to help." He paused, fidgeting with his spoon. He remembered the weight of the tree's slumbering thoughts. "I tried harder. I reached out and sensed a mind, but it was slow and heavy like a sleeping ... elephant or something." He looked up and found Kim's attention riveted on him.

"And then what?" she demanded. She was leaning forward, her tea forgotten.

"Well ... " Brendan shrugged. "I kind of ... yelled at it with my mind. I woke it up and asked it to help me.

That's when that crazy tree grabbed Greenleaf. You know the rest."[24]

Kim's head snapped toward Greenleaf. "I thought he made the roots grow around you. That is possible with the Green Art."

"No," Greenleaf said. "He didn't cause any new growth. I believe he spoke to the tree itself."

"But … " Kim was flabbergasted. "That's impossible!"

"I saw him do it," Greenleaf insisted. "Furthermore, I don't believe he merely spoke to the tree. I believe he Compelled the tree to protect him."

Kim stared, her mouth open in surprise.

"Whoa, whoa, whoa," Brendan interjected. "What's the big deal? So I talked to a tree. So what? I talk to birds and bugs and stuff. What's the difference?"

Kim leaned back in her chair and shook her head. "There's a big difference. A huge difference." She sighed, frowned, and looked around the room. At last, she grinned and reached up to unhook a hanging ivy plant from its place above the table. Setting it on the tabletop, she lovingly ran her fingers through the trailing leaves. "The Green Art. An adept can use it to influence plants. That means I can change growing things. I can make them grow." She laid a hand on the handle of her field hockey stick while closing her eyes. As Brendan watched, the ivy began to sprout and grow. Tendrils of vine wrapped themselves around her fingers. It was like watching the time-lapse films of growing plants

---

[24] Please, unless you are a Faerie, do not yell at trees. One: people will think you are odd. Two: they are very hard of hearing. You'll end up with a sore throat. Three: if you do manage to get their attention, they'll talk endlessly about itchy bark and acorn fungus. Bo-ring.

they showed on the science channel. New stems unfurled from the pot. The stems sprouted new leaves, and within a few seconds, Kim's hand was completely covered by a drapery of new growth. "I can make them die back." The leaves began to curl and shrink. The stems shortened and disappeared. The plant withdrew into itself until only a single branch sprouted from the top of the pot, drooping forlornly into space with a scraggle of yellowed leaves. "That's about as far as it goes. I can make plants grow, cultivate them, and even heal them. That's what the Green Art is in a nutshell."

"So?" Brendan was still confused. "What's the point? That's what I did, isn't it?"

"Not at all," Kim said emphatically. *"You talked to the tree!* You just don't understand the significance of what you've done."

Brendan didn't know how to react. He hadn't thought about what he was doing at the time—he'd just done it. Ever since he'd first learned of his true identity, he'd been experiencing similar things. He heard the voice of the wind, and sometimes plants and trees, and there had been the weird incident with the Snoring Rock, too.[25] He was about to open his mouth to tell them about how the rock had spoken to him, but something made him keep quiet. They were already freaking out about the tree: he didn't need any more grief at the moment.

"So, I don't understand," Brendan grumbled. "What's new? I'm in a state of almost permanent confusion."

---

[25] In Book One, Brendan had a strange experience with a large black rock that graced the front lawn of Lord Lansdowne School. He swore he could hear the rock snoring, hence his name for it, the Snoring Rock. I hope you are reading these footnotes as there may be a quiz later.

"You don't get what we're saying," Kim insisted heatedly.

Greenleaf laid a calming hand on Kim's arm. "How could he? He hardly knows what he's doing. He hasn't had the benefit of growing up with his powers the way we all have." Greenleaf turned his attention to Brendan. "Brendan, a gift like yours is vanishingly rare. I'm not sure if anyone has ever had the ability to speak directly to trees. Not since the old times. Perhaps Pûkh … or the Old Man."

Brendan sat up. "Who? And Who?"

Greenleaf frowned, a cloud crossing his features. "Pûkh is one of the Ancient Faeries, born before the Pact was struck, and a leader of the Dark Ones who fought to enslave the Humans. He was given the choice of imprisonment or surrender. He chose surrender and founded a realm he called Tír na nÓg, the Everlasting Lands. He lives there with other Fair Folk who dislike living among Humans."

"And the Old Man?" Brendan prompted. His mind went back to the old Faerie he'd seen just a moment ago.

"Let's not dwell on the past. Suffice it to say that according to legend, the True Ancients had the gift. They were in tune with the universe in a way we aren't today. Much has been lost. You appear to have a sensitivity. Nowadays, the trees have retreated so far into themselves that they have become impossible to rouse. Today, you seem to have reached in and woken that tree up."

Brendan groaned. "Oh great! Now I've done something else that makes me weird. Y'know, I thought I was a misfit in the Human world. Here's another excuse for me to stick out like a sore thumb in the Faerie world, too. Will I ever get a break?"

"Stop feeling sorry for yourself, can you?" Kim said, shaking her head.

Greenleaf chuckled. "Believe me, every Faerie would give anything to have your problems. Seriously, you have discovered an amazing new gift. You mustn't feel that it's a bad thing. Unfortunately, we will have to work much harder if we hope to have you ready in time."

Brendan stopped in the middle of spooning whipped cream out of his mug. "In time for what?"

Kim and Greenleaf exchanged a glance. Kim shrugged. "I guess you'll find out soon enough. We wanted you to concentrate on your training and not worry about anything else, but you might as well know: a Gathering of the Clans has been called."

"A gathering?" Brendan frowned. "What does that mean?"

"The People of the Moon are divided into Clans, descended from the first great tribes of the Fair Folk. Every few decades, a Gathering is called. Faeries come from all over the world to tell stories, share news, and compete in Contests of the Arts."

"Like the Highland Games?" Brendan asked. "You throw logs and dance over swords and stuff?" Brendan had gone to the Highland Games in Fergus, Ontario, when he was a child. He remembered a lot of men in skirts, some of them throwing logs.

"A bit like that," Kim agreed, then shook her head. "And nothing like that. Some of the most brilliant Artificers come. The Artisans' Fair is pretty incredible. But there's one major thing you need to worry about … "

"I knew this couldn't be all good," Brendan said glumly.

"There's been a lot of debate about you in the Faerie world," Kim explained. "You've been quite a hot topic."

"Oh." Brendan brightened. "That doesn't sound so bad. It's nice to be popular."

"I didn't say popular. I said that Faeries were talking about you a lot. There's some debate among our people about whether your initiation was valid."

"But Ariel accepted it!" Brendan cried. "Isn't he the big cheese around here?"

"Around here, yes," Greenleaf replied. "But there are many more cheeses of the same size or larger around the world, and some of them insist that he was negligent. He didn't witness the initiation. You came back to us fully fledged, and we had to accept your story."

Brendan didn't respond. He'd never told anyone what had happened, how his Faerie father, Briach Morn, had come from the Other Side and performed the initiation. He'd kept that to himself. Now he was going to suffer for that choice.

"So what does this mean for me?" he asked.

"The Council has decided you must be tested," Greenleaf said. "You will go through a Proving, a series of Challenges to determine if you are truly one of us."

"And what if I fail these Challenges?"

"I wouldn't advise you to fail. You'd end up as an Exile, doomed to live on the fringes of our society. Like Finbar."

Finbar was now living at the Swan of Liir on the Ward's Island, doing odd jobs until Ariel decided whether he should be reinstated as a Faerie. Finbar had lost his Faerie status when he'd revealed his true nature to a Human, a woman he'd later married. He'd lived in Exile for almost two centuries, until the opportunity came through Brendan to appeal for a return to the Faerie world. Now he waited in an agonizing limbo.[26]

"*That* sounds bad," Brendan groaned. "That sounds really awful."

Greenleaf finished his café au lait and placed the bowl lightly on the tabletop. "Come, come! You have no need to worry, Brendan. I'm sure you will pass the tests with flying colours, once we get past the mental block you seem to be building for yourself. I must admit, I've never seen anything quite like it, and I've had my fair share of pupils."

Brendan slumped forward, his elbows on the table and his chin on his fists. "I can't help it. Whenever I try to use my gifts, it's like I can't concentrate hard enough. Somehow, they don't seem real to me. If I hadn't done that thing with the tree today, I'd think I didn't have any abilities at all."

"I'm sure we can overcome this obstacle." Greenleaf smiled. "You are a most extraordinary and sensitive person. That is both your strength and your weakness. You think too much about what you are doing and how it will affect others. At this point in your training, you should worry only about yourself."

"Things would be a lot easier if you weren't around those Humans you call your family," Kim pointed out.

"Well, I'm staying with them and that's just the way it is," Brendan snapped. "They are my family. I don't care if they're Human or Faerie or monkey. They're mine, so get used to that."

Brendan's Human family was always a bone of contention. His father and mother had adopted him as a baby,

---

[26] A state of being neglected or simply left awaiting some kind of decision. Not a dance involving a bamboo stick and a bongo drum (although limbo dancing *can* be agonizing).

thinking he was no different from any other infant. They'd raised him and loved him as their own. Though he'd come to learn they weren't his real parents and he wasn't Human at all, they still held the place in his heart that true parents should. Many Fair Folk insisted that he cast them aside, but he refused. Although trying to live in two worlds was difficult and perhaps ultimately impossible, he loved his family and couldn't leave them behind—even his sister, Delia, who made his life a constant trial.

"Peace, please." Greenleaf raised his delicate hands in a placating gesture. "Ki-Mata, we must respect Brendan's wishes and his choices. If Ariel allows it … well, let's just say he's wiser than either of us can ever hope to be."

Kim leaned back until her chair bumped against the wall. Crossing her arms, she chose not to reply. Brendan glared at her. She glared back.

"I know what Ki-Mata said is distasteful to you, but she does have a point, Brendan," Greenleaf continued. "You face challenges that most Faeries have never had to deal with. Most Faerie children grow up knowing of their powers and exercising them daily. Their powers are second nature to them by the time their initiation ceremony comes around. Yours, however, were suppressed by powerful magic. Your father made sure you would seem in every way to be Human, and so you are unfamiliar with the very essence of yourself. That's a large mountain to climb."

"Can't I just wait until the *next* Clan Gathering?" Brendan asked hopefully. "By then, I'm sure I'll have everything under control. I'll totally kick ass in the tests."

"Sadly, that's not an option. The Council would not bend on their ruling. The Proving will take place at the coming Gathering. Don't worry. You'll be fine."

"We hope," Kim said softly.

Brendan felt his stomach sink. "Thanks for that. You really know how to make me feel good."

Kim winced. "I'm sorry. I'm just worried about … "

Suddenly, the tabletop jumped as something struck it from below. The cups rattled with another impact.

"What the … " Brendan began.

A streak of light shot out from under the table. BLT corkscrewed into the air like a miniature stunt plane, smashing into a hanging plant and setting it swinging wildly.

"BLT, stop that!" Brendan cried. "Have you been eating sugar?"

"Found a couple of chocolate chips under the TAAAA-BLE!" BLT shrieked happily as she dive-bombed table after table.

"That's all I need," Brendan groaned.

HOME LIFE

By the time Brendan took the streetcar along College and arrived back home, it was already past three. He'd had to wait while BLT came down off her sugar high and passed out. She'd slept in his jacket pocket all the way home. He trudged up the steps and reached for the door handle.

"So, this is where you live?"

"Whhaa?" Brendan leapt like a scalded cat.

Charles was sitting in a wicker chair on the front porch. Brendan's father hadn't gotten around to taking the chairs down to the basement for the winter. She was curled up, her legs tucked under her, watching him. Her big violet eyes crinkled at the corners as she smiled.

"It's a cute little house," Charlie said. "I like it."

"What are you doing here?" Brendan demanded. "This is my family's house. It's off limits."

"I just wanted to talk to you again. See if you'd changed your mind about being such a stick in the mud."

"Well, I haven't. So buzz off."

"You are a very rude boy."

For some reason, being called a boy was extremely irritating. He glared at her, summoning his will, and said, slowly and clearly, "Leave me alone."

She stiffened. Moving jerkily like a broken puppet or a faulty robot, she stood, tottered across the porch, and stumped down the steps.

Brendan sighed with relief. He'd done it! He'd Compelled her!

No sooner had he thought that than she laughed and did a little jig at the bottom of the steps. "Nice try! You've got some power, I'll admit that." She smiled and curtseyed prettily, holding out the edges of an invisible dress. "I'll go, then. But I'm not giving up. You can't get rid of me that easily." With a little wave and a wink, she headed off up Montrose Avenue.

Brendan grunted, annoyed and disappointed. He had to admit that he was a little glad his Compulsion hadn't worked. He didn't like having that kind of control over other people. After what he'd unwittingly done to Chester … He shuddered at the memory. He pushed the thought from his mind and entered the warmth of the house.

"Brendan? Is that you?" his mother's voice called from the kitchen. She stuck her head around the door. "Where have you been? Dmitri and Harold waited for you for an hour."

Brendan's stomach sank. "Oh no! I forgot." He'd invited his friends over to work on their social studies presentation. It had completely slipped his mind. *There's another reason for your friends to hate you.* Shaking his head, he kicked his shoes off and hung his jacket on a hook. He'd have to call them and apologize.

"Do you want a snack or something?" his mother asked.

"Not really," Brendan answered, entering the kitchen. His senses were flooded with the rich scent of fresh bread. His mother was baking, as she did every Saturday afternoon. He ruefully remembered using her baking as a bribe to get the guys to come over. What an idiot.

Brendan loved her bread, so she made sure she baked plenty to last through the week. She also made muffins and cookies for Delia's and Brendan's lunches. She loved to bake: it was her way of unwinding after the week at the office. She was a promotions and events manager at an advertising firm. She was always rushed and under pressure. "Baking takes time. You're forced to move slowly and carefully. I need that in my life," she often explained as she churned batter or greased a pan.

She held out a plate laden with chocolate chip cookies. "You sure?"

Brendan couldn't resist. "I guess I could have one." He plucked a cookie off the plate. It was warm in his fingers, the chocolate melting onto his fingertips. He took a bite and grinned. "Me likey!"

"Me happy!" his mother answered. They had gone through the ritual since he was a child. She put the plate down on the counter and opened the oven door a crack to check on her bread. Brendan leaned against the counter and savoured his cookie.

"Everything all right?" his mother asked.

"Yeah."

"You don't often forget things."

"Well, I've been a little busy lately."

"Busy with what, exactly?" His mother closed the oven door and fixed him with an inquisitive look.

"Uh … lots of stuff. School. Stuff. You know." He couldn't very well tell his mother he'd been undergoing a rigorous training program in the Faerie Arts.

His mother raised an eyebrow. "Stuff. Does some of this stuff have to do with a girl?"

Brendan froze with the cookie halfway to his mouth. How had his mother known about the girl following him around? Had she seen her on the porch?

"What?" Brendan bleated.

"I wasn't born yesterday." She laughed. "You're a normal teenage boy. It has to happen sooner or later."

He relaxed. She didn't know about Charlie. She thought he had a girlfriend! *Oh, how wrong you are, Mum.*

Out loud, he said, "Mum! No. Come on."

"I was your age too, you know, many, many long years ago. I know how things are."

"Mu-um … " Brendan began to protest his innocence, but then a thought occurred to him. If his mum thought he had a girlfriend she might not be suspicious, and that would give him a little breathing room. He didn't have to deny anything, but he didn't have to confirm it, either. The truth was, though a few months ago he'd thought he was in with his dream girl, Marina Kaprillian, nothing had happened. Kim had put her foot down and demanded that he leave Marina alone. Brendan had reluctantly complied. He really didn't have the time for romance right now, anyway.

"You don't have to be embarrassed, Brendan." His mother ruffled his hair and laughed. "It's a natural thing. You're only human."

Not really, Brendan thought ruefully.

"All I want is for you to be careful. Girls grow up faster than boys in a lot of ways. You have to be sure you don't get in over your head."

You have no idea how far over my head I am already, Mum.
Not for the first time, Brendan wished he could bring his mother into his confidence. The Faeries had strict rules about giving information about the Faerie world to Humans. Finbar had paid dearly for sharing his secret with his wife. Brendan was tempted to tell his mother anyway. He needed advice. She wouldn't believe him at first, but he'd convince her and then she'd probably freak out. But, in the end, she would try to help, he was sure. Even if she wasn't his flesh and blood, she was his mother in every other way. And he felt as though he were betraying her somehow by keeping his troubles from her.

"Whoa." His mum laughed as he enveloped her in an impulsive hug. "What was that for?"

"Do I need an excuse to love my mum?"

"Barf!" Delia's voice was filled with loathing. "Barf and barf!"

Brendan released his mother from the embrace to find his sister standing in the kitchen doorway. "Hey, Delia. Not very nice to see you, I must say."

"Ditto, Nerd." She sneered and picked a cookie off the plate. "Your nerd friends were here polluting the air all afternoon."

"Plate, Delia. Plate!" Mum scolded. In response, Delia rolled her eyes and stuffed the entire cookie into her mouth.

"I'm gonna go up and call the guys," Brendan announced. His mother turned back to check the oven. Delia stuck out her tongue, covered in half-chewed cookie. "Nice, Dee. Really nice." He pushed past Delia into the hallway and grabbed his jacket from the hook. He started up the stairs with Delia at his heels.

"Where've you been, Brendan?" Delia demanded. "What's going on?"

"Nothing's going on. I was just out."

"Your friends didn't know where you were," Delia insisted. "You've been disappearing a lot lately. What are you up to?"

They reached the second floor. Brendan faced her. "What's it to you, super-pest? I don't have to tell you where I'm going. What are you, the CIA?"

"Worse." Delia smiled sweetly. "I'm your sister.[27] At least according to the law." Delia was always pointing out that they weren't really related. She seemed to take a sadistic pleasure in reminding Brendan that he was adopted. "You can't put anything past me. I'm all over you like a bad smell."

"I agree with the bad smell part."

"Ha-ha!" Delia leaned into him, jabbing a finger in his ribs. "If you're hiding something, I'm gonna find out. You can't escape me, Brendan. I've got my eye on you." She pointed at her eyes with two fingers and then stabbed the same fingers at Brendan. "Believe it!"

Threat delivered, she spun on her heel and marched into her room. Brendan caught a glimpse of the clothing-strewn lair that was Delia's sacred inner sanctum before she slammed the door. Filled with apprehension, he stared at the closed door. Delia was tenacious. If anyone could expose his secret, he'd bet on her. He would just have to be very careful around her. *Very* careful indeed.

---

[27] I think most brothers would agree that sisters are terrifying and to be avoided until at least the age of forty and then approached only with great caution.

I suppose I could have her killed, he said to himself. He shook his head. *I pity any assassin sent after my sister.* Laughing softly, he climbed the ladder-cum-staircase to his attic room.

Brendan's room had become the one place in his world where he could completely relax. He flopped down on the bed, tossing his jacket onto the floor. He was exhausted. Greenleaf had pushed him hard today. Brendan knew Greenleaf was concerned about his lack of progress. But every time Brendan tried to exercise his abilities, he found himself unable to focus on the task at hand. No matter how he tried, the results were mediocre at best. A headache threatened at the back of his skull.

"Oi! Oi!" BLT's muffled but indignant voice rose from the floor. "Get offa me! I'm suffocatin'!"

Brendan swung his feet to the floor. His jacket was practically hopping around the floorboards as BLT battled to escape from the pocket. He grabbed the garment and opened the flap for her. Instantly, she rocketed out of her cloth prison and smacked into the bedside lamp. The fixture toppled. The old Brendan would never have caught the lamp before it shattered on the floor. Without thinking, the Warp Warrior speed flared in his nerves and he snatched it from mid-air and placed it back on the nightstand.

"What's the big idea?" BLT demanded, lighting on the lampshade and shaking her fist at Brendan. "You tryin' ta kill me?"

"Quiet!" Brendan hissed. "Someone will hear you. My sister is suspicious enough as it is."

BLT stuck out her tongue at him. Her eyes were bloodshot and her hair was tangled. She began to massage her temples. "My head is killing me."

"Serves you right," Brendan said, lying back down. "I told you, no sugar."

"What a downer you are." BLT flitted down and stood on Brendan's chest with her arms crossed. "You oughta lighten up."

"How am I supposed to lighten up? I've got to learn how to use my powers."

"You know how to use your powers!" BLT marched up his chest and placed a tiny booted foot on Brendan's chin. "When you ain't thinkin' too much, you just do it naturally." She slapped his nose. "Stop thinkin'!"

"Ow!" Despite her size, BLT packed a wallop. "Quit hitting me!"

"Who are you talking to?" Delia's voice sounded from the bottom of the stairs. "Who's up there with you?"

Brendan scrambled to his feet in a panic. "Nobody!" He heard Delia mounting the stairs.

"There's someone up there with you! I heard you talking to someone."

In a split second, Brendan scooped up a squirming BLT and stuffed her into the drawer of his bedside table. "Be quiet," he hissed at the little Faerie before slamming the drawer shut. He turned just as his sister's head rose up above the floor.

"Who's up here?" She glared around the small room.

"I'm up here, idiot. Who do you think?" Brendan tried to look innocent. He prayed that BLT had the sense to keep her mouth shut.

Delia narrowed her eyes, studying his face. "You're lying! I heard you talking to someone just now."

"I was doing some homework ... for Drama Club. Rehearsing lines."

"Since when are you in Drama Club?"

"Since when is it any of your business?"

"Since you started acting all weird."

"I'm not acting weird. I'm *acting*. Now get out of my room."

"I know you're up to something. And I know I heard you talking to someone."

"Get out! You aren't allowed up here. Get lost!"

"Make me!"

Brendan was about to do just that. He made it two steps across the floor when the nightstand rattled loudly. Brendan froze. The table rattled again, practically leaping off the floor.

Delia stared in shock. "What was THAT?"

"What?" Brendan asked innocently.

"The nightstand moved."

"I didn't see anything."

With a bang, the drawer shot out of the stand and hit the opposite wall. In a shower of sparks, BLT came whizzing out of the drawer and buzzed around the room like a miniature comet.

"Oh no!" Brendan groaned.

Delia shrieked as BLT swooped toward her face. Throwing up her hands for protection, she lost her balance and fell backwards down the staircase. A loud thud told Brendan she had landed on the floor in the hallway below. He rushed to the opening and looked down to see his sister lying flat on her back on the carpet, her eyes wide with surprise and her mouth a round little *o*.

"Are you all right?"

Delia blinked up at him once. Twice. Then, she began to shriek and point at Brendan. "It's on your SHOULDER! WHAT IS IT? A BUG!"

Brendan turned his head to see BLT squatting on his shoulder, a half-eaten M&M in her sticky hands and a mad grin on her face. Her eyes were glossy as marbles.

"Look what I found in the drawer!" She took another bite of the candy and zipped off to resume her circuitous transit of Brendan's bedroom. Delia shrieked and leapt to her feet. "MUM! MUM!" She ran off down the stairs. "There's some kind of KILLER BUG in Brendan's room!"

Brendan felt a wave of relief. Delia couldn't see BLT's true appearance.[28] He'd have far less trouble explaining a big bug than explaining a Faerie. He shook his head and descended the staircase to help calm his now-hysterical sister.

He smoothed things over with Delia, convincing her he'd driven the wasp out of the open window of his room. In a sense, he was telling the truth. He'd shooed BLT out his window and told her to stay away for the rest of the night. She could stand the cold. She just didn't like it. On nights when she was banished from the house, she'd fly off to meet up with other Lesser Faeries in the park or go hunting for sweets. She always managed to take care of herself.

He went downstairs to find that his father had arrived home from work at the café and it was time for dinner. He suddenly realized he was absolutely starving. Time flew by as he sat with his family and listened to his father regale

---

[28] All Faeries have glamours or magical disguises to hide their true nature from Humans. While Greater Faeries take the Human form to move among us, as Brendan does, Lesser Faeries are forced to take on appropriate disguises for their size: mice, insects, birds, etc. BLT, being a contrary sort of individual, settled on an ugly, hairy fly, but she could have been a butterfly or a hummingbird. I think we agree that wouldn't be in keeping with her personality.

them all with his impressions of the customers he'd served that day. Even Delia seemed to relax and forget her scare, laughing in spite of her protestations that her father was the least funny man in the world and that his stories were the dumbest in the world.

When he was with his family, he could almost forget about the weirdness of the Faerie world and his place in it. He could forget about the Art, Gatherings of Clans, and Proving Challenges. Here, at the kitchen table, eating meatloaf with his mother and father and even his annoying sister, he belonged. He was home.

Weary but content after a couple more cookies, Brendan trudged up to his room with no thought in his mind but sleep. He peeled off his clothes, donned his T-shirt and pyjama bottoms, and lay down on the bed. He was almost asleep when he remembered he still hadn't called Harold and Dmitri to apologize. He reached for his Faerie phone. His fingers rested on the smooth grain of the wood for a moment before he pulled his hand away. He decided he was too tired to face explaining his screw-up to his friends. He lay back and was asleep in minutes.

Charlie stood in the shadows, watching as the light in the attic went out. It was chilly but she didn't feel a thing.

"He's going to sleep," she said softly, seemingly to herself. No one was with her in the lane. "He still does that. It's very strange. He's so tied to his Human habits. It's sad but kind of sweet, too, his feelings for these people."

There was a rustle of wings. A hawk with snowy white plumage lighted to perch on the fence beside Charlie. The bird of prey blinked bright blue eyes and hooted softly.

Charlie nodded. "That's true. His attachment to his Human family is the way to get close to him."

The hawk flapped its broad wings and the air around it smudged and smeared. The shape of the bird stretched and its plumage darkened. The next instant, an old man stood leaning against the fence. He wore a rumpled tweed suit and a flat cap. "It's his greatest weakness but perhaps his greatest strength, too. That's the key to his passion. It's what will set him apart."

"He's very reluctant to let me in," Charlie explained. "He distrusts strangers."

"Few could resist your charms, my dear Charles."

"He's doing just fine," she snorted, hanging her head.

The old man raised Charlie's chin and looked into her eyes. He smiled. "Show him how wonderful our world can be. You will succeed, I'm sure."

Reluctantly she nodded. "I have an idea that might work." Her brow furrowed. "Have you found out any more about my family?"

"No," the old man said sadly. "I haven't given up, but the trail is centuries old. It will take some time.

"Now, I must be gone," he said. "Don't worry. You will wear him down." As he raised his arms, his form melted down and collapsed. The bird sat in his place on the fence post. The hawk clicked its beak and rose with a powerful snap of its wings, throwing itself into the frigid night sky.

"Yes." She nodded and held out her bare arm. A weasel-like shape stretched from her elbow to her wrist, etched into her skin with black ink. The tattoo shivered, writhed, and then detached itself from her skin, thickening and expanding until the creature it depicted had become a separate entity, dark as the shadows under the fence.

The creature chittered softly and swarmed up her arm until it wreathed her shoulders like a living scarf.

"Yes, Tweezers. It's time to take the gloves off."

PART 2

The Shadow Dancer

Another Note
from the Narrator

Ha! Things are certainly heating up. Mysterious hawks in the dark of night! Sisters spying on brothers! Chocolate chip cookies! Oh, what a tangled web of intrigue and deception.

The story is really starting to get rolling now. The pieces are in place, as it were. Who is the mysterious old man? Old men are always interesting. In stories, they fall into one of two categories: Wise Old Sage or Mad Old Weirdo. I prefer the old men characters that are a little bit of both. Old Mad Wise Weirdo has a nice ring to it.

So, Brendan is having a crisis of sorts. He is alienating his friends and failing in his training, and an annoying girl is trying to weasel her way into his life. Little does she know he already has an annoying girl in his life.

I have come under criticism from readers for Delia being unreasonably mean to Brendan. But anyone who has a sister will not find fault in my portrayal of Delia, for they'll know I am more than likely not being harsh enough.

Sisters can be extremely annoying. I have a sister who is never satisfied until she's driven me slightly mad. When we were children, she used to sneak into my bedroom and glue my pyjamas to my bedsheets. Very annoying. Then there was the time she mailed me to France. What can I say? I'm a very deep sleeper. I woke up in the mail-sorting office in Paris. The supervisor almost choked on his croissant.

Surely, my sister was an extreme and sadistic case. (She is currently in prison serving five years for mail fraud.) But the stakes are high for Brendan, and a nosy sister is the last thing he needs. He is keeping a lot of balls in the air, and those balls are of different weights and sizes. Every once in a while, another ball is tossed to him and he must react swiftly or risk dropping everything. Sometimes he has to pass one ball under his leg or behind his back …

All right. I'm exhausted with this juggling metaphor. Shall we continue? Let's throw some more balls at Brendan.

EVISCERATION

The next day, Sunday, Brendan awoke to find BLT tapping at the window. The temperature had dropped and snow had fallen overnight, the first of the season. Christmas was just over a week away. He let the tiny Faerie in out of the cold.

"About time!" BLT grumped.

"It's not like you feel the cold, anyway," Brendan pointed out.

"Not the point!" She shook snow off her wings and burrowed under his duvet, refusing to respond to his apologies.

It was one of those rare days when both his mother and father were home. He joined them for breakfast at the kitchen table while listening to them making their plans for the day.

"We have to get the tree put up," his mother said, referring to her to-do list on the table in front of her. "And I need you to get the decorations out of the bins in the basement."

"Absolutely, dear," his father answered absently. He was preoccupied by the highlights from last night's game on SportsCentre. The tiny TV on top of the fridge held at least half of his attention. "Decorations."

"Hey, Dad," Brendan interrupted. "Did they win?"

"Lost in a shootout."

"Bummer."

"They played hard, though."

"Sure." Brendan shook his head. Part of being a Toronto Maple Leafs fan was hoping against hope that this season would be better than the last, though it rarely was. Still, you stayed with your team through the good and the bad. When they actually did win, the victory would be worth waiting for. That was his father's philosophy, at least. Brendan thought it sucked to be a Leafs fan, but his father had left him no choice. He'd been indoctrinated since he was a baby.[29]

"What have you got on for today, Brendan?" his mother asked.

"I'm gonna try and get together with Harold and Dmitri. And maybe do some Christmas shopping."

"That's good. They were really down when you didn't show up yesterday." His mother raised an eyebrow. "Friends are important, Brendan. And not just girlfriends, either."

"Mu-um." Brendan was pleased that his mother seemed to be buying the girlfriend ruse, which might give him a little more time to work with Greenleaf and Kim in the days before the Challenges. "Where's Dee?"

"She said she had some errands to run. Probably shopping at the mall with her friends. She left a few minutes ago." His mum stood up and put her coffee cup in the sink. "I'm going to take a shower and then we're going to get a tree." She waited for her husband to respond. "Edward?"

"Hmm?" His father tore his eyes from the television. "Oh, okay. Fine. I'm ready any time."

Satisfied, Mum kissed Brendan on the forehead and went upstairs, leaving him alone with his father. Brendan

---

[29] Being a Toronto Maple Leafs fan can now be used as a mental disability claim and a legal defence.

chewed his toast, watching the game highlights in silent companionship with his dad.

Finally, the show ended and his dad turned off the TV. "What a miserable shootout. Our goalie couldn't stop a beach ball with a piano tied to it," he said glumly.

Brendan had a sudden thought. "Dad, can I ask you something?"

"No," his dad answered flatly. Brendan looked at him in confusion until his father laughed. "I'm kidding. What do you want to know?"

"Just some advice, kinda," Brendan said.

"I'll kinda try and help if I kinda can."

"Right." Brendan thought for a moment then struggled to form his question. "When you're doing something difficult like, say, trying to learn a new song … "

"Yeah?"

"Have you ever just not been able to do it, no matter how hard you tried? I mean, for some reason, no matter what you do, you can't play the song or whatever?"

"You mean, like having a mental block?"

"Something like that." Brendan nodded. "In fact, exactly like that."

His father frowned. "That's happened before, sure. Sometimes, for whatever reason, your mind just can't absorb something. I remember trying to learn 'American Pie.' Long song. Lotta words. Kind of annoying. I had to perform it at somebody's wedding and I didn't have it down the night before."

"What did you do?"

"Well, I'd been killing myself trying to get it perfect and I'd spent hours and hours poring over the words, but I just couldn't play it through perfectly. So … I convinced them to let me play another song."

Brendan had been anticipating some words of wisdom. His face fell.

"Again, I'm kidding," he laughed. "Although I think 'American Pie' is a pretty lame song for a wedding. I mean, you want to immortalize your union by singing a song about a guitar player who died in a plane crash? Buddy Holly's great and everything, but come on. Turns out they'd met to that song and so … "

"Dad!"

"Sorry. Yeah, okay." His dad smiled. "You know what I did? I did nothing. I stopped practising. Obviously, it was all there in my head and I was so worried I was going to fail that I was making myself fail. I put down the guitar and didn't touch it until right before the ceremony."

"Did it work?" Brendan asked. "Did you get it right?"

"Turns out I forgot a verse but they didn't notice. Love tends to preoccupy people when they're getting married. And the fact that they're trying not to wet themselves with terror. My point is, you have to trust that you've done the work and let it go. Does that make sense?"

"Sure." Brendan nodded, but inside he was disappointed. His father had no idea what the stakes were. Brendan couldn't make any mistakes or they might be his last. There was no room for error. He didn't want to worry his dad, though. "Thanks, Dad. I'm gonna get dressed and go out. See ya later."

"Okay," his dad answered, reaching for the paper. "What are you so worried about? What do you need to learn? Can I help?"

"Nothing," Brendan replied, heading for the stairs. "Just something for school. Later, Dad."

Brendan showered and dressed quickly, but by the time he came downstairs, the house was empty. His parents were gone. He'd called Harold and Dmitri but got their voice-mail. He'd left apologetic messages for both and begged them to call him back. Pulling on his parka, he headed out the door.

He walked down the street to wait for the streetcar. BLT was content to nestle in his inner pocket out of the cold. Brendan felt his spirits rise a little bit. His breath gusted out in a white cloud. He liked the cold, and he especially liked the first big snowfall. He loved the way the entire city looked clean and fresh. He loved how all sound seemed muffled by the layer of white. He contentedly scuffed at the fluffy snow, sending puffs of flakes in front of him, savouring the squeak of the compressed snow beneath his boots. Snow-flakes drifted in front of his face, and with his acute Faerie Sight he could see the intricate shape of each one. He could almost hear the tinkling as they collided with the ground.

"Beautiful," Brendan breathed softly.

"You can keep it," came BLT's tiny, grumpy voice from his coat. "Cold. Wet. Blah!" She snuggled deeper.

Brendan was looking forward to spending the day doing normal (and by normal, he meant Human) things. He hadn't been able to set aside any time for Christmas shop-ping. He wasn't really sure if Faeries observed Christmas, but he decided he would get gifts for his new family, too. That meant double the gifts that he'd had to buy last year. Luckily, he had a little extra money saved.

He took the streetcar to Queen Street West and wan-dered in and out of the shops, searching for the right things for everyone on his list. His dad was easy: CDs. Mum was easy, too: she always wanted some new tool for the kitchen. Delia he could fob off with a gift card at a clothing store. The real difficulty was buying for his Faerie family. What did one buy as a gift for an immortal? A tie? Some tea? Nice-smelling soap?

He searched and searched but came up empty. The sun was already going down when he headed back to the subway. He was frustrated and tired from fighting the crowds, but most of all, he was a little worried. He couldn't shake the feeling that somebody was following him. He found himself looking over his shoulder, stopping and turning around suddenly or even ducking into shops and watching the people passing by on the street. But no matter what he did, he couldn't catch anyone tailing him. Perhaps the anxiety and pressure of the coming Challenges were making him paranoid.

He'd just decided to let go of his fears and head home on the subway when he came out onto the platform and found Charles waiting for him again.

She was leaning against a pillar, a latte in her hand, smiling.

"Fancy meeting you here," she said.

"So *you* were following me!"

She frowned in confusion. "I don't know what you're talking about."

"Leave me alone," Brendan said flatly, walking past her.

"But I like you," she giggled, following him.

"Well, I don't like you," Brendan snarled.

"You have to get to know me," the girl said, tossing her empty cup in a trash can. "I'm really quite fun."

Brendan felt the rush of air that announced the arrival of the subway train. Light shone from the tunnel and the squeal of metal wheels on the tracks filled the air. He whirled, waving a finger in the girl's face. "I'm not interested in getting to know you, and I don't like being followed."

Before Brendan could pull his finger away, the girl nipped his fingertip.

He yelped in pain and snatched his hand back. "You bit me."

"It's not polite to point!" She smiled, revealing strong white teeth.

The train arrived. Brendan stepped through the doors as they whooshed open. He turned and said angrily, "Leave me alone."

She frowned prettily as the doors closed.

"That ain't no way to talk to a girl." A homeless man sitting on the train, bulging shopping bags piled around him, gave Brendan a reproachful look.

Brendan ignored him. No one else was on board so he had his pick of seats. He plunked down on a bench facing the platform, well away from the homeless man. The train started to roll. The girl jogged along until she was even with him, waving as she ran alongside. Brendan tried to ignore her. The train picked up speed. The girl kept pace, running with ease and grace. She puffed out her cheeks and pretended she was having trouble keeping up. Despite his annoyance, Brendan found her performance amusing. A small smile tugged rebelliously at the corner of his mouth.

Suddenly, she threw up her hands in alarm and dropped headlong from sight. Brendan leapt up to see if she was okay, pressing his face against the window beside the homeless man. The girl popped up and banged on the glass, scaring Brendan so that he staggered back and fell in his seat. She pointed and laughed, once again keeping pace with the train. Brendan rolled his eyes. She stuck out her tongue.

The end of the platform loomed. The girl waved goodbye and dropped back out of sight. Brendan didn't wave back.

The homeless man had been watching the whole thing. "She can sure motor," he said, eyes wide. "That's some girl, there."

"Yeah," Brendan had to admit.

He took the subway north to Spadina. Rather than take the streetcar from the station, he decided to walk home through the softly falling snow. People were bundled up against the weather, but Brendan hardly noticed the cold. The sun was low in the grey sky.

By the time he got to what he'd taken to calling the Snoring Rock, it was already dark. Brendan came level with the black stone and found himself compelled to stop. Lately he'd avoided this place. Something about the monolith sitting in the schoolyard made him uneasy. He read the little brass plaque that decorated the stone.

THIS BASIC IGNEOUS ROCK WAS FOUND AT A DEPTH OF TWELVE FEET DURING THE COURSE OF EXCAVATION FOR THIS SCHOOL. THE COMPOSITION IS OF A VERY RARE TYPE AND IS ASSUMED TO HAVE BEEN CARRIED HERE FROM CARIBOU LAKE NORTH OF PARRY SOUND BY A GLACIER DURING THE GREAT ICE AGE 12,000 YEARS AGO.

Brendan could barely imagine the force required to transport a stone over such a distance and bury it so deep in the ground. Thinking about it made him uncomfortable, perhaps because the rock reminded him of the first terrifying and confusing day when he'd stumbled into his new life. He and Dmitri had been walking past this very spot when he'd heard the stone "snoring." He remembered the harsh warning the stone had barked in his mind, telling him to stay away.

So why was he here? He could have easily taken another route. He stood in the yellow light of the street lamp with the snow gently falling around him, staring at the mottled black surface of the stone.

The world faded from his awareness. The surface of the stone swam before him. What at first seemed to be a chaos of bumps, gouges, and cracks began to shift and resolve into patterns. Brendan struggled to make sense of the markings, but their meaning was just beyond his perception. He felt that if he could just concentrate a little more, he'd be able to puzzle them out.

He heard a voice whispering his name. The voice was soft, insistent, and hypnotic.

Breandan.

Breandan.

I am waiting.

Breandan.

"Brendan!"

The voice was suddenly loud. Brendan came to his senses to find that he had climbed over the little fence surrounding the black rock and had laid his bare hands on its rough surface.

"Hey, Brendan!" His father stood on the sidewalk looking at him, concern plain on his face. "Are you okay?"

Brendan dropped his hands to his sides, embarrassed and confused. He didn't remember climbing the fence and approaching the stone.

"Hi, Dad," he said lamely, stepping back onto the sidewalk. "Where are you coming from?"

"Work. They called me in to cover a shift at the café. And I had to pick up some stuff your mother ordered." He held up a couple of shopping bags. He cocked his head to the side and looked at Brendan again. "Are you okay?"

"Yeah! Yeah!" Brendan said. "I was, uh … I just thought I saw some graffiti tags on that rock. But it wasn't anything. Just a shadow." He smiled lamely.

"Oh, okay," his father said slowly. "That's good. All right, then, shall we go home and see what's for dinner?"

"Sure!"

Dinner was sloppy joes and homemade french fries, Brendan's favourite. There was also a big salad, since his mother always forced him to eat at least one plate of greens as well. He demolished two joes in short order, suddenly famished. He still felt weird after his latest encounter with the Snoring Rock. He guessed he had to call it the Talking Rock now. He pondered the experience while he ate, his mum and dad chatting happily about their days.

Toward the end of the meal, he noticed that Dee was quieter than usual. He kept catching her looking at him.

"What?" he demanded.

"Nothing," she sneered.

"Then stop looking at me."

"I'm not."

"Good!"

"Good!"

"Wow," his father laughed. "Some siblings have trouble communicating, but you two are so in sync. It's heartwarming."

"Time to decorate the tree!" His mother was eager to defuse any brother-sister meltdown. "Let's get to it."

The next hour was spent re-enacting a ritual that occurred every year. His father would string the lights and mildly curse when he couldn't find the one bulb that was burnt out and keeping the whole string from shining. Then there was the argument over tinsel placement: throw or drape carefully. Then taking the ornaments out of the boxes, finding which ones had broken and which were just too plain ugly to use this year and should be retired.

Finally, all that was left was the star on the top. His mother climbed the ladder and placed the antique silver star that had been in her family for generations on the spindly top bough of the blue spruce. The star meant a lot to his mother. The year before his grandmother had passed away, she'd handed it down to his mum. His mother and his father had no living parents, so any token that reminded them of those who were gone was special.

His mother was just climbing down the ladder, helped by his father, when the doorbell rang.

"Who could that be?" she asked.

"Beats me." His father shrugged. "Are you expecting anyone, Dee?"

"No." Delia shook her head.

"Brendan?"

Brendan shook his head. The bell rang again.

"Well, I know one way to find out who's at the door." Brendan's father pushed back his chair and stood. "I'm going to open it. Don't try and stop me."

Brendan followed his father down the hall to the front door. After peeking through the curtains that shrouded the tiny window in the top of the door, Brendan's father grasped the handle and swung it open.

Brendan's heart sank. Standing on the front porch in the glow of the porch light was Charles. She was the picture of thin teenage waif in ragged jeans and a Clash T-shirt. An oversized leather jacket draped her shoulders. She carried a backpack encrusted with patches and band buttons, held together with safety pins. Seeing Brendan's father, she grinned shyly, completing the helpless persona.

"*Allo*," she said, affecting a heavy Quebecois accent. "Is Brendan at 'ome?"

"You're in luck. He's right behind me," Brendan's father said. He stepped aside to reveal Brendan, whose face was a mask of shock.

"I 'ope you don't mind my just coming over but I was passing by," the girl said shyly.

"Who's this, Brendan?" said his mother, coming out of the living room.

"She? Uh … " Brendan stammered. "Uh … "

The girl laughed prettily. "I can't believe Brendan 'asn't mentioned me. My name is Charlie Lutine."

Getting over his shock, Brendan felt anger bubble up in his stomach. This was way out of bounds! This was breaking all the rules!

Brendan's mum raised an eyebrow at Brendan. "I'm sure he was working up the courage to introduce us to his new girlfriend."

"Girlfriend?" Brendan's dad was beaming. "Well, isn't this nice?"

Brendan's jaw dropped. Girlfriend? His heart sank. His conversation with his mum had backfired. He tried to think of a way out but he was stuck.

"You should have called," Brendan said, trying to hide his fury with a light tone.

"I'm sorry." She smiled sweetly. "My cellphone, she die an hour ago. Like I said, I was 'oping to surprise you."

"Oh, it's a surprise all right," Brendan muttered between gritted teeth.

Delia shouldered her way between her parents. "Who's this?"

"I'm Charlie," the girl said with a smile. "You must be Delia. Brendan's told me a lot about you."

Delia managed to look disgusted, surprised, and suspicious all at the same time. "He has?"

"Oh, yes!" Charlie assured her. Then she shivered theatrically.

Brendan's father practically leapt to take her arm and draw her into the house. "Come in out of the cold. We'll make you some tea."

Brendan didn't know what to say. He didn't know what to do. All he could do was stand by helplessly as his parents ushered the girl into his home.

HOME INVASION

Half an hour later, the Clairs were sitting around the kitchen table watching their visitor devour leftover sloppy joes.

For such a scrawny little runt, she can sure put it away, Brendan thought bitterly, watching his alleged girlfriend mopping her plate with a piece of thick white bread. He had no idea how he was going to get her out of the house. She was playing the part of the new girlfriend meeting the parents to a T. One sure way to get into his mother's good books was to show a healthy appreciation for her cooking. Charlie didn't demur when offered something to eat and even asked for seconds, making her a superstar in his mum's eyes. Brendan watched, despairing, as his mother made sure the girl didn't run out of food. His father was conducting a mild interrogation, but Brendan could tell that he was utterly charmed as well. The only one who looked unconvinced was Delia, who leaned in the doorway watching with intense interest, like a hawk examining a mouse in an open field.

"So how did you meet Brendan? At school?" his dad asked.

"*Mais oui.*" She stopped chewing long enough to grin at Brendan. "I 'ave just moved to the area, and Brendan was kind enough to show me around."

Brendan glowered back. *What a barefaced liar!* he wanted to shout in her face, but instead he just smiled, choking back his anger.

"He hasn't mentioned you at all," Dad said. "I would've thought he'd want to let everyone know he had a girl as pretty as you."

"Oh, come on," Charlie said, blushing.

"I had an inkling something was up." Mum smiled knowingly. "He was probably just embarrassed."

Brendan kept a straight face but inside he was seething. He wanted to yell at her, *Who are you, really? What are you doing in my family's house? Get out of here!*

Instead, he bit his tongue and listened as his father asked her: "Where are you from? You don't sound like you're from around here."

"Montreal," she said, finally pushing back her plate. "My father is in banking. 'E was transferred."

"I'm sure Charlie has to get going," Brendan said, looking to move her along. He just wanted to get her out of the house before she said something that didn't ring true for his parents. "I'll walk you to the streetcar."

"Brendan." His mother glared at him. "You'd think you didn't want us to get to know her. You have nothing to be embarrassed about."

"So, what are you into?" Brendan's father asked, offering the girl a chocolate chip cookie. "Do you like music?"

She took a cookie. After popping a piece into her mouth she shrugged. "I like the music, me. I play the guitar and sing. I like busking in the street sometimes."

"You busk?"[30] Brendan's father's eyes lit up. He loved performers like himself. "Are you any good?"

---

[30] *Busking* is the art of street performing. In my opinion, busking should be avoided at all costs. If you are a performer, try to perform indoors. First of all, one doesn't get rained or snowed on. Second, there's usually a stage or some other sort of platform

"I like to think so." She grinned at Brendan.

"We have to jam sometime. I've tried to interest Brendan in music but it's really not his thing."

"Thanks, Dad," Brendan said flatly, annoyed that his father would volunteer personal information.

"Oh, I don't know," Charlie said, with a wink at Brendan. "Brendan 'as a lot of 'idden talents. 'E could surprise you."

"He already has." Mum laughed, punching Brendan's arm lightly. "We had no idea he had a girlfriend."

"It's not like that," Brendan groaned. "We're friends. That's it."

"Then, my son," Dad said, shaking his head, "that only proves what I've thought all along: you're crazy."

"Thanks, Dad," Brendan said. "I appreciate your support."

"I'm just saying," Mr. Clair laughed. "If I had a girl this cute, I'd be bragging to everybody!"

"Edward," his mother warned.

"I'm just saying!"

"Brendan," Charlie said, giggling before he could respond, "I never imagined you 'ad such a nice family." Brendan could tell this act of hers was working on his parents. They'd been so worried about him since they'd told him he was adopted. Finding a girlfriend would be a good sign that he was a "normal" teenage boy and not suffering some secret pain. Whoever this Faerie named Charles actually was, she was playing his parents like a violin. And

---

to perform from. Third, any performer who plays for spare change and the odd half-sandwich from a passerby is not really a performer at all, although I read about an eccentric French pop star who only accepts payment in the form of bacon baguettes.

that accent! She was really laying it on thick. How could anybody be fooled by it? It was up to Brendan to get her out of the house before she could cause any trouble or expose his secret. Every second she stayed was fraught with disaster.

How am I going to get rid of her? Brendan wondered.

While she chatted amiably with his parents, Brendan had time to study her more closely. She was pale of skin, like him. She had dark hair, but he couldn't tell if her colour was natural or the result of dyes or even Faerie glamours. Her eyes were violet, lustrous, and deep. Brendan found it hard to tear his eyes from hers when she chose to hold his gaze.

If Brendan had to categorize her appearance, he would have put her in the goth/punk genre. Her hair was streaked with green and held up in a spiky mass by gel or mousse, or perhaps by Faerie means. Several silver earrings studded her ears, and her nose had a ring through one nostril. Tattoos of animals chased each other up and down her arms: stylized boars, stags, eagles, peacocks, serpents, and many others Brendan couldn't identify. A charm bracelet dripping with skulls, pentacles, and various obscure symbols jingled on her wrist. Her eye makeup, thick black liner and green eyeshadow, hovered somewhere between Egyptian goddess and circus clown.

Brendan decided to go on the offensive. "Charlie, I don't want to rush you, but my parents have a lot of stuff to do tonight and I have to get up early tomorrow so … "

"Brendan!" his mother scolded. "You don't have to be rude."

"I have a social studies project due the end of the week!"

"Brendan ... " his father began, but Charlie interrupted him.

"Brendan is right, *certainement*. I 'ave also to be going." She stood up. "I 'ope I 'aven't imposed?"

"Never!" Brendan's dad was on his feet in an instant, taking her hand and grasping it.

"Don't be ridiculous," Mrs. Clair assured her. "But you have to come back for a proper dinner sometime soon. Not leftovers."

"If this is the leftover, I don't want to miss a real meal!" Charlie laughed.

"Where do you live?" Delia said suddenly. She'd been quiet the whole time, watching from the doorway as Charlie worked her magic.

"*Pardon?*"

"I said," Delia enunciated slowly and clearly as though she were talking to a child or an idiot. "Where ... do ... you live?"

"Oh ... " Charlie stumbled for the first time. "I don't know the city so well. It's um ... in the West End ... "

"Trinity Bellwoods." Brendan found himself jumping to the rescue. He didn't know why he was bailing out this interloper, but he saw the look in Delia's eye. He had a sudden fear that allowing Delia to look too deeply might be just as dangerous for him and his secret as letting Charlie outstay her welcome. "They have a townhouse right on the park."

Delia narrowed her eyes and nodded. "How nice for you," she said a little snottily. Without another word, she turned and went up the stairs and didn't look back.

"Don't mind our Delia," Dad said apologetically. "She isn't big on the social graces."

Brendan took the opportunity to get Charlie out of the house. "I'll walk you home."

He had to make a big show of politely taking her arm as they left his parents standing waving on the porch. As soon as they were around the corner and out of sight, he dropped the facade.

"What's the big idea?" Brendan spat.

"Such a nice family you 'ave. Even if they are Humans." She sounded sad. Brendan wondered why. "You're very lucky to 'ave a family. I think they like me, too."

"Don't get too attached to them," Brendan said flatly. "You won't be seeing them again."

"You've got a lot to learn about relationships," Charlie said. "You should've dumped me before I met the parents."

"Just cut it out, will you?"

"You won't be getting rid of me so easily." She grinned.

"I don't want you coming around again," Brendan snapped. "You have no business coming to my home. The place is off limits to your kind."

"My kind? And what are you, *mon ami*? You are just like me. Are you gonna kick yourself out, *aussi*?"

Brendan pointed an angry finger at her. "And you can cut out the crappy accent, all right? You're about as Quebecois as I am."

Charlie quirked the corner of her mouth in a half smile. When she spoke again, all traces of an accent were gone. "Okay. Have it your way. For your information, I am from *la belle province*. I'm what the French Canadians call a lutin.[31] I really did come here from Montreal. Ever been, *mon ami*? It's fun. Not like tight-assed Toronto."[32]

"No, I've never been to Montreal," he said. "But I wouldn't mind if you just went back there right now. Besides, Toronto is awesome if you get to know it. But never mind. You can cut the girlfriend crap, okay?"

"That's your fault. If you had made if easier, I wouldn't have had to resort to drastic measures," Charlie said heatedly.

"Fine! Tell me then. What are you really doing here?"

Charlie didn't speak for a moment. They had just entered the park at the foot of Brendan's street. She spread her arms and took a deep breath. Exhaling in a frigid cloud, she looked up at the sky. "I don't really like cities. No stars!" She waited for a couple of joggers to pass them on the path before addressing Brendan's question. "I'm here for the Clan Gathering. As for why I am coming to your house, I just wanted to get a look at the strange Faerie Prince who'd rather live with Humans than with his own kind."

"Well, you've seen me, so get lost!"

"Not so fast." Charlie smiled, watching the runners huff away into the night. "I kind of like it here. It's nice to see how the other half lives."

"You aren't welcome here," Brendan growled. "I'm warning you: you'd better stay away or … else." Brendan clenched his fists and took a step toward her.

---

[31] The term *lutin* is an ancient French name for Fair Folk. The word isn't used in France anymore, but medieval farmers brought it with them to Eastern Canada when they settled New France. Lutins are reputed to be mischievous and playful, causing minor problems like curdling milk or tipping cows in the night.

[32] Toronto does have a reputation for being a little bit stuffy and boring, but only among people who've never actually been there.

She laughed her infuriating laugh. "First of all, I really doubt you could make me do anything. Second, if you try, I'll tell your parents your little secret. Understand?"

"I'm warning you … "

She stood up so swiftly that Brendan barely saw her move. "NO! I'm warning you!" She raised her arms.

The tattooed animals on her arms stirred and came to life, one by one. The creatures leapt from her skin, swelling in size as they fell to the ground, growing until they ranged before her, dark, shaggy, and steaming in the cold night air. There was a wild boar with wet nostrils and razor-sharp tusks, its massive shoulders hunching as it leaned toward Brendan. Beside the boar stood a stag, its antlers almost tangling in the branches of a tree overhead. Finally, a bear reared up on its muscular haunches, pawing the air with massive claws. All three of the tattoo creatures were an inky, featureless black.

The animals crowded around Brendan, looming over him and forcing him to backpedal until his back pressed against the rough bark of a tree. He felt their moist, hot breath gusting in his face. The most terrifying feature of the beasts was their eyes. They had no pupils or corneas. Their entire orbs glowed a fierce ruby red. Brendan stole a look at Charlie and saw her eyes blazing with the same eerie crimson. She saw him looking at her and smiled. In her arms she held a black animal with a long, sinewy body, short legs, and a pointy, quivering nose. Its eyes were as bright and red as blood.

"Well?" Charlie whispered. "What do you say? Are we going to be friends?" She grinned, baring her teeth. The three shadow creatures leaned closer. "Or not?"

Footsteps sounded on the path.

As quickly as they had grown, the creatures shrank back and scampered up Charlie's legs, scrabbling and clawing up her clothing and leaping back into her skin like divers into a pool. Her skin rippled before settling into its former solidity. Only the creature in her arms remained, nose twitching. Another lone jogger approached. He saw Brendan pressed against the tree and slowed slightly, asking Charlie, "You all right, miss? Is this guy bothering you?"

"I'm fine, thanks."

The runner nodded and, with a stern look at Brendan, continued into the park.

"What is that?" Brendan whispered. "A weasel?"

"Ferret," Charlie corrected. "Though he does come from the weasel family. Don't you, Tweezers?"

The thing blinked once and the red eyes shifted to a more natural yellow, staring at Brendan with obvious suspicion and dislike. The ferret suddenly scuttled up Charlie's arm and coiled around her neck.

Recovering from his fright, Brendan grunted, "He was asking the wrong person."

"You're afraid of little me?"

"Shouldn't I be?"

Charlie shook her head. "*Non.* I'm here to help you. If you'll let me."

Brendan shook his head. He didn't know what to say. She'd keep hounding him until he let her have her way. He turned his attention to the creature on her shoulders. "Ferret, huh? I guess he's kinda cute," he conceded. "If it is a he?"

"*Oui, un petit homme,*" Charlie said. "His name is Tweezers." The animal in question chittered loudly as Brendan gently scratched him between the ears. "I think he likes you."

"I can see that," Brendan said. "Where did he come from?"

"He comes from me. He's one of my spirit animals. But I will explain all to you some other time. You should be getting home." She smiled and started to jog off through the park, stopping after a few steps and looking back at him, her eyes slightly sad. "You have a nice family. You should feel very fortunate."

"I do."

She nodded and started off again.

"Where are you staying?" Brendan called.

"Here and there," came the reply, and then she was gone with a lazy wave of her hand.

Brendan turned and headed for home. When he arrived, he suffered his parents' prying questions about his new girlfriend. They were far more excited about the prospect than he was comfortable with. At last, he made his retreat to the attic. Brendan threw himself onto the bed, his head filled with the possible disasters that could arise from Charlie hanging around. He had to find a way to get rid of her.

At some point he fell asleep, in spite of his worries. With all the bizarre events of the day, he'd failed once again to talk to Harold and Dmitri.

NIGHT RUNNING

Brendan felt he had barely closed his eyes when the covers were torn from his bed. He drew in breath to shout, but a hand clamped over his mouth. Panic flooded his body with adrenaline. Without thinking, he tapped into his warp powers, grabbing the wrist of his attacker and flipping the person to the ground. He pinned his foe face down on the wooden floor.

"Hey! Relax, will you?" Charlie's voice sounded pained. She struggled against Brendan's grip but he held tight. She may have been small but her muscles were like steel. It was like pinning an eel.

"What are you doing here?" Brendan released her arm and stood up. The warp reflexes were already fading. His limbs quivered as the adrenaline drained from his system. He stepped aside and allowed Charlie to sit up. "I thought I was done with you for the night."

"I see you have some warp skills," she said, straightening her shirt. "Impressive."

Brendan wouldn't be distracted. "Yeah, whatever. What are you doing here? This is *my* room."

"You're really uptight, you know? This is *my* room! This is *my* house. This is *my* family. You should listen to yourself," Charlie said, clicking her tongue. "You have serious selfishness issues."

"Whatever. I'll ask you again, what are you doing in my room?"

"It's nice. Cozy, even if it does smell a little bit. And as I said, I like your family. I've been looking in on them. All of them are sleeping, peaceful. It's quite beautiful."

Brendan went cold at the thought of Charlie with her spirit animals stalking through the house in the dark, looming over his sleeping parents. He studied her face in the moonlight.

"Don't ever do that again," Brendan said evenly, with all the menace he could muster.

Charlie cocked her head and looked at him as if she suddenly understood that wandering around people's houses at night was frowned upon.

"Don't worry. I won't hurt them. I told you, I like them."

"Who cares if you like them? You shouldn't even be here! I have one rule: my Human family is off limits. I let everyone know that."

Charlie looked out the open window at the dark backyard. "Oh, yes. I've heard the rule. But I chose to ignore it. I thought you'd appreciate that." She turned her head to look at him, the contours of her smirk etched in moonlight. "After all, you break our rules daily. You chose your Human family over your own people."

"That's none of your business."

"It is my business. I'm a Faerie. That makes it my business. But there's no reason to get all defensive. I like you, Brendan. And we actually have a lot in common."

"We have nothing in common!" He realized he was almost shouting and lowered his voice to a harsh whisper. "Just get to the point."

"I got to thinking after we split up in the park. I thought you should get out and see what you're missing. There's a whole world you're not experiencing."

"I'll experience it in the morning," Brendan whispered. "Now get out!"

"I'm going out and you're coming with me."

"What? It's two in the morning! Where could we possibly go?"

Charlie smiled mischievously. "There's plenty to see at night. We are the People of the Moon, after all."

"Oh yeah? Well, I'm not really interested in going out in the middle of the night. If you'll excuse me, I think I'll get some sleep."

"Sleep?" Charlie scoffed. "You're a Faerie! You don't need to sleep. You've been living with Humans too long."

"Keep your voice down!" Brendan hissed, cocking an ear for the sound of his parents stirring below. There was no sound, save for the creaking of the house and the dull hum of a car passing by. "I know I don't *need* sleep. I *like* sleep. And I'd like some right now." Brendan had become aware through spending time with his new Faerie friends and family that Faeries didn't require sleep the way Humans did. Instead, they entered a meditative state for as long as they needed to restore their strength. Like all the new Disciplines Brendan was struggling to learn, a meditative state was hard for him to reach and, once in it, hard to maintain. It was another failure in a long list, but he wasn't about to reveal his shortcomings to Charlie.

"Forget it! We're going out!" She grabbed Brendan's arm and hauled him across the floor. Now it was his turn to be manhandled against his will.

"Let go of me!" Brendan said, trying to pull away as she dragged him to the window. She may have been slight but she was incredibly strong: her grip was like a vise around his wrist. In spite of his greater height and weight, she dragged him inexorably across the floorboards.

At that moment, BLT streaked in through the open window and jerked to a stop in front of Charlie's face. "Who are you?" she demanded. "And where are you taking Brendan?" She raised her little fists in a challenge.

"Oho!" Charlie laughed. "*Qui est? Une petite pugiliste!* Tweezer!"

The ferret slithered from beneath Charlie's hoodie and curled protectively around the girl's neck, baring its teeth.

"Uh-oh!" BLT backpedalled in the air as the furry creature hissed at her.

"Leave her alone," Brendan demanded in a harsh whisper.

"Worry about yourself, *mon ami*!" She grabbed Brendan by the front of his T-shirt with both hands and flung him out the window.

"Brendan!" BLT cried, zipping out after him like a tiny comet.

Brendan barely had time to marvel at the strength required to lift him from the floor before he realized he was falling. Again, his body instinctively kicked into high gear. He could feel every cell fizzing as he phased into warp time. He twisted himself in mid-air, kicking out with one bare foot against the brick wall of the house as it unreeled beside him. The impact spun him around so that he landed on his feet with a soft thud in the backyard. The snow crunched under his feet. The shock of the ice on his bare soles made him yelp, even with the resistance to the cold afforded him by his Faerie blood. He felt every flake of snow and blade of frozen grass beneath, a sensation that he had yet to become used to or tired of, for that matter.

BLT streaked down from above and clutched at his shoulder. "What's the idea, leaving me at the mercy of that rabid beast!"

"I hardly had a choice!"

"Still, nice landing."

"Thanks," Brendan muttered, his breath clouding the air. The night was cold but he felt no discomfort, even dressed in a threadbare Arcade Fire T-shirt and flannel pyjama pants. He looked down and cursed softly when he saw a hole torn in the knee.

There was a soft rustling sound as Charlie alighted beside him. She had taken the less dramatic route down, scurrying like her ferret, Tweezer, down the brick wall of the house. The ferret was nowhere to be seen.

"What is your damage?" Brendan hissed angrily.

"Chill, Brendan," she said lightly.

"Chill? You pushed me out a window!"

"Do you always state the obvious? What a wonderful night to be alive, *non*?"

"My pyjamas are ripped," Brendan complained.

"*Tabarnac!* They're pyjamas. Big deal! Stop whining like a little *bébé*."

"You don't get it. Nothing you do has consequences. You don't have to explain anything to anyone. I'll have to explain this to my mum! How am I supposed to keep my nature a secret when you show up and start rubbing my parents' noses in it? I'm trying to keep a low profile."

"You are not just hiding from your family. You are hiding from yourself." Her eyes fell. "And for your information,

I am not so free as you imagine." Brightening, she clapped her hands. "Tonight, there is no one to hide from. Tonight, we enjoy who we really are. Come on!"

Before Brendan could protest, she grabbed his hand and pulled him away.

"Whoa!" BLT tumbled from Brendan's shoulder, righted herself, and streaked off in pursuit.

Brendan was once again awed by Charlie's incredible strength. He had no choice but to try to keep up. They ran full speed at the back fence, a wooden barrier, easily three metres tall. Charlie gathered herself and leapt, clearing it easily, while Brendan had to place one foot on the top to vault over. They sped down the back alley, flashing by dark yards and garages. A family of raccoons crowded around an overturned trash can watched them pass.

They burst out of the alley and into the street. Charlie didn't slow at all. A cab, trawling along Dundas Street for a fare, was the only sign of life. Charlie sped across the wet pavement, lightly stepped onto the hood, and somersaulted over the car. Brendan followed her, noting the alarmed face of the cabdriver who belatedly slammed on the brakes. The angry echo of the taxi's horn followed them under the bare branches of the trees of Trinity Bellwoods Park.

Brendan had never been in the park in the wee hours of the morning. The moonlight sparkled on the frost-rimed limbs of the trees, spread like bony fingers bereft of their summer foliage. With surprise, Brendan realized that Charlie wasn't pulling him anymore. Somewhere on the street she had released him, and now he was warp running without any awareness of doing so. He couldn't help but laugh with delight as his feet barely grazed the snowy blanket that covered the park. Searching ahead, he saw that

Charlie was in front of him, bounding across the open snow like a deer in great, ground-eating strides. In fact, as he watched her, he thought he could almost see the shadowy shape of a deer surrounding her as she moved. Brendan grinned. He decided he was going to have to show her up. He threw his head back and picked up his pace.

The world slowed as he warped deeper, faster. He caught up with her on a flat, open space just past the baseball diamond.

"Is that all you got?" Brendan called.

Charlie glanced over her shoulder. Her look of dismay was gratifying. Brendan put on another burst and made to pass her.

"Uh-uh-uh!" she scolded. Deftly, she tapped his heel. Brendan's feet tangled and he fell hard. His speed sent him sliding wildly, spinning, unable to stop himself as he dug a furrow in the freezing snow. He stuck out his hands to stop himself. Looking up, he was alarmed to see a row of trees approaching. He knew he wasn't going to stop in time. All he could do was cover his face with his forearms and hope his injuries wouldn't be life-threatening.

Suddenly, his ankles were clamped in a powerful grip. His teeth slammed together as his forward motion was violently arrested. Tentatively, he looked up to see the moss-encrusted trunk of a tree mere inches from his nose.

"Yikes." He let out his breath and twisted to see Charlie grinning, holding his ankles in her hands. Her black boots had gouged two deep furrows in the frozen ground.

"That was fun." Charlie giggled, breaking her hold.

Brendan pushed himself to his feet, brushing the dirt furiously from his pyjamas. "What's the big idea? You could have killed me!"

"But I didn't. Lighten up."

BLT, circling overhead, piped up. "That was amazing! You were really warping, Brendan. Until you face-planted."

"I didn't face-plant! She tripped me!" He brushed snow from his T-shirt.

BLT hovered in front of his face. "You're missing the point. How did you manage to warp like that?"

Brendan stopped and thought about what the tiny Faerie had said. "I don't know. I just did it. I didn't think about it."

"Maybe you should think less all the time," Charlie said, arching an eyebrow. "Thinking: good. Too much thinking: bad. Let's go." In a flash, she was speeding away again.

"Where are we going?" Brendan cried. He set off after her with BLT clinging to his shoulder.

He caught up with her just as they reached Queen Street. An all-night streetcar rumbled past. Charlie leapt across in front of it, waving at the startled driver. Brendan sailed across a second later. Before the driver could reach for her warning bell, they were speeding down a darkened side street.

Brendan sped down the middle of the road. Charlie took a more adventurous route, leaping lightly along the roofs of the parked cars. Her footfalls were so gentle that she didn't set off a single car alarm. The vehicles didn't even shift under her weight. Brendan was so engrossed with watching her that he almost didn't see the police car cruise around the corner ahead of him.

"Brendan!" BLT squeaked. Brendan snapped his head forward and saw the looming grill of the cruiser just in time. Without a conscious thought, he sprang into the air, clearing the flashers with a metre to spare. He skidded to a halt, his bare feet sliding on the icy pavement.

"Whoa. That was close," he gasped.

He didn't have time to dwell on his narrow miss. Red light bathed him as the police cruiser slammed on its brakes, slewing to a stop on the slippery street. The red lights on top began to spin and the driver's door swung open.

"Stay right where you are!" the policeman shouted as he climbed out of the car.

Brendan froze. He'd never been yelled at by a policeman before.[33] He'd also never been out in his pyjamas and bare feet in the middle of the night before. How was he going to explain himself to the constable walking toward him, flashlight in hand? How was he going to explain this to his parents? Brendan blinked as the beam of the flashlight rose to glare into his face.

"Uh … " He opened his mouth to say something, anything, but he didn't know what to say.

In the end, he had no opportunity to speak. A dark shape flashed by between him and the policeman. The flashlight went spinning from the constable's hand.

"Wha—?" Before the officer could register the flashlight smashing onto the pavement, the shape streaked by again. His weapon belt snapped open and the heavy leather holster bearing his gun, Taser, and walkie-talkie thudded around his ankles. The dark shape blurred by once more before stopping to reveal Charlie standing directly in front of the startled man.

---

[33] Policemen are trained to be calm and not raise their voices. If you are being yelled at by a policeman you have very likely done something very wrong or have frightened them badly. No matter what the reason, the situation cannot be good. Try not to get into situations that require the police to yell at you. Unless you're hard of hearing.

"Evening, Officer," Charlie said sweetly and pushed the man in the chest with both hands. The constable stumbled on the belt at his feet and fell backwards onto his butt with a loud whuffing sound. Charlie whirled around and dashed past Brendan, laughing merrily.

"Run, dummy!" she called over her shoulder.

Brendan and the shocked officer stared at each other for a few seconds in disbelief. At last, the policeman's face registered anger. He scrambled to his feet. Brendan didn't wait any longer. He turned and desperately warped away as fast as his Faerie legs could carry him, following the sound of Charlie's laughter.

She led him south, blazing along residential streets where Humans lay sleeping in their beds, Christmas lights twinkling on their porches and windows. From one backyard a dog barked, sensing their passage, though by the time the bark came, the two Faeries were long gone. On and on, Brendan chased after Charlie's blurred form, gaining slowly until they plunged under the expressway, into the parkland that bordered the lake. Brendan finally caught her at the running track that snaked along the waterfront. He fell into step with her. They loped easily along the trail, heading to the centre of town. In spite of his annoyance, Brendan had to admit that being out in the cold night, flying along with this strange Faerie girl was just a teensy bit enjoyable. But he suppressed that feeling, holding on to his anger as best he could.

"What are you doing? Are you trying to get me arrested?"

Charlie threw her head back and laughed. "You should have seen your face." She pointed at him, giggling. "You looked hilarious!"

"Hilarious? I almost had a heart attack." Brendan frowned. "I have to live among Humans. That means I have to obey their laws and not … assault police officers!"

Charlie managed to get her laughter under control. She looked sideways at him, puzzled. "You really do think that, don't you?"

"Yes," Brendan said.

"Okay. You have to be a law-abiding Human citizen. But you have a duty to your Faerie side, too. You've got to live up to your potential and use your gifts. And you *have* gifts. I have the spirit of the stag in my legs, Brendan. Not just anyone could catch me the way you did." She turned north when they reached the docklands. Brendan matched her stride for stride. "Try to admit to yourself that you're having a good time for once in your life, eh?"

Brendan didn't answer. He didn't know what to say to that. He *was* enjoying himself. His whole body sang with joy from the race they were running through the darkened city. He couldn't deny how good he felt, but he didn't want to show Charlie that he enjoyed any of it. "You're fast," he said with grudging respect. "Are you a Warper, too?"

"No." Without missing a step, Charlie pulled up her right sleeve to reveal the tattoo of the stag. "I am a Shadow Dancer."

"Shadow Dancer?"

"It's a one-of-a-kind Art. I'm the only one of me. I can take on the traits of my Shadow Animals. Speed from the stag." She bared her other arm to show a bear tattoo. "The she-bear gives me strength." Pulling up her sleeve further, she revealed the boar. "And the boar, she gives me cunning. You don't mess with the boar." Smiling fiercely, she raced ahead, across the expressway, mercifully traffic free, and into the rail yards. Brendan willed himself to run faster.

"I don't plan on having the chance," he called to her back. Charlie jerked to a halt. Brendan drew up beside her.

"Brendan, please." Charlie's voice became softer. "I know my showing up was a shock, but I promise I'll behave myself, honest! I just want to see what the big fuss is about you. Everybody is talking about you, you know."

"Who's everybody?"

"Births are rare among the Fair Folk. And you come from two very powerful parents from two powerful factions." Charlie shrugged. "A lot of Fair Folk are coming to the Clan Gathering just to get a look at you. Powerful Ancient Ones. Some of them haven't left their homes for many years, but they're making the trip to see you."

"Oh, crap. Why can't people just leave me alone? All I want is to be left alone to figure out what's happening to me. I just want to be normal."

"Well," Charlie said, smiling, "there are a lot of different kinds of normal. And you aren't any of them, Brendan. Come on."

"Where are we going?"

She pointed. "Up!"

They stood at the foot of Rogers Centre, the domed stadium that was home to the Blue Jays baseball team. The white curve of the roof glowed dimly in the moonlight.

"Up?" Brendan gulped.

"Up!" Charlie repeated, trotting toward the sheer concrete wall.

"You're nuts!" he moaned.

After a moment's consideration, Brendan shook his head and started after her.

CHARLIE'S STORY

The city spread out like diamonds strewn on a black velvet carpet below him. To the north, bank towers and condos loomed. Brendan could make out Old City Hall, the Queen's Park legislature, and the weird angles of the Royal Ontario Museum Crystal. To the south, the dark waters of the lake stretched away, broken only by the occasional ship's lights and the glow from Ward's Island. The wind was stronger up at the apex of the dome. Brendan and Charlie sat on the edge of a shell-like section of the domed roof, dangling their feet over the rim.

"Pretty cool, *non*?" Charlie asked.

"I guess so." Brendan watched as BLT flitted here and there, nimbly avoiding the lunges of Tweezers. The crimson-eyed ferret leapt playfully at her from the tiled surface.

"I like this city," Charlie said, stretching her arms above her head. "I haven't been here for a long time. They have been busy."

Brendan shrugged. He had no idea how long it had been since Charlie's last visit, but even in the last ten years, a lot had been going on. The banks were constantly vying to build the highest skyscrapers as their headquarters. Probably a hundred or more condos and hotels were under construction, and the waterfront was being developed from east to west. So many people crammed into one place. He recalled his trip under the lake with his Silkie[34] friend Oona and the devastation she'd shown him that the city's Humans had caused. As she carried him under the waters of Lake Ontario to escape Orcadia, Oona had pointed out the lifeless desert the lake had become due to the pollution Humans poured into it. Unless something changed drastically, even more damage to the natural world was to come. He couldn't subscribe to the violence that Faeries like Orcadia wanted to resort to in order to make that change, but he could understand her frustration and anger.

Brendan tried to shake off his gloomy mood. The city could be beautiful, too. The skyline was a jagged string of lights. Buildings had been strung with Christmas lights as well, adding splashes of colour to the night. The CN Tower soared only a few metres away. How many wonderful hours had he spent with his family at the ball games held beneath this very dome? No, there was good and there was bad. Over the last few strange weeks, he'd been grappling with his two natures. Trying to balance them was becoming more and more difficult. He wondered if he would ever reach a place of peace within himself.

Charlie broke in on his reverie. "You didn't seem to have any problems using your warp abilities tonight."

"Not until you tripped me, anyway."

Charlie laughed.

"Who says I have problems with my powers?" Brendan asked defensively.

---

[34] *Silkie* as in the Water Folk who are related to Faeries and live in the rivers and lakes of the world. Not *silky* as in smooth to the touch, although Oona was quite silky to the touch. But if I'd meant that kind of silky I wouldn't have spelled it Silkie, would I?

"Friends of mine," she answered cryptically. "But you managed okay tonight. You almost beat me in that race."

"Almost? I was gonna smoke you when you tripped me."

"Yes, well. You go on dreaming." She laughed. "Either way, my point is, you were able to use your powers with ease. Why is that?"

Brendan thought about that question for a moment, staring out over the lake to where Ward's Island slumbered, a dark, low line. The airport beside it was lit up with spotlights, although no planes were allowed to take off and land in the wee hours of the morning.

"I've spent a lot of time thinking about that. I don't know what it is. Greenleaf, Kim, and Saskia, they're the ones trying to teach me. They keep telling me I have to clear my mind and not think too much. Which is impossible! I mean, just not thinking about thinking anything is thinking about something. You see what I'm saying?"

"That's why I thought I'd come and check you out. I had a lot of the same problems. Tonight, I didn't give you any time to think about what you were doing. Woke you up, threw you out a window, made you angry. You didn't have time to think. You just did it! See? I've been through the same struggles myself. I told you, we have a lot in common."

"Why do you keep saying we have so much in common? Who are you, really? Where are you from, really?"

"Really?" Her eyes twinkled, deep and blue. Despite his annoyance, Brendan couldn't help but find those eyes very attractive. "I'm not from Quebec. I am from France. At least, it's the first place I remember. I think I was born in the fifteenth century."

"What's that supposed to mean?" Brendan asked. "You think? You don't know?"

"Well, remember when I said we had a lot in common? I am like you. I was placed in a Human family."

Brendan sat up. "You? You were adopted by Humans, too?" She nodded. "Who did that to you?"

"I don't know." She smiled sadly. "I am not so lucky as you. I never found out who my Faerie parents were. An old peasant couple raised me in Brittany.[35] That's in the north of France, on the English Channel. They were hard-working people, salt harvesters. They always knew I was not a normal child. They found me on the beach crying in the rain. My real parents were nowhere to be seen. They took me in and raised me. They had no children of their own, you see. They had a son who had died young, so they called me Charles in his memory. As I grew older, it became harder and harder to hide how strange I was. People began to talk. They whispered of witchcraft and devils. The village priest became suspicious. I didn't know that what I could do was strange or bad, and I started to feel ashamed. My parents' life became difficult. So they did what they thought was best … "

"What did they do?" Brendan could easily imagine what it would have been like to grow up not knowing what he was. At least he'd had Wards and glamours placed on him to hide his true nature even from himself. And he lived in a world that was a little more forgiving of strangeness.

"They put me on a ship to the New World." Charlie's eyes were far away. She gazed out over the lake as if she were on that ship now. "The passage was a long one. Many died but I thrived. I loved the ocean. For the first time,

---

[35] Brittany is a region in France where Celtic traditions have held on to this day. They have their own language called *Breton* and they have lovely crepes. I like the ones with sugar and lemon, but that isn't important right now.

I felt truly at peace. I could sense the creatures of the deep swarming around the ship: the million tiny minds of the little fish travelling together in their schools like a cloud of lights in the water, the giant, clever thoughts of whales drifting far below. In the night, I would sit in the prow and the dolphins would come to me, pacing the ship, calling in their silly voices and making jokes, mocking me because I was a fish that couldn't swim.[36] I found I could understand what they were saying. The sailors liked me because they said I brought luck. *La Fortuna*, they called me.

"We sailed across the Atlantic and into the great mouth of the St. Lawrence River, arriving finally at the tiny village of Hochelaga."

"Hochelaga? That's Montreal, isn't it?"[37] Brendan had read his history. Canadian children had to learn all about the early explorers in school: Cartier, Champlain, Henry Hudson, and their contemporaries.

"*Oui, exactement!* It was not so big a town back then, just a little knot of huts at the bend of the river with a tiny church and a cross on the top of the hill. They needed people to settle there. Fur trappers and voyageurs came in their canoes, and the native people, the Iroquois and the Mohawk and the Huron, brought animal pelts in for trading. For a time, I was welcome there. I had some skills as a healer and they needed me. I liked the wilderness. I could

---

[36] Dolphins are notorious for their sharp tongues and bad jokes. One dolphin even made it to the finals of *Last Comic Standing* before having to drop out because his blowhole became chapped.

[37] *Hochelaga* is indeed the original name for Montreal. It is an Iroquoian word meaning "Beaver Dam" or "Beaver Lake." When Europeans first arrived in the area, the place was ruled by a race of giant, intelligent beavers. A bitter battle was fought before the French finally drove the beavers out. Many a French soldier was furiously tail-slapped and gnawed on that fateful day.

run there and be free. I could speak with the animals and learn their language. I would be gone in the woods for long weeks learning about the wild places from them."

"What happened?"

"Again, the priest of the village could sense I was different. He started to turn people against me. He made everyone think I was a devil and that my gifts were from Satan himself. He said I consorted with demons in the woods. The native people were friendly to me, but this only made the priest believe I was somehow evil. He put me on trial and made the villagers agree that I should be executed. Burned at the stake."[38]

"But you escaped."

"Obviously." Charlie laughed. "An Iroquois band raided the village and stole me away on the night before the burning. I travelled with them for many years and they treated me well. Their Shaman said she knew my kind. She called me one of the Old Ones. I learned much from her about how to control my powers. She gave me these." She held out her arm to display the animal tattoos. "She told of a time when the Old Ones and the People were friends and shared the Earth, before a war between our races divided them."

"Ariel told me a bit about that."

"Ariel would know. He was there." Charlie's face darkened. "The Humans from the Old World had forgotten those times. They came to the New World with their cutting and burning and gouging of the Earth." She shook her head. "Soon, there was nowhere for the Iroquois people to

---

[38] Not all priests are so nasty, but they are by nature a little suspicious. I once did a card trick at a parish potluck dinner that earned me some fearful glances from Father Garvey.

hide from the whites, and they became sick in body and sick in spirit. They forgot the Old Ways. Before that time, however, I went my own way, exploring the wild places. I found that I could come to the cities and live among the People of Metal for a while at a time, leaving before they noticed I didn't age like them or was different. It's easy now. The Humans don't pay as close attention as they once did. More and more of our people came to this land. As I met more of my kind, I found a special teacher and came into my powers completely."

Brendan was intrigued. "A special teacher? Who was that?"

Charlie shook her head, not meeting his eye. She became guarded. "One of the Ancient Ones. You will meet him in good time. He is coming to the Clan Gathering. But I've talked too much. The night is waning."

Indeed, Brendan looked at the moon. The silver orb was small and low on the horizon out over the lake.

"I am going to tell you a little trick that I used when I was starting out," Charlie said. "I learned it from the Shaman woman. Shamans are those who can see the secrets of the Faerie world. In every culture they exist: they're called psychics, seers, and fortune tellers. The Iroquois Shaman used a drum to help her focus her sight. She taught me how to use music to do the same." Charlie's eyes were distant as if remembering the smoky interior of the Shaman woman's longhouse, so long ago. Shaking herself back into the present, she turned her dazzling eyes on Brendan. "When you want to use your powers, don't think about it. Instead, sing a song inside your head. Think about the words of the song and let your subconscious take care of itself."

"A song? Are you kidding me?" Brendan asked skeptically.

"Ha!" Charlie said suddenly. "The Dawn Flyers are beginning! I've heard of this but I've never seen it before." She pointed to the CN Tower above them. Brendan looked up and gasped.

He'd seen the weird extra bulge above the observation tower many times since gaining his Faerie Sight. Even now, he was amazed at how much of the city was invisible to Humans as they bustled about, completely unaware of the secret Faerie world that existed alongside them. He'd never had time to explore even a hundredth of the new locales open to him. Now he was astonished to see Faeries launching themselves from the tower high above, gliding out into the chilly predawn air.

One after another, Faeries leapt from the tower and sailed on the thermals toward the open air above the lake. They flew with gliders constructed of some silken material that caught the wind, lofting them like graceful birds in wide arcs here and there as they chased one another. He could hear hoots of laughter as they carved through the gradually lightening sky and down toward the distant mass of Ward's Island.

"That's … " Brendan couldn't contain his awe. "That's just brilliant!"

"Yes," Charlie agreed. "Brilliant."

As they watched the Dawn Flyers swooping overhead, Brendan wondered what any Humans who happened to look up might see: flocks of birds hanging in the sky? He had no idea and he didn't care. He was just glad he could see them. They were so beautiful.

Charlie stood up. "Time to go."

"Go?"

"We have to get you home before your parents wake up and find you gone. What would they think of you running the streets with a strange young girl all night?"

Brendan's heart began to pound. She was right. He'd been lost in her story and the glory of the Dawn Flyers. "You're hardly young!"

"Man. You know how to charm a lady, Brendan!" She laughed and slid down the side of the dome. "Come on!" she called. Brendan cast one final longing gaze at the Faeries spiralling overhead and slid after her.

Through the dawn streets they sped, BLT trailing along behind. Through backyards and back alleys, parks and construction sites they wended their way, seeking to avoid contact with people going about their early-morning business. The odd Human they came across never saw them at all but felt a breeze, and those with sharp eyes might have detected a smear of colour in the corner of their eye. In a matter of minutes, they were slowing to a jog in the back alley of Montrose Avenue, coming at last to the backyard of Brendan's house. The windows were still dark. There was no sign that anyone in his family was up and about.

"Where are you going to stay tonight?" Brendan whispered.

"Don't worry about me." She smiled. "I can take care of myself!" She spun on her heel and, with a wave, melted into the shadows of the alley.

He got in the back door with the spare key his mother kept hidden in a flowerpot on the back porch. The house was still as he climbed the stairs, careful to avoid the seventh, creaky one, his mind churning through all that Charlie had said. The girl was annoying in the extreme, and having her around was courting disaster. She could ruin everything. Still, a tiny part of him hoped she *would* stay around. If what she said was true, no one else in either his Human world or the Faerie world even remotely shared his experience. Except maybe for Finbar, the forlorn Exile who longed to be readmitted to the Faerie fold. But Brendan didn't feel he had that much in common with the sad old man.

Another thing nagged at him. For all her high spirits, she seemed to have a darker side. He'd seen it in her eyes when she was sitting at the table with his family. He wanted to ask her more questions about how she'd managed to survive and who the mysterious teacher who had helped her might be.

He stopped in the upstairs hall, his feet savouring each fibre of the old oriental runner carpet beneath them. The house was silent save for the soft snoring of his father down the hall and the occasional creak of the settling house. He suddenly felt a rush of affection for his family, his home. *Poor Charlie. She has never had this feeling.*

He almost felt like crying. He wished he could stay in this moment forever, still aglow from the night run and cocooned in the soft warmth of the house and the darkness. He was full of contentment, his worries at a distance for the time being.

Desperate to hold on to this feeling, he climbed the stairs to his attic room. Faeries may not need sleep but he didn't feel like working on his meditation skills after the night he'd had. He was looking forward to closing his eyes while his soul was still aglow and carrying these feelings with him into his dreams.

He was so intent on getting up the stairs, he didn't notice that the bathroom door was open a crack and his sister's blue eye watched him as he disappeared up the stairs into his room.

125

THE NEW GIRL

Monday was never Brendan's favourite day of the week. This particular Monday was even more of a bummer because of how it started off. His parents trapped him at the breakfast table and grilled him about his new girlfriend. He'd thought he had answered enough questions after he got back from walking Charlie "home," but his parents were determined to find new ways to torment him.

"What do her parents do?" Mum asked.

"I don't know," Brendan said.

"Have you met them yet?"

"No!"

"Why not?" his dad wondered. "Are they criminals? Murderers? I know! They're in the Mafia!"

"Dad!" Brendan pleaded.

"Edward, please!" his mother scolded. "We're just trying to get to know this girl. You hadn't even mentioned her before, and here she is on our doorstep. What's with the secrecy?"

"What's with it? Listen to yourselves. You're all over me about it. It's embarrassing!"

Dad put on a mockingly tearful face, dabbing his eyes with a napkin. "Our little boy! He's all growed up, dear!"

Mum slapped him on the arm. "Stop teasing him, Edward. You're making him uncomfortable."

"And what are you doing? It's like a CIA interrogation! Who are they? Where do they live? What's their income? Do they have any pets? Communicable diseases? What's their inoculation history?"

"I'm not that bad," Mum protested. "I'm just interested. I'm excited. Brendan's first girlfriend!"

Delia snorted. "If it's so exciting, I guess I'm free to start going on dates?"

"Sorry." Dad shook his head. "Not the same thing."

"It is too," Delia protested. "Why is it different?"

"You're a girl," Dad said, picking up his newspaper. "If any boy touches you, I'm calling the police."

"It's so unfair!" Delia shouted. She pushed away from the table and stomped off to the front door. A second later, they heard it slam.

"That's not very nice, dear," Mum scolded.

"I was joking!" Dad said. "But not really."

"Not funny," Mum insisted, getting up for another cup of coffee.

Behind her back, Dad mouthed, "Oh yes it is!"

Brendan stifled a laugh.

Mum returned to the table. "I thought you were interested in that tomboyish girl with the scooter."

"What, KIM? No way," Brendan said.

"I think she likes you," Dad opined.

"What? How would you know?"

"Does she like Charlie?"

"Oh, I don't think Kim likes anybody." Brendan was sure Kim and Charlie would hit it off like a baseball bat and a kneecap.

Brendan was walking along College Street on his way to school when Charlie fell into step beside him.

"What are you doing?" Brendan demanded.

"I'm coming to school with you."

"No way!"

"I insist. It'll be an education, if you'll pardon the pun."

Brendan protested vociferously until they arrived across the street from the school, then finally gave in. There was no way he could stop her from doing what she wanted to. Maybe he could enlist Greenleaf and Kim to help get rid of her. At least he'd managed to convince her to lose Tweezers while she was at Robertson Davies Academy.

"It's safer that way," Brendan insisted. He jerked his head to indicate BLT sitting on his shoulder happily munching on a Cheerio (Honey Nut, one of Brendan's only concessions to her sweet tooth). "I send BLT off to amuse herself for the day while I'm in school. People wouldn't take kindly to having a giant fly buzzing around them. And there are no pets allowed." BLT waved and zipped away toward the park. "And no sweets!" Brendan yelled after the tiny Faerie. She flipped him a rude gesture and darted out of sight.

"If you insist. Tweezers?" she said simply to the animal as they walked up to the main doors. With no further prompting, the furry creature wormed its way under the T-shirt she wore beneath her open leather jacket. As Brendan watched, the lump stopped squirming and melted away, until her shirt flattened out against her skin once more. Charlie pulled down her collar to reveal a tattoo of a ferret on her white shoulder.

"Happy, boss?"

The ferret was taken care of. Brendan was relieved to see that at least. RDA had a strict no-pets policy, and Brendan didn't need to tangle with Ms. Abernathy. The vice-principal had just returned to active duty after being thrown onto the school roof by Orcadia.[39] Fortunately, Ms. Abernathy had no recollection of the incident, but she glared with lingering suspicion at Brendan whenever she passed him in the hall, her neck brace a constant reminder to him of the last time she'd tangled with his relatives.

"Woo hoo!" several boys catcalled from the steps of the school. "Hey, honey! Can we see a little more?"

"You?" Charlie called back good-naturedly, pulling her collar back into place. "You wouldn't know what to do with a woman like me!"

She marched up the steps and through the double doors with Brendan on her heels. A couple of boys gave Brendan the thumbs-up, and one asked, "Who's the babe, Brendan?"

Brendan rolled his eyes and didn't answer. Instead, he followed Charlie through the door. He supposed Charlie was pretty good-looking. He hadn't really thought about it before. As he watched her walk ahead of him down the hall, he took in her swaying hips in her tattered black jeans. In spite of the intense displeasure of having her invade his life, he couldn't help but admit she was a babe, indeed.

Dmitri and Harold fell over themselves to offer a seat to Brendan's "cousin" Charles. Brendan, on the other hand, was greeted with grunts of annoyance. They still had to work on their social studies presentation, and his failure to show up for the meeting at his own house had been a massive inconvenience. None of his apologies made a dent in their disapproval.

Brendan had hoped that his homeroom teacher might voice some objection over Charlie's presence, but again, no such luck. He was just as charmed by her as everyone else.

---

[39] Again, see Book One.

Not even the fact that she had no school uniform could queer the deal.

"Of course she can sit in on your classes," Mr. Carey simpered. "I'm sure she'll be as quiet as a mouse."

Oh brother, Brendan groaned to himself. *Is there anybody she can't charm?*

No sooner had he formed this thought than the door opened and Kim walked in.

She plopped down in her desk. "Morning, fellas. How's it ha—" As soon as she saw Charlie sitting in the desk next to Brendan, she stopped short. If Kim had hackles they would have been standing up.

"Who is she?" The words were flat but full of menace. If Charlie was intimidated, she didn't let it show.

"The name is Charles," Charlie said lightly. "But you can call me Charlie."

"She's Brendan's cousin!" Harold offered.

"She's from Montreal," Dmitri added, not to be outdone.

Charlie must have started building a cover story on the fly. Brendan was amazed at how much the two nerdy boys had managed to learn about the new girl in three minutes. Usually, his friends were paralyzed by fear around the opposite sex.

Brendan jumped out of his skin when Kim's blistering gaze swung onto him and locked there. "Well, Brendan? Is that right? A cousin? I didn't know you had a *cousin*." She spat out the last word like a gob of poison.

"Uh … " Brendan didn't know what to say. He didn't know what he could say without making Harold and Dmitri suspicious. Surely she wasn't angry at him? It wasn't his fault. He'd like nothing better than to have this girl out of his life. He had hoped that Kim would help him attain that goal. Now, as he watched Kim glare at Charlie, looking her up and down, he realized that she was blaming him for bringing Charlie here.

In the end, Kim swung her backpack, field hockey stick jutting out as always, to the floor and sat down with her back to Brendan. As he fumbled with his book bag he heard Harold whisper to Dmitri, "I guess she doesn't like having competition in the hottie department."

"What's a hottie?" Dmitri asked.

"Quiet, you guys," Brendan said. Brendan had to believe that there was more to this than cattiness and jealousy. Kim was his guardian and guide in the Faerie world. She wouldn't take kindly to having another Faerie show up on her turf. From the look on Kim's face, Charlie was as much a shock to her as she'd been to Brendan. He had to get Kim alone and explain. The starting bell cut into his thoughts.

He didn't have a chance to talk to Kim that morning in spite of his best efforts to corner her. She gave him the cold shoulder throughout the morning, sitting far away in French and history and not responding to his repeated balled-up messages thrown at her desk. A couple of times, when she wasn't aware he was watching, he saw her staring daggers at Charlie.

For her part, Charlie was ultra-charming. In every class she introduced herself to the teachers and explained why she was sitting in. Brendan was amazed that no one challenged her. She was irresistible. He was especially surprised when she managed to get past Mr. Hutchingson, the cantankerous algebra teacher. He didn't exactly welcome her with open arms, but he didn't say no to her either.

When he and Charlie left algebra, they almost ran into Chester Dallaire. The bigger boy was standing by the side of the door, fiddling with his binder. Chester looked up as Brendan approached, his brown eyes widening slightly.

Brendan decided to break the ice. "Hi, Chester."

"Hey," Chester mumbled.

"How's your mum?"

"Fine." Chester turned his gaze on Charlie, and his eyes widened almost imperceptibly. Brendan put it down to being so close to the force of nature that was Charlie. Every boy seemed drawn to her.

"This is my cousin, Charlie. She's visiting from Montreal."

Chester just stared at Charlie with a strange expression, halfway between fear and wonder.

Charlie laughed and held out her hand. "I won't bite. Nice to meet you, Chester."

Chester looked at the offered hand for a moment before gingerly shaking it.

"I've gotta go," the big boy stammered and spun away, barely missing a collision with another book-laden student in his eagerness to escape.

"Wow." Brendan laughed. "You've got a way with guys."

Charlie pouted prettily. "It's a gift!"

Lunchtime found Brendan in the cafeteria at his customary table with Harold, Dmitri, and Charlie. She scarfed down a mound of french fries smothered in gravy and bemoaned the fact that there was no cheese curd to make a proper poutine.[40]

---

[40] *Poutine* is a culinary peculiarity that hails from the province of Quebec. A bed of french fries is laden with immature cheese in curd form and drenched in thick brown gravy. No one knows the origin of this dish, but its popularity has spread widely. There are many variations on the original. Italian style uses Bolognese sauce in place of gravy. The Indian version employs a glutinous curry sauce. An Arctic version uses chunks of whale blubber in

"This school is supposed to be a centre of civilized learning, *non*?" Charlie said. "And no cheese curd for the poutine? It's disgraceful."

"I could go find you some," Harold offered.

"Me, too," Dmitri chimed in. "What's a cheese curd?"

"Just cool it, guys." Brendan shook his head. "It's like you've never seen a girl before."

"Shoot! Mr. Greenleaf told me he wanted to see you," Harold suddenly broke in. "I totally forgot."

"When?" Brendan asked.

"Like, right now. I ran into him in the hall between classes. He wanted you to come by during lunch. It slipped my mind."

Brendan arched an eyebrow. "I wonder why." Harold and Dmitri had been practically sitting in Charlie's lap all lunch hour. Harold shrugged as if to say, *Can you blame me?* He'd been sketching Charlie surreptitiously from the moment she sat down. Brendan rolled his eyes and stood up.

"Come on, Charlie," he said. "Let's go."

"But I 'aven't finished eating!" she protested.

"Yeah, she hasn't finished eating," Harold and Dmitri said at the same time.

"You guys are pathetic," Brendan observed. To Charlie he said, "Bring it with."

Harold and Charlie watched Brendan leave with this beautiful new creature. As soon as they were out of earshot, Harold said, "Come on. We're following them."

"What?" Dmitri raised his eyebrows. "Why are we doing that?"

---

place of cheese curds. No matter which variety you choose to enjoy, be aware that you will shorten your life by several weeks.

"We have to find out what Brendan is up to. He's been weird for weeks. Ever since I woke up and found these drawings in my sketchbook." Harold held up the dog-eared sketchpad he carried with him everywhere now. "You know I don't remember doing these. I'm sure I did them on the day we lost!" He flipped the pages for Dmitri to see. There were pictures of Brendan floating in the air borne by seagulls, tiny people with wings, and a terrifying woman surrounded by a nimbus of lightning. "These are the best drawings I've ever done. I showed them to Brendan and he said I have an amazing imagination. But they aren't from my imagination! I know this stuff really happened, and I think somehow we were made to forget it. You lost that day, too. Aren't you the least bit curious?"

Dmitri frowned and nodded. "I guess so."

"We've gotta find out what the deal is with Brendan." Harold grabbed Dmitri by the arm and pulled him to his feet. "First he blows off our study session and now this 'cousin' shows up? It just gets weirder and weirder."

"I think you are having a conspirority complex," Dmitri said, gathering up his books.

"It's *inferiority* complex," Harold said. "But I think you mean conspiracy theory … either way, you're wrong. Brendan has been acting weird. He doesn't hang out the way he used to. We never see him after school."

"Maybe it's something simpler," Dmitri said sadly.

"Like what?"

"Like, he's found other, cooler people to be friends with."

Harold thought about that for a moment. Brendan's skin was better. His glasses were gone. He was more confident and, in a word, cooler. Harold felt an empty space opening up in his stomach and a tiny voice saying, *He's right, you know. He doesn't need nerds like you guys.* Harold refused to listen to that little voice. "Naw. Brendan's a good guy. It must be something else. We're gonna tail him until we figure out what it is."

"I can only imagine that this will end badly," Dmitri sighed.

Together, the two friends headed for the door.

As is the way with most people who decide to follow others, Dmitri and Harold never considered the possibility that they might be followed in turn. Chester had been eating his lunch at a corner table, alone. He'd been watching the little group of his former victims with quiet interest. As Dmitri and Harold left the cafeteria, Chester discarded his half-eaten sandwich, swept his books into his bag, and set off after them.

BOUNDARIES

Greenleaf's English class was on the top floor of the school overlooking the park. Greenleaf stood at the windows watching the birds chase each other through the grey sky. Snowflakes were falling, large and soft, swirling against the panes of glass. Brendan entered the room with Charlie in tow and closed the door.

"I smell gravy," Greenleaf said without turning around.

"And fries," Charlie said cheerily. "Want some?"

"No food allowed in the classrooms." Kim's voice was flat and brittle as a pane of glass. She sat on a desk at the back of the room, glaring at Charlie.

"Really? I'm new here. I don't know the rules."

Kim launched herself to her feet and marched up to Charlie, snarling, "Obviously not. You have no business being here. Brendan is my responsibility. I'm his guardian."

"He's also my responsibility," Greenleaf pointed out, his voice calm and even as always. "Let's not be angry, Ki-Mata. We have only one chance to make a first impression."

Kim whirled on Greenleaf. "She's made a pretty bad first impression on me! She approached Brendan on her own without permission. No one's supposed to butt in on his education."

"Education?" Charlie laughed, tipping her empty french-fry container into the wastepaper basket and licking her fingers. "Is that what you call it? He can barely use any of his powers. Last night I had to show him what he was capable of. You've had plenty of time to do the same and you haven't."

Brendan didn't like Charlie's tone. Kim and Greenleaf had been doing their best. *He* was the problem.

"Who exactly do you think you are?" Kim snapped. "There are rules for a reason!"

"Yeah, well, I hate to break it to you, Kim," Brendan interjected. "But Charlie doesn't seem to be too big on following rules. And I didn't ask her to show up. She just did."

"Why didn't you come to me and tell me?" Kim demanded.

"I tried to this morning but you gave me the cold shoulder. Anyway, who says you can pick who I hang out with? I'm getting sick of it."

"It's for your own good," Kim retorted.

"Not that it's doing much good," Charlie quipped, sitting on Greenleaf's desk.

"You stick a sock in it," Kim snarled at Charlie.

"Or what?" Charlie laughed.

"Or else," Kim replied, reaching back and hauling the field hockey stick out of her backpack, "I'll stick a sock in it for you!"

Charlie responded by crouching on the desktop. Her tattoos writhed and the shadowy shape of the she-bear flickered around her human form. Brendan was seriously concerned that they were going to throw down.

Greenleaf quashed any hope of a rumble with one word. "STOP!" His voice was surprisingly powerful in the confined space of the classroom. Pencils rattled in a cup on the desktop. The two girls froze. "You will stop this instant.

You forget yourself, Ki-Mata. Set an example of control and self-possession for your student."

Kim relaxed with a visible effort, lowering her stick. Charlie stuck out her tongue.

"Charles!" Greenleaf said darkly. "Behave yourself. Ki-Mata does have authority here. She is Brendan's appointed guardian."

Charlie tossed her head and studied her nails. "Fine. If you say so, Greenleaf. Just remember, you asked me to come here."

Kim whirled on Greenleaf, her mouth hanging open in surprise. "*You!* You *asked* her to come here?" Fury turned her voice into a rasp.

"You?" Brendan repeated. He was angry, too. "What's the big idea?"

Greenleaf heaved a heavy sigh. He ignored Brendan and addressed Kim's wounded pride. "Ki-Mata, we needed help. The kind of help that only Charles could give us."

"What kind of help could she possibly give us?" Kim demanded. "Some backwoods lutin?"

"I'll take that as a compliment." Charlie smiled, leaning against the desk.

"That's jealousy talking, Ki-Mata. You know we have to help Brendan at all costs, even if that means a bruised ego. And Charles has a special past. She was raised in a Human family. She knows things about Brendan's situation that may help him make a breakthrough," Greenleaf said evenly. "You have to admit, we've been less than successful."

Kim's shoulders bunched with repressed fury, but she managed to hold back her anger. "Why wasn't I consulted?"

"I had no time," Greenleaf answered. "I consulted with Ariel and detailed the trouble we were having. On his own authority as the Eldest in the region he called Charlie's teacher."

Kim simmered in silence, her eyes narrowed in mistrust of Charlie. Charlie, for her part, took Kim's hostility in stride. Brendan supposed that the threat of being burned at the stake made most other forms of disapproval pale by comparison. Then his mind hooked on something that Greenleaf had said. "Charlie's teacher? Who's that?"

"You'll see soon enough," Charlie said, leaving him hanging. She addressed Greenleaf. "He made a breakthrough last night, I think."

"What kind of breakthrough?" Kim demanded. She was intrigued in spite of her annoyance.

"With a little prompting from *me*, he was able to enter and maintain a warp state on his own. He outran me." She arched an eyebrow in Brendan's direction. "Almost! And I watched him leap over a police car.[41] Has he ever shown *you* ability like that?"

Kim glared at Charlie but didn't speak. Instead, she jammed her stick back into her backpack and sat down with a snort of disgust.

"Hey," Brendan said, breaking the angry silence, his voice dripping with sarcasm. "I don't mean to interrupt yet another discussion where you talk about me like I'm not even here, but … I thought I'd laid down some rules of my own. No one was supposed to come into contact with my family without my permission."

"I realize we bent the rules a little bit … " Greenleaf admitted.

---

[41] I once leapt over a police car. It belonged to my nephew, who is three.

"Yeah, I'd say so. And if anybody has a right to be angry," Brendan said, aiming a pointed look at Kim, "I'd say that would be me."

Greenleaf sighed another world-weary sigh. He took a moment to gather himself, plucking a bit of lint from his otherwise immaculate green vest. Finally, he sat in the chair behind his desk. "Brendan, we didn't tell you everything about the ceremony."

"Oh really? What an unbelievable surprise!"

"No need to be so dramatic, Brendan," Greenleaf sniffed. "It's only a little bit dangerous."

"Oh great!" Brendan slumped down in a chair. "Here we go! More horrible things I didn't know about. Awesome! Kill me now and get it over with."

Greenleaf chuckled. "Death is not to be feared, Brendan. It is a natural transition from one state of being to another. However, there are … "

"Don't tell me! Don't tell me!" Brendan interrupted. "There are worse things than death and they could happen to me if I don't pass some weird tests devised by weird Faerie weirdos that I don't know?"

"Am I that predictable?" Greenleaf laughed. "You seem to have a grasp of the situation. The Proving is only a part of the ceremony. Once you complete the Proving and survive, you must submit to be chosen by a Clan. Clan membership is very important, Brendan. As soon as you are chosen, you have the protection of that Clan and access to all of its resources. You gain powerful allies. To be without a Clan is to be truly alone in the world, which is not only sad but can be very dangerous."

"Can't I be a free agent? Neutral or something?" Brendan demanded.

"It's very rare," Kim said with a frown. "Only the most powerful can survive outside of a Clan."

"Won't I just join your Clan?" Brendan asked Greenleaf.

"Clan has very little to do with family," Greenleaf explained. "Though Og and I are brothers, we are in different Clans. The Clan system is a sort of support network. In Ancient times, the Clans were constantly feuding and fighting. Fair Folk banded into Clans for safety and to pool resources. Now we don't fight anymore … "

"Much!" Charlie interjected.

"Much," Greenleaf agreed ruefully. "But being part of a Clan is important because it provides support and protection from the Dark Ones, the rogues who seek out the weakest and turn them to the Darkness. Being outside of the Clans means that Dark Faeries like Orcadia will prey upon you with impunity. You'll be on your own. Even if we chose to break the Law and try to help you, we wouldn't be able to guarantee your safety or your family's—there aren't enough of us."

"Fine," Brendan said, exasperated. "Another reason I have to pass these tests. So can anyone just tell me what they're going to be? Shouldn't I be studying them to make sure I pass?"

"I wish things were so easy." Greenleaf shook his head regretfully. "The highest-ranking Faeries present choose the tests. No one knows what they will be until the ritual begins. That makes preparation incredibly difficult."

"Great." Brendan threw up his hands. "Do I at least get to know who the judges will be, or is that a big secret, too?"

"No, the judges are no secret." Greenleaf smiled.

"I assume Ariel will be a judge, since he's the head honcho around here?"

"Ariel is the head of his Clan. But he is acting as the chairman, so he's neutral. But Kitsune Kai from Japan will be there. It's a great honour to have her as a judge. She is a strange one and quite … eccentric. Her test will be a bit odd, no doubt. You'll have to be on your toes. Happily, my sister will be a judge, too."

"Aunt Deirdre is the head of a Clan?" Brendan asked, amazed. He had no idea she was old enough to be considered a Clan leader. She hardly seemed older than his Human mother, but Faeries' looks were very deceiving. Charlie had lived for centuries and still appeared to be a teenage girl. The same went for Kim.

"Indeed. She was born only eight minutes before me." Greenleaf grinned. "We're twins. A very rare occurrence among our kind."

Kim piped up, "The last judge is a big deal. Pûkh himself will be there. He calls himself the King of Tír na nÓg, the Everlasting Lands."

"Never heard of it. Sounds like a Japanese cartoon."

Charlie burst out laughing. "Oh, Brendan, you are a real treat. Japanese cartoon. Ha! That's good." She continued to laugh despite glares from Kim and Greenleaf. She wiped her eyes with the hem of her T-shirt. "Sorry. That's just funny."

"Tír na nÓg is a stronghold of Faeries who wish to follow the Old Ways," Greenleaf explained. "Pûkh was one of the Dark Faeries who lost the battle of the Final Alliance between Humans and Faeries. He chose to lead his followers into a sanctuary outside the realm of Humans. The Faeries of Tír na nÓg rarely venture outside their kingdom, but Pûkh put his name forward as one of your judges. This is a great honour, Brendan."

"Lucky me! He sounds like a really great guy," Brendan said glumly. "I guess I should be flattered?"

"I don't know." Kim shook her head. "I'd be suspicious. Who knows what he really wants. Maybe he just wants to get a look at you. Or maybe he has something else in mind."

"He won't make it easy, will he?" Brendan said.

No one said anything. Finally, Charlie smiled a lopsided smile. "Don't count on it."

Brendan felt his heart fall into his shoes.

Outside Greenleaf's classroom, Harold and Dmitri strained to hear the conversation on the other side of the door. For some reason, though the door wasn't particularly thick, they couldn't make out a single intelligible word.

"What are they saying?" Dmitri whispered.

"What, have I got better ears than you? You tell me." Harold's round face was red and sweaty from the effort of squatting out of sight beneath the window, although he found maintaining his awkward position easier than he might have a few weeks before. He was eating less since he'd found this new obsession with Brendan. "It's weird. They've been in there for half the lunch hour. What could they be talking about?"

"Beat me," Dmitri whispered.

"Beats me. It's beats me, you goof." Harold had less patience with Dmitri's English slang vocabulary than Brendan did.

"Sorry." Dmitri shrugged. "What do we do now?"

"I don't know. We gotta find out what Brendan's been up to. And this super-babe cousin of his shows up outta nowhere? Did you see the way Kim reacted when she saw Charlie? She was really angry."

"Yes," Dmitri agreed. "There's more to this than greets the eye!"

"Meets the eye! MEETS! OW!" Harold cried out as what felt like a vise gripped his ear and hauled him to his feet. It wasn't a vise but a vice-principal. Harold and Dmitri had been so occupied with their eavesdropping that they'd failed to detect Ms. Abernathy's stealthy approach. She clamped Dmitri's ear in her other pincer and pulled him up, too.

"A little birdie told me you were lurking around up here," Ms. Abernathy snapped. "The upper halls are off limits during lunch hour."

"Yeah … uh … we … "

"No excuses. We are going to the office and you'll be assigned punishment duties. I think a couple of hours after school scrubbing the floors in the boys' washrooms should teach you some respect for the rules."

"We were just trying to … " Harold stammered. "I mean, Mr. Greenleaf asked us to … "

"What? Polish his keyhole with your ears?" she sneered. "You're coming with me."

Harold and Dmitri groaned as she dragged them away. Chester was careful to stay in the shadows of an alcove as they passed. Satisfied that the eavesdroppers were taken care of, he sidled away, whistling.

Inside the classroom, Mr. Greenleaf's head turned as he heard the commotion. "We had some eavesdroppers, but thanks to my glamour and the trusty Ms. Abernathy, they've been dealt with." He turned to Brendan. "We have explained what's coming as best we can. I don't want to frighten you, but you need to be prepared for the tests ahead. Ki-Mata … " He addressed the sullen Faerie who sat with arms crossed at one of the desks. "I know you are upset. But I've done this for Brendan's benefit. I hope you can forgive me and learn to get along with Charlie. You are more alike than you know." Both girls snorted at that but didn't speak. "All right. We've talked enough. The bell will ring soon and I have my lesson to prepare. I'll see you tonight at the Swan."

Kim, Brendan, and Charlie stood up and headed for the door.

"Oh, and Charlie?"

Charlie turned.

"Try not to do anything too outrageous, please?"

"Me?" She grinned. "Never."

THE CIRCLE

The winter solstice, the time when the sun was farthest away from Toronto's latitude, would fall on December twenty-first, a Friday. That Friday would therefore be the shortest day of the year. It might also be the last day Brendan ever saw. Everything else seemed insignificant beside the Challenges. Brendan had four days until the Proving ceremony, and he was completely terrified.

According to Greenleaf and Kim, strong Wards, Compulsions, and glamours were being woven to keep the Human residents of Toronto away from the Island of the Ward. Weather glamours would freeze the lake to discourage travel, and the ferries would cease to run. Island residents would be convinced that they should spend the weekend away or ensconced in their homes.

Brendan couldn't imagine the power required to work such a massive glamour. But he could easily imagine the worst coming to pass in the days ahead. In the four days he had left, he had to prepare for any possible test the judges might throw at him. *And* do his social studies project, although the wrath of Mrs. Scott, his teacher, paled in comparison to a fate worse than death. Brendan couldn't believe how much his perspective had changed over the last few weeks. Before then he'd had a healthy fear of his high school teachers. Now he was standing across the sparring circle from Saskia, part-time bartender and full-time Warp Warrior, who was getting ready to hand him yet another beating as part of his training.

"This is completely hopeless!"

"Naw, it ain't, lad! Ye were better tha' time," Og urged him. "Ye almost touched her once."

"I missed by a mile," Brendan grumbled.

"Och, aye. But still, it was closer than last time!" Og sat at the bar of the Swan of Liir, swigging from a mug of brown ale the size of Brendan's entire head. Despite the glass's size, his gnarled fist hefted it with ease. "Ye can't give up." He burped.

"Nope!" BLT cried, waving a tiny fist. She sat on the lip of a glass of diet cola, her feet dangling down and her free hand clinging to a drinking straw. "You show her who's boss!"

Brendan was still gasping for breath after the last round. They'd been at it for an hour now, and he didn't feel that he'd improved at all. His T-shirt was soaked with sweat and his hair plastered down. Saskia looked as if she'd just rolled out of bed, fresh as a daisy.

"You think too much, Brendan," the Faerie said. "Your thoughts slow you down. Clear your mind and react, only react."

Easy for you to say. Brendan tried to free his mind of all stray thoughts. The fact that he had an audience didn't help. Kim and Greenleaf stood at the railing on the balcony above, witnessing his humiliation.

Kim had been very cold to him when he'd arrived at the Swan. She was still angry about yielding her authority to Charlie.

"Where's What's-Her-Face?" she'd sneered when he had come in the door for his training session with Saskia.

147

"You mean Charlie?"

"Who else would I mean? Or do you have another girl I don't know about?" At that, Kim had spun away and left him speechless.

As for Charlie, she had declined when he'd asked her to come along to the Swan.

"I have a few errands to run before the Gathering. Besides, I don't think Kim is all that thrilled with me at the moment. I'll see you later tonight, *non*?"

Her absence annoyed him, which was strange because he'd found her incredibly annoying when she'd first shown up. Now he was mildly shocked to find that her presence was reassuring. She always had good advice. She was right about one thing, though: Kim was not fond of her at all.

Finbar was hard at work polishing the wooden tables. He pretended not to watch, but Brendan could see the old man stealing glimpses of him as he rubbed oil into the worn, gleaming surfaces.

Finbar had become a fixture at the Swan ever since he'd led Brendan to the amulet he'd stolen from Brendan as an infant. Though the old Exile had caused him a lot of trouble, Brendan had spoken up for him, taking his part in a bid to be reinstated in the Faerie Fellowship. Brendan knew what being an outsider felt like, so he sympathized with the white-haired, haggard man with the haunted blue eyes.

Still, the way those eyes followed him whenever he came to the Swan disturbed him. He saw a hunger there, a plea for help. Brendan had done all he could to plead Finbar's case to Ariel. He imagined what it would be like to be an Exile himself, always knowing that another world existed and never being able to see it. He felt a sharp sadness for the old man wiping the table so doggedly.

"Hey, Finbar," Brendan said with a little wave. Finbar raised his sad blue eyes from the table he was polishing. "You okay today?"

"Right as rain, young Prince. Right as rain." The answer didn't match the emptiness in Finbar's eyes. "You just keep yer mind on yerself. I'm just fine."

Brendan smiled and looked around the room. The rest of the audience was made up of a few early-evening patrons. Monday was a slow day at the Swan. That was why Saskia had the time to spar with Brendan. Leonard, usually the doorman and bouncer, was keeping an eye on the bar for his love, Saskia. They made a formidable couple: she a Warp Warrior and he a shape-shifter. Brendan had never seen the big man transform into a lion, and he wasn't sure he wanted to. Leonard grinned at Brendan, his golden teeth glittering against his dark skin. "Don't let her scare you, Brendan. She ain't such a hard one, deep down." Saskia bared her teeth at her man in a feral grin and growled deep in her throat. Leonard's booming laugh rolled out across the bar like thunder.

"Ready, Brendan?" Saskia asked.

"I guess … " He barely got the words out before she blurred across the circle on the attack. Brendan dove out of the way, brushing against the invisible barrier of the fighting circle. The barrier flared with a purplish light, and his shoulder stung where he'd brushed against it.

The fighting circle itself was amazing, though Brendan was too busy getting his butt handed to him to really marvel at it. Prior to their sparring match, as she had done before every session, Saskia had cleared the floor of furniture and drawn a circle on the seamless wooden floor with what appeared to be a piece of purple chalk. Satisfied with her work, she tucked the chalk in her trouser pocket. They were confined within the circle.

Saskia closed her eyes and took a deep breath, held it, and let it out. Brendan had seen many Faeries perform similar rituals to focus their minds before employing their powers. He envied her concentration. No matter how hard he tried, he could never seem to block out the world around him and see what he wanted with his mind's eye. Saskia then clapped loudly once at each of the four points of the compass, north, south, east, and west. Suddenly, a shimmering cylinder of energy sprang up from the chalk line, reaching from the floor to the ceiling high above. The energy shimmered and then faded.

"That's so cool," Brendan had said the first time she'd created a fighting circle. He'd reached out to touch where he thought the barrier was. His fingertips brushed a flexible, elastic, yet impenetrable surface. Instantly, his hand sang with pain and went numb. A flare of purple light accompanied the agony. "Ow! MAN!"

"The circle is a holy shape, sacred to our people," Saskia had explained. "It is simple. It is perfect. It is eternal. Within this circle, I will attempt to teach you how to defend yourself. The circle will contain you. You may not leave until I permit you to leave."

"What if I have to go to the bathroom?" Brendan had quipped on that afternoon, weeks ago.

Saskia didn't laugh. She flexed her fingers, stretched her neck until it cracked loudly, and then began to mercilessly thrash Brendan. When she'd finally let him out of the circle by scratching away a section of the chalk, Brendan was barely able to limp to the Faerie Terminal. He'd spent two hours in a hot bath at home before going to bed.

Now he was about to take a beating again. He watched Saskia crack her knuckles and his heart sank. He'd never so much as laid a finger on her in ten sessions. She was just too fast and far too experienced for him.

"The circle is in place," Saskia said. "The pain is a distraction. Avoid the barrier. Defend yourself!" The sparring match commenced.

Another hour of punishment followed. Though he was aching from a hundred carefully aimed blows, Brendan believed he was beginning to follow Saskia's movements a little better. She came at him from every angle. Her movements were so fast that her limbs were mere blurs.

Brendan was having less trouble staying in warp mode. He found he could connect with something inside him, like a current of energy running under the surface of his skin. He realized that apart from being a pain in the butt last night and keeping him from getting a good night's sleep, Charlie had perhaps helped him see what he had to do.

In the meantime, Brendan had been scorched, whacked, slapped, and tripped more times than he could count while never landing a solid blow on his opponent. Saskia looked as fresh as ever. Her skin was flushed and slick with sweat, but otherwise she seemed unaffected. Now she was stalking him around the circle in an effort to lay yet another beating on him.

Brendan was exhausted. He was bruised. He was more than a little sick of being a punching bag. He tried to imagine himself moving faster, warping more efficiently, but he couldn't concentrate. He was in too much pain. He couldn't turn off the part of his mind that shrilled in his ears that he wasn't able to beat Saskia and shouldn't try.

Then he remembered what Charlie had said as they sat on the dome under the stars, watching the Dawn Flyers. *Sing a song inside your head.* Brendan thought about that. *It sounds crazy. I'll probably just get my head knocked off, but at least there'll be musical accompaniment.*

He decided to sing a song that his father loved. One of Brendan's earliest memories was of his dad rocking him to sleep and singing the song as he drifted off. It was a Scottish folk song, and probably the only song he knew all the words to. As Saskia crouched for a new attack, Brendan struggled to remember the lyrics.

In his head he sang,

> *Oh, you'll take the high road and I'll take the low road*
> *And I'll be in Scotland before you*
> *But me and my true love will never meet again*
> *On the bonnie, bonnie banks of Loch Lomond.*

He'd been thinking so hard about the words that he almost failed to see Saskia's attack coming. He ducked under a roundhouse kick and stepped aside. Even so, she managed to clip him on the shoulder. His arm went numb to the fingers. Still, he'd dodged the worst of the blow. Saskia's yellow eyes registered the slightest surprise before narrowing.

> *But me and my true love will never meet again*
> *On the bonnie, bonnie banks of Loch Lomond.*

The words were coming easier now. Brendan could hear his father's voice in his ear. He grinned, imagining what his dad would think if he knew that his son with the tin ear was singing, even in his head.

He tried to block out everything but the song. He tried to conjure the sound of it. His pain faded. He was vaguely aware that Saskia was swinging her fists at him, but her blows were so slow. So slow! His head wove from side to side as the song rumbled on in his head.

By yon bonnie banks, and by yon bonnie bonnie braes
Where the sun shines bright on Loch Lomond
There me and my true love spent many happy days
On the bonnie, bonnie banks of Loch Lomond.

He was dancing along now. He shuffled and whirled in the circle, avoiding kicks and punches. He kicked into the chorus and felt the glory of the song fill him.

O ye'll tak' the high road and I'll tak' the low road
And I'll be in Scotland afore ye
But me and my true love will ne-er meet again
On the bonnie, bonnie banks o' Loch Lomon'.

Suddenly, a Moment crystallized. He saw Saskia, and it was as though the fierce woman were swimming in syrup. She ducked under a kick and prepared to rise at him with her right hand flat as a blade, driving for his chest.

Brendan almost laughed. It was too easy! He reached out with his left hand and grasped Saskia's wrist, pulling her toward him. With his left he made a fist and, ducking low, drove it straight out from his shoulder, folding her over with a perfectly placed punch. There was a satisfying *whoof* as Saskia doubled over, falling backwards. Time returned to normal.

"I did it! I did it!" he crowed. Immediately, dismay flooded through Brendan. "Oh NO! What have I done?

153

Saskia? Are you all right?" Instead of replying, Saskia lashed out with her leg and swept his feet out from under him. He fell to the floor with a loud crash. "Ooof."

"Don't let your guard down," she wheezed. She forced herself to stand up.

Brendan pushed himself painfully to his feet, panic and remorse filling him at once. "Are you okay?" He turned to the spectators. "She needs help!" He ran to get a glass of water from the bar and ran smack into the circle barrier.

The flare of pain singed his nerves from head to toe. He fell to his knees, shivering. Still, his head was full of worry for Saskia. He looked down at the chalk line on the floor that was the circle's boundary. His urgency made him see it clearly. The chalk line wasn't solid. He could see each particle of chalk on the wooden grain of the floor, making up a seemingly unbroken line. But he could now see a break, a place where a minuscule span of floor was free of chalk dust. Without thinking, he reached over and wiped the chalk away on both sides with his index finger. He felt the circle collapse, the power draining away, a blizzard of bits of energy dispersing into the air of the Swan. He leapt to his feet and dashed to the bar. "A glass of water and a bag of ice, please, Leonard. Hurry!"

He knew immediately that something was up the way Leonard was staring at him. Nothing ever surprised Leonard. He was the bouncer in a Faerie bar, after all. But he was staring now.

Brendan mistook Leonard's surprise for anger. Apologies tumbled out of his mouth. "I'm sorry I punched your girlfriend! It was an accident."

That's when he noticed the silence. Even BLT didn't speak. She sat staring from the lip of her glass of diet cola, the straw in her hands forgotten. He realized that there was no sound in the bar save for the low drone of a golf game on one of the big screens. He slowly turned around to see that Saskia hadn't moved from the centre of the circle.

"What?" Brendan asked. "What is it?"

"How?" she said.

"How what?"

"How did you break the circle?"

"I don't know," he answered, confused. "Did I do something wrong?" He looked up to see that Kim and Greenleaf were also staring at him. "Oh no. You all have that 'Brendan did something impossible' look on your faces."

"It *is* impossible to break a circle drawn by another," Saskia breathed.

"Oh." Brendan winced. "By 'impossible' do you mean unlikely or … "

"Impossible," Greenleaf repeated, coming down the stairs from the balcony with Kim at his side. "A Faerie circle is a sacred thing tuned to its creator. No other can break it without permission."

"Well, uh … How did I do it then?"

Greenleaf shook his head and smiled. "You really are a mystery to me, Brendan. You constantly confound all expectations." He sat down on the stool beside Brendan. "What did you feel when you broke the circle? Do you remember?"

"Not really," Brendan admitted. "I was tired. I was angry. I was fed up with that stupid barrier. I had to help Saskia."

"What else?"

"I can't think of anything else," Brendan said, annoyed at the whine in his voice. "I just … "

"Yes," Kim prompted. "It's really important."

Brendan tried to remember the moment when he'd broken the circle. "I just saw the line. I saw that it was a little thinner at one point than everywhere else, and I wiped it away."

"Well." Greenleaf raised his eyebrows in amusement. "You are full of surprises, Brendan."

Brendan snatched the glass of water from Leonard's giant hands and took it to Saskia. "Here. I'm sorry."

Saskia took the water and drank gratefully. She finally smiled and patted his cheek with her palm, a short, stinging slap. "Don't worry about it. You think this hurts? I've had worse. You should be proud of yourself."

"Proud?" Brendan said incredulously.

"Let's just say you've made a breakthrough and leave it at that." Saskia shrugged.

Brendan was about to apologize again when his eye caught a glimpse of the wristwatch Og had made for him.

"Holy crap! Is that the time?" Brendan said. "My mum is gonna kill me. I've gotta get home for dinner." He grabbed his bag from the floor. BLT flitted to his shoulder. He called to Kim and Greenleaf, "I'll see you in school tomorrow."

Brendan hefted his school bag over his shoulder. He had a load of geometry to get through before he went to bed. Of course, he might not get to sleep if he went to bed. He didn't know how long Charlie would let him rest tonight. As he walked out the front door, Finbar caught his eye. The old man winked at him and gave him the thumbs-up. Brendan merely shrugged and waved before leaving the Swan.

Greenleaf watched Brendan go. "I am at a loss as to how to help him. He seems so helpless most of the time, and then quite out of the blue he accomplishes something extraordinary."

Saskia raised a section of the bar and returned to her duties beside Leonard. "I see flashes with him. It's been a long time since anyone landed a blow like that against me."

"I think he be fine." Leonard nodded, his dreads bobbing. "He got a good heart and somehow tings turn up right for him."

"We can't leave everything to chance," Kim insisted. "The Proving is going to be fierce. He isn't prepared."

"We still have three more days," Greenleaf said softly. "Perhaps Charlie will be able to work a miracle."

Kim merely scowled in answer. "I wouldn't hold my breath."

Greenleaf chuckled softly.

"What's so funny?" Kim demanded.

"I never thought I'd see you like this."

"Like what?"

"Jealous."

"Jealous? Ha! Of that … " Kim searched for a word scathing enough but failed. "You really are losing it, Greenleaf." She spun on her heel and stomped up the stairs to the balcony.

Greenleaf watched her go with a wistful grin on his face. "Oh, to be young. Or at least young*er*." He bent to examine the chalk circle on the floor.

ALLIANCE

"Here he comes," Harold whispered. "Get down."

They were hidden in a clump of juniper bushes off to the side of the main road leading to the Community Centre on Ward's Island. From where they crouched, they had an unobstructed view of both the road and the building.

"Where did he come from?" Dmitri asked, puzzled.

"I don't know," Harold answered, equally confused. They had followed Brendan across to the island and all the way to the Community Centre. They had to be careful because the ferry wasn't very big. Luckily, the boat was crowded with commuters on their way home from work on the mainland. Winter wasn't high season on Ward's Island. The amusement parks were closed and the tourists didn't come. Only island residents were in evidence, people who lived here all year long.

It was a stroke of luck that the pipes in the girls' washrooms on the third floor burst. Ms. Abernathy, in crisis mode, had been forced to let Dmitri and Harold leave without serving their detention. They'd been free to tail Brendan as he made his way to the island.

They had managed to hide at one end of the ferry, hopping on at the last possible minute. Brendan hadn't looked back to discover them among the island commuters. He stood outside in the raw wind and stared straight ahead as Ward's Island approached, lost in thought.

After they arrived at the island, they had followed at a safe distance until he reached the white clapboard Community Centre. He'd walked around behind the building and then disappeared.

Harold and Dmitri had waited for him to emerge on the other side. After fifteen minutes, they'd tired of waiting. Where had he gone? After debating the pros and cons they decided they had no choice but to go and take a closer look. Dmitri darted from tree to tree while Harold, red-faced and puffing, followed as quickly as he could. They arrived at the front door to find it securely locked.

Inching around the building, they circumnavigated the whole structure. There was a side door. Locked. They made their way to the back door on the side of the building where Brendan had disappeared, only to find another door that was boarded shut.

"I don't get it," Harold said, scratching his head. "Where did he go?"

"Perhaps we missed him somehow," Dmitri suggested. "Maybe he went farther into the woods." He pointed to the sparse forest behind the building.

"No way, Dmitri. We would have seen him. He must have gone in here somehow." Harold laid a hand on the cracked and peeling paint of the wooden wall. "Do you think there's a secret door?"

"What do you think this is, the Hardly Boys?"

"Hardy Boys, not Hardly Boys. Geesh!"

"Whatever. So what do we do now?"

Harold frowned and thought for a moment. "We wait."

"For how long?" Dmitri asked. "It's getting cold out here."

When they left the mainland, it had been a sunny if chilly day. Here on the island, the weather was different. Grey clouds were gathering and the air was far colder. It was almost as if the island had its own weather system, distinct from that of the city across the channel. Somehow, it felt unnatural.[42] The prospect of hunkering down in the deep cold didn't excite either of the boys.

"I don't know. As long as it takes," Harold vowed with grim determination. "He has to come back this way to get to the ferry, so we watch the road." He pointed a chubby finger. "There!"

And so they found themselves in the clump of juniper bushes when Brendan emerged from behind the Community Centre. Harold was relieved. He'd been hungry before they'd begun their stakeout. Now he was positively ravenous. Sitting still in the cold and damp had only made his discomfort worse.

"Look at him," Dmitri said. "He isn't wearing his jacket." Harold grunted. It was true. Brendan walked along with his coat tucked under his arm and his school bag over his shoulder. He didn't seem the least bit uncomfortable, though the temperature was well below freezing. The sun was just about gone and it was getting dark. He walked up the road toward the boys' hiding place. They sat very still, trying not to breathe.

Brendan came even with them and stopped suddenly. Harold and Dmitri sat stock-still, willing even their heartbeats to silence. When Brendan started talking, they

---

[42] Of course it's unnatural. It's the beginning of the Ward that will shield the island from Human eyes during the Clan Gathering. Duh!

thought he had discovered them. But then they realized he wasn't talking to them.

"Don't be ridiculous," Brendan said. "I just got lucky. I doubt if I could surprise her like that again."

Who was he talking to? He was alone, wasn't he?

"All right! All right! I'll put my coat on. There's no one to see me. After that workout, I'm sweating like a pig."

Harold and Dmitri peered through the branches of the juniper bush and watched as Brendan dropped his bag to shrug on his coat. His head steamed gently in the cold air. His hair was wet. What workout was he talking about, and who was he talking to?[43]

Then they saw the bug.

"What is *that*?" Harold whispered in amazement.

The bug looked like a big hairy beetle, kind of a cross between a housefly and a bumblebee. Its shiny wings hummed as it hovered in front of Brendan's face.

"Oh, sure," Brendan laughed. "And who's going to see me out here? Never mind. I'm gonna be late for dinner. Let's get going. Climb in." Brendan held his coat pocket open, and to the watchers' amazement, the bug thing flew in. Brendan started off down the road again.

---

[43] These days it's hard to tell who is mad and who is talking on a cellphone. It's not unusual to see people walking down the street and talking at the top of their voices to no one in particular. It used to be that you knew such a person was mad and they were best avoided. Now, people have these little ear thingies and they're most likely holding a phone conversation, closing a big deal or planning dinner. I long for the old days when you knew whether a person was mad. Sometimes, just for fun, I put a little ear thingy in my ear and walk up and down the street saying strange things like, "Tell them we need it delivered to Atlantis by noon tomorrow!" or "The bears were completely covered in electronic strawberries!" I find it very liberating.

They waited until Brendan was a safe distance away before starting off in pursuit. The gathering darkness made their task easier. They crept from tree to tree, keeping Brendan in sight.

"What kind of bug could that be?" Harold hissed.

"Insects are not fond of the cold," Dmitri whispered back. "I must admit I'm stamped."

"Stumped."

"Right."

They were surprised when Brendan turned away from the road to the ferry terminal.

"Where's he going?" Dmitri asked.

"I don't know," Harold whispered. "Just keep quiet."

They came to the spot in the road where Brendan had turned off. The snow was uniform and white. There were no footprints or any other indication that Brendan had left the road at that spot. Harold looked off into the darkness.

"Are we sure this is where he left the road?" Harold whispered.

"I think so," Dmitri said uncertainly. "But where are the footprints?"

They heard the unmistakable sound of Brendan's voice in the trees calling, "Wait up!"

"Come on," Harold hissed. They set off in the direction of Brendan's voice, torn between speed and stealth. The snow helped dampen the sound of their footfalls.

"Look!" Harold said, pointing to the ground in front of them. Brendan's footprints were now easy to see. They led toward a cluster of birch trees. Obviously, the tracks had been there all along, but for some reason they'd been unable to see them. "Why couldn't we see them from the path?" Harold whispered.

"Very weird," Dmitri agreed.

"This whole island's a little weird," Harold said.

The boys entered the stand of birch trees in the deepening gloom. Their breath puffed out in huge clouds. They moved as quickly as they dared, finally emerging from the trees to find themselves at the edge of the lake.

Ice had formed along the shore. There was no sign of Brendan anywhere. The only sign of Human habitation was a rickety old wooden dock that jutted out into the gelid[44] black water. Like a stumpy finger, it pointed toward the Toronto skyline glittering in the distance.

"Where did he go?" Harold asked in complete confusion.

"Where could he have gone?" Dmitri shrugged. "There is nowhere to go. He vanished like a thin hair!"

Harold was about to correct Dmitri again when a female voice did it for him. "It's thin air, you geek." Harold and Dmitri spun around to find Delia Clair standing at the edge of the trees. "And why am I not surprised he gave you the slip?"

"What are you doing here?" Harold demanded. "You were spying on us!"

"And what were you doing following Brendan?" She let that question hang in the air. Harold and Dmitri hung their heads sheepishly.

Finally, Dmitri said, "We're worried about him. He's been behaving kind of strangely."

"We wanted to find out what he's doing," Harold added. "He hasn't been around much lately."

"Maybe he just realized you two are the biggest losers in the universe?" Delia suggested. Harold clenched his fists

---

[44] *Gelid* means on the verge of freezing, for word fans out there.

but said nothing. "You guys are pathetic spies. I've been watching you for at least an hour and you didn't even know I was there."

"Oh yeah?" Harold retorted. "What are *you* doing here? I suppose you just happened to take a trip to the island in the freezing cold?"

Delia's eyes narrowed. "I'm doing the same thing you are. I'm trying to figure out what Brendan is up to."

"Spying on your own brother?" Harold shook his head. "That's pretty low."

Delia grabbed Harold by the front of his jacket and pulled him close until she was staring into his eyes. "He isn't my brother. Not really! And I want to know what happened to me. I think he had something to do with it."

"What do you mean, what happened to you?" Dmitri interjected.

"I mean … " she stopped. Disgusted, she let go of Harold and turned away. "Never mind." She started to walk back into the trees.

"Is it about the day you lost?" Dmitri shouted at her back.

Delia froze. Slowly, she turned around and looked at the two boys. "What did you say?"

"I said, 'Is it about the day you lost?'" Dmitri watched her face. She didn't speak.

Harold jumped in. "We lost a day, too, a few weeks ago. We just can't seem to remember anything about this one day."

"We believe Brendan had something to do with it," Dmitri added.

Delia stared at them. At last, she whispered, "Why? Why do you think he's involved?"

"We can't be sure," Harold said. "It's just a feeling we both have. And, well … " He hesitated, his hand resting on his book bag. "I have these pictures I drew."

Delia's eyebrows rose. "What pictures?"

"In my sketchbook."

Delia grinned a hungry grin. "Let me see these pictures."

Later, they sat in a café drinking hot chocolate and comparing notes. On the ferry from the island, Delia had pored over the bizarre sketches that Harold insisted he'd done but couldn't remember drawing. They showed Brendan flying with birds, and an old man with a grizzled face and a slouch cap. There were pictures of a magnificent but terrifying woman with fierce eyes. Her hands were alight with some form of energy. On another page, weird creatures that seemed to be half man and half dog slavered and snarled.

Delia was captivated. "If you'd seen someone like that, you'd think it would stick in your mind."

They sat in silence for a few minutes, trying to make sense of what they'd seen so far.

"I've been following him for days now," Delia said at last. "I even followed him when he was Christmas shopping."

"What did he do?" Dmitri asked.

"Went Christmas shopping," Delia snapped sullenly.

"Nice work, Sherlock," Harold scoffed.

"Why don't you just shut up?"

"Please!" Dmitri interjected. "Let's not fight. We have to figure out what's going on."

"Okay, so we all agree," Harold said. "Something weird is going on and Brendan is at the centre of it. So what do we do?"

"We keep doing what we're doing," Delia announced. "Only now, we join forces."

"Join forces?" Harold repeated, mystified. "You'd work with dorks like us?"

"Though it makes me dry-heave just thinking about it, yes. Three heads are better than one. We can cover more ground this way. Coordinate our efforts. Are we agreed?"

Dmitri and Harold exchanged a glance. After a moment of silent communication, they nodded.

"Okay." Delia smiled fiercely. "There are two conditions."

"What?" Dmitri asked.

"One: I'm in charge."

"Okay," Harold conceded. "The other?"

"You guys gotta get some deodorant. Really!" Delia grimaced. "I mean, come on. Grow up."

"One question," Dmitri said.

"What's that?" Delia asked.

"What's deodorant?"

"Are you kidding me?" Delia snorted.

"Yes," Dmitri answered and grinned.

PART 3

Preparation

Another Note
from the Narrator

Well! If you like stories full of mystery and excitement, this is your lucky day! Brendan has once again surprised everyone with a new ability, but his friends and his evil sister have formed an alliance to spy on him. What a tangled web! What intrigue! What a twisted tale!

Certainly, Harold and Dmitri are more worried about their friend and less bent on his destruction than Delia is. They've all lost a day of memories, and one can sympathize with their confusion and desire to figure out what exactly happened to them on the fateful day that disappeared. I'd be worried if I lost a day, wouldn't you? I mean, anything could happen in twenty-four hours. You could eat a bag of worms, dance naked in a shopping mall, grow a moustache and shave it off, mail it to your parents, and grow another one. I have done all these things, but I have the pleasure of remembering them: that's the difference.

Some of you may think it's a little harsh to insist that Delia is bent on Brendan's destruction. All right, maybe his sister is not evil in the strictest sense. There are many gradations of evil. At the top of the Evil Food Chain are the

Evil Dictators who hold their people in an iron grip of fear. Below the Evil Dictators are the Criminal Masterminds who plot the downfall of society to advance their own evil agenda. The next tier is the Corrupt Official who exploits the public for his or her own evil gains. Then there is the average murderer, although murder is hardly average. Finally, there is the Big Sister bent on destroying her sibling in retaliation for the borrowing of a sweater unasked or in revenge for an imagined slight.

Of all of these, the Big Sister is the most unpredictable and terrifying. One may never know when one will become the target of her wrath. One must cringe through life in a constant state of ulcer-inducing fear.

I remember once, when I was twelve, I accidentally spilled a glass of milk on my sister's favourite woollen skirt. She accepted my apology after a massive tantrum, but she never forgot. It took her twenty years, but in the end she got her revenge. She had me pantsed at the altar on my wedding day. She then posted the pictures on a website she created, entitled www.youruinedmyfavouriteskirtyoulittlecreep.com.

I never saw it coming. I'll never live it down. I thought she'd forgotten but she hadn't. Big Sisters are like elephants ... with access to the Internet.

MUSIC

Brendan made it home late for dinner. He needn't have hurried. A note was stuck on the fridge: his mother was out Christmas shopping, his father working an evening shift. Of his sister there was no sign. He was glad to have the house to himself. His mum had left a pan of lasagna in the oven. Peering in at the expanse of cheese and noodles, he was suddenly aware of how desperately hungry he was. Happily carving off a chunk, Brendan sat down at the kitchen table to enjoy a solitary meal. He was sore from the sparring and a bit light-headed. His mind was spinning with thoughts of how he'd broken Saskia's circle and managed to knock the formidable Warp Warrior down.

Somehow, I did it. I have to figure out how to do it again. He tried to force his mind to recapture the feeling he'd had when the warp had taken him, but his tired mind rebelled.

"This is hopeless," he said aloud to the empty kitchen. "I can't do it!"

"Sure you can!" Charlie's voice answered. He whirled, knocking his chair over. Charlie was leaning in the kitchen doorway, smiling cheekily. "What is it we're talking about, exactly?"

"What are you doing here?" Brendan demanded. "How did you get in?"

"You left the door unlocked." She walked over to the table and pinched a lasagna noodle between her fingers and popped it into her mouth. "Mmm. Tasty."

Brendan snarled and snatched the plate away from her. "You shouldn't be here."

"But I am." Charlie shrugged. "What will you do about it?"

Brendan carried his plate to the counter. He plunked it down and turned to snap an angry retort at Charlie, but she wasn't there. He looked around in confusion and then saw that the basement door stood open.

"No way!" Anger flushed through him. "That's my dad's place." He stomped across the floor, fists clenched, and headed down into the cellar.

When he got down to his dad's music studio he found Charlie playing a song on his father's electric guitar. The original 1952 Gibson Les Paul was his dad's pride and joy; he'd found it at a flea market and had lovingly restored it. Brendan would never have dared to touch the instrument for fear of damaging it in some way, but here was Charlie, uninvited, handling his father's prized possession. She sat on a stool with her back to him, her attention focused on the guitar. Her dark hair, he noticed, was set differently today. Normally, it was teased up into a rooster's comb, held in place by glamours or more mundane hair products. Now it hung in a curtain around her pale face as she concentrated on her fingers. Brendan was on the verge of yelling at her for coming down here and handling his dad's stuff, intruding on his family's space. But just as he opened his mouth, she began to sing and his anger was forgotten.

At first, he couldn't understand the words. They were just sounds, surprisingly rich and plaintive. Brendan had always thought of her as a young girl, a teenager like himself. Now, listening to the emotion in her voice, he realized she was old, centuries old, and she'd seen a great deal of joy and sadness in that long span of time. She sang in French. Brendan had never been any good at languages, but as he listened the meaning began to come clear to him. The song was melancholy and reached into his heart, touching something inside him.

This world is not for me.
I am just biding my time.
One day I'll be set free.
And my spirit will climb.
There's a place I need to go.
But I don't know the way there.
Someday I'll find the road.
It may take a while but I don't care.
I belong in the stars.
I belong in the sky.
Won't be long 'til I'm up there.
Won't be long 'til I fly.
And I'm gonna find you.
And I'm gonna hold you again.
And I'm gonna tell you.
All of my tears at an end.
And I'm gonna find you.
I'm gonna hold you again.
And I'm gonna tell you.
All of your tears are at an end.

Charlie's voice trailed off. She played a last lonely note that hung in the musty air of the basement. Brendan felt he could almost hear her breathing, the beat of her heart. As she turned her head, he saw that her cheeks were wet with tears.

"Oh! *Allo*," she said softly, wiping her face with her sleeve. "Have you been standing there long?"

Brendan shook his head. He couldn't trust his voice not to crack. Finally, he said, "You're a good singer." He felt like an idiot saying that, but he couldn't think of anything else. He was undone by her sadness.

"You were crying … "

"Just the song. It made me sad," she said evasively.

She placed the guitar on the stand and arched her back like a cat, stretching her arms above her head. She looked perfectly at home with herself, perfectly beautiful. Brendan longed to be like her. She saw him looking at her and smiled again. "What?"

"How? How can you play the guitar? Don't the strings burn your fingers?"

"They are copper wound. The harder part is not blowing out the amplifier. It takes concentration. Really, you shouldn't worry about me. Worry about yourself." She looked at him directly. Brendan saw her eyes were swimming with tears again.

"What's wrong?" Brendan said with alarm. She'd always been so annoyingly confident. He'd never seen such weakness in her before.

She turned her face away, wiping at her eyes. "I don't know," she said softly. She ran a finger over the strings of the guitar, releasing a ghost of a sound that whispered through the room. "Just feeling a little lonely, I suppose."

"Lonely?"

"You're lucky," she said, wandering around the studio, letting her fingers trail over the instruments on the wall and the unfinished artwork. "You have a family. You have a place you belong. I wish I could say the same."

Brendan was about to protest that he was as much of an outsider as she was, but he realized that was wrong. His Human family loved him … even Delia in her own weird way. He could count on their support. He tried to imagine Charlie, young and without full knowledge of who she was, being forced to leave the only family she'd ever known and sail to a world of strangers.

"I wish I knew my real family. Who they were and why they left me. Was I such a disappointment? Was I so repulsive to them?"

"Charlie, I'm sure that they had their reasons … "

"And why did they never come for me? All these years? All these centuries? Why did they leave me alone?" She sat on a stool and began to sob, her face in her hands.

Brendan froze. He didn't know what to do. This was such a turnaround. He was the weak one, the emotional one. He was the confused little boy. Seeing her like this dissolved something inside him. He took a step closer and gingerly wrapped his arms around her. She leaned into his chest and wept some more. Brendan, not knowing what to do with his hands, gently stroked her hair. He didn't know how long he held her like that: minutes, hours. Finally her sobs lessened and she regained control. She tried to push him away.

"You shouldn't be so kind to me," she said fiercely. "I don't deserve this from you."

"Why not? Everybody needs help sometimes. I know I do."

She stood and looked into his face, her eyes red and her cheeks streaked with tears. "Oh, *mon cher*." She wrapped her arms around him. At first he stiffened but she didn't let go. She kept on holding him and he relaxed. "You have a good heart. I was sent to help you, but you are the one comforting me. Forgive me."

"It's okay." Brendan shrugged.

"Oh, Brendan. Whatever happens, remember I never wished you harm," Charlie whispered softly in his ear.

"Why do you say that?" Brendan asked.

She was silent for a moment. "I just don't want you to misunderstand me in the time to come. You have such difficult days ahead. So much for one heart to bear. It's not fair, is it?" Her breath on his neck was soft and warm. She pulled away and looked into his eyes. "Be true to that good heart. Promise me!" She held him so that she could stare into his eyes. Her face was deadly earnest.

"Relax, Charlie … "

"No! Promise me!"

"Okay! Okay! I promise!"

"Good. And you aren't alone." She smiled and leaned forward, kissing him softly on the cheek, gentle as a feather fall. "You have a lot of good friends."

"Like you."

She smiled sadly and nodded once.

Brendan's whole body felt light as air. All of his fears and worries receded. He looked into Charlie's face. He'd never felt anything like this before. He felt hot and cold, light and more substantial, powerful and weak at the same time. He gazed into Charlie's eyes and found he had nothing to say. Not a single word.

DOUGHNUTS

Brendan lay on his bed that night trying to tune out the terrible ache of his muscles and quiet his thoughts. He was already confused by the coming Challenges. Now he found that his mind kept twisting around Charlie. She was annoying. She was infuriating. Her visits to his house threatened to expose his secret to his family. Despite all that, she could be totally disarming and attractive. He found he couldn't stop thinking about her.

"Hey," Charlie's voice suddenly whispered in his ear. "Penny for your thoughts."

Brendan sat up so fast that he slammed his head on the angled ceiling above his bed.

"Ow!" he grunted, clutching his forehead. "You scared the crap out of me."

"Can you keep it down?" Charlie whispered. "You'll wake everybody up."

Brendan bit back a retort, partly because he didn't want to make any more noise, and partly because he felt oddly nervous. It was as though by thinking about Charlie, he'd somehow summoned her.

"Come on. There's someone I want you to meet."

"Now?" He looked at his watch. He must have fallen asleep. It was past 3 A.M.

"*Oui!* Now!"

"Can I at least put on some real clothes this time?"

Charlie giggled. "Just hurry. I don't like to keep this fellow waiting."

"Who is he?" Brendan asked, reaching for a sweatshirt.

"You'll see."

Brendan hesitated before taking off his pyjama bottoms. "Do you mind?"

"Don't worry." Charlie smiled. "I won't laugh."

"Just turn around!"

"Fine." And she did.

Brendan pulled on his jeans, grabbed his jacket, and slid open the top drawer of his dresser. BLT was curled up in a nest of socks and underpants. He gently lifted the little Faerie in his palm.

"Wha?" BLT mumbled. "What's happening?"

"We're going out," Brendan whispered.

She shook her head. "Wake me when it's summer."

When he was ready, Charlie eased the window open. Brendan scooped BLT into his coat pocket and leapt out into the night.

The city, muffled under a fall of new snow, was as quiet as it ever got. The yellow light of the street lamps shone down on the pair as they trotted easily through the streets. Tweezers ran ahead, leaping and rolling in the soft snow, pausing every few seconds to stare back at them, whiskers twitching. They made their way through the park again, passing the outdoor skating rink, its glassy surface glimmering faintly with reflected moonlight.

"Where are we going?" Brendan asked.

"Not far," Charlie answered. She smiled cryptically and picked up her pace. Brendan matched it easily. He was beginning to discover how close to the surface his power lurked, like water flowing under the ice of a frozen river. He could break through more easily now. Was it just practice? Or did the presence of Charlie make it easier?

He looked over at her face as she ran, her prominent nose and pale cheeks flushed with the cold and exertion. Her profile was strong and angular, like one of those portraits from the Renaissance painters.[45] She was smiling slightly, breathing through her open mouth, sending out gusts of frosted air and running through them. She sensed him looking at her and turned her blue eyes toward him. "Are you all right?"

He nodded and smiled.

She smiled back. "I'm sorry for my moment of weakness."

"Don't be sorry." Brendan laughed. "My whole life is a string of them."

She grinned.

They left the park and turned onto Queen Street. Charlie slowed and came to a stop in front of the steamy window of a twenty-four-hour doughnut shop. Brendan had often passed it but had never gone in. The shop had always looked a little seedy in the daylight, but now, glowing with warm yellow light, it appeared cozy and inviting. The window was painted in swirling letters surrounded by shooting stars.

> ## COSMIC DOUGHNUTS
> OUT OF THIS WORLD
> 24 HRS A DAY!

---

[45] Renaissance painters were very fond of women with big noses. Leonardo da Vinci was quoted as saying, "A woman is really just the ideal life support system for a large and wonderful nose." Granted, he was a weirdo.

"Here we are."

"A doughnut shop?"

She opened the door, sketching a mock bow. "*Après vous, monsieur!*"

Brendan stepped past her into the warmth of the shop.

Before him a glass counter with metal racks displayed a few lonely fritters. More racks held an assortment of doughnuts. Two pots of coffee simmered on burners, one decaf and one regular. On a stool by the counter, a man wearing an old-fashioned paper busboy's hat sat reading a newspaper. He looked up when Brendan and Charlie came in.

"Hello." He set aside the paper. "Pardon me, but ain't you two a little young to be out and about at this hour?"

"They're with me!" a voice announced from a booth near the window. Brendan looked over and saw an old man in a woollen suit with a herringbone check pattern. A flat cap lay on the table beside an open box of doughnuts and a steaming cup of coffee. On the bench beside him a dark overcoat was folded neatly. A walking stick made of polished wood leaned against the seat.

He smiled when Brendan looked at him.

"I know you!" Brendan cried. "I saw you in the Hot Pot!"

"Yes." The old man nodded. "I couldn't help myself. I had to get a look at you."

His face was a nest of wrinkles over strong cheekbones. A neatly trimmed grey beard brushed the front of his worn linen shirt, and his sky-blue eyes were clear and sharp. They held Brendan in their grasp and didn't let him go as he crossed the floor and slid into the bench opposite.

Brendan had never seen an old Faerie before. Certainly, Ariel was ancient. Ariel had an aura, a gravity, as though the years crowded around him, but in appearance he seemed no older than Brendan's dad or mum. The Faerie sitting across from him was elderly. Thick purple veins crawled over the backs of his liver-spotted hands. His white hair was thinning on top, and his shoulders were slightly stooped. But for all his aged appearance, the man didn't seem the least bit frail. Somehow, his age was his power, and Brendan felt the weight of it bearing down on him.

Charlie stooped and kissed his wrinkled cheek. "*Mon Seigneur, bienvenue.*"

The old Faerie reached up and ran the back of his fingers against her rosy cheek. "*Ma belle Charles.* I've missed you."

Charlie sat down beside Brendan. "Here he is. Brendan Morn."

"Hello there, my lad." The man turned his smile on Brendan. Those blue eyes looked him up and down before resting on his face. "I see old Briach in you, and your mother, too."

"You knew them?"

"Oh, yes. He was a handful. She was a sweet thing."

"Uh … " Brendan suddenly felt awkward. "You know who I am but … "

"But who am I?" The old man smiled. "Forgive me. Very rude. My name is Merddyn. At least in the Old Tongue, that is my name. It means 'hawk.' You might know me by a more popular name: Merlin."

"Merlin?" Brendan croaked. "You're *Merlin*?"

"Yes."

"*The* Merlin? The *wizard* Merlin? *Sword in the stone* Merlin?"

"Guilty! Though it wasn't a stone, really. It was an anvil. Still, that was me."

"I can't believe it," Brendan said softly. "You're the Ancient One Greenleaf was talking about. Charlie's teacher."

Merlin nodded. "Would you like a doughnut?"

Never in his wildest imaginings had Brendan ever thought he might be sitting in the presence of the legendary Merlin. Never in his most bizarre dreams had he ever imagined that the greatest wizard in history and counsellor of King Arthur would be offering him a doughnut.

"Uh," Brendan finally managed. "A doughnut?"

"You do like doughnuts, don't you?" Merddyn asked. "I mean, as a pastry, they are quite delightful. Consider their variety: so many types to choose from. I am partial to the Hawaiian, myself. All those different-coloured sprinkles. Truly spectacular! Though I don't see why it's called Hawaiian. There's no pineapple in it at all. Or poi. Or roast pig, for that matter. Still, one shouldn't question perfection. And consider its shape." He nimbly plucked a plain doughnut from the box and held it in his long fingers. "A circle: the symbol of eternity. One wonders if the Humans realized this when they chose the shape or whether they stumbled upon it by accident, as they so often do. Creatures of instinct, are Humans. Why not make doughnuts square, one might ask? They'd certainly fit better in a box."

Merddyn shrugged and, chuckling, bit into the doughnut with his strong white teeth. Brendan didn't know what to say. He watched as the old Faerie chewed happily, dabbing the corners of his mouth with a paper napkin.

"Are those doughnuts?" Brendan had forgotten all about BLT. She was hanging out of his pocket, eyes wide as saucers. He could practically feel her blood fizzing with desire.

"Oh no you don't … " Brendan began, but Merddyn waved a hand. He broke the doughnut in two and gave half to BLT.

"Sweet!" BLT saluted cheekily and sped away with her prize. The man at the counter opened the door for her and she rocketed out into the darkness. Tweezers scampered out of Charlie's jacket and dashed after BLT.

"They get along pretty well, *non*?" Charlie laughed.

"Is he … ?" Brendan asked, pointing at the counterman.

"Edgar's one of us, yes." Merddyn waved. The man smiled, displaying an even set of green teeth, and went back to his newspaper. "Now, forgive me," Merddyn said, placing the rest of his doughnut back in the box. "You must have many questions, and I'd hazard a guess that none of them are about doughnuts."

Brendan had a million questions, and he couldn't begin to choose just one. He decided to start with the simplest. "Why me?"

"Why you?" Merddyn's eyebrows rose like bushy caterpillars. "That's fairly broad. Can you be more specific?"

"Why are you here, right now, talking to me?" Brendan asked. "I mean, I'm hardly the only Faerie in the world and you must be a busy guy. You're Merlin, right? Come on!"

"You know, it never ceases to amaze me how the truly important people I have dealt with throughout history haven't understood their place in the grand scheme of things. I don't know if it's humility, ignorance, or wilful pigheadedness. Take Arthur, for example. He was a lovely boy, perceptive, kind, and clever, but slightly foolish. When he pulled the sword from the stone, or anvil I should say, he was ready to give it to anyone who was willing to take it from him. He needed so much cajoling, but in the end he became the man and the king he was meant to be in spite of himself."

"If I remember, things didn't work out too well for him," Brendan pointed out.

"How so?"

"Well, he got killed, didn't he? By his own son?"

"Not exactly killed, but that's beside the point. And was he a failure? People everywhere revere him as a great king. The name of King Arthur is symbolic of nobility and righteousness. Everyone remembers Arthur. Very few remember his son."

"Mordred?"

"Yes. Annoying little twerp," Merddyn snorted. "But to the point: why you specifically? Many reasons, most of which would only confuse you." Merddyn frowned. "Let me just say this: you are uniquely positioned to make a real difference in the world."

"Me? How could that be possible?" Brendan cried. "Ask Charlie! Ask Greenleaf! Ask Kim! I can barely manage to control my powers. How could I make a difference in the world?"

Merddyn smiled. "I have asked Greenleaf. He has kept me apprised of your progress, and it was he who sent for my help. I assigned Charlie to assist with your training."

"You sent her?" Brendan asked in disbelief. He glared at Charlie, who gave him a pained smile in return. "So then you know what a washout I've been. She must have told you."

"Your lack of confidence in yourself would be charming if it weren't so dangerous. Charlie has a great deal of faith in you, you know. I'd say she has become quite fond of you, in fact. Oh my. She's blushing. It takes a lot to make Charlie blush."

"Merddyn, please." Charlie rolled her eyes.

She's fond of me? Brendan didn't know how to feel about that. He was kind of annoyed at her but a little excited by the thought. *Why didn't she tell me who sent her? Would it have made any difference? Probably not, but still … it was a matter of trust, right?*

"Brendan, you must take my word for it. You are very special. That's why I came here to meet you," Merddyn said.

"I don't feel special. If you mean 'special' as in I should be in a class with kids who need extra help, then yeah, maybe. I feel like an idiot most of the time."

Merddyn smiled. "Well, Charlie thinks you're quite gifted. As I said, I've been receiving reports. I've heard about what you did with the tree. And how you broke the circle."

Brendan nodded.

"I find the incident with the tree particularly fascinating. Can you tell me about it?"

"I don't understand it myself." Brendan shook his head.

"Tell me in your own words," Merddyn said, placing his elbows on the table. "Describe what it was like with the tree. Just take your time."

Brendan closed his eyes. He tried to remember exactly how he'd felt that day. He sighed and began to talk. He told Merddyn of his frustration, of how Greenleaf had transformed into Orcadia. He recalled how scared he was when BLT was threatened and the fear he felt for his own life. He related how he'd groped for help as he had done before, and the slumbering mind of the tree had stirred at his entreaty and defended him.

"It was like talking to the birds or bugs," he concluded. "I've done that before. It was a matter of focusing harder,

I guess. I wasn't able to get the tree to let Greenleaf go afterwards. I couldn't get that focus back no matter how hard I tried."

Merddyn had hardly spoken as Brendan recalled the events. He asked the odd question now and then, prodding him for details. Mostly, he listened. Looking into those soft blue eyes, Brendan felt he could be entirely honest, entirely at ease. It felt good to talk to someone who seemed to understand him so completely. When Brendan finally finished, Merddyn leaned back in his chair and silently contemplated the boy across the table. Brendan found it quite disconcerting.

"Well," Brendan asked impatiently. "What's wrong with me?"

"Wrong?" Merddyn blinked and then laughed as if he'd never heard anything so ridiculous. "Wrong! Nothing is wrong, my dear boy, nothing at all. In fact, I suspect that a number of things are exactly right. Difficult but right."

"What's that supposed to mean?"

"Forgive me, Brendan. I'm just trying to figure out how to explain this to you. You see, I haven't met anyone in centuries, perhaps longer, who has been even remotely capable of understanding."

"Are you talking about me? I don't understand anything!" Brendan threw up his hands in frustration. He looked into Merddyn's blue eyes and saw sympathy there, and a little sadness, too.

Merddyn said, "Brendan, please. I know this is overwhelming. I'll tell you what I know and what you can understand."

Brendan hesitated. He looked to Charlie, who smiled encouragingly. Reassured, he sat back.

"Greenleaf wasn't exactly right when he said that you exhibited a new kind of Talent. It's really quite an old Talent. And I should know, Brendan. I am one of the oldest of the Ancients. There are few of us left who remember the time before the Pact. Even fewer remember what it was like when the People of the Moon and Metal lived in harmony at the dawn of the world."

Charlie rose from the table. "I have heard this tale many times. I'll leave you two to talk. It's snowing!" She went to the door and opened it, breathing deeply. "I love the snow." She dashed out into the night.

Merddyn chuckled softly. "She has a lovely spirit. She had a hard start in this life, much like your own."

Brendan nodded. "She told me."

"Indeed. I see you two have become close."

Brendan reddened. "It's not like that."

"Of course not," Merddyn chuckled. "It never is like that until the moment when it suddenly *is* like that, and then it's too late." Merddyn sighed, suddenly melancholy. "I feel sorrow for the girl."

"She's like me. She never knew her parents. It's worse for her, though. She never even knew who they were."

"Yes, it weighs upon her heavily. I have promised to find out who her real parents are. Not as easy as one might expect. It's a real mystery, in fact."

Brendan sighed. "I met my father, if only for a few moments … "

For once, Merddyn looked astonished. "You met your father? How is that possible?"

"I'm not exactly sure. He came to me for only a moment, and he said it was very hard for him to do. He came when I was fighting Orcadia."

"Aha! So that's how you were initiated!" Merddyn clapped his hands. "Old Briach Morn managed to zip over from the Other Side, did he? The old fox."

Brendan silently cursed himself. "I haven't even told Kim that. Why did I just blurt it out to you?"

Merddyn laughed, winking slyly. "You have to get up pretty early in the morning to get anything past old Merddyn." He laughed again and it was an infectious sound. Brendan found he couldn't help but join in.

"Are you sure you wouldn't like a doughnut?" Merddyn said at last, tipping the box toward Brendan.

"No thanks," Brendan declined. "You were talking about the People of the Moon and Metal."

"Yes." Merddyn plucked out a doughnut with pale brown icing. He took a dainty bite and closed his eyes with pleasure. "Mmmm. Maple. I do love it so. Who could imagine a tree might produce such a delightful flavour?"

"Sir?"

"Oh, yes. Two tribes."

Merddyn began his tale.

HISTORY

"The People of Metal and the Fair Folk lived together then. The jealousies and fears that caused the later fracture were yet to rear their ugly heads. The two tribes of Sun and Moon complemented each other, shared each other's strengths. The balance was kept for many eons."

"What happened?" Brendan asked. He was having trouble grasping the expanses of time Merddyn was speaking about. Could there really have been a time when Humans and Faeries shared the world?

"What always happens when the world seems too simple and peaceful: there were those in both tribes who grew to mistrust the others. Some of the Fair Folk tired of the People of Metal's appetite for change and disrespect for the Earth: the digging, mining, burning, and cutting of the forests to build their homes and towns. Among the Humans, some assumed that the Fair Folk harboured secrets and riches that they refused to share with their Human brethren."

"What was the truth?" Brendan asked.

Merddyn sighed. "The truth is never simple. The Humans tended to take what they needed when they needed it. They lacked the insight of the Fair Folk. They couldn't feel the harm they did to the Earth. They were like children, unwittingly devouring the world around them as they multiplied and spread to fill its open spaces.

"For our part, we Fair Folk tended to remain aloof from the Humans. Many of us began to look upon them as a nuisance and a burden to be avoided. We started to seek our own company in the wild places, out of reach of the Humans. That was a mistake, but an honest one. It only served to make our actions more mysterious and arouse further suspicion in the Humans. They began to fear us.

"The conflict started with small incidents. Here and there, individuals clashed. Hatred grew. Soon there was open warfare between our tribes. The destruction was terrible and the loss of life unspeakable. Something had to be done to return the peace before one side or the other was destroyed.

"I gathered a council of Fair Folk and Humans and we formed an alliance. We'd fight together to restore order. We knew accommodation with the Humans was necessary. The People of Metal multiplied much faster than we ever could, and one day they would vastly outnumber us. If we didn't strike some form of pact with them, we would be doomed.

"Others among the Fair Folk believed the opposite. They were determined to subjugate the Humans or annihilate them. These fell-minded Faeries we called the Dark Ones. They marshalled their forces and brought ruin upon the Humans, enslaving or destroying all in their path.

"There was a great battle. The very Earth was reshaped beneath the titanic blows that were struck and the powers that were unleashed on that dark day. In the end, we defeated the Dark Ones. We imprisoned their leaders, the ones who refused to accept defeat, with our strongest Wards. Those who repented of their ways were allowed to go free provided they worked to repair the damage they had wrought.

The Pact was struck and we Fair Folk faded from memory, remembered only as demons and ogres in children's stories. We clung on in the cracks of Human society, and that is where we find ourselves today."

Merddyn stopped speaking, staring out into the dark night where snowflakes had once again begun to fall. He shook himself. "Forgive me. Wool gathering! I am definitely getting old. Now, I'm sure you're wondering what all this history has to do with you. Well, bear with me. Everything is connected, you see."

Merddyn gently pinched the bridge of his nose. "Ah," he said wearily. "We lost so much on that horrible day. So many Ancients went to the Far Lands, or what Humans call heaven. Many others were maimed and chose to pass to the Other Side, cutting themselves off from this world and its woes. Few of us were left, and very few of the truly Ancient Ones like myself survived. Much deep knowledge was lost."

Merddyn looked up at Brendan and smiled sadly. "How can I begin to describe to you the heartbreak I felt at such waste? You couldn't grasp it." He fell silent again.

"What does this have to do with me?" Brendan prompted. "And the tree?"

"Oh." Merddyn roused himself. "Everything. You see, the Fair Folk who had survived and remained on This Side after the Pact was struck were younger, without the experience of the Ancient Ones. Much lore and wisdom was lost. They scattered far and wide, some passing out of contact with their brethren altogether. I tried to keep us all connected as best I could, but there were few who could help me. Whereas before the Fair Folk had instinctively understood the ebb and flow of the energy that is the lifeblood of the universe, they now comprehended it only in fragments. In the passing centuries, the idea that a Faerie could master only one Talent became the accepted norm."

"That's what Greenleaf told me," Brendan confirmed. "And Ariel, too. Everybody is unusually good at one Talent."

"But you have more than one. Why?"

"You're the expert. You tell me!"

"In the Old Times, there were no specialties, no specific Talents or Arts. There were no such distinctions. The universe is full of energy. It's alive with it. We could tap into it readily and manipulate it to do anything we wished. Let me explain." Merddyn waved a hand at Edgar. "A glass of water, if you don't mind, Edgar!"

Edgar complied, filling a tumbler from the tap. He brought it to the table.

"Many thanks," Merddyn said. Edgar went back to his paper. Merddyn pushed the glass of water into the centre of the table. "Tell me, Brendan. What do you see?"

Brendan shrugged. "A glass of water."

Merddyn nodded. "That's one answer. I think there is a better one."

Though he was seated across from the legendary Merlin himself, Brendan couldn't help but feel completely exasperated. "Oh, come on, will ya? Does everything have to be some kind of Zen riddle?"

"I like Zen riddles. 'Koans' they're called, by the way. Buddhism has some wonderful mystical traditions. And Buddha himself was a very sweet fellow. So curious and good-hearted. A wonderful student."

"You're telling me you taught Buddha?"

"For a brief time. He had the idea already. I just gave him a nudge in the right direction."

"Buddha was a … one of us?"

"Oh, no! He was a Human. Like Jesus and Mohammed and Zarathustra. Enlightened Humans who saw that there was a pattern underpinning the world we think we know. But that is beside the point. What we have here is a difference in perception. You see a glass of water. I say that within this glass is all the water in the world."

Brendan just stared. "I don't get it."

"You have to see all the water in the world as one thing, no matter how it's parcelled up. Those partitions—a glass, a lake, a river, an ocean—are all boundaries we place on a thing so that we can better understand it. What they actually do is make it impossible to understand that thing completely."

Brendan thought about that. "But I can't possibly hold the image of all the water in the world in my mind. It's too huge."

"Better philosophers than I could and would elaborate on this idea, but for our purposes, it isn't necessary. I just want you to think in a new way."

"So I'm thinking in a new way," Brendan conceded. "How does this relate to me, exactly?"

"The energy Faeries draw upon, the energy that fuels our glamours and our Wards, is like that ocean. In the distant past, we were able to see this ocean of energy as a continuous thing, without a beginning and an end. We could manipulate the energy and make the universe do our bidding.

"Now that perception is gone. We've lost our ability to see. The Fair Folk now dip a bucket into that proverbial sea and believe that the bucket of water is all there is. There is a problem with our thinking."

"But I don't even have a bucket," Brendan said in exasperation. "I haven't even got a cup!"

"You're wrong, Brendan." Merddyn smiled. "You grew up without the mindset a Faerie usually has when he's raised in our world. You have no preconceived notions about Talents and Arts. You are having trouble because you can't understand the restrictions we have come to set upon ourselves. You are unique."

"I am? I don't get it. I can't seem to master any skill."

"No. You don't seem to *need* to master those skills. Because your mind is unrestricted, you can manipulate the energy of the universe spontaneously. When you are pushed by necessity or danger, you just draw on that energy and create what you need to overcome the problem.

"Allow me to illustrate another point. Watch." He plucked a chocolate-glazed doughnut out of the box. "What is this?"

"A doughnut."

"Yes, but it is also anything I wish it to be because it is made of energy. I can manipulate that energy with my will." Merddyn closed his eyes and concentrated. The doughnut shimmered, melted, swirled, and then solidified into a pebble. The small stone remained for only a moment before it, too, transformed into a handful of feathers. The feathers crackled and turned into a blue flame that danced in Merddyn's wrinkled palm and finally disappeared, rising as smoke toward the rafters. "They are all the same. The doughnut, the stone, the feathers, the flame."

"Mass is energy," Brendan said with hushed awe. "Einstein."

"A clever fellow, Albert. I guess someone has been paying attention in physics class." Merddyn smiled.

"What about living things?" Brendan said suddenly. "Why not change the doughnut into a bird or something?"

Merddyn frowned. "That's very difficult. Life is very complicated. To create it means that you must have the insight and wisdom to construct a soul for your creation. Very arrogant and very dangerous."

"So ... what does this mean for me? I can do things because I have no preconceived ideas? I'm some kind of Faerie freak? I'm ... what do they call those people ... an idiot savant?"[46]

"A savant, perhaps," Merddyn agreed. "An idiot? I think not. I believe you are like the Fair Folk when they were in their infancy, in the most Ancient of times. You're a throwback but a wonderful one. I believe you are what all Faeries should be. When I first heard of you, I was intrigued. I asked Ariel to keep an eye on you and inform me of your progress. What I learned excited me. I've been looking for someone like you for a long time. I thought our Charlie might have been the one."

"Charlie?"

"Yes. She grew up in the Human world, ignorant of our ways. I thought she might be the clean slate I was looking for. Alas, I found her too late. She'd already been partially trained by a native Shaman. Her mind had been set. Her ability is quite unique and beautiful, don't you think? Quite unlike anyone else's in the Faerie world."

---

[46] The term *idiot savant* is old-fashioned now. It was used to describe someone who was capable of accomplishing one very complicated task, despite being of below normal intelligence or mentally challenged. For example, a person whose brain was faulty in some way and couldn't speak might perform extremely complicated mathematical functions in his or her head. I once knew a beaver that could slap out pi to the three-hundredth decimal place. It wasn't an idiot savant, however; it was merely amazing.

"She's kind of terrifying. I wouldn't want to cross anyone who could turn into a bear if I got them upset," Brendan said. "Wait a minute, though. Isn't she a shape-shifter? There's a guy at the Swan of Liir on the Ward's Island who can change into a lion."

"Ah, yes. Leonard! Charming fellow. You're right, he is a shape-shifter, but shape-shifters can assume the shape of only one animal. Charlie has several in her repertoire."

"Oh." Brendan nodded. "I see. Okay, I'm unique. I understand that. I don't mean any disrespect but … so what?"

The old Faerie became serious. His pale blue eyes locked on Brendan's and held him fast. "Brendan, I have stood by and watched for countless years as this world has gone on its way. I've tried my best to tweak things onto a better course, to forestall a dark future that haunts my dreams. We are living in a dark time. The balance is slipping. The Earth is suffering. She is sick from centuries of neglect and exploitation to the point that she may fail completely. Something must be done."

Brendan felt a cold fist clench his heart. He held up his hands in protest. "No. Don't do this to me. Don't tell me I'm the only hope for a dying world. Are you kidding me? I'll lose it, I promise you."

"No, not the only hope. But I believe you are a part of a solution," Merddyn insisted. "Together with others who share our wish for a better world, we can possibly reverse the damage before it's too late."

"Do you people ever stop?" Brendan shouted. "You're all trying to drive me insane. 'You've gotta find an amulet!' 'You've gotta master your powers.' 'You've gotta pass a test or die trying.' 'You need to save the world!' Seriously? I'm just a kid. I should be hanging out with my friends and playing video games. Instead, I'm running from psycho Faeries! Oh, and of course a girl who can change into a deer, a bear, and a wild pig!" Brendan stood up and marched for the door. He whirled and pointed at Merddyn. "Who do you people think you are? None of you care about me! You all have your games you're playing, and you want me to jump in and join you. Well, I don't want to. I wish I'd never found out about all this stuff. I wish Deirdre had just left me alone and let Orcadia kill me."

"It's no game, Brendan." Merddyn's voice was soft. He gently shook his head. "I wish things were different, easier for you. I have no right to ask anything of you. I am only appealing to you who have family in both worlds to think about helping me. I need you. Your families, both Human and Faerie, need you."

Brendan felt the anger drain out of him. He looked at Merddyn and saw not a powerful wizard out of legend, but a desperately weary old man asking for help.

"I'm sorry," Brendan said. "It's just … so much. I have to think. Will you be coming to the Proving?"

"I haven't decided yet," Merddyn said. "And Brendan? Can you keep our little meeting just between the two of us? Like you, I value my privacy."

Brendan nodded. Then he turned and fled into the night.

Edgar folded up his newspaper, picked up a pot of coffee from the warmer, and came over to Merddyn's table. "More coffee, sir?"

"A little. Thank you, Edgar."

Pouring the coffee, Edgar said, "He's a nice kid. He'll come around."

"How can you be sure?"

"I run a doughnut shop. You get a feel for people."

Merddyn smiled. "I guess I'll just have to have faith in your judgment, Edgar."

"I'm never wrong."

"I used to think the same thing a few thousand years ago." Merddyn smiled sadly and turned his attention to the important task of choosing another doughnut.

DAWN FLYERS

Brendan had left the doughnut shop intending to go home. Instead, he'd found himself running, faster and faster. At first, he had no idea where he was going. He just needed to move. He didn't want to think about anything but speed. It was the only way he could wipe his mind and exhaust himself to the point where he could fall asleep. At last, he went home and crawled into bed without even changing into his pyjamas.

For the next three days, he was irritable and distracted. His parents were too busy with work and Christmas preparations to notice his mood. Delia, surprisingly, stayed out of his way. He went to school and sleepwalked through classes, alone. Charlie didn't come around, as if sensing that the meeting with Merddyn had left him needing some time and space to himself. Each night he waited until he was sure everyone was asleep and then, once again, he raced through the streets, trying to banish his worry and confusion with the burning sizzle of the warp singing in his blood.

On the third night, the night before the Proving, he followed the Humber River north into the countryside. As he left the blaze of city lights behind, he could see the stars wheeling above him. Now and then, a star raced steadily across the blackness: a satellite, his father had told him years ago. He was always amazed that the works of Humans were visible in space, a sign that they were constantly reaching for more in the universe. Brendan turned and swung across the top of the city, ghosting along just outside the reach of the halogen lamps that lit the freeway, until he reached the Don River and headed south.

South he flashed, keeping to the back alleys, staying in the shadows and away from the people who frequented the nighttime streets. The speed didn't come easily to him now. His mind was troubled, turning over what Merddyn had told him. How could he be so important? How could he be the key to anything? He looked up to the stars but could barely see them in the wash of light pollution.

Humans have no idea how much more there is to the world. Even my parents, with their recycling and green habits, will never see it the way I can, the pain and the poison. I can feel it in the air. I can feel it my lungs when I breathe. If I think too much about it, I'll go insane!

He staggered to a halt in the shadowed doorway of St. Michael's Church, in the heart of the winter city. The streets were quiet save for a few late revellers. He couldn't see them but he heard the mobs heading along Church Street. They shouted back and forth, sang at the top of their lungs. He envied them their easy mood. He found himself sliding dangerously toward self-pity.

He leaned back against the weathered wooden door of the cathedral. Christmas with his family was probably his favourite time. His mum and dad were big fans of the holiday and tried to impart its traditions to their kids. There was midnight mass on Christmas Eve, though they rarely went to church any other day. They came here, to St. Michael's. Brendan closed his eyes and tried to remember the smell of the incense and the sound of the choir as it filled the vaulted space.

He needed some peace. He couldn't catch his breath. Everything was just too much: the revelation of his true heritage, and now the pressure of the Proving. To top it all off, here was Merddyn, the great Merlin himself, telling Brendan that the fate of the world might rest on his shoulders. How could he hope to bear such a heavy burden? Only weeks ago, the biggest thing he'd had to worry about was his crush on Marina Kaprillian. Now he wasn't sure if he'd live to come back to this church with his family on Christmas Eve.

He didn't hear Kim's approach. Suddenly, her voice was in his ear.

"There you are!" Kim melted out of the shadows and trotted toward him. "I've been looking everywhere for you. People were worried sick."

"Oh," Brendan grunted. "Well, you've found me. You can go tell everyone I'm fine."

"Wow. Hello, Grumpy-Pants! It's nice to see you, too."

Brendan didn't speak as she settled down next to him on the steps.

"Look who's talking," Brendan shot back. "You haven't exactly been all sweetness and light, you know!"

Kim glowered but said nothing. They leaned against the door in silence for a moment, listening to the people laughing and singing.

"What's wrong?" she asked.

"What's wrong?" He laughed bitterly. "What isn't wrong?"

"It's not that bad, Brendan."

"You don't think so? I may die at the Proving!"

"You probably won't, though."

"Why not?" Brendan said softly, hanging his head. "What makes you so sure?"

Kim smiled her lopsided smile. "You always manage to surprise everyone. I believe in you."

"Well, that makes one of us."

"And … "

"And what?"

Kim took his chin in her hand and lifted his head until he was looking into her almond-shaped brown eyes. "And I won't let anything bad happen to you. I promise."

As Brendan studied her familiar face, the angle of her chin, her high cheekbones, the dark, glossy hair falling over her forehead, he realized suddenly how glad he was to see her. Charlie had shown up and stolen his attention. The lutin had stepped into his life and pulled him into her orbit. He'd neglected not only his friendship with Harold and Dmitri, but his friendship with Kim, too. He saw that she'd been hurt by that, and he felt ashamed.

Kim sensed his discomfort and mercifully let go of his chin. "All right, pal. It's time to blow off some steam. I know just the thing. Follow me."

She set off across the churchyard, her field hockey stick swinging back and forth on her back like a pendulum. After a moment's hesitation, he followed her.

He didn't know where they were going until she turned down a street and the looming spire of the CN Tower rose into the night before them. Year-round, the tower's elevator shafts that crawled up the sides were lit up, but during the holidays, the lights were bright green and red, transforming the grey concrete finger into a gargantuan candy cane. Even through the cloud of his tension and worry, the sight lifted Brendan's spirits. He felt a swell of fondness for the city he called home.

As they drew closer they were joined by others heading to the tower. Faeries emerged from the alleyways and side streets until a small group of colourfully dressed travellers coalesced into a throng. Some carried bundles on their backs, tightly rolled tubes of bright fabric and sticks that looked like tent poles.

"Hey, Ki-Mata! How's it going?" a Faerie called, falling into step with them. She was carrying a multicoloured bundle on her back. She smiled at Brendan. "Hey, Brendan! I've never seen you out here before."

Brendan recognized Cassie, the barista from the Hot Pot. Gone was the bland apron and Human disguise. She was out in all her Faerie glory. Her hair was aglow with filaments of silver wire woven into her dark tresses. She wore a tight jumpsuit of muted sky-blue and grey. "Hi. No, I guess not," Brendan admitted. "What's going on? Where are all these people headed?"

Cassie shared a sly look with Kim and slapped his back. "You'll see!"

They jogged up the ramp by the baseball stadium and down into the open space at the foot of the tower. There they found a metal door propped open. The band of Faeries entered a dark room, hooting and shouting at one another, sending echoes all around. As Brendan's eyes adjusted to the gloom, he realized they were at the bottom of a winding staircase. He looked up but the top was hidden from sight.

A Faerie man with a bright vermillion mohawk waving from the top of his head shouted, "Last one to the top is a Dwarf's underpants." Then he sprinted up the stairs out of sight. The others catcalled and shouted after him before setting off in hot pursuit.

"Come on, Brendan," Kim laughed. "Believe me, you don't want to be a Dwarf's underpants!" She pushed him toward the stairs, and soon they were taking the treads two at a time.

Brendan had been to the top of the tower before, but only on one of the super-fast elevators. Running up in the dark was a totally different experience. He'd read somewhere that the staircase had thousands of steps: it was over half a kilometre high.[47] In his old life, he would have succumbed to exhaustion after a hundred, if he hadn't already tripped over his clumsy feet and bounced all the way back down to the bottom. Now he took the steps with ease. He fell into an easy rhythm, pumping his arms and breathing easily. He started to enjoy himself, losing himself in the physical exertion. He easily matched Kim's pace and even had to hold back a little to avoid outpacing her. Soon they caught up to the pack. They joined the jostling, laughing mass surging upwards through the dark.

Moments like these made him forget the new responsibilities that weighed on him. His worries over his family, the upcoming Proving, the conversation with Merddyn all dissolved in the simple pleasure of his physical existence. He relished being alive and being part of the joy of the Faeries around him.

All too soon, the group reached the top of the stairs. The last runner was jeered good-naturedly as he arrived

---

[47] It's actually 553.3 metres tall. I don't mean to be a stickler, but …

on the landing. He was a short, wiry Faerie with luminous grey eyes. "I ain't got long legs, ya know. Gimme a break."

They were standing at what appeared to be a blank concrete wall. The stairwell simply ended.

"What now?" Brendan asked.

"Watch!" Kim said. The group reached out and grasped hands. Brendan took Kim's and Cassie's hands in his. Once all of the members of the group had established physical contact with someone, they began to sing.

The song had no recognizable words. They merely opened their mouths and uttered a soft, breathy sigh. Brendan tried to follow the lead of the others. He was self-conscious at first, but as the moment stretched out, he let himself go. The sound began as a single note sung in unison. Then individuals diverged, some sliding up, some sliding down, until the concrete space was vibrating with a lush, achingly beautiful chord that reverberated through Brendan's body. He'd never felt anything so gorgeous, and he wanted to stay in that moment for as long as he could.

The chord crescendoed, and suddenly the wall before them shuddered and flowed away. A fresh, bitingly cold wind washed over them. The singers stopped and shouldered their burdens once more. Together, they stepped out onto an open platform. Brendan's jaw dropped. The whole of the city, the lake, and the islands spread out before him.

"Neat, huh?" Kim laughed at his dumbstruck expression.

"The Dawn Flyers?"

"You got it, Brendan." Cassie smiled. People were shrugging their bundles off and unwrapping them. Brendan watched as they assembled what amounted to broad kites, like the outstretched wings of gulls with harnesses at the centre. Brendan wandered around the platform, watching the work with undisguised fascination. As the wind whipped around them, they constantly struggled to keep the gliders from being plucked away.

Brendan walked to the edge of the platform. The ledge ran all the way around the central column of the tower. A roof of opaque resin or crystal kept the snow and some of the wind off the fliers as they prepared their equipment. Brendan gripped a support post and leaned out to look down. A hundred metres below, he saw the roof of the observation platform. He'd been there before with his parents and had stood on the glass floor and felt his stomach drop away as he saw the ground so far below. This platform was higher still and nowhere near as safe or enclosed. He should have felt pure terror, but instead he felt exhilarated. He was higher than any Human had been on the tower since a helicopter had lowered the spire four decades ago.

"Brendan!"

He turned to see Kim pulling a set of the wings onto her back. The others were pulling straps and tightening harnesses. The wings could be folded in close to the body like a bird's wings. Elaborate hinges and joints tensed and loosened as the fliers tested their contraptions.

Kim walked toward him. "There are a couple of extra sets of wings here. You wanna come?"

Brendan shook his head. "Are you kidding me? I'd totally kill myself. Or barf. It's a mile to the ground."

"C'mon! Don't be a big baby!" Kim cajoled.

"No. No way! I'll walk down and see you on the ground."

"All right. Have it your way." Kim suddenly pointed out toward the islands. "What's that?"

Brendan turned to look. He saw only sky and the dark hump of the Toronto Islands. Lights twinkled here and there. "I don't see anythioooof!"

Kim slammed into him from behind and pushed him out into space.

THE WILD HUNT

Brendan's heart was hammering against his ribs. He wanted to scream in terror, but he couldn't get any air into his panic-constricted lungs. He heard Kim's hysterical cackle close to his ear. She had her arms wrapped tightly around his chest.

"Here we go! WOOOOOOOOOOO!"

"Are you insane?" Brendan screamed, but the sound was whipped away by the air ripping past his face as they plummeted toward the base of the tower.

"Relax, granny!" Kim shouted. "I just need to find an updraft!"

The ground was rushing at them very fast now. The grey concrete was expanding to fill Brendan's vision. He just had time to wonder if Kim had been hired to kill him when wings snapped open on either side, and with a crackle of taut silk they were swooping up again, skimming over the sidewalk at a height of about a hundred metres. The wind was lifting them steadily. They rose higher and higher up over the rail lines and the expressway, with its trail of red tail lights snaking by below. Then they were over the condos on the waterfront and the lake itself.

Brendan's stomach unclenched. When he was confident that he wouldn't lose the dinner he'd eaten earlier, he turned his head to see Kim's madly grinning face. "What is wrong with you? Are you crazy?"

"Lighten up, Brendan. Isn't this amazing?"

"It might be more amazing if I hadn't wet my pants. I almost had a heart attack, you insaniac nutcase! Couldn't you warn me?"

"Where would the fun be in that?" Kim tipped her right wing slightly, sending them curving out and banking even higher, moving out farther over the lake. "Look! They're closing off the island."

Brendan looked down and saw that the surface of the lake nearest the island, usually rolling with whitecaps, was still and smooth as glass. The flat area spread slowly out toward the city beyond. He suddenly understood. "They're freezing the lake!"

"Yeah," Kim confirmed. "It takes a lot of Faeries to weave some pretty intense weather Wards together, but it's the best way to isolate the Ward's Island."

Brendan watched as the ice continued to radiate out from the island. He peered closer. He saw tiny figures out on the ice. "Who are they?"

"Fair Folk are starting to arrive. The Gathering starts when the sun goes down tonight ... or tomorrow. You know what I mean."

Kim tipped her wings forward and they rose higher. The island became more and more indistinct below. Brendan looked around and saw other Dawn Flyers dipping and diving, their wings silvered by the moonlight. The sky was remarkably clear, especially so high up and out of the reach of the city lights. The stars twinkled with cold brilliance.

Kim hung in the air, slowly turning in a circle, like a hawk lazily floating as it waited for prey to break cover below. Brendan became keenly aware of her arms wrapped around him. Her body was pressed against his back, and he could feel every tiny adjustment she made with her shoulders and legs to keep them aloft. For the second time in the past week, he was close to a very attractive girl. Even as he savoured the sensation, he felt a weird pang of guilt. Only a few days before he had held Charlie and comforted her, and now here was Kim with her arms wrapped around him. Why did he feel guilty? He didn't know; he just did, that's all.

"Are you sure this thing can hold two people?" he asked.

"The Artificers guarantee them. But don't worry, if we start to lose altitude, I'll drop you and save myself."

"Thanks, Kim. I appreciate it."

"No problem."

They were silent for a long time. The wind whistled an eerie tune through the flier's rigging. He took in the stars and the moon hanging almost full in the sky. He looked over his shoulder and saw the city shining below. Brendan suddenly laughed out loud.

"What?" Kim asked.

"Nothing," Brendan said. "It's just … this is awesome!"

Kim laughed. "Yeah." After a moment she said, "I wanted you to see this. I wanted you to see … "

"What?"

"I wanted you to see that there are great things about being one of us, Brendan. It isn't all bad. It isn't all Proving and tests and Quests and trouble. It's beautiful, too."

Brendan thought about that. He looked out over the lake and the city. He was seeing it in a way he never would have if he hadn't met Kim and learned about his Faerie family. And it was beautiful.

He realized something else, too. He hadn't been aware of how much he'd missed Kim. He felt bad.

"I'm sorry, Kim."

"For what?"

"I haven't been there for you at all."

"You have a lot to worry about. Don't sweat it."

"I have a lot to worry about and so do you. But more than that … " He swallowed. "I've … I've missed you these past few days."

"Don't be an idiot," she said, but her grip around his chest tightened slightly. Brendan hadn't thought she could hold him any closer than she already was.

"Holy stars," Kim said sharply. "Look."

Out over the lake, there was a loud rumble followed by a clap of thunder, reminding Brendan of a fighter plane at an air show breaking the sound barrier. An explosion of bright light erupted about a mile above the lake, igniting the sky in a flash. The glow started moving across the sky like a comet, cycling through every colour in the spectrum, a hot swirl of shifting light that grew in intensity as it approached. "What is that? A plane?"

"That's no plane," Kim called in his ear. "That's the Wild Hunt! Pûkh has arrived."

"The Wild What?" Brendan cried. He was having trouble hearing Kim. He became aware of a high keening not unlike the sound of a jet engine.

"The Wild Hunt. When Pûkh travels outside the realm of Tír na nÓg, he always brings his retinue," Kim explained. "They travel as the Ancient Faerie Lords once did. Pûkh, or Lord Pûkh as he prefers to be called, tries to keep the Old Ways alive."

The light drew closer, descending from the sky like a comet with a rainbow tail trailing behind. As the Hunt approached, Brendan saw it was composed of many Faeries, at least fifty of them. They were attended by countless Lesser Faeries who swarmed around them in a glittering crowd.

The Faeries were dressed in clothing that Brendan thought wouldn't have looked out of place in a fantasy movie. Cloaks and capes of brilliant hues streamed out behind them. The men wore tunics of rich brocade and beautiful patterns that changed as the light caught them. Elaborate jewellery of gold, pearls, and glittering gems dripped from their throats and wrists. They rode their mounts with casual grace that was beyond any Human's ability to imitate.

The animals were another shock. Some of the Faeries rode horses that glowed faintly in the moonlight. Others came on powerful stags bedecked in tack and harness, their massive racks of antlers beribboned and hung with delicate silver bells. The stags put Brendan in mind of Santa's flying reindeer, but these creatures were not benevolent and lovable. Their nostrils flared and smoked. They tossed their heads and rolled their eyes as if the beings on their backs terrified them. Brendan felt sorry for them.

At the front of the cavalcade rode a trio of Faeries. One was a woman so small that Brendan thought she was a child until he looked at her face. Her eyes were wild with a mad intensity that filled him with dread. She grinned, displaying teeth that had been filed to points, and shrieked in a wild lament that made Brendan's hair stand on end. On a massive horse, the biggest that Brendan had ever seen, sat a freakishly tall man with long silver hair and cold blue eyes. Slung loosely under his arm was a long lance, its tip flashing in the starlight. His face was long and grim.

Between these two bizarre figures and slightly ahead rode a dark Faerie with long chestnut hair caught up in a clasp of gold and diamonds at the back of his neck. He wore a light suit of silver armour that rippled like the surface of a moonlit pool. He threw his head back as he laughed out loud. His slightly slanted eyes and cruel mouth were smiling as if he was enjoying the spectacle he was making.

"Holy cow," Brendan shouted. "Is that … "

"Lord Pûkh has arrived," Kim confirmed, a sneer in her voice. "In all his pompous glory."

Brendan could sense the disapproval in her voice. He watched as the Wild Hunt swung wide over the city, descending swiftly toward the Ward's Island below to disappear beneath the trees.

"It's time to get you home," Kim said in his ear.

Brendan was about to protest when he saw that the horizon to the east was growing pale. He would have to be back before his parents awoke. He nodded to Kim and she banked away toward the city, dropping toward the lights below.

Kim landed them in the park near Brendan's home. They swooped down over the snow and slid to a stop amid a stand of trees, managing to avoid smashing into any tree trunks. Kim removed the wings and laid them on the ground. At her direction, they piled snow over the bundle. Satisfied that the wings wouldn't be discovered, they walked together through the park and crossed the street into the alley that led to Brendan's house.

"You're quiet," Kim said.

"Yeah, I guess. I suppose I don't know what to say. The Proving and the Gathering are tomorrow. Seeing the kind of people who'll be judging me doesn't exactly fill me with confidence."

They reached the back gate. Kim grabbed him by the arm and turned him to face her.

"Brendan, I know you must be worried. Maybe even a little scared … "

"Try pants-crapping terrified."

"But I know you can do this."

"How can you be so sure?"

Kim smiled her lopsided smile. "I know a good heart when I see one."

Brendan didn't reply. Charlie had said the same thing in his dad's music studio. Did a good heart matter in this insane world he grappled with? He hoped Kim and Charlie knew what they were talking about.

Then Kim did something totally out of character. She leaned over and kissed him on the cheek. Brendan was so surprised that he just stood there looking at her.

She laughed. "I've missed your silly face. Charlie's a lucky girl."

Before Brendan could say a word, she turned and dashed off down the alley. He stood staring at the place where she'd melted into the night. She thought that Charlie was … what? His girlfriend? Was Kim crazy? He raised a hand and touched his cheek where she'd kissed it. *Twice in one week? I must be doing something right.*

"That was weird," he said to no one at all. He opened the gate and stepped into the yard.

STAKEOUT

"Maybe he isn't coming back tonight," Dmitri suggested. Harold had fallen asleep an hour ago, his head nestled on Dmitri's shoulder. A healthy gob of drool had collected on Dmitri's jacket.

"He'll be back. He has to be back for breakfast," Delia said.

They had turned Dmitri's father's tool shed into a make-shift surveillance HQ for Operation Eye-On-Brendan, as they'd taken to calling it. For the past three nights they had met at Dmitri's house because both of his parents were working night shifts. Only his bedridden grandmother was at home, confined to a daybed in the family room. They had free rein without any fear of parental interference.

The shed was cold despite the little space heater Harold had rigged up. Dmitri and Harold huddled together under a sleeping bag, fighting to stay awake. Harold had lost the battle. Delia had declined the offer of shared body warmth, opting to shiver on her own while sitting on a sawhorse[48] draped with an old blanket that smelled vaguely of barf.

---

[48] I've always wondered why they call them *saw horses*. Why not *saw cows* or *saw pigs* or some other four-legged saw creature. I mean, cows are much less skittish than horses. A cow would certainly stay still while you were sawing something. I wouldn't expect any such cooperation from a horse. Still, I'm not in charge.

Harold and Dmitri, both adept at computers, had set up a remote webcam that was trained on the backyard of the Clair house. They'd seen Brendan and Charlie emerge from the back window three nights before and then seen Brendan return alone. The following nights, Brendan had gone out by himself. Delia wondered why. Had they had a falling out of some kind? They watched the footage again and again, unable to believe the agility of the famously clumsy Brendan as he tumbled into the snow and dashed off. After that, each night was a long, cold vigil in the shed, staring at nothing but a snowy expanse of back lawn until Brendan returned and climbed through the window. They needed more if they were going to understand what was going on. Sure, sneaking out at night would get Brendan in trouble if his parents knew. But what was he doing? They had to find out. More importantly, Delia had to find out. Three boring nights passed in freezing discomfort, but Delia refused to call it off.

"Do you want something to eat?" Dmitri asked, rummaging in a paper bag decorated with ominous grease stains.

"No!" Delia snarled. "Keep that stuff away from me." Dmitri had provided snacks. Weird snacks, according to Delia. Cabbage rolls and perogies[49] heated in the microwave. "I don't know which is worse: the smell or the taste."

"I guess it's a required taste," Dmitri shrugged, stuffing a perogy in his mouth.

"AC-quired! Not RE-quired!"

---

[49] A *perogy* is a Polish dumpling containing any number of fillings, ranging from potato and cheese to minced meats to pickled cabbage. I've heard rumours of a dessert perogy filled with chocolate pudding and even a Mexican-style perogy stuffed with candies and small trinkets, hung from a tree and beaten with a stick. Or it might have been a piñata. I don't get invited to a lot of parties.

"Ac-quired then," Dmitri said. "If you don't mind my saying so, I prefer spending time with your brother. You are not a very pleasant person."

Delia sneered. "Well, if he's such a great guy, why are you two spying on him?"

"I don't think we're doing this for the same reason as you," Dmitri suggested.

"What does that mean?" Delia demanded.

"Brendan is my friend and I worry about him. He's been acting strangely. I want to make sure he's okay. So does Harold, even if he can't manage to stay awake. But it seems to me that you hate Brendan a little bit."

"Oh, really." Delia rolled her eyes. "And why would I hate him, Sigmund Freud?"

"You tell me," Dmitri said sweetly. "He's your brother."

"You don't know what you're talking about."

"Maybe not," Dmitri conceded. He picked out another perogy and nibbled it in silence. For a moment, they didn't speak. There was nothing but the soft snoring of Harold in the dim shed. Dmitri wondered if Delia might have dozed off. But then he saw the light of the laptop screen reflected in her open eyes.

"Nobody understands what it's like," Delia said softly in the darkness. "Everybody loves him. He can do no wrong. He's sneaking around and doing who knows what, but my parents think he's just the best thing ever. And he isn't even their *real* child."

"I don't understand why you're so angry at him," Dmitri ventured. "It isn't his fault he was adopted. It just happened. He would change it if he could."

"What do you know about it? You don't have any brothers or sisters."

"I did have a brother," Dmitri said softly. "He died."

Delia fell silent.

"I don't remember him very well. He was older than me. He had a cancer of the blood."

"Leukemia."

"Is that the English word? As I was saying, I was very young and I barely remember him. I remember playing soccer in the street with him once. His name was Albin."

"Well," Delia said in the awkward silence. "That's too bad."

"Uh-huh. I wish I had a brother still. I think you're lucky to have Brendan. Even if he's not your *real* brother," Dmitri said pointedly and lapsed into silence.

Delia didn't respond. She sat in the darkness, glaring at the screen and trying to ignore what Dmitri had said. Maybe she was being insane. Brendan was an annoying freak, but he was her brother. Maybe she should be worried about him instead of suspicious. Still, she couldn't forget how she'd lost that day. She knew he had something to do with it. And Charlie was a part of it, too. When she saw the two of them climbing down from the window on the webcam, her suspicions were confirmed. Even if her parents were fooled, Delia wasn't.

She gritted her teeth with new resolve. She wouldn't let Dmitri's sentimental opinion distract her from her path. She'd get to the bottom of this. If she and Dmitri had different reasons for doing this, so be it.

She glared into the greenish glow of the laptop as if willing Brendan to appear. She just had to keep her focus despite the fatigue that was beginning to set in. She couldn't count on the two boys. Harold was already out for the count. That left her and the little kid, Dmitri. She would have to make sure she didn't succumb to the heaviness that was pulling at her eyelids. She had to stay sharp … Had to …

Delia's head snapped up. She was still sitting on the sawhorse, but now she was wrapped in a scratchy woollen blanket.

Harold and Dmitri were eating steaming bowls of oatmeal in chipped white bowls. They smiled at her.

"Why did you let me sleep?"

"You were tired," Dmitri explained. "We've been watching, don't worry."

Delia shrugged off the blanket fiercely. "What time is it?"

"Six-thirty," Harold said. "It's gonna be dawn in an hour or so. He's gotta be back soon."

"Thanks, Sherlock," Delia snarled.

"Geez." Harold whistled. "You really are a total … "

"He's back!" Dmitri sat bolt upright. He pointed at the screen.

Delia shouldered her way between the two boys. There on the screen was Brendan, closing the backyard gate. The picture was too grainy to see his face, but it was undoubtedly him. His coat was open despite the cold. He walked across the yard.

"He's alone," Harold pointed out. "Again."

"Yeah," Dmitri agreed. "Where has he been all night?"

"What's that?" Delia asked.

A small mote of light darted into the picture. It moved like a bumblebee or a hummingbird but it was larger. Again, the picture wasn't clear enough for details. Brendan stopped and appeared to be speaking to the speck of light. Suddenly, it raced at the camera and, for an instant, filled the lens. Then the screen dissolved into electronic snow.

"What the heck was that?" Delia demanded. Her heart leapt. This could be the break they were looking for.

"Hold on!" Harold tapped the keyboard and the video began to scroll backwards. He stopped when the screen was full of the glaring white thing only inches from the camera. He made a few more taps and the image dimmed and became more defined. Though it was still fuzzy and burned out, the thing on the screen was clearly a tiny human figure. It was obviously female. She wore a tightly laced old-fashioned vest and red trousers. Her little face was frozen in a snarl and her fists were clenched in fury. A smear of colour at her back indicated wings that were moving too fast for the camera to capture.

"What is that?" Delia gasped.

"Hold on!" Harold cried. He dug into his backpack and produced a leather portfolio crammed with papers. He flipped through a few sheets of scribbles and finally said, "Aha!" He laid the picture on the keys of the laptop and pointed to a drawing. "That's her! I drew her! I knew these pictures were of real people and things. I knew it!"

The drawing was just a rough charcoal sketch, but it undeniably portrayed the creature on the screen.

"It's a little person?" Delia couldn't believe her eyes. "Is this some kind of joke? An optical illusion?"

Dmitri shook his head. "How could it be?"

"How could I draw this before I saw it on the screen?" Harold asked. "I must have seen her on the day I lost."

"But … " Delia struggled. "But … she's tiny! There aren't people that small! It's impossible. It's crazy!"

"Crazy or not, it would appear to be true," Dmitri decided. "You can't deny it. She's there before our sight."

"Before our eyes!" Harold and Delia snapped together.

"Whatever," Dmitri conceded. "So the question is, what do we do now?"

Delia stood up. "I'm going to confront Brendan."

"No!" Dmitri grabbed her arm. "You can't do that. We need to know more."

"Get your cabbagy hand off me." Delia tore her arm away. "I have to make him tell me what's going on. My family might be in danger."

"You don't know that," Harold pointed out.

"I don't think Brendan would ever do anything to harm you or your family," Dmitri said. "He's a good person."

"How do you know? You obviously don't know him at all!" Delia shouted. She turned and flung the door open. "What … ?"

Standing in the doorway was an old woman, her head wrapped in a shawl. Her face was ancient and wrinkled but her blue eyes were bright. She wore a thick woollen dressing gown over her nightclothes and a pair of fluffy blue slippers on her bare yellow feet.

The woman croaked in words in a strange language. She pointed at Delia and croaked again, more insistently.

"Babka!" Dmitri cried in alarm. "What are you doing out of bed?" He leapt up and went to the old woman, taking her arm. He spoke a few words in the same strange language and tried to guide her back to the house. She struggled against him, shouting again.

"What's with her?" Delia asked. "What's she saying?"

"She's my babka, my grandmother. She's speaking Polish. She seems quite upset. She keeps saying, 'The Prince is going to the island.'"

"The island? What Prince?"

"She could mean Ward's Island. Where we followed Brendan," Harold suggested.

"But who is the Prince?" Delia asked. "Brendan?"

The old woman pointed a gnarled finger at Delia. *"Tak! Tak! Prinz* Brendan!"

"How does she know?" Delia said, skepticism clear on her face.

"She is what we call a *vrooshka*," Dmitri explained. "A psycho."

"Psychic," Harold corrected.

Delia looked at the old woman. She had a thought. "Ask her this. Tell her we followed Brendan to the island but we lost him there. How can we follow him?"

"She should be in her bed," Dmitri said. "In fact, I don't think she's been up on her feet for months … "

"Just ask her!"

Dmitri shook his head and turned to his babka. He spoke in Polish and the old woman nodded. She answered in a rapid stream of words. When she was done, Dmitri translated. "She says we must find one who can see. She is too old to make the trip but there is another. He was an enemy but now he's a friend. The Prince gave him Sight, though the Prince was not aware of the gift. Find the former nemesis."[50]

"The former nemesis?" Delia was confused. "Who could that possibly be?"

"Excuse me," Harold interjected meekly.

"What?" Delia barked.

Harold swallowed. "I, uh … I think I might know who the nemesis is."

---

[50] A *nemesis* is a person's arch-enemy. It's an old Greek word. Every hero has his nemesis. Peter Pan had Captain Hook. David had Goliath. My personal nemesis is a parrot named Crackers who curses me every time I walk by the pet shop down the street. Curse you, Crackers! Curse you!

THE LAST DAY

Brendan tried his best to meditate in the Faerie style. He didn't have enough time to sleep before going to school. But he found he couldn't settle his mind because of what had happened when he'd come back to the house this morning before dawn.

He had parted with Kim and come through the back gate to find BLT waiting for him. She was very upset.

"Where did you go?" she demanded, zipping up to his face and bopping him painfully on the nose with one tiny fist.

"Ow! That hurt!"

"Serves you right. I was worried sick!" the little Faerie sniffed. She crossed her arms and hung in the air, her wings whirring. "Well?"

"I … " he stammered. "I needed some time to think."

"Some time to think?" She whizzed in a circle. "And you left me out in the night alone again?"

"I thought you'd be able to handle yourself," Brendan said, hoping to appeal to her pride.

"Of course I can. I was worried about you." She seemed slightly mollified. "Where did you go?"

"Kim and I went Dawn-flying. We saw Pûkh arrive."

BLT's eyes went wide. "You saw the Wild Hunt. Was it marvellous?"

"It was … pretty impressive." Brendan had meant to say "terrifying," but he didn't want BLT to think he was afraid. "Anyway, it was nice to see Kim. I've missed her."

BLT arched an eyebrow. "Oh you have, have you? She missed you, too, you know."

"What do you mean?"

"Oh, he is blind," she cried to the stars. "Well, obviously …"

Brendan expected her to keep speaking but she stopped dead, her entire body tense. She began searching the yard with her tiny eyes. "What? What's the matter?" he asked.

Her voice came out in a tense whisper. "We are being watched." Suddenly, she screeched and rocketed off into the air. She made a beeline straight for a telephone pole that overlooked the Clairs' yard. She slammed into the pole and tore at something with her hands. It came away from the wood with a snap. Carrying it in her hands, she brought it over to Brendan. He held out his hand and she dropped a small webcam into his palm. It was cracked and broken but still recognizable. They could be bought at any electronics store.

"What was that doing there?"

"Spies!" BLT hissed.

"Who would want to spy on me?" Brendan asked in shock.

"Not a Faerie spy. This is Metal Folk work."

On that note, they had gone inside. BLT refused to budge from her lookout spot by the window and stayed up muttering until she fell asleep and began to snore noisily. Brendan couldn't stop worrying about the camera. As he tried to meditate, he turned the question over in his head.

Who would want to spy on me? Mum and Dad? Maybe. But no. His dad could do stuff with his amps and knew a little bit about computers, but he only knew music software. His mum didn't know much about computers at all. She could type, but that was it. Besides, it wasn't their style. They'd just ask him if they had a problem with him. They wouldn't sneak around.

His sister. Oh yeah. Could be her, but she didn't like computers and couldn't have rigged up a webcam to save her life.

Maybe Harold and Dmitri. Would they resort to spying on him? He found it hard to believe. Had their friendship slid so far that they would do something like that? Maybe.

Or maybe it's even worse. Maybe it's someone I don't know who's trying to learn my secret.

That thought made him really worried. He gave up trying to calm his mind and got dressed.

At breakfast, Delia was behaving strangely. She refused to even look at him. There were dark circles under her eyes as though she hadn't slept either. When Brendan asked for the jam, she passed it to him without a word or a glance. She was usually sullen in the morning, but this was a new level of frigidity. He decided he couldn't be bothered figuring out what was wrong with her. His mind was buzzing with other thoughts. Last night, being with Kim had given him a little distance from Charlie. He now looked at the lutin more critically. The meeting with Merddyn had opened his eyes. She was Merddyn's … what? Apprentice? Lackey? Servant? The Ancient Faerie had instructed her to befriend him. Was she really a friend? Her tears when she'd visited his dad's music room had seemed genuine, but how could he know for sure? Although Kim was annoying, bossy, and disdainful of his attachment to his Human family, he was certain that everything she did was meant to help him adjust to his new life. With Charlie, he wasn't sure if he was just a part of Merddyn's agenda, a pawn in some larger game.

His father had just finished talking about a UFO that had supposedly been sighted in the wee hours of the morning over the lake.[51] Condo residents reported hearing a sonic boom and high-pitched shrieking, and seeing bizarre lights in the sky. Officials were saying the phenomenon was likely heat lightning or some other weather anomaly that was related to the unprecedented cold snap that had fallen on the city. Brendan knew that residents had actually seen the Wild Hunt arriving at the Ward's Island, but he didn't share his knowledge with the table.

"What are you going to do today, Brendan? Plans?" his dad asked.

"I don't know. We only have a half day today. And there's a Christmas assembly. Not much of an actual school day," Brendan said. "I'm free for the afternoon. I was thinking of going out tonight."

"With Charlie?" His mother's face was eager for news on the Charlie front.

"Maybe," Brendan conceded. Again, the girlfriend ruse was coming in handy. Having Charlie as an excuse

---

[51] On a side note, I wonder why UFOs always appear to people of doubtful credibility—drunk men, the insane, hillbillies, etc. If aliens really wanted to abduct humans and experiment on them, why wouldn't they abduct articulate people who might elucidate them on the finer points of humanity? Why not abduct authors, scientists, or (yes, it must be said, though I disdain the limelight) narrators like myself? I would like nothing more than to be abducted by interstellar travellers and spend some idle hours shooting the breeze with them telepathically. Let this be your invitation, Starpeople! I will be waiting in an empty field just outside of Poughkeepsie, New York, after 7 P.M. each Wednesday.

was going to be helpful tonight when he had to attend the Gathering.

"I hear the Toronto Islands are a nice spot for a date," Delia said suddenly, breaking her silence.

"That might be a no go," Brendan's mum said. "There was a cold snap last night. The harbour is frozen and the ferries aren't sailing. They're trying to break up the ice but they haven't got an icebreaker heavy enough."

Brendan stared at Delia. Why had she suggested the islands? It was weird. She was focused on her waffle again, studiously avoiding his gaze. She must know something, he decided. But what? Was she the culprit with the camera? He wouldn't put it past her. He'd have to be careful. He tried to put it out of his mind. He had to concentrate on the Proving to come and save any worries about Delia for later … if there was a later.

"We'll probably go to the movies or shopping or something."

"Yeah," Brendan's dad agreed. "It's a real freak weather system. So wear your heavy coats, guys. It's gonna be super cold." He picked his parka off the hook and pulled it on. "And don't lick any frozen pipes!"[52] With that advice, he opened the back door and was gone.

"I gotta go, Mum," Brendan said. He lifted his backpack off the floor and bent to kiss his mother. "See you tonight."

Brendan and Charlie walked along College Street, past the hospitals and the cafés that served the university.

---

[52] Though such advice seems obvious, thousands of children are stuck to cold metal pipes by their tongues each year. Please give generously to "Don't Lick It, Kids!," a non-profit organization that I have founded.

"What's the matter with you?" Charlie said finally. She'd appeared at his side moments before. "You haven't said two words in a row since I showed up."

"I don't know," Brendan mumbled. "Don't feel like talking, that's all."

Brendan's father was right. The city was gripped in an arctic chill. BLT took refuge in Brendan's parka pocket, refusing even to poke her head out. The very air seemed to crystallize around them. He focused his Faerie Sight and saw the minute particles of ice glittering in the clouds of his breath. All the people around him were bundled up against the cold, only their eyes peering out between scarves and hats. The clouds hung low and grey with the promise of more snow.

They turned up a side street, cutting across to the Spadina loop.

"Merddyn likes you," Charlie said. "I can tell."

"Good for me," Brendan grunted.

"Come on," Charlie chided him. "It's quite a thing to impress that guy. He's seen everything, that one."

Brendan stopped and faced her. "Why should I care? I have enough people who like me. I have my family and my friends. And they don't expect me to save the world for them, either."

"So angry all the time." Charlie shook her head. "What have I done?"

"It's not what you've done, it's why you're doing it."

"I'm just trying to show you how to use your power."

"Because Merddyn told you to."

"*Oui*," Charlie agreed. "He told me to get close to you and help you. But after a while, I did it for me. I envy you, Brendan. I don't know who my family is, or if they're even alive. I like your family."

"Do you?" Brendan said angrily. "You've come into our lives and told them lies and they believe you. They don't even know who you really are. What's worse, I think they want to believe you for *my* sake, to make me happy."

Charlie hung her head, her dark hair hiding her face. When she raised her head again, he saw that she was crying. Tears shimmered on her cheeks. "You're right. What you say is true. I'm sorry, Brendan." She turned and walked away.

Brendan suddenly felt ashamed of himself. So what if she was helping him to help herself? Did that make her so terrible? Did that give him the right to attack her? He reached out his hand, about to call her back …

"*BRENDAN!*" A voice suddenly pierced his head like a spike driving between his ears. He cried out and fell to his knees. "*BRENDAN! COME TO ME NOW!*"

Brendan fell on his face on the frozen sidewalk. When he rolled over onto his back, he saw that he was in front of Lord Lansdowne School. The black rock loomed over him. It seemed huge, about to topple down and crush him with its infinite weight.

"No!" Brendan cried out. "NO! Get away from me!"

"*BRENDAN!*" the voiced howled in his head. "*YOU MUST HELP ME! I'M TRAPPED IN HERE!*" The voice filled his whole mind and soul. It was rife with need and pain and anger. There was something else. Beneath the pain and anger was blackness, an abyss of unnatural hunger.

"LEAVE ME ALONE!" Brendan shouted at the top of his lungs. He could feel something clawing at his consciousness, trying to unravel the edge of his mind like a cat tugging at a ball of yarn. It was a sickening feeling.

"Brendan! Brendan!" A voice spoke nearby. "Brendan? Are you all right?"

"LEAVE ME ALONE!" Brendan screamed, pushing the speaker away. Suddenly, the voice was gone and he could think again. Charlie had fallen over the low fence that surrounded the stone. He must have pushed her without realizing. Instantly, he reached for her hand and helped her to her feet again.

"I'm sorry," Brendan said automatically. "I heard a voice. That rock … It spoke to me."

"Spoke to you?" Charlie said in surprise. She turned and cast an appraising eye on the rough surface of the stone, her focus suddenly on it rather than Brendan. "Has this happened before?"

Brendan got to his feet. He felt shaky. "Once or twice." He raised a hand to touch Charlie's arm but she absently batted it away.

"And it was with this rock? Only this rock?"

"Yeah. What's the matter with you?"

"I must go," Charlie said suddenly.

"Where? What's going on?"

"Nothing. I just forgot I had to do something." Charlie turned to go.

Brendan grabbed her arm and pulled her back. "I'm sorry I hurt you. Why are you acting so weird all of a sudden?"

She pulled away from him, flowing effortlessly from his grasp. "See you at the Gathering tonight, Brendan." Before he could speak again, she raced away.

Puzzled, Brendan stood watching the place where she'd disappeared from sight. "That was weird," he said to no one in particular. He looked once again at the rock, fearful of hearing that insistent voice once more, but it seemed to be inert now, a simple lump of stone. Finally, Brendan went on his way. He was late for school.

The last day of school before the Christmas break had a festive air. Students in the halls greeted Brendan cheerfully as he went from class to class. The classes themselves were lax and easy (except for algebra, which sucked as much as ever). The teachers had brought in baked goods and candies, and the physics teacher even brought a punch bowl full of eggnog. Brendan would normally have enjoyed the light mood, but his mind was weighed down with fears of the upcoming Proving.

He would have liked to talk to Harold and Dmitri. Although he couldn't have told them everything that was bothering him, just talking to them would have been nice. But they weren't in school today. When Brendan asked his homeroom teacher where they were, he was told that both had called the office to say they were sick. They weren't the only ones. A lot of kids had decided to start the holiday early, but Harold and Dmitri never cut class. Even stranger, today they'd been scheduled to present their social studies project. Brendan couldn't believe they'd bailed, but he was relieved. He'd forgotten all about the dumb project and now he was off the hook.

Bereft of their company, Brendan drifted through French and chemistry, listening in as other kids talked excitedly about what they'd be doing over the holidays: visiting family, going to Florida, skiing. Their plans sounded simple and wonderful. He wished his life were like theirs. Instead, he'd be going through an ordeal at the hands of beings from legends.

Failing the Challenges would be bad. Aside from the fact that he might actually die at the hands of the judges, the consequences of failure if he survived weren't much better: Exile. An Exile from the Faerie community was completely alone. Brendan would have to live in the Human world knowing all that was closed off to him. He'd only just begun to explore the many gifts his Faerie heritage offered him. Though he'd been confused at first, as his senses expanded, heightened, and changed, he realized that living without his Faerie abilities would be a bleak existence. Watching his family and friends age and die while he hung on, frozen while the world changed around him, filled him with dread.

Also, he was now just beginning to understand what was at stake for the whole world, Humans and Faeries both. The world wouldn't survive if Humans continued to poison it and Faeries remained aloof. He'd begun to see a place for himself in the battle ahead to change the future. He didn't want to lose that opportunity.

Finally, he had grown to love his Faerie family: Uncle Og, Auntie Deirdre, and Uncle Greenleaf. They were all a bit mad, but he'd miss them if he were Exiled. They really were his family now.

And Kim, Brendan thought. *She's been there the whole way, even before I knew who I really was. She's more than a friend ...* He let that thought hang, afraid to examine his feelings for her more closely.

After a lunch eaten alone in the cafeteria, he went to the washroom. He was hoping for a moment of peace away from all the other students. With a sigh of relief, he found the boys' room empty.

He'd forgotten that BLT was in his jacket pocket, so when she suddenly spoke, he jumped about ten feet.

"What are you so mopey about?" she said, crawling out of Brendan's pocket as he splashed water on his face at the sink.

"Do you mind?" Brendan asked. "This is the boys' restroom."

"Relax, pal," she said. "What's the big deal?"

"Well," Brendan said, at a loss. "It's just not cool."[53]

"What's the problem now? Your face is so long you might step on it."

"I'm just worried about … well, everything, and I think I have a right to be."

"You've gotta get your head in the game, boyo!" BLT flew out of his pocket and up onto his shoulder. "If you go into the Proving this worried then you're halfway to failing already. Look in the mirror."

Brendan raised his head and looked at his face. A year ago, he would have seen a pimply, gawky kid with braces. But now the face looking back at him was hardly recognizable. He willed his glamour to drop and saw how much he'd changed. His hair had been a dirty blond before but now was a deeper, more lustrous gold. His eyes sparkled deep green with flecks of amber. His face was leaner and the bones more refined, and there wasn't a pimple in sight.

Sure, he'd changed on the outside, but the changes on the inside were much more profound. He had learned more about his heart and his soul in the last few weeks than he'd ever thought possible.

"Do I have the strength to pass these tests? Am I good enough, B?"

BLT tugged on his ear. "Never doubt it, Brendan. Never doubt it."

---

[53] I have to say, I sympathize with Brendan on this point. The washroom is not a place for chatting. One should be allowed to evacuate one's bladder in peace without any casual conversation or distractions.

"Who are you talking to?" said a voice behind Brendan.

BLT dove into Brendan's pocket to avoid detection. Brendan whirled, raising his glamour. He found a senior student standing on the bathroom tiles with a confused look on his face. He must have been in one of the stalls when Brendan had come into the bathroom. Brendan cursed himself silently for not being more careful. "Huh?" he stammered. "Uh, nobody! I was talking to myself."

"Yourself?" The older boy frowned. "What are you doing that for?"

"A play!" Brendan said quickly. "Auditioning for a play for next semester." Boy, *that excuse is getting worn out!*

"Yeah? Well, rehearsing in the men's room is a little weird, dude. Why don't you … ?"

The boy didn't finish his suggestion. He stopped speaking and just stood, staring, his eyes slightly out of focus. He had a dreamy, peaceful expression as though he were trapped in the middle of a daydream.

"Hey," Brendan said. Then louder, "Hey!" He waved his hand in front of the boy's face but he didn't react.

"What's the matter?" Brendan asked. "Are you okay?"

"This is a Faerie glamour," BLT said, climbing out of Brendan's pocket. "It's a powerful one, too. Can't you sense it?"

Brendan closed his eyes and concentrated. He did sense it, a tingle of energy or ambient power like a charge of static electricity hanging in the air.

"You're right," Brendan said softly. He opened his eyes. The boy was still staring dreamily into space. Brendan felt confident the boy wasn't in any danger of hurting himself, but just to be sure, he took him by the arm and gently forced him to sit on the tile floor with his back to the wall. Satisfied, Brendan left the bathroom.

The hall was full of people in the same state of bemusement. Students and teachers shared the same vacant gaze, their eyes slightly unfocused as if they were straining to see a speck of dust on the tips of their noses. Brendan made his way up the hall, weaving through them as he sought out the source of the glamour. He could feel a current of energy in the air that led him on as though he were a piece of iron seeking a magnet. As he walked down the hall, he passed Chester Dallaire outside the library doors. The large boy stood, eyes half closed. Brendan glanced at Chester's face as he walked by, wondering who had caused this mass dream state.

The current led him down the main hall and into the principal's office. At the front desk, Miss Conacher, the secretary, sat looking blankly at her pen while a female student stood in dreamy silence holding a doctor's note limply in her hand. Brendan walked past them and into the open door of Ms. Abernathy's office.

The vice-principal sat behind her desk. Her mouth hung open. She was staring into space, her glasses slightly askew, but otherwise seemed unharmed. She wasn't alone in the room. Standing at the window with his back to Brendan was a tall, slight Faerie in a finely tailored, shimmering blue suit. His chestnut hair hung loose over his shoulders.

"Ah," the Faerie said musically, without taking his eyes off the vice-principal. "You are here. How lovely."

"What's going on?" Brendan demanded. "Who are you? What have you done to them?"

The Faerie turned lazily around to face Brendan.

Tall and lean, he radiated power, setting Brendan's nerves jangling. It was like standing next to a massive electrical transformer. The Faerie's face was beautiful, but there was a cruel twist to his smile as he gazed at Brendan with coldly amused brown eyes.

"You're … "

"Lord Pûkh." The Faerie smiled, bowing deeply. "At your service, Brendan Morn." Without waiting for Brendan to respond, Pûkh spread his arms and did a little spin. "What do you think? It's an Armani. The fabric and workmanship are not quite up to my usual standard but the Humans have certainly made strides."

"What have you done to them?" Brendan demanded again. He felt ridiculous and powerless next to Pûkh, but he tried to keep the fear from his voice.

"Don't worry." Pûkh waved dismissively. "They are quite safe. Their senses are fogged with glamours. For them, the moment is frozen. They will remember nothing. They'll wake up quite refreshed, in fact. Your concern for them is touching, though. Like a child caring for his pets."

"They aren't pets," Brendan said angrily. "They're people."

"Well, I'd disagree with you there, I'm afraid. They make a mess everywhere they go. They are ignorant of the true nature of the world, like animals. And I must say, they have a very unpleasant stink. I'm sure you're used to it by now, having lived among them for so long."

"They are cute," a childish voice lisped. Brendan whirled to see the tiny female Faerie who had ridden at Pûkh's side the night before stroking the hair of the secretary, Miss Conacher. "So fragile." The stroking hand sprouted long, razor-sharp claws and she drew their tips along the secretary's vulnerable throat.

"Stay away from her." Brendan took a step to intervene, but suddenly his wrist was clamped in a powerful grip. He turned to find that it was the tall, silver-haired Faerie he'd seen at the head of the Wild Hunt the night before.

This guy was fast. Brendan hadn't even sensed his approach. He was just there, looming over Brendan with his silver head brushing the ceiling. Brendan looked up into the cold grey eyes and saw no spark of Human emotion. *He's a Warp Warrior*, Brendan thought with some dread.

"Don't touch me," Brendan said evenly, grateful that his voice didn't crack.

"Lugh! Mâya!" Pûkh's voice intervened. "Don't be rude. These are Brendan's people, though why he should consort with People of Metal when he is a Prince of the Fair Folk is quite beyond my understanding."

Brendan ignored the comments, though inside he seethed with anger at the insult to his friends and family. "Why are you here?"

The Faerie sauntered around the desk toward Brendan. "Why, to see you, of course. You are the talk of the Faerie world, young Brendan. Everyone wants to know about you. Even I, in the Hidden Kingdom of Tír na nÓg, have heard of you. The Faerie who prefers the People of Metal to his own Folk."

"You shouldn't be here. My Human friends and family are off limits."

Pûkh's eyes darkened. For an instant, Brendan saw something reptilian stir behind the beautiful mask of his face. Just as quickly, Pûkh composed himself, and the darkness passed. "You really can't expect to tell me what to do, Brendan. I am quite simply beyond your ability to command. But you needn't be so angry." The Ancient Faerie smiled and chucked him under the chin as if he were a little child. "I merely wished to see what you found so attractive in this Human world. Frankly, I understand how a sentimental attachment might develop, but look at these creatures." He threw out an arm to encompass the school. "You aren't like them. As I said, I don't know how you can bear the smell." Pûkh laughed lightly.

Brendan clenched his fists in rage. Pûkh was one of the most stunning people he'd ever seen. His presence inspired awe. When he'd first entered the room, Brendan had been tempted to fall to his knees like a supplicant. Yes, Pûkh was beautiful, but his words sickened Brendan.

"I'll say this again because you didn't seem to hear me the first time: they aren't pets. They are people. My people."

Pûkh laughed again. "Then why am I here? I have come to judge you at your Proving. I thought this meant you wanted to be a member of your true family and a part of the Faerie world. Am I wrong?"

Brendan didn't know what to say. Pûkh was right. The Ancient Faerie smirked, seeing he'd scored a hit. Pûkh opened his mouth to speak but was interrupted by the arrival of Greenleaf and Kim.

They barged into the outer office ready for a confrontation. Lugh and Mâya instinctively interposed themselves between the new arrivals and Pûkh.

"Leave Brendan alone," Kim snarled, her stick levelled.

"This is an outrage," Greenleaf spat. Brendan had never seen his teacher show such strong emotion. He looked ready for physical violence, his grey eyes alight with fury. "Release these people immediately."

"No need for hysterics," Pûkh tutted, leaning back against the desk and crossing his arms. "They aren't in any discomfort."

"You know this is not permitted, interfering with Humans in any way. Even you in your isolated little princedom are aware of the Pact and the rules we must follow if we are to survive."

"I was there when the Pact was struck, lest you forget, Greenleaf. We fought on different sides on that day, but I hope you'll let those old grudges rest. Just as you and your sister have set aside your differences."

Greenleaf didn't answer. With a barely perceptible nod from Pûkh, Lugh and Mâya stepped aside, allowing Greenleaf and Kim to join Brendan.

Kim turned to Brendan. "Are you all right?" Her face was full of concern. Brendan was reminded of the kiss last night and blushed.

"I'm fine. We were just talking."

"Good."

"Disperse this glamour immediately and get away from here," Greenleaf demanded.

Pûkh stood up to his full height and his head seemed to brush the ceiling. Underlying the exquisite face was dire threat. The temperature in the room dropped as if a window had been opened onto the frigid winter. "You have no power to tell me where to go or what to do," he said, his voice heavy with menace. Brendan took an involuntary step back, disgusted by his own cowardice.

Pûkh seemed to sense he'd tipped his hand a little too much. The darkness faded from his face and the atmosphere lightened. In the blink of an eye, the cheerful smile returned to his perfect mouth. "Let's not fight, my friends. I beg your indulgence. I am not accustomed to the Human world and perhaps I overstepped my bounds. This Clan Gathering is a happy occasion. Let's not spoil it with recriminations, hmmm?"

Pûkh casually stepped between Kim and Greenleaf and walked out of Ms. Abernathy's office. "Come along." He gestured and his mismatched companions fell in behind him. Mâya brushed past Kim and sneered. Kim returned the sneer with interest. Kim and Greenleaf followed the trio warily with Brendan bringing up the rear.

Out in the main hall, Pûkh paused and looked about him at the students standing looking blankly into space. He shook his head. "So this is where the People of Metal teach their children? A school they call it. How can they have such places and still remain so ignorant of the world all around them? They know enough to destroy the Earth but not to sustain her." He sighed theatrically and strolled toward the doors at the end of the hall.

Brendan looked around at the people in the hall and felt something nagging at the edge of his perception. Something was different. He scanned the hallway but couldn't figure it out.

Pûkh reached the doors and turned. He smiled at them and sketched a bow. "Lovely to see where you spend your days, Brendan. Most enlightening, if not inspiring. I shall see you all later at the Gathering. I look forward to judging your Proving." Opening the door, he let Lugh and Mâya pass through. Then, he casually spoke a word Brendan didn't understand and passed an open hand before his eyes as if waving away a fly.

Immediately, everyone began to move and talk, picking up conversations in mid-sentence. The entire school came to life without any awareness that they'd been standing in a daze for the past quarter hour. Brendan stood dumbfounded as the students went about their business, girls in giggling groups, boys trying as always to look as cool as possible and failing, all of them completely unaware that their lives had been interrupted.

"No sporting equipment in the halls." Ms. Abernathy's brittle voice jarred Brendan out of his thoughts. The vice-principal stood in the doorway of her office, hands on hips. "I have warned you before. Don't think because it's the last day of school before the holidays I won't keep you for detention tonight."

Kim lowered her stick. "Yes, Ms. Abernathy. I'm sorry."

Ms. Abernathy nodded curtly and retreated to her office.

"That guy, Pûkh," Brendan said, "he's a piece of work."

"He's always been what we call a Rogue Spirit," Greenleaf said mildly.

"He's what I would call a psychopath," Brendan remarked.

Kim stuffed her stick into her backpack with practised ease. "He has no respect for authority."

"In Tír na nÓg, he *is* the authority. He answers to no one," Greenleaf explained, his eyes on the door where Pûkh had disappeared.

Brendan suddenly didn't want to be in school or any-where near other people. "I'm going home."

"They won't be back, Brendan." Kim looked concerned.

"I'm not worried about that," Brendan said.

"You'll miss the Christmas assembly," Greenleaf pointed out.

"Well, much as I'd like to hear some Christmas carols sung by the Robertson Davies Academy Glee Club," Brendan announced, "I think I may just go home early."

"I'll tell Ms. Abernathy you were feeling a little under the weather," Mr. Greenleaf offered.

"You won't be lying," Brendan said with a pained expres-sion. "See you tonight."

Brendan headed for the door. Passing the library, he suddenly realized what had been bothering him.

What happened to Chester? He was standing right there when I went into the office, but he wasn't there when I came out. That's weird.

He shrugged and pushed his way through the doors and into the cold. *Just one more thing that I can't explain or do anything about.*

He headed for home.

NEMESIS

Harold and Dmitri had decided to take the day off. They were both exhausted by their vigil over the past few nights. In the end, Harold had just crashed on a futon in Dmitri's room. He'd already called his parents and told them that he'd be spending the night. Delia had gone home but made them promise they would meet at noon to confront the person Harold believed was the nemesis.

Dmitri had managed to calm his babka after she burst in on them in the shed. She kept babbling about Princes and Enemies and Little People until Dmitri finally convinced her to lie down on her daybed in the living room. He made her some tea and toast, but by the time he carried them into the living room, she was asleep as if nothing had happened. Dmitri left the tray on the coffee table and went up to bed himself.

Noon found the three conspirators in the BQM Eatery on Ossington Street. Harold had suggested it because he knew that the nemesis lived nearby. They could stake out the streetcar stop. Also, he was quite fond of their burgers. They sat on stools, faces to the window with an eye on the transit shelter across the road.

"How do we know this guy's going to come?" Delia said. She picked at a salad with a plastic fork. "How do we even know he is the nemesis or whatever? How do we know that the old lady isn't completely nuts?"

"That isn't very nice," Dmitri said sulkily.

"She has a point, though," Harold admitted. "I just think this is the guy. I can't think of anybody else who fits the bill."

"So when will we see him?" Delia asked. "Are you sure he'll come here?"

"I take my piano lessons nearby," Harold said through a mouthful of low-fat turkey burger. "I ride the same street-car as he does lots of times. He always got out here. His mum works in the Pizzeria Libretto across the road."

"Why do you know all that?" Delia wondered.

Harold shrugged. "I dunno. I'm an artist … Or at least I want to be an artist and one of the things artists are supposed to do is observe people. You know."

"So he comes here to meet his mum," Delia said. "What if she isn't working today?"

"She is," Dmitri interjected. "I called and asked for her an hour ago. I hung up when they went to call her to the phone."

"Wow." Delia nodded, impressed. "You guys are good. And a little bit creepy."

Before Harold could respond, Dmitri sat up higher on his stool and exclaimed, "There he is!"

Their eyes swung to the other side of the street, where a streetcar had just stopped. The door opened and passengers stepped down onto the road. An old woman was struggling with a shopping cart in the narrow folding doorway when a large, broad-shouldered boy lifted the cart and carried it to the curb for her. The old lady smiled and said something to the boy, who merely nodded and turned toward the BQM window.

Chester Dallaire had changed a great deal since the bizarre episode that had made news headlines. He was leaner and his skin was clearer. His hair was neatly trimmed. The cruel smirk he'd habitually worn when he picked on Harold and Dmitri during their first weeks at RDA was gone. His expression was guarded and his eyes wary.

"*That's* the nemesis?" Delia asked. "I was expecting someone … I don't know, scarier?"

"He was indeed more frightening before the incident," Dmitri explained.

"Incident?" Delia asked.

"He had some kinda breakdown and ran away. Wouldn't stop running," Harold told her. "They say it was like he was possessed or something. It was on the news."

"That's the guy?" Delia cried in disbelief. "I remember that story. He doesn't look crazy."

"He had therapy and he's only just come back to school," Harold said.

"He used to pick at Brendan and us," Dmitri continued. "But now he's a different person."

"Pick *on* us," Delia mumbled. "Okay, let's go."

"What?" Harold cried. "Go where? What are you gonna do? Just walk right up to him and ask him if he's the nemesis of Brendan? You'll sound totally crazy."

Delia shrugged on her coat. "You guys stay here and try not to wet your pants, okay? Just leave it to me."

While they were talking, Chester had entered the pizzeria. Delia took her time, crossing at the light and entering the restaurant through the steam-glazed glass door.

Inside, a few customers were enjoying their pizza and pasta at a long bar. Long tables full of lunchtime diners stretched toward the back of the narrow restaurant. The room buzzed with conversation and the clatter of plates as people met for lunch before the holidays. Delia scanned the room for Chester but couldn't find him. Moving deeper into the restaurant, she passed beneath an arch that was covered in a chalkboard. Customers had scrawled messages praising the food in multi-coloured chalk. She paused to read a couple of comments, and when she dropped her eyes again, she almost ran into Chester.

He was carrying a plate full of pasta in one hand and a pizza in the other. For an awkward second Delia was nose to chest with him. She looked up into his face.

Everything about him was big. He was easily a head taller than Delia. He looked down at her warily.

"Hi," Delia said at last.

"Hi," Chester answered. "Do you mind?"

"Oh, sorry." Delia stepped out of his way. He passed her and went to an empty stool at the end of the bar nearest the window. He sat down and unrolled a knife and fork from a napkin. For a big person, his movements were careful and precise. He cut his pizza into wedges and then into smaller pieces. Lifting a piece to his mouth, he stopped, his brown eyes aimed at Delia.

Delia realized she'd been staring at him and tried to cover her gaffe with a winning smile. She walked over and stood beside him.

"Hi, again. Sorry I was staring at you. I think I might know you from somewhere."

He put the pizza into his mouth and chewed thoughtfully. "No, I don't know you."

"I think you know my brother, though. Brendan Clair."

Chester paused with another morsel of food halfway to his mouth. What passed over his face? Fear? Worry? Delia pushed on.

"I'm Delia." She held out her hand.

He ignored it. "Brendan Clair, huh? I know him but we aren't friends." He stared straight ahead at the mirror behind the bar.

"Why not?" Delia asked.

Chester turned his head and glared at her. "What do you want?"

"Me? Nothing. I don't … " Delia stammered. She decided on the direct approach. "Fine. Just tell me, has anything weird happened to you lately? Anything connected to Brendan?"

Chester laughed bitterly. "Don't you follow the news? I had a breakdown! I lost my crap for a whole day. Ended up in the psych ward. Are you just trying to make fun of me or something?"

"Can you remember if Brendan had something to do with it? It's important." Delia put on her best pleading look, her big blue eyes wide.

Chester just stared. At last, he said, "How could you know that?"

Delia leaned in closer and gripped his arm. It was hard and muscular. "Because I had the same thing happen to me," she whispered. "I lost a few hours of my life. A couple of my friends lost a whole day."

Chester licked his lips. Nervous sweat beaded his brow. "It happened to you, too?"

"I'd like you to meet my friends and talk to them. Something weird has been going on with my brother, and I think you can help me get to the bottom of it. Will you help me?" She amped up the pathos, calling on all of her hours of teen-drama TV viewing to mimic a girl in need of a friend.

Chester was about to answer when a woman with dark hair greying at the temples and Chester's brown eyes approached from the other side of the counter. "How's your food, Chess?"

"Great, Mum. Thanks," Chester answered.

"And who's this?" Chester's mum asked, smiling at Delia.

"A friend."

"A girlfriend?"

"Come on, Mum."

Delia came to his rescue. "I'm Delia Clair."

"Clair?" The woman's face lit up. "You wouldn't be related to Brendan Clair, would you?"

"Yeah," Delia confirmed. "I'm his sister." Delia watched in surprise as tears filled the woman's eyes.

"He was so sweet to Chester when he was in the hospital. He was the only one who came to visit him and I swear that after he came, Chester began to improve immediately."

Delia caught Chester's eye and raised an eyebrow. He frowned and looked away.

"Do you want something to eat? Or drink?"

"No thanks, Mrs. Dallaire. I just ate."

"Well, if you want anything at all, you let me know." A waiter waved a hand to summon her back to work. "And you tell Brendan I said hello!"

"I will!" called Delia to her retreating back. Turning to Chester she said, "Finish your pizza. We have to talk."

An hour later, the four of them sat around a table in the Communal Mule, a café not far away. When Chester saw Dmitri and Harold, Delia had to turn on all her charm to keep him from turning tail. He eyed them warily and said nothing. Over the last hour, though, his guard had slowly come down as he listened to their accounts of their lost day and their conviction that Brendan was somehow responsible or at least involved. The clincher was the drawings.

"You drew these?" Chester said, impressed. "They're pretty good."

"Thanks," Harold said. "They're some of my best work. The only problem is, I can't remember drawing them."

"And then there's this." Delia laid the grainy image from the webcam on the table. The little figure was blurry but recognizable as a female dressed in oddly old-fashioned clothing. Brendan stood behind her in the frame, looking up at the camera, his face frozen in an expression of surprise.

Chester stared at the photo for a long time. Then he mumbled something under his breath.

"What did you say?" Dmitri prompted.

Chester looked up, his face pale. "I said, she's with him most of the time."

"Who? Who is she?" Delia demanded.

"More like what," Chester answered. "She's a tiny person … with wings like a bug or a dragonfly. She flies around him. Usually she's hiding in his pocket."

"Wait a minute," Delia interrupted. "Are you saying you've seen her?"

"Lots of times." Chester nodded shyly. "And other ones like her, too. Big ones. Little ones. They're all over the place."

"What are you talking about?" Delia said, mystified.

Chester sighed and rubbed his eyes with the heels of his hands. "I don't remember anything from that day when I tried to run away. It was like I was hypnotized or something. I only remember waking up in the hospital. My mum told me Brendan had come to see me there. It didn't make any sense. I mean, all I ever did was pick on him and these guys." He jerked his head at Harold and Dmitri.

"Why should he come and see me? And there was something else. I felt more at peace with myself than I had since my dad died. I felt better. My mum forced me to see a therapist and talk about why I'd had that episode and stuff, but I knew I was going to be okay. They finally let me out of the hospital and then … " He paused, as if deciding whether he should tell them, but continued. "That's when I started seeing them."

"Who?" Dmitri asked softly, not wanting to hurry him.

"The beautiful people. They glowed sort of, like they were shining from the inside out. There weren't many of them. I'd just see them once in a while on the street, as if they were trying to pass themselves off as normal people. At first, I didn't know how no one else could see them. They were impossible for me to ignore. I asked my mum if she could see them, but she said she couldn't see anything special about the people I pointed out. I stopped asking her 'cause I didn't want her to think I was losing it. The thing was, I didn't feel crazy. I felt special. I could see things that other people couldn't. I just had to keep it to myself.

"I started to see impossible things, little people in the trees and in the grass running around right under people's noses. There was one guy who hung out with a pack of squirrels, and people must have thought he was a squirrel 'cause they never batted an eye. I should have been scared but I wasn't. I loved it."

Harold and Dmitri listened with rapt attention to Chester's story, both of them wishing they could see these people he was talking about. Something about what he was saying seemed to resonate with them. They never even contemplated disbelieving him because deep down what he was saying rang true.

"Do you see any of these people right now?" Delia said suddenly.

Chester frowned and looked around. He looked out the window of the café. "There. The guy on the corner with the hat."

They all craned their necks and looked out to see a man in an overcoat and a wide-brimmed felt hat standing at the crosswalk waiting for the light. He didn't seem in any way unusual. He held a newspaper under his arm and was talking animatedly into a cellphone.

"He doesn't seem weird to me," Delia scoffed.

"Okay," Chester said. "How cold is it today?"

"What does it matter?" Delia asked.

"It's minus ten Celsius," Harold offered.

"Minus eighteen with the wind chill," Chester confirmed. "Look at his hands."

The man wasn't wearing gloves. His hands were bare. "And that jacket?" They saw now that the guy was wearing a thin spring jacket that couldn't possibly have kept him warm in the subarctic chill.

"They put up some kind of illusion so they look like us. At least that's my theory. If you could really see him, you'd know that the cellphone he's using is a piece of wood and his hair is blue and shines like one of those fibre optic lamps."

The light changed and the man set off across the street.

"You're asking us to believe that you see things we can't," Delia said.

"I'm not asking you to believe anything." Chester raised his coffee and slurped it noisily while leaning back in his chair. "You came to me, remember. Believe me or don't. Couldn't care less."

Delia chewed her lip. "Tell me about Brendan."

"He's one of those people. So is your other friend. The girl with the stick."

"Kim?" Dmitri and Harold gasped at the same time.

"Uh-huh." Chester nodded. "And that new teacher."

"Greenleaf!" Harold and Dmitri said together.

"Wow," Chester laughed. "You guys are good at that. You should start an act."

Delia smacked the table, setting the cups clattering in their saucers. "Listen! So Brendan is one of these … people? Things? The bigger question we need answered is what are they and what do they want?"

"Why do you want to know?" Chester asked, leaning back and cracking his giant knuckles. "They aren't doing you any harm."

"I live with one of them in my house," Delia spat. "It's disgusting."

"You know two of them, actually. That French chick who just showed up? The hot one? She's one of them, too."

"No way!" Harold exclaimed. "That's cool."

"No, it isn't. It isn't cool!" Delia shouted angrily. Other patrons of the café jerked their heads around to stare at her outburst. She sneered at them and turned back to her companions. "We have to find out what he's doing."

"I know what he's doing," Chester said mildly. At their shocked expressions, he shrugged. "This dude showed up at school today with two other scary ones and sort of froze everybody, put them to sleep on their feet. He was different from any of the others I'd seen. He was, I don't know, really powerful, a total badass. All the other ones I see are sort of quiet, harmless, you know? Not this guy. He scared the crap outta me. And the other two with him, a guy and girl, had that psycho vibe, too. It's the only time I've ever seen one of them interfere with people in any way. I pretended to be dazed like everybody else. I heard them talking about some gathering that starts tonight on Ward's Island, only they called it something weird: 'The Island of the Ward.' Kim and Greenleaf were seriously mad at this dude they called Puck."

"Puck! As in hockey puck?" Harold asked, confused. "What kind of name is that?"

"I only know of one Puck and he's in *A Midsummer Night's Dream*," Delia said thoughtfully.

"A midsummer's what?" Harold asked.

"*A Midsummer Night's Dream*," Delia said disdainfully. "Shakespeare, dumbwad. And Puck is a character in the play. He's a fairy who causes all kinds of trouble for some people who go into the woods."

"Sounds dumb," Harold grumbled.

"Well, it isn't!" Delia spat.

Dmitri cleared his throat. "Perhaps this Puck is in some way related to the character in the play by Shakespeare. Maybe … " He paused as if his theory were taking shape in his mind. "Maybe the character was based on one of these people that Chester can see?"[54]

"There's only one way to find out," Delia announced. She looked into each of their faces in turn. "We're going to this gathering tonight! And Chester is going to take us."

---

[54] Indeed, Puck in Shakespeare's play is based on Pûkh, Lord of Tír na nÓg. Pûkh actually commissioned the play from the Bard of Avon. In the end, Pûkh defaulted on payment because he didn't like the way he was portrayed. Shakespeare went on to mount the play in London with great success.

THE GATHERING

"You guys are going to be all right?" Brendan's mother asked for the tenth time as she allowed her husband to help her on with her coat. The Clair parents were dressed up for a party at the Matador, a seedy bar not far from their home.[55] Brendan's dad was playing in the band so he was dressed in his vintage tuxedo.

"What is it tonight, Dad?" Brendan asked. "Jazz? Rock?"

Edward Clair smiled. "Rockabilly! The Matador will be shakin'! It's the last night before they close it down. They've actually gotten a liquor licence for the occasion!"

"What is the world coming to?" Mum said, laughing. "We'll be home by midnight."

"Or maybe two," Dad suggested hopefully.

"Midnight. And there's food in the fridge. Just nuke it in the microwave. I'll be on my cell so if there are any problems ... " Mum instructed.

---

[55] The Matador is a decrepit old building with a red brick facade in Toronto's West End. It has seen countless after-hours parties and is a favourite of Faeries and Humans alike because of its rich history and character. A fixture of the honky-tonk scene in Toronto, it was opened by Ann Dunn, a mother of five who needed a little extra cash. A tall Faerie in a Stetson hat has adult beverages on hand for the right price. Fortunately, the city is trying to close it down and replace it with a twenty-space parking lot. Thank goodness someone can still see the value of a good parking lot.

"There will be no problems." Brendan's dad rolled his eyes. "We have to go!" It was still early, only five o'clock, but they were going to have dinner before the sound check. Despite the early hour, darkness was falling fast. This was, after all, the shortest day of the year: the winter solstice, the day of the Clan Gathering and Brendan's Proving Ceremony.

He watched his parents prepare, happy and carefree. He wished he could go with them and forget about what was coming that night. Why did life have to be so complicated? Delia interrupted his train of thought before he could spiral into self-pity.

"Mum, I'll be staying at Katie's tonight, remember?" Delia stood by the door with her arms crossed. "I told you this afternoon."

"Oh yeah." Mum nodded. "Fine. Just be sure you leave her number on the fridge."

"Okay," Delia agreed, heading away up the hall for the stairs. She'd been weirder than usual during dinner. She seemed reluctant to even look at Brendan. She kept her head down and ate her food and left the table as soon as she was done. Brendan wanted to ask her what her problem was and confront her about the webcam but decided he could do without a fight. He wanted to be calm and collected when he went to the Gathering and Delia had a way of setting him on edge.

"Goodbye, Mum. Bye, Dad. Have fun."

"Bye, son." Brendan's mother kissed him on the cheek. His father opened the door and there, on the porch, finger poised to press the doorbell, was Charlie. She was ridiculously underdressed for the cold weather.

"Charlie!" Dad smiled. "Nice to see you! Don't you have a coat?"

"I'm naturally warm! Good to see you too, Mr. Clair. Mrs. Clair!"

"What are you two up to tonight?" Brendan's mother asked.

Brendan jumped in. "Movies. Going to the movies."

"I see," his mother said, archly. "Well, have a good time and don't stay out too late."

And with that, his parents were gone, out the door into the falling snow and the falling darkness.

"They are very sweet," Charlie said.

"They're like kids sometimes." Brendan shook his head, smiling. He watched his parents head down the street arm-in-arm and felt a pang of loss. He had a sudden fear that he might never see them again. He wished he had said something more meaningful than just goodbye. He tried to shake the melancholy mood that fell over him.

The question Pûkh had posed him earlier that day still rankled. Why was he risking his future with his Human parents to be accepted into the Faerie world? But he knew the answer. He couldn't forget about the Faerie world. It was a part of him now, and he couldn't unlearn what he had mastered so far. He had to see it through. Maybe what Merddyn said was right. Maybe he did have a responsibility to Humans and Faeries. Maybe by living in both worlds, he could bring the two sides together.

I'm just one person, though. What can one person do to make any difference in the world?

"Are you okay?" Charlie asked, breaking his reverie.

He'd been trying to avoid being alone with Charlie today. He wasn't sure why. He still felt awkward about their moment in his dad's studio. Now, with his parents gone and his sister out of the room, there was nowhere else to look.

"Yeah," Brendan mumbled. "Nervous about the Gathering and the tests and everything."

Charlie nodded. "Nothing else?"

Brendan looked up into her blue eyes and his stomach flipped a bit. "No. Not really."

Charlie laughed. "You are such a terrible liar, Brendan. That's one of the reasons I like you so much. Are you ready to go?"

"I think so. Let me get BLT." Grateful for an excuse, he ran up the hall and mounted the stairs. Charlie watched him go. As soon as she was alone, her shoulders sagged. A tortured look twisted her face.

Footsteps on the stairs forced her to recover her smile. She expected to see Brendan and was surprised when Delia rounded the corner, dressed to go out, ski jacket in hand. On seeing Charlie, she stopped. For a second Delia's face held a look of undisguised wariness, but it was immediately replaced with a smile.

"Oh," Delia said. "Hi!"

"*Allo*, Delia," Charlie said. "What are you doing tonight? Party?"

"Yeah," Delia said, a guarded look in her eyes.

Brendan returned, pulling on his jacket. "Ready to go?" Seeing Delia, he said, "Hey, Dee." Suddenly, impulsively, he reached out and hugged his sister. Delia stiffened as if he'd zapped her with a Taser gun. Brendan let her go. Delia stared at him blankly and then spun, ducking out the door into the gathering darkness without another word.

"Wow." Brendan laughed. "I guess that's one way to get rid of her. Or maybe I have cooties."

"Cooties?"[56] Charlie asked, confused.

"Never mind. Shall we go?"

"All right."

Brendan insisted that they ride the streetcar and the subway to the waterfront and walk the last block through the frigid air. A light fog had congealed over the lake, casting an eerie, otherworldly glow upon the condo towers and throwing golden haloes around the street lamps. Brendan knew the fog was part of the glamour woven to distract Humans from the Clan Gathering on the island. Though unnatural, it gave the concrete buildings a spectral loveliness and made the coloured Christmas lights strung in the trees shimmer with magic.

"Christmas," Charlie said as they reached the Harbourfront complex, a cluster of shops, restaurants, and concert venues clumped around the ferry docks and the small boat marina. In winter there was a skating rink. "It's a Human celebration of the older Faerie Festival of the Solstice. They have adopted many of our customs without knowing any of the truth behind the day."

"They have their own reasons to celebrate," Brendan said defensively. "Just because they don't know about us and our world doesn't mean their holidays don't have value on their own."

"I know. I wasn't criticizing."

"Sorry," Brendan mumbled. He was on edge.

They passed through packs of people looming out of the fog. Humans were enjoying the deep freeze as best

---

[56] Cooties, like mumps or measles, is usually a childhood affliction that renders a person undesirable to other Human Beings. In adults it can be much more serious, leading to paralysis or even death.

they could, bundled up against the cold and sipping from paper cups of hot chocolate and cider. Some carried skates slung over their shoulders or hanging from hockey sticks as they made their way to the open-air rink by the water. Brendan envied their happiness and wondered if he'd ever feel as comfortable in his life as these people did in theirs. Certainly, they had worries, but they knew what they were and who they were. Brendan hoped he might have that kind of simplicity in his life again one day.

Faeries, too, mingled among their Human cousins, making their way to the Ward's Island for the Clan Gathering. They flared like torches among the throngs of Humans in Brendan's Faerie Sight. The Fair Folk were in good spirits, some of them a bit tipsy as they made their way to the Faerie Terminal. The Faerie Terminal was at the end of a pier at the foot of the quay. Only a small piece of red cloth fluttering on the top of a pole indicated its existence. Faeries walked past the flag and disappeared into a denser fog. Humans who approached the same threshold paused and then walked back the way they had come.

Brendan and Charlie passed the pole and found themselves in a dense crush of Fair Folk huddled together on the pier. Brendan had never seen so many Faeries in one place before. The Swan was always full of Faerie clientele, but this was more like a Faerie convention. They were a diverse crowd, too. Skin colours varied from pale like Brendan's to brown, golden, or deep red, but there were more unnatural hues as well. Brendan saw several with blue skin, some with green, and one with frosty silver.

Their costume also ran from the traditional kimono to high-fashion couture and everything in between. Brendan felt very plain in his parka, jeans, and hoodie.

"Is this 'im, then?" A Faerie with a thick Cockney accent sloshed a can of beer as he pointed at Brendan. "The one oo's got to be Proved?"

"I guess that's me," Brendan affirmed. The Faerie smelled quite strongly of the ale he'd been imbibing. He wore a red ball cap back to front and had a glow stick dangling from a string around his neck.

He squinted at Brendan and laughed. "A lot of trouble fer such a runt!" A gust of beery breath wafted into Brendan's face.

"Leave off, 'Enry!" A female Faerie jabbed the drinker in the ribs with an elbow. "'E don't need you slobberin' all over 'im." Henry's companion was a robust-looking Faerie in a miniskirt and tube top with a sparkly jacket thrown over her shoulders. Her massive blond bouffant threatened to topple as she teetered on ridiculous stiletto heels. "'E ain't 'alf cute, neither."

"Wha'evs," Henry grunted. "Where is the Ferryman? Opening ceremony's in 'alf an hour and I could use the toilet."

"Oo, me too. I definitely gotta take a slash."

"'Spose we could walk?"

"Across the ice? In these 'eels? Are you daft?"

They wandered away arguing.

A bell rang in the fog and the pier quieted slightly. All the Faeries turned to face the lake. Out of the mist a shadow loomed, eventually resolving into the broad prow of a barge. Brendan was amazed to see that the frozen surface of the lake flowed like water around the vessel. The boat slowed and bumped into the pier with a dull, ominous thud. All the Faeries fell completely silent as a figure strode out from the foggy deck.

The Ferryman was tall and thin. Only his chin was visible beneath the yellow rain hat he wore. The hat's brim was crusted with rime.[57] An oilskin coat and heavy Wellington boots crackled with frost as he moved toward the dockside. He took up his place with one foot on the barge and the other on the pier, a wooden bucket dangling from his bony fist.

"Come aboard!" the low, raspy voice intoned. He raised the bucket.

Faeries surged forward. Charlie and Brendan joined the queue. One by one, the passengers filed onto the barge, dropping some small gold or silver trinket into the bucket as they passed the Ferryman. When Brendan had first ridden on the ferry, he had no money for passage and so had promised to repay the Ferryman with a service performed in the future. He dreaded the day when the cadaverous creature might call in that debt and determined never to be without payment for passage again. His Human grandfather, whom he could barely recall, had left Brendan a coin collection when he died. The coins were mostly silver dollars from the States and Canada. Brendan never left the house without a handful in his pocket.

He dug into his pocket and came up with a silver coin, dropping it into the bucket when his turn came. The Ferryman made no acknowledgment of the payment, merely staring into the space over Brendan's head as he passed.

---

[57] Not *rhyme*, as in a word that sounds the same as another word, but *rime*, as in a crust of frozen sea water that clings to ships' rigging in cold weather. Granted, the water was not sea water but lake water, but I like the word *rime* and I'm going to use it anyway. If you don't like it, call the word police.

Soon everyone was aboard and the Ferryman pushed off from the pier. The barge made its way through the frozen harbour. The Island of the Ward heaved into view. Conversation among the Faeries picked up again, and soon the barge had a party atmosphere in spite of the chilling figure looming at the tiller.

Standing together in the prow, Charlie and Brendan didn't speak. They watched the dark line of the island become more distinct as the fog thinned. Shimmering lights hung over the island, reminding Brendan of the northern lights he'd seen once on a family camping trip up north in Algonquin Park. He wondered again at the Fair Folk's ability to hide in plain sight and marvelled at the power of their Wards and glamours.

With an unnatural abruptness, the fog ended and they came out into the open water surrounding the Faerie Terminal on the Ward's Island. As the barge nestled up to the dock, Brendan stared in awe at the transformation of the shore. Torches lined the paths leading from the dock into the woods. The bare branches of the trees were strung with glowing crystals that flickered as they reflected the torchlight. Lesser Faeries wove in and out of the trees, immune to the bitter cold as they chased one another and called out in merry voices. Food and drink stalls erected along the path offered a bewildering variety of refreshments.

As soon as the Ferryman secured the barge, the new arrivals disembarked, many rushing to the vendors to purchase drinks or food. The rest made their way up the path. Hanging in the air with no visible means of support was a glowing sign that read

FAERGROUND

An arrow pointed up the path in the direction of the Community Centre.

Brendan could hear music wafting from the centre of the island. In spite of his trepidation at the upcoming tests, he felt uplifted by the strains of the pipes, harps, and fiddles and the sound of voices raised in song.

Realizing he was standing on the barge alone save for Charlie, he shook himself and made for the dock.

As soon as their feet hit the wooden planks, the Ferryman pushed off. Brendan watched the barge drift into the mist. He wondered if the Ferryman was the same one he'd been forced to make the bargain with on the night of the Quest. No sooner had the thought crossed his mind than the figure raised a bony finger and pointed straight at him.

"You are remembered," the deep voice intoned. Having delivered this message, the Ferryman and the boat were swallowed in the fog.

"What was that about?" Charlie asked, mystified.

"Long story," Brendan muttered. "Let's go," he said, wishing to avoid further explanation.

They headed up the path past the food stalls, following the throngs on their way to the Gathering.

FAERGROUND

As soon as Brendan left the house, they'd gone into action. Delia had followed Brendan and Charlie at a safe distance. She called the others, conferencing in all three boys and telling them where Brendan was heading. She informed them when the targets had boarded the streetcar. Harold was waiting across the street from the subway station. Upon seeing Brendan and Charlie alight from the streetcar and enter the station, Harold informed Dmitri, who was waiting down on the platform. They had guessed right. Chester had said they were going to the island and that seemed to be what was happening.

In the subway the cell reception died, so they had to trust Dmitri to get on the same train without being seen and call them when Brendan got off at his destination. Dmitri wasn't good at lying and was nervous about spying on his friend, but he convinced himself that he was doing this for Brendan. He hung back behind the newspaper kiosk and waited for Brendan and Charlie to pass. They wove their way among the holiday shoppers that clogged the station until they were halfway down the platform. Dmitri had little trouble following them in the noisy crowd without being seen.

When the train arrived, he hopped on the car next to theirs and sat down between a woman and an off-duty transit driver. Dmitri watched Brendan and Charlie through the glass door between the cars. Station after station slid past, but they didn't budge. The pair looked serious. Sitting side by side on a bench, they didn't speak.

As they headed south, Dmitri's conscience started to bother him again. No matter how he tried to convince himself that he was following Brendan for his own good, he knew deep down that he was driven by relentless curiosity about the day he had lost. Whenever he thought about those missing hours, he was consumed with a longing he'd never experienced before. Inexplicably, he was certain that he had seen and done things that he needed to know about. It was as if he'd woken from a dream just at the moment when he was about to figure out what he was supposed to do, get the reward, truly understand the point of everything.

The screech of the train wheels as they rounded a corner jarred him from his reverie. The train was approaching the bottom of the U that made up the Yonge-University line, pulling into Union Station. Dmitri was sure Brendan would get off the train there. He was probably headed for the waterfront and from there to Ward's Island. Dmitri would call Delia and Harold and tell them to head to the harbour, where Chester was on duty. They had no idea how Brendan and Charlie planned to get to the island with the lake frozen and the ferries not running. They'd just have to wait and see.

So here they were. Dmitri and Chester had followed Brendan and Charlie along the quay to the point where they'd suddenly disappeared. The fog was too thick to see them and the wharf ended.

"Where did they go?" Dmitri demanded in confusion. "They were right there ahead of us and then they were gone."

"Tell me," Chester said softly. "What do you see exactly?"

Dmitri frowned. "I see the boardwalk. It ends at that pole there with the red ribbon on it. Then the fog. Why? What do you see?"

Chester didn't answer. He just chewed his lip, nervously. "Let's wait for the others."

Delia and Harold joined them a few minutes later, having shared a cab from College Street. When they heard that Brendan had given Chester and Dmitri the slip, they couldn't believe it.

"He did it again," Harold said in amazement.

"Where did he go?" Delia hissed, furious that Brendan had escaped their carefully planned tailing operation.

"Relax," Chester grunted. He eyed the wall of fog before turning to them. "I'll show you how they hide themselves. Dmitri, I want you to walk that way, into the fog."

"What?" Dmitri squeaked. "I'll fall into the lake."

"You won't," Chester said. "It's an illusion. There's a dock out there. I can see it."

Dmitri frowned. "I can't see anything."

"It's there," Chester insisted.

"Oh, come on!" Delia snarled. "I'll do it." She took a few steps toward the fog, her face rigid. With each step, her progress became more difficult. Suddenly, just as she reached the pole with the fluttering cloth, she stopped. Her face was a mask of confusion. She turned on her heel and started walking in the opposite direction.

Chester caught her by the arm. "Where are you going?"

Delia stared at him. "I'm … I'm going home."

"Why?"

"I don't know," Delia said. She frowned. "I just suddenly wanted to go home."

Chester turned to the other boys. "See? They make you see things that aren't there. They make you do things that you don't really want to do. Listen to me. I told you before, I can see things, all right?"

Delia was shaking off her daze. Her eyes shifted to the fog and the end of the boardwalk. "So? What do you see?"

Chester took a deep breath. "I see … a dock. It's made of wood and looks really old. It juts out into the water a ways."

"That's impossible," Harold scoffed. "There's nothing but fog and empty water."

"If that's what you want to believe," Chester said angrily, "we can just call this off right now. Otherwise, you're just gonna have to trust me."

Harold, Delia, and Dmitri exchanged glances. Delia spoke. "What do we do?"

"I don't know what's going to happen. I don't know if this will work. It's just a hunch," Chester said. "But I think we should all join hands."

"Why?" Dee demanded.

"If I see what's there and I walk out onto that dock and you're with me, maybe we'll all make it onto the dock."

"And if we don't?" Dmitri shook his head. "We end up in the lake with hypotherminus."

"Hypothermia," Harold corrected.

"Whatever," Dmitri retorted. "We could die."

"That's the only way I see us doing this together," Chester insisted. "Either we try it my way or I go on alone."

Delia rolled her eyes and stepped forward. "I'm in. Don't be such little girls!"

She reached up and grabbed Chester's hand, holding out her other hand to Dmitri. When given the chance to hold a pretty girl's hand, Dmitri decided death by frigid drowning was a small price to pay. He grabbed the proffered hand. Harold reluctantly reached out and took Dmitri's other hand. Thus linked, Chester faced the edge of the board-walk and, smiling grimly, stepped past the pole with the red ribbon fluttering on top.

One by one, the little group followed him. Each in turn disappeared into the wall of fog.

They emerged on a rough wooden dock. The boards creaked beneath their feet. They were all alone. The frozen lake vanished into the fog.

"Holy crap," Harold breathed.

"This is amazing!" Dmitri gasped.

"It worked!" Chester laughed.

"Now what?" Delia demanded.

As if in answer, they heard a bell ringing out over the lake. The sound of waves slapping on wood came to them an instant before a boat emerged from the mist. The craft was like a boat out of a storybook with a high prow carved in the shape of a dragon.[58] A tall man in an old-fashioned rain hat and oilskin coat stood in the stern. They watched in trepidation and wonder as the boat glided, propelled by no

---

[58] I'm sure there are some clever clogs out there wondering why this boat is different from the barge that took Brendan and Charlie across to the island. It is a peculiarity of the Ferryman's guild, "The Brotherhood of the Ways." Their vessels are changeable, growing bigger or smaller as needed to convey people across boundaries. As an aside, Ferrymen aren't the only members of the Brotherhood of the Ways, or at least the Brothers don't all appear as Ferrymen. They are elevator operators, train engineers, balloon pilots, taxi drivers, tollbooth operators, wagon drovers, or any other person who drives some kind of vehicle. Just so you know. An entire book could be written about the Brotherhood, and maybe it will be someday if any Brother ever consents to an interview.

obvious means, and bumped against the dock. The tall man placed one foot on the planking of the dock to secure the vessel before addressing them.

"The Ferry is here," he rasped. "I am the Ferryman, Brother of the Ways. What payment shall you offer?"

"Payment," Harold squeaked. "What kind of payment?"

"You must pay the fare. Gold. Silver or precious stones."

Delia was the only one of them who seemed nonplussed by the situation. She dug in her jacket pocket and came out with a handful of change. She held it out for the Ferryman to see. "How much is it?"

The Ferryman shook his head. "Gold. Silver or precious stones."

"But this is money!" Delia insisted.

He merely shook his head.

"I get it!" Dmitri said suddenly. "There's no silver in coinage anymore. It's mostly nickel and other alloys."

"So it has to be real? Okay." Delia fumbled at her wrist. She was wearing a charm bracelet. With a little effort, she managed to detach a silver snowflake charm. She held it out to the Ferryman, who plucked it from her palm with nimble fingers. He held it up under the brim of his hat. He sniffed the metal and nodded. "Board."

"Great," Delia said. "I have charms for everybody."

The Ferryman raised a palm. "No. Each one must pay his way with his own coin. That is the Law."

"What Law?" Delia demanded.

"The Law of the Brotherhood of the Ways. There are no exceptions. Each must pay the fare."

Delia opened her mouth to argue but closed it again as if she suddenly realized whom she was talking to. She stepped off the wharf into the boat.

Harold reached into his backpack. After a bit of digging, he pulled out an old-fashioned fountain pen. Unscrewing the cap, he revealed a shiny metal nib. He held out the pen to the Ferryman. "It's gold."

The man took the pen, held it up, and sniffed. He nodded once. "Board."

Harold sidled warily past him. Dmitri reached into his jacket and drew out a silver chain. He tugged gently, snapping the chain from his neck and holding it out. "My Saint Christopher medal."[59]

The Ferryman's head tilted slightly to one side as he took the chain and held it up glittering before his face. "A Brother of the Ways. Board."

Dmitri scuttled over to join Delia and Harold in the craft. Only Chester stood on the dock. Chester just stared evenly at the tall figure without making any attempt to search for payment.

"I haven't got anything to pay you."

"A Boon then," the Ferryman rasped. "A Boon in exchange for passage."

"Boon?" Chester frowned. "What's a Boon?"

"A bargain," the voice intoned. "A promise. I will ask for a service in the future and you must do what I will or thy life is forfeit."

Chester didn't say a word. He just stood on the wharf, thinking it over.

"Don't do it," Harold urged him. "Are you crazy?"

---

[59] Saint Christopher is a Catholic saint who is the patron of travellers. Medals are worn by those who hope that he'll look out for them on long journeys.

"It isn't wise," Dmitri agreed. "You have no idea what he'll ask of you."

Delia didn't speak. She just stared at Chester, waiting. Chester returned her gaze. Something in her face made him decide.

"I agree," Chester announced.

"Board!" The Ferryman instructed in his cavernous voice. Was there a hint of satisfaction in his tone? It was impossible to tell. Chester stepped past him onto the boat with his companions, and the Ferryman pushed away from the wharf into the fog.

"I was expecting more," Brendan said as he walked along the path. He and Charlie were heading to the Community Centre where the Swan was hidden. So far, there had been a few stalls selling food, the kind of thing you'd see at a county fair, with sandwiches and cider, hot drinks and sweets.

"Just wait." Charlie smiled. "We aren't at the Faerground yet."

"Fairground? There are rides and stuff?"

"Not fair with an i. Faer with an *e*."

"What's the difference?"

They emerged from the trees into a clearing. Brendan caught his breath. They had crossed some kind of invisible barrier. The island had been grey and bare the last time he'd been here. The park surrounding the Community Centre had been utterly transformed. A city of magnificent tents and pavilions crowded around the white clapboard building. The entire space was ablaze with torchlight. Multicoloured flames sprouted from torches planted in the ground on long poles. The tents were a riot of different cultural designs: wigwams, yurts, teepees, brocaded silks, and billowing Arabian fantasies, all in bright and festive hues. There was no rhyme or reason to the layout. It was as though a caravan of insane nomads had fallen from the sky and decided to set up camp.

"Wow," Brendan breathed. Then he had a thought. "What do the Humans who live on the island think of all this stuff?"

"They won't see any of it." Charlie laughed. "They've been convinced to stay in their homes by glamours."

The variety of tents was exceeded by the variety of Fair Folk frolicking among them. Every imaginable national costume was represented, and every historical era. Each Faerie had dressed extravagantly in order to stick out, and the result was jarring to the eye. Brendan had never seen so many Fair Folk in one place. The effect was overwhelming.

He looked up and gasped again. Faeries had strung cables from tree branches and stretched a maze of colourful high wires across the entire open space. Faeries dashed and somersaulted along the tightropes performing amazing feats of agility. Everywhere, Lesser Faeries swarmed and chased one another at dizzying speeds.

Brendan noticed something else. "Hey ... Am I crazy, or is it suddenly warm?"

"As balmy as a spring day," Charlie agreed. "Part of the glamours. We don't feel the cold, but why not just have a bit of spring in the heart of winter?"

Brendan couldn't argue with that. Still, he was dumbfounded and his expression must have been goofy because Charlie laughed again. "Come on," she said, tugging him back into motion. "Let's go to the market."

They plunged into the heaving throng, shouldering their way through the press. Brendan's ears rang with a barrage of languages: English, French, German, Chinese, and others that he couldn't place. Musicians added to the din, playing impromptu concerts on a bizarre array of traditional and incomprehensible instruments. DJs were spinning club mixes in tents filled with gyrating dancers. In the alleyways between the pavilions, Faeries blocked the way in knots, pausing to dance whenever they felt inspired.

Brendan's worries melted away. He had been concentrating on the Proving so fiercely, he hadn't given a thought to what a Faerie Clan Gathering might actually be like. He found himself caught up in the insanely joyful mood of the Faerground. As they made their way through the chaotic maze of cloth tunnels, he found himself dancing with a number of partners, singing songs he'd never heard before, and being embraced by total strangers. He was only slightly aware that people were pointing at him and whispering. He tried not to feel self-conscious. By the time they reached the lawn-bowling green beside the clubhouse in the centre of the tent village, he was feeling a lightness of heart that he'd never realized he'd been missing these last few weeks.

When the Faerie convention wasn't in town, the bowling green was a flat, manicured lawn bordering the Community Centre. Now it had been appropriated as a marketplace. Stalls had been set up all around the perimeter, selling a bewildering variety of wares. Toys, clothes, jewellery, hats, books, and antiques with indecipherable purposes were laid out on velvet pillows to be pawed by potential buyers. Potion sellers hawked their wares, professing the beneficial health effects of their herbal infusions and ointments. Souvenirs were on offer just as they would have been in a Human flea market. Faeries haggled with merchants. Coins were exchanged along with insults and jokes.

Everywhere Faeries wandered, singly or in raucous groups. In the centre of the green, a large tent sheltered a temporary extension of the Swan of Liir. Huge wooden kegs were suspended on sawhorses, and the ale flowed liberally. Charlie led Brendan into the tent. As they arrived, Og was just topping off a foaming mug. He turned, slopping the amber contents of his tankard as he raised it to his lips. He saw Brendan and his heavy face split open in a grin.

"Well, well, well! Here he is himself. Welcome, Brendan, me boy!" He made his way through the throng toward them.

Brendan's stomach fluttered. Everyone nearby had heard Og's booming greeting. Most eyes turned to search for him and he wished he could disappear. Some of the faces were filled with curiosity, a few were unreadable, and a few revealed undisguised disdain. He tried to cling to the happy mood and ignore the worry that gnawed at his mind once more.

Og found them a rough trestle table and they sat down.

"Will ye have a pint of ale, then, Brendan? Put hair on yer chest?"

"No thanks, Og," Brendan declined. "My mum wouldn't approve."

"She wouldn't even know!" Og declared.

"Gotta stay sharp," Brendan insisted.

"Suit yerself," Og conceded. "What do ye think of the Clan Gathering, me lad? Impressive, what?"

Brendan nodded. He cast his gaze about the clearing, marvelling at his surroundings. *If only Harold and Dmitri could see this. They'd flip!* Brendan immediately felt a stab of sadness. He could never share this with them. He'd made that decision when he'd Compelled them to forget. Now he was alone. Well, not exactly alone. He had Greenleaf, Deirdre, Og, and Kim. He had Charlie.

He watched her as she waded through the crowd to the bar. She had really wrapped herself around his life in such a short time. He didn't know how he felt about that. She was certainly very beautiful. She was fun to be around. But he'd seen another side of her: she was desperately lonely and sad. He remembered her crying in his arms and saying, "I never wished you harm." What did she mean by that?

She sensed him staring at her and turned her head to smile at him. His heart tightened. He was about to wave at her when his eye caught a sharp movement behind her shoulder.

Brendan saw Lugh, the tall, sinister Faerie companion of Pûkh. The silver-haired Faerie bent over and spoke angrily into Charlie's face. The revellers parted for an instant, long enough for Brendan to see that Lugh had a huge hand clamped on Charlie's shoulder.

Brendan was out of his seat in an instant and forcing his way through the crowd. After a few curses and well-placed elbows he reached Charlie. Just as he arrived, he heard Lugh's sharp voice.

"You must reconsider. Pûkh will not be pleased if you refuse him."

Charlie shook her head fiercely, her jaw jutting out. "I don't care what he threatens me with."

"Let go of her," Brendan demanded.

Lugh stared hard at Brendan with his cold grey eyes. Finally, he said, "This does not concern you, Princeling. Begone."

"She's my friend." Brendan tried not to let the fear jangling in his heart show in his voice. "So it does concern me. Let her go."

Lugh continued to stare at Brendan, hand firmly clamped on Charlie's arm.

"Let de girl go," said a deep voice, echoing Brendan's demand.

Leonard stood with a wooden keg on his shoulder. His muscles bulged from the strain of holding the barrel upright. His dark face was serious as a gravestone as he stared Lugh down.

Lugh's lip hovered at the doorstep of a sneer. He let go of Charlie's arm and without a word stalked off into the crowd.

"Thanks, you guys," Charlie said. "But you didn't have to worry. I'm fine."

"What did he want?" Brendan asked.

"It was nothing." Charlie waved the question away, but Brendan saw the lingering fear in her eyes.

"It didn't seem like nothing. What did he want?"

"Nothing I could give him."

"That Lugh is a creepy dude."

Charlie's face clouded. "Yeah, he's creepy, all right. You should stay away from him. He's dangerous."

"Believe me," Brendan said, "I'll keep a healthy distance from that guy. I just don't like the way he was bugging *you*."

"I can take care of myself," Charlie said. "Lugh and Pûkh do not have your best interests at heart, Brendan. Believe me."

"How do you know?"

Charlie looked down, boring a hole in the sandy ground with her foot. She seemed about to say something, but Kim's arrival interrupted her.

276

"Hey, everybody," Kim said with a wave.

Kim was decked out in clothes that Brendan had never seen her wear before. She was usually a T-shirt and jeans type, but today she was total Faerie. She wore skin-tight green leather trousers and a tight embroidered silk tank top that showed off her elaborate vine tattoos. Her hair was dusted with gold and her feet were bare. Her field hockey stick was slung over her shoulder with a green leather strap.

Brendan found he could only stare, speechless, his mouth hanging open. Kim smirked.

"And hello to you, Brendan." Kim was obviously delighted at Brendan's reaction. She smiled in turn at Charlie. "Hello, Charles."

Charlie merely smiled, a little insincerely.

"Come on, everybody," Kim said, clapping her hands. "It's time!"

"For what?" Brendan asked.

"The Solstice is minutes away," Kim explained. "Deirdre is the Greeter. And after that, the Proving."

Brendan's stomach fell away. At that moment, a bell began to toll.

SOLSTICE

"What's going on here?" Delia asked. "Some kind of hippie festival, or what?"

"Keep your voice down," Harold begged. "We're trying not to attract attention."

Though they didn't know it, they were following in Brendan's footsteps along the path. Since Chester had managed to open their eyes back on the wharf, they could now see the Beautiful People, as he called them.[60] The people had a vibrancy and a glow that normal Humans didn't, and their clothing was more outlandish and exuberant. The little troop waited until the last of the strange people had made their way along the path and then dashed in, darting from tent to tent for cover.

---

[60] Most Humans see what they want to see, what is easiest to believe. We explain away the amazing by convincing ourselves that magical, bizarre, or impossible events have mundane causes. UFOs are weather disturbances. Ghosts are hallucinations brought on by indigestion. Faeries use our willingness to disbelieve our eyes to help their glamours work. Brendan, an untried Faerie with little control of his powers, seems to have left an unconscious suggestion in Chester's mind that allowed Chester to see the Faerie world. Now Chester has transferred his power of Sight to his friends, not because he has any Faerie abilities himself, but because he has made them *want* to see. No amount of will can turn me into a cat, however. Believe me. I've tried. A lot.

"Do you hear that?" Chester said suddenly. They all listened as a clear, high tone rang out across the island. As soon as the sound began, the Beautiful Ones hurried up the path.

"Let's go!" Delia cried, heading off in pursuit. The boys hesitated a moment before setting off after her.

They followed the crowd and soon found themselves in the clearing where the Community Centre was. They stopped short in astonishment at the impossible village of tents.

"Holy crap!" Harold breathed.

The bell changed in tone, rising slightly.

"Come on," Delia said. "We'll be late."

"For what?" Dmitri asked.

"I intend to find out." Delia smiled fiercely and moved forward. The three boys shared a look and then started after her.

Brendan stood in the midst of the hushed, breathless throng. The reverberation of the bell overwhelmed all other sounds, cutting through the din of voices and instruments with insistent clarity. All who heard the bell turned their heads toward the source of the chime. A hush fell over the Gathering. Even the Lesser Faeries, normally prone to constant nattering, had fallen into a respectful silence. All stood (or fluttered, in the case of the Lesser Faeries) facing west toward the red wash of the sunset sky and the fiery orb of the sun hanging just above the frozen lake. Brendan held his breath. The bell continued to chime, and presently a procession approached.

They seemed to emerge out of the dying sun. Brendan was relieved to see a familiar face in front. His aunt Deirdre led the way, dressed in a shimmering silken gown of the purest white. In her hand she held a long pole. From the top of the pole dangled a bell that reflected the torchlight in its polished golden surface. As Deirdre walked into the Gathering place among the silent Faeries, she gently swung the pole so that the bell tolled with each step.

Ariel followed her. He was dressed in an exquisitely tailored suit sewn from golden cloth. His pale face and hair glowed softly, whether from the sun, the torchlight, or some inner illumination, Brendan couldn't tell. He was the most senior of the Faeries in this part of the world, and so he was the host of the Gathering. The entire crowd ducked their heads in respectful greeting. Ariel raised a hand in response.

Behind Ariel, Pûkh smirked at the crowd as if he were a king among peasants, mildly amused by their quaint behaviour and customs. Pûkh had discarded the Armani suit in favour of a more traditional costume: a cloak encrusted with minute pearls and a plain white tunic with hose.

Walking behind him was a creature that made Brendan want to rub his eyes to make sure he wasn't dreaming. She looked as if she'd just stepped out of a Japanese anime cartoon. She wore what looked like a white sailor suit that had been splattered with green paint applied via shotgun blast. Her makeup was stark white with one black tear drawn at the corner of her right eye. Her hair was dyed a vibrant red and stood up like a cock's comb. She was tiny in stature, almost childlike, and yet the look in her eyes was anything but innocent. The eyes in question were shaded by pink sunglasses. She was chewing a pink wad of bubble gum. The most bizarre aspect of her appearance had nothing to do with what she wore. A rich and glossy foxtail swished behind her as she walked.

"Kitsune Kai and her bodyguards," Charlie whispered in his ear. He started. He'd forgotten she was there at his side.

Walking in attendance close behind Kitsune Kai was a pair of stout, dark-haired Japanese men. Their heads were oddly flat and the tops of their scalps glittered in the torchlight.

"What's on their heads?" Brendan asked.

"They're Kappa. They are tremendously strong. They wrestle their opponents to the ground and snap their limbs with powerful arms. However, they are vulnerable. They have to carry water from their home lake in a hollow at the top of their heads. If the water spills, they lose their strength and may even die."

Brendan watched in silence as Kitsune Kai and her odd bodyguards came to a halt in the centre of the Faerground with Pûkh and Deirdre.

The bell tolled one last time and fell silent. The crowd held its collective breath. Ariel stepped forward and raised his hands, the dying sun tinting his pale skin crimson.

The four Faeries formed a circle and raised their hands so that their palms faced downwards. They opened their mouths and sang out a single, achingly beautiful note. They sustained the chord and it grew in depth and power. Harmonics quivered in the air, making the sound more elaborate and complex. The air in the centre of their circle thickened and curdled into a glowing fog that seeped into the ground. The sound of their voices was joined by a deep rumbling.

The ground heaved and crumbled as a massive stone, a chunk of the island's bedrock, emerged like the back of some long-buried, petrified beast. The stone rose, shedding crumbling earth, until it stood two metres high, a flat slab that could serve as a platform or stage.

The small circle of Faeries stopped singing and dropped their hands. The crowd cheered. Ariel stepped up onto the rock and addressed the assembly, calling for silence.

"O Mother Sun! On this the Solstice night, we beg you to return," he cried. "The time is come to turn your face upon us once more."

"Return!" the crowd exclaimed in response.

"Renew the Earth and bless the world with your power and warmth!"

"Return!"

"We await the kiss of spring, the spread of leaf, the burst of blossom!"

"Return!" Brendan shouted with the rest. He felt the magic of the incantation. He felt the tingle of power seeping into the cold ground beneath his feet. He felt the power of the promise of rebirth in the coming spring.

Ariel dropped his arms and swept his grey eyes back across the crowd. "Welcome all the Clans from near and far, Greater and Lesser, Silkies, Trolls, Kappa, and any others who gather to celebrate the death of the old year and the dawn of the new. All those who seek fellowship and kinship, we welcome you."

He bowed his head and stepped back. This was Deirdre's cue to hand the pole and the bell to Greenleaf, who stepped out of the throng to accept it. Another attendant handed Deirdre her harp with a deferential bow. Thus equipped, she stepped up onto the stone platform. She stood for a moment, her head bowed, lightly plucking the strings as though to confirm they were in tune. Satisfied, she raised her face, eyes closed, and strummed a chord.

The crowd sighed as one. Brendan felt his heart lift on the resonating sound of the harp. All at once, Deirdre's fingers exploded in a flurry of movement. She was joined by instruments of every description played here and there throughout the gathered crowd. The sound was overwhelming, consuming. It drove deep inside Brendan, taking control of his body. He began to dance with abandon, flailing his limbs like a maniac. It felt good!

He was aware that others were dancing, spinning, and whirling around him. He paid no attention to individuals. A particle in a hurricane, a dust speck in a tornado, he lost himself in a gyre of pure joy. All his worries melted away. He was aware of only the pulse of the music and the beat of his heart.

The music swelled and sped up. He was a spinning top, a planet rotating, the slowly turning galaxy. Everything was moving like a giant clock, and he was a part of that vast timepiece, tiny but still important. He belonged.

Then the music stopped dead.

He staggered to a halt, streaming with sweat. All around him Faeries were panting and laughing, utterly spent. Lesser Faeries littered the ground like fallen leaves. Exhausted laughter wafted up from all over the Faerground as people caught their breath.

Brendan felt elated. It was as though all the tension in his body had been burned away. He looked around at the Faeries as they clasped hands and laughed, sharing the experience, and he felt joy at being a part of this world. There were good things in it if he let himself enjoy them. In this new state of mind he felt unafraid, even of the Proving, whatever that should turn out to entail. He felt happy.

He looked around to find Charlie to share the feeling but she was nowhere near. He cast his gaze wider. *Where did she go?* He spun around slowly, trying to pick her out of the crowd.

That's when he saw Delia.

She was standing at the very edge of the Faerground in the shadow of a tent. The sun was down now so she was partially obscured by darkness, but there was no mistaking her blond hair. She was wearing the pink ski jacket she'd had on back at the house when she'd gone out. She wasn't even trying to hide herself. Obviously, from the disbelieving look on her face, she'd been watching the ceremony. Hundreds of people in a dancing frenzy was probably a pretty weird thing to walk in on.

Any peace that had existed in Brendan's soul was replaced with terror. What happened to Humans who walked in on Faerie rituals? He didn't know but it couldn't be good.[61]

"That was amazing, wasn't it?"

Brendan turned to find Kim beside him. She was flushed from dancing and her hair was dishevelled. In spite of his terror, some part of his mind was aware that she looked very beautiful. She was smiling brightly and her eyes danced. When she saw his eyes, however, her smile vanished.

"What's wrong?"

"My sister's here," Brendan whispered.

"Your sister!" Kim practically shouted.

Brendan grabbed her arm and pulled her away from the closest Faeries. "Quiet!" he hissed urgently. "She's over by the tent with the red stripes. See her?"

Kim scanned the area and nodded. "How?" Kim asked. "How did she get to the island?"

"If I knew, I'd tell you. I've got to get her out of here before someone else sees her."

---

61 Indeed, it is not good, as we will soon discover.

"You can't leave. They're about to call you forward for the Proving."

Brendan groaned. "What am I gonna do?"

At that moment, three boys joined his sister. Brendan recognized Harold and Dmitri. He took an instant longer to recognize the third boy as Chester Dallaire. "What is he doing here?"

Brendan's thought was interrupted by Ariel's voice.

"Brendan, Son of Briach Morn. Step forward."

Brendan froze. He didn't know what to do.

Kim took his face in her hands. "Go. I'll take care of this. Good luck."

She whirled away, weaving through the crowd to where Delia and the boys stood.

Dazed, filled with worry, Brendan tore his eyes away from her progress and turned to face the judges. He took a deep breath and walked through the crowd. The Faeries parted to let him pass.

Delia couldn't believe what she was seeing. It was like a scene from a movie or an insane dream. She had run ahead of the others through the maze of fluttering tents, following the eerie, throbbing music until she arrived on the edge of an open space filled with these bizarre people, all in the throes of a frenzied dance. A woman in white stood on a large stone. She played a harp with furious passion. Other instruments accompanied her from here and there in the crowd. A DJ at a table supplemented the sound. The scene reminded Delia of a rave, only the music was so much more hypnotic and compelling. She felt the urge to leap out among the dancers and join them in their state of abandon. She was on the verge of doing exactly that when the music suddenly stopped.

Delia felt bereft, as if someone had torn a part of her soul away. She longed to hear the music again, but the woman in white was stepping down from the stone. Delia tried to focus. She scanned the crowd, looking for Brendan. Chester, Harold, and Dmitri arrived.

"Holy crap," Harold whispered.

"What's going up?" Dmitri asked in wonder.

Chester didn't say anything. He just took in the whole sight, mouth slightly open and eyes wide.

Delia ignored them, searching for Brendan. At last, she picked him out. To her chagrin, he was staring straight at her. Kim was with him. She swung her head and locked eyes with Delia.

"Uh-oh," Delia breathed.

At that moment, someone called out Brendan's name. Delia's adopted brother reluctantly turned away to answer the summons of the pale guy who now stood on the rock. Kim, on the other hand, started weaving her way through the crowd. She wore a look of grim determination. She was heading straight for the little group of spies.

"Run!" Delia cried. Turning on her heel, she followed her own advice.

She didn't have a plan. She was just trying to get away. Harold, Dmitri, and Chester set off after her. They wound their way through the maze, walls of silk funnelling them along.

"Stop!" Kim's voice called to them. "Guys, wait!"

They paid no attention. All of them were driven by a desire to be far away from this place as soon as possible. They were on the verge of panic.

Suddenly, a young girl stood in their path. She wore a hoodie and jeans. She was Human. One of them!

"Come," the girl said urgently. "Hide in here." She held open the flap of a tent and motioned them inside. Something about her inspired trust. Delia made a decision. She didn't want to be caught. It was hard to think. Something was keeping her from concentrating.

"In here, guys," the girl cried and led the boys into the tent. Delia ducked in after her.

Kim pelted around a corner to find the way empty. She had been gaining on the little group of interlopers. All she wanted to do was get them away from the Faerground and off the island before they were discovered. Now they were nowhere to be seen.

Puzzled, she stood in the alleyway between the tents, wondering how she could have missed them. Without any other options, she decided to retrace her steps. Slowly, listening hard, she jogged back toward the Faerground, passing the closed flap of the tent where the group was huddled, waiting for her to leave.

When they were confident Kim was gone, the group of Humans let out a collective sigh of relief. In the gloom of the tent's interior they allowed themselves to relax.

"That was close," Delia said.

"She almost caught us," Harold added.

Dmitri frowned. "Would that have been so bad?" They all looked at him, confused. In response, he shrugged and continued. "I mean, why did we get so panicked? We just ran. Doesn't that strike you as an odd thing to do? There was no reason to assume that Kim meant to hurt us."

Harold thought about that. "Yeah, I guess that's true. I just felt this total panic. I had to run."

Delia realized they were right. "I don't know."

"Something made us do it," Chester said heavily. "Or someone. Where is she?"

"Who?" Delia asked, confused.

"The girl," Chester said. "The one who told us to hide here."

"Uh … " Delia couldn't concentrate.

"Here I am!" came a playful voice from the gloom. A girl danced out into the light of the single lamp that hung from a tent pole. In the golden light, all pretense of Humanity was gone. As she came out of the shadows, she cast aside the hoodie. Beneath it she wore a ragged black dress, and her hair stood out in a wild tangle around her pale, child-like face. Her eyes had a mad gleam. She grinned, displaying glittering pointed teeth. "Who wants to play with me?"

Instinctively, the group backed toward the tent flap. They turned to flee but found the opening filled with the bulk of a tall, silver-haired man with cold grey eyes.

Chester stepped in front of the others and raised his hands in a defensive stance.

"Let us go," he demanded.

The silver-haired man tilted his head to one side and stared at the boy as if considering the challenge, then said a single word.

"No."

PROVING

Delia! Always manages to be annoying. Now she's annoying in two different worlds! I'll kill her if somebody hasn't already. So it was Harold and Dmitri who'd been spying on me, but Chester? How did he get involved? And how could my sister possibly stand dealing with my friends? She wouldn't normally be caught dead with such nerds.

With effort, Brendan pushed the questions from his mind as he made his way through the crowd of silent Faeries. He had to have a clear head if he was going to succeed. The crowd watched him pass with watchful, appraising eyes. Here and there he saw someone he recognized.

Leonard stood with his massive arm around Saskia's waist. He flashed his gold teeth in a smile and Saskia winked.

Og patted Brendan on the back, almost knocking him off his feet. "Good on ya, lad."

BLT flitted out of the crowd. She didn't speak. She merely tugged on his earlobe with both hands and zipped away.

Brendan was almost at the rock when Finbar reached out and took his arm. The old man pulled him close in a rough embrace. Brendan was surprised at this show of emotion. The Exile barely spoke to anyone. A hug was quite out of character.

"Good luck, lad," the old Exile whispered in his ear. Finbar let him go and melted back into the crowd before Brendan could react.

Brendan's eyes turned to Pûkh. The Lord of Tír na nÓg stood beside the rock, smiling enigmatically. Brendan didn't return the smile, keeping his face as straight and determined as he could. This only seemed to tickle Pûkh more, broadening his grin. Brendan started forward again, covering the last few metres to the rock and stepping up beside Ariel. Ariel nodded, acknowledging his arrival.

"Brendan Morn." Ariel spoke loud enough for all in the Faerground to hear. "You have been called forth to be Proven." He turned to Pûkh, Kitsune, and Deirdre. "Who will judge Brendan Morn?"

Pûkh stepped forward and smiled his irritating cocky smile. "I will. Lord Pûkh of Tír na nÓg."

Deirdre stepped up beside Pûkh and said, "I will judge him. Deirdre D'Anaan: Weaver and head of the Clan of D'Anaan."

Kitsune Kai waved a hand dismissively, blowing a pink bubble and popping it loudly as she studied her nails. "Let's get on with it."

"Very well," Ariel said gravely. "Let the Proving begin."

Ariel stepped down from the rock, leaving Brendan feeling horribly exposed and alone. He looked out at the sea of faces and felt faint. They all had the same eager look in their eyes. Brendan imagined that this was what convicted criminals felt like when they stepped out onto the gallows. His eye was drawn to a flicker of movement at the edge of the crowd. He saw Kim returning. She met his gaze and shook her head, shrugging. Kim hadn't managed to catch Delia and the others. Brendan supposed that was a good sign. Perhaps they were gone, out of reach of any reprisal. He had to hope that was true.

His aunt Deirdre handed her harp to one of the attendants and mounted the stone, graceful and sure despite the long gown she wore. Brendan mentally crossed his fingers that she might go easy on him. Then he remembered how she'd terrorized his dreams when he first found out about his true heritage. Brendan glumly braced himself for the worst.

Before she turned to face the throng awaiting her Challenge, her eyes met Brendan's. His aunt always made him a little uncomfortable. She was a powerful personality, and he sensed that she had to work to keep hidden a strong current of emotion that flowed close to the surface. It made her hard to be around. Brendan had often interpreted this as disapproval or anger. Today, in her eyes, he saw that emotion clearly as deep, irrevocable sadness and loss. He longed to reach out to her, here in front of everyone.

She turned away and addressed the crowd in her clear, powerful voice.

"This Proving was never necessary in my mind. I know this is my sister's son. He has her eyes, her smile, and most importantly, her kind spirit. Bir-Gidha lives in him. He is my only link to her. I merely wish to show you how I know."

With that, she began to sing.[62]

---

[62] Hearing Deirdre D'Anaan sing is one of the greatest pleasures in the Human or the Faerie world. Her rare recordings and live performances for the People of Metal are treasured, though she is careful to weave glamours into her music that discourage the attention of critics and award committees. Even among Faeries, her voice is a legendary force. It is said that she can split stone or call down lightning with a well-turned melody.

Her song was light and plaintive, a lonely little melody that twisted around Brendan's heart and tugged at it, trying to unravel it.

He couldn't understand the words, if they were words at all. They were sounds, merely, nonsense but fraught with meaning. He found himself joining in.

Any fear of embarrassment was absent. He matched her note for note, instinctively following her lead and then soaring away on his own into harmonies that came as naturally as breathing.

At some point in their duet, Brendan reached over and grasped her hand. The connection crumbled his final reserve of self-consciousness. He sang with abandon now, lost in the ecstasy of the sound they were creating together. He had never felt so free. He closed his eyes and revelled in the glorious feeling of being alive and completely involved in this single moment.

He had no idea how long their song went on, but finally the melody wound down and dwindled into silence.

Brendan opened his eyes. The entire Faerie throng stared in wonder. There were tears on some faces. Kim had moved through the crowd and stood directly below him, her face shining.

Brendan turned to his aunt. She was smiling at him.

"This is my nephew, Brendan. He sings with his mother's voice. I am satisfied."

The crowd erupted into applause and wild cheering as she wrapped him in her arms. Brendan hugged her back, breathing in the lavender of her golden hair.

"I'm proud of you," Deirdre whispered in his ear. "And she would be, too."

Brendan felt an ache in his throat as he let Deirdre go. He'd never understood how painful it must have been for Deirdre to see him, the image of her lost sister, knowing that Brendan's birth had taken her away. This was a proving for them both. He smiled at her and she returned the smile. With a final squeeze of Brendan's hand, Aunt Deirdre stepped down.

And Kitsune Kai stepped forward.

Brendan had no idea how she managed to stay upright on her stylish shoes. Without the shoes, she would have stood well under five feet. Even with them, she had to crane her neck to look up at Brendan perched on the rock.

"Okay," Kitsune said, planting her hands on her hips. "You want to prove to me that you are one of us? It won't be easy!" She glared up at him, her dark eyes tinted pink by the lenses of her sunglasses. She seemed to be expecting an answer.

Brendan shrugged. "Okay."

"Yeah, you're right it's okay! I say so. I am Kitsune Kai, the Number One Fox Spirit. I am going to test you. Are you ready, Brendan?"

"Uh, yeah."

Kai narrowed her eyes. She snapped her elegant fingers. "Kappa! Fetch the tea!"

One of her bodyguards jogged forward carefully carrying a porcelain cup in his hands. The liquid inside steamed. The cup was filled almost to the brim. She accepted the tea and the Kappa bowed, retreating to join his fellow. She turned, holding the cup, and with a flick of her tiny feet that was almost too fast to see, she removed her shoes. They tumbled through the air into the hands of her Kappa servants.

"Tea?" she asked Brendan, holding the cup out to him.

Brendan shrugged. "I guess?"

"Do not guess!" she snapped. "Do you like tea or not?"

Puzzled, Brendan nodded his head. He took the cup. She bowed to him. He returned the bow.

"Okay," she said. "Your test, Brendan, son of Briach and Bir-Gidha, is to hold the teacup and not spill a drop. Do you understand?"

"I think so, yes."

She locked his eyes with her steady black gaze. For an instant, he could see how ancient this creature before him was. In her eyes was a feral flicker of hunger, a cold animal stare.

"Sounds easy, no?"

"If I've learned anything from becoming a Faerie, I've learned this: if it sounds easy, it will probably be one of the hardest things I've ever done."

She smiled, revealing sharp, white teeth. "Ha! That's good! You're not as stupid as you look. Don't spill a drop." With that, she leapt at him with a wild scream. He clumsily ducked her attack and staggered backwards. He looked down at the cup and was relieved to see that it hadn't spilled. Then he looked up in time to dodge a punch aimed at his nose.

Uh-oh! Brendan cried in his mind, ducking as fast as he could. The punch went high and he felt the familiar sizzle in his blood as he forced his body into warp mode.

He held the cup in both hands and did his best to keep ahead of the wild Fox Spirit who was trying to smack him.

After half a minute, she hadn't managed to land a blow.

Brendan was quite pleased with himself until he saw Kitsune Kai stop, stretch, and smile. "Okay. The warm-up is over. Let's begin in earnest." She coiled her whole body like a panther about to spring.

"Crap." Brendan gulped.

With a snarl, she launched herself at him again.

Fists and feet came at him with blinding speed. It was all he could do to avoid her flurry of blows. She held nothing back. Brendan had to warp faster than he ever had before or he was finished.

Come on! Come on! he screamed in his mind. *You can do this!*

Then he remembered what Charlie had suggested. He started to sing.

"Who taught you to live like that?" he sang suddenly. *"Who taught you to live like that? Who taught you to live like that?"* It was a song by Sloan, one of his favourite bands.

"What are you doing?" Kitsune Kai frowned.

Brendan ignored her and concentrated on the lyrics, singing them in his head.

> *She came through inspections*
> *Towards me in sections*
> *The life disappeared from the room.*
> *She asked me politely*
> *May I put this lightly*
> *The death that you thought was exhumed*
> *It's buried beneath us*
> *Since I wrote the thesis*
> *I think I know better than you.*

He felt the fizz of the warp begin in his blood.

Kitsune Kai seemed to sense the onset of Brendan's warp powers. She hissed and redoubled her efforts. The song was in his hands and his feet now, driving him on, kicking him into high gear. He sang only in his mind now, the lyrics and the melody second nature as he balanced the cup and avoided Kitsune Kai's blows.

He leaned backwards and avoided a roundhouse kick. He was astonished that a woman so tiny could reach his face with her equally tiny foot. He backflipped away from her while desperately trying to keep the tea from spilling. He managed to land safely on the very edge of the rock, teetering on the verge of losing his balance.

"Faster!" cried Kitsune Kai. "Faster!"

Oh no! He cradled the teacup in his hand even as the mad little woman leapt at him again, her tail whipping back and forth ferociously.

He dodged as best he could, twisting his torso to miss the kicks and punches she hurled at him. He was vaguely aware that the crowd around him was hooting and cheering. As soon as he let that outside sound distract him, Kitsune Kai swept his feet out from under him. He went head over heels.

Suddenly, his warp powers kicked in full force. He was frozen in the moment. Time stretched out like taffy. He could see the expressions on the faces of the Faeries closest to him shifting from eager excitement to shock. Kitsune Kai's eyes bored into his as the world rotated one hundred and eighty degrees.

Strangely, Brendan felt no alarm. Everything was slow and beautiful. He had time to savour his flight. With ease, he rotated his wrist so that the teacup was upright. Even so, a drop spilled out of the bowl. The droplet hung in the air, a glittering globule rotating with him. He felt weightless, like an astronaut in orbit. He smiled at the sensation. Slowly, he started to descend toward the rock beneath his head. He strained his neck forward and opened his mouth, catching the droplet of tea easily. Realizing he'd crack his skull if he didn't take appropriate action, he stuck out his hand, palm down, and landed on it, balancing himself upside down while cradling the teacup in his other upturned hand. His legs were splayed out for balance.

The warp state dissipated and he was left poised on the rock. Throughout the Faerground, silence reigned supreme. Kitsune Kai stood with her hand cocked on her hip and a look of cool appraisal on her delicate face. Her tail twitched once. Twice. Then she nodded, a single dip of her pointy chin.

"Yeah, okay. I am satisfied."

The crowd roared approval. Kitsune Kai plucked the teacup from Brendan's hand and hopped down from the stone. Brendan gratefully lowered himself to the stone and got back on his feet. He was starting to feel that he might get through these tests after all. His elation died when he saw Pûkh step up onto the rock.

The Lord of Tír na nÓg took a moment to gaze out over the crowd. Pûkh had a sense of the theatrical, letting the tension build and the crowd slowly cease its chatter. Finally, when he had absolute silence, he raised his hands. "I have thought long and hard about this Proving. It is said that you are descended from the line of Morn. I was a close compatriot of Briach Morn. I was his comrade-in-arms in darker times." A whisper stirred the crowd before he continued. "But it is contested that the great Briach Morn was your father." He paused here for effect, looking out over the crowd solemnly. "True, I can see his face in yours, Brendan, but I must be sure. Thus, my test!" He waved a hand and two Faeries moved forward carrying a long, narrow wooden box between them. The box was simple and rough-hewn with two rope handles at either end. From their staggering approach, it was clear that the box was quite heavy. They set the box on the grass with a dull thud.

"As you may or may not know, Brendan," Pûkh said, pausing to arch an eyebrow at the audience, emphasizing Brendan's ignorance, "Faerie weapons and armour are keyed to the energy of their owners. By lucky chance, I happen to have an item that once belonged to my dear friend Briach." Pûkh flicked a wrist at the bearers and they bent to flip open the lid of the box. Lying inside was a long object wrapped in black silk. Pûkh lifted the bundle easily in one hand and joined Brendan on the rock.

Brendan was torn between dread at being so close to the Lord of Tír na nÓg and curiosity about the object.

Pûkh continued to speak as he gently unwrapped the bundle with his long, elegant fingers. "When Faeries die, their armour and weapons lose their power and quickly dissolve. Your Father, however, is not dead. He merely chose, in his grief over his wife's death, to go to the Other Side. Therefore, his weapons and armour remain intact. He left them in my safe-keeping until the ..." Pûkh stopped suddenly, then affected sorrow. "Alas! So sad. So much potential lost. He was an old friend and I miss his counsel." He pulled the cloth from the object, revealing a beautifully wrought sword. He was careful to keep the hilt wrapped in silk as he held it. "This was his favourite blade. I'm sure you wouldn't be able to pronounce the name in the Old Tongue, Brendan. In English, it would be called *Dawn Cleaver*."

Brendan held his breath. The weapon was exquisitely crafted. The blade was a metre long with a single cutting edge. Sunlight danced along the razor-sharp edge, dazzling Brendan's eyes. The hilt was a simple cross. The entire weapon seemed to be formed from one continuous piece of smoky, translucent crystal. It was a beautiful, deadly object.

More fascinating to Brendan was the sound. He could feel rather than hear a deep, rich humming as though the sword were vibrating to music only he could hear. It was like a tuning fork struck by a celestial finger.

"The sword is tuned to Briach, but if Brendan is really his son, he should be able to hold the weapon without undue harm," Pûkh explained.

"NO!" Deirdre cried. "It's too dangerous!" Ariel placed a hand on her arm to restrain her.

"Deirdre," Ariel said. "Pûkh has chosen the test. He is a judge. You cannot interfere."

"But he is young in his powers," Deirdre insisted. "Even though he is Briach's son and Morn blood flows in his veins, the imprinting of the blade upon his mind may drive him mad. Or worse. If the blade rejects him, it could be fatal!"

Ariel's face was hard. He glared at Brendan. "He must be Proven. I, for one, would have Brendan Prove beyond a doubt that he is of the line of Morn and that his initiation was valid." Ariel's authority was at stake as well. He had accepted Brendan's initiation and must have found it humiliating to have his judgment questioned by the Proving ceremony.

"What's the point if he doesn't make it through the Proving?" Deirdre insisted.

Brendan laid a hand on his aunt's arm. "It's okay, Aunt Deirdre. I have to do it. Otherwise people like Pûkh will never stop finding new reasons to doubt me. If I do this, it's over."

He could see the concern in Deirdre's eyes. She opened her mouth to speak, then closed it without a word, nodded, and stepped back. Brendan smiled with a reassurance he didn't quite feel himself and turned to face Pûkh.

"What is the harm?" Pûkh smiled. "If he is truly the son of Briach and Bir-Gidha, he should be none the worse. But if he isn't … " Pûkh's smile darkened. "Well, then, I've done my job." Pûkh held the sword out to Brendan in both hands, being careful to handle only the black silken cloth.

Brendan hesitated. The hum emanating from the sword was a siren song to him. His hands itched to grasp the weapon so that he could hear its voice more clearly. He forced himself to pause and consider the consequences. Touching the sword might end this ordeal once and for all, but it might also be the last thing he ever did.

He looked up into Pûkh's face. The handsome features were fixed in a state of friendly detachment, giving nothing away. Brendan had a flash of insight then. He suddenly realized who had protested Ariel's acceptance of his initiation. Pûkh had forced this Proving, made him jump through hoops and live through this terrifying ordeal. He looked into that blandly smiling face and felt a rush of anger. Brendan understood that he'd been manoeuvred into a corner for some purpose that only the Lord of the Everlasting Lands knew. He had a sudden desire to show the smirking Faerie that he wasn't afraid of him. Without another thought, he reached out and grasped the sword.

The hum sang bright and clear, filling his head as soon as his hands touched the smooth, cool surface of the blade. Brendan closed his eyes and listened to the sweet tone.

Is this all? he thought. He'd never heard such a beautiful sound. The note was pure and clear, resonating in every fibre of his body, every bone and blood vessel, every hair on his head. Ecstasy! He had heard the word before and thought he understood it, but this was ecstasy distilled into sound and poured into his soul through his palms.

Suddenly, his entire body ignited in agony. Lightning jagged along his nerves, and the hum escalated into a shriek that threatened to tear his head apart. Together, the pain and the sound grew to fill Brendan's entire universe. Blinding white light flared, though he couldn't tell if his eyes were open or shut. For that matter, he couldn't tell if he was up or down, in or out. Brendan didn't care. He just wanted it to stop.

He realized then that the shriek was coming from the blade itself. The sword wasn't dead like some Human creation. No, it was a living thing with a mind and a soul of its own. The sword felt Brendan's foreign touch and was attacking him. The sword wanted to destroy him.

"Stop!" he shouted, not knowing whether he screamed aloud or only in his head. The tiny part of him that could still think reasonably wondered how much time had passed and whether he was dead or not. That's when he heard the voice.

"Breandan. Can you hear me?"

He recognized the voice, though he'd heard it only once before.

"Father?"

"Yes, son."

"What's happening?"

"You hold Dawn Cleaver. It is tuning itself to you. The sword served me and will serve you now. We are connected for a very short time."

"Where are you? How can I hear you?"

"We may speak now, if only for a moment."

"Pûkh brought the sword for my Proving."

"I am aware. Dawn Cleaver told me what is happening."

"It speaks to you?"

"Yes, as it will to you. Listen to me. We haven't long."

"But I have questions." Brendan couldn't believe he was talking to his father. He had so many things he wanted to ask him about, things that he'd thought of since the last time they'd met in the basement of the orphanage.

"I know you have, my son, but I need to speak to you now. I cannot maintain the link between us for long. Listen to me. Do not trust Pûkh. He has plans that serve only himself. No matter what he says, he does not have your welfare in mind."

"I figured that out for myself."

"Clever boy. Do you remember the name I gave you?"

Brendan remembered the afternoon in the basement, when Orcadia fell and Briach breached the veil between this world and the Other Side to initiate him. He remembered the secret name his father had whispered in his ear. He'd never told a soul, just as his father instructed.

"I'll never forget it."

"Share it only with the one you trust most."

"How will I know who the right one is? And why is my secret name so important?"

"It is the key to controlling your heart and soul. Those who know it can make you do what they wish, even bring about your death."

"Seems like a dumb thing to have then. Why did you even tell me?"

Brendan sensed Briach laughing. *"Breandan, you are a delightful boy. I wish we had more time. Just keep the name safe."*

"How will I know when it's time to share it?"

"You'll know. Finally, do not tell anyone about the rock."

"The Snoring Rock."

"Exactly. Tell no one. Especially Pûkh. Now I must go. I haven't the strength to hold on."

"Father!"

"Yes?"

"I … I wish you were here."

"I wish I were there, too. Take care, my son. Farewell."

"No! Wait! Don't … "

The next Brendan knew, he was on his knees on the platform, the sword held in both hands in front of him. His cheeks were wet with tears. He blinked his eyes clear and looked up into the face of his aunt Deirdre.

"Are you all right, Brendan?" Her grey eyes were full of concern. She helped him to stand.

"I'm fine, I think," Brendan croaked. He looked at the sword. The blade glowed with a soft green fire. The humming had faded to a faint echo, a ghost of itself, still present but muted. Brendan lowered the blade and saw that Pûkh was looking at him, the deep brown eyes blazing with a disturbing light. It was the hungry gaze of an animal that promised to devour Brendan if he wasn't cautious. When Pûkh saw that Brendan was returning his stare, his face resumed its mask of amusement.

"You passed my test, Brendan," Pûkh said with a mocking bow. "I am satisfied." He turned to step down from the rock but stopped and shot a smile over his shoulder. "I believe the sword is yours now. I look forward to the day when you come to Tír na nÓg to claim the rest of your father's possessions."

"Don't hold your breath," Brendan muttered. Deirdre crushed him in her arms, planting a wet kiss on his cheek.

"Gross, Aunt Deirdre," he groaned, but secretly he didn't mind at all.

"If the judges are all satisfied … ?" Ariel broke in. He looked first to Kitsune Kai, flanked by her Kappa guards. She nodded. He looked to Deirdre, who merely smiled. Pûkh assented with a wave of his hand. "Then we have heard from all concerned, and—"

"Not all!" a voice called from the crowd.

"Who speaks?" Ariel said sternly. "Show yourself!"

"Gladly!" There was a murmur from the Faerie throng that swelled as a path cleared to allow a single person through. "Give me a moment. I'm not as young as I once was."

The crowd buzzed with excitement as Merddyn clambered up onto the stone. He was dressed in the same tweed suit he'd worn in the doughnut shop. He looked every inch a doddering, elderly man afraid of a fall that might break his hip.

Brendan sprang forward to offer his hand to the Ancient Faerie.

"Thank you, dear boy." Merddyn gratefully took the proffered hand. His knotty hand was surprisingly strong. Brendan realized that any show of frailty was just that: a show.

"You were never young, Merddyn," Pûkh quipped. "But you were always a little feeble."

"I enjoyed your test, Pûkh." Merddyn smiled back. "Test the boy and do some spring cleaning at the same time."

"Well, Merddyn," Ariel said, recovering from his shock at Merddyn's surprise appearance. "I wish you'd told us you'd be here. You could have presided over the Proving. You are the most senior."

Merddyn raised a hand. "Not at all. You've done a wonderful job. I wouldn't have dreamed of usurping your place.

No, not at all. I think everyone has performed their duties extremely well. Kitsune, very entertaining display." Kitsune bowed slightly, hands pressed together. Her guards bowed with her. "Deirdre, very moving. Love a good song!" Deirdre nodded and smiled. "And Pûkh, crafty. I wouldn't expect anything less."

The crowd watched the old man's every move. He made a small circuit of the rock, his head down, seemingly deep in thought. Finally, he stopped in front of Brendan. The sky-blue eyes locked onto Brendan's. They were as kind and as deep as Brendan remembered from the night they'd met in the doughnut shop. Merddyn gave him a wink and turned to the throng.

"You have done very well, Brendan. These tests were difficult and you have passed with flying colours. I, however, would like to claim my right to test you. I am the most senior here. Are there any who dispute my right?" Silence greeted his query. None would dare question the renowned Merddyn. He smiled. "Excellent."

Merddyn stood blinking at the crowd, his eyes watering, as though suddenly confused about what he was doing there.

"Any time, old fellow," Pûkh called. There was a smattering of laughter. Pûkh smirked and acknowledged his admirers.

Merddyn puffed out his cheeks and blew out a breath. "Quite right. A Proving, is it? What shall it be?"

"How about a memory test?" Pûkh suggested, winning more titters.

Merddyn chuckled. "Indeed. Not very spectacular, however. People love a show. How about fire?"

He raised a hand and a sheet of flame leapt up from the ground to surround the rock. The crowd scrambled back to avoid the fire. Brendan felt his eyebrows singe. Just when Brendan was having difficulty breathing in the baking heat, Merddyn dismissed the flames with a flick of his wrist.

"Too gaudy, I think, eh, Pûkh?" The crowd laughed. Pûkh was silent. He gave a little shrug, obviously annoyed.

"Lightning?"

He raised a hand and out of the overcast sky, a fork of purple light scorched the air, slamming into the stone platform between Brendan and the old Faerie. The sonic boom as the lightning struck was deafening. Brendan had trouble keeping his feet, and many in the crowd were knocked to the ground or threw themselves down, covering their heads. Brendan's nostrils sang with the metallic smell of ozone.

Merddyn stood completely unaware of the effect his display was having on the crowd. He shook his head slightly. "No, too heavy-handed. Can't savour lightning. It's over too quickly." He looked at Brendan, his blue eyes no longer the watery orbs of an aged man but instead sharp, clear windows to a well of impossible power. Brendan dreaded to contemplate what the old man might finally decide on.

Finally, Merddyn snapped his fingers. "I know. A test of stone."

Merddyn clapped his hands once, sharply. Suddenly the stone beneath Brendan's feet became like water. In a split second, he sank into the liquid rock. He barely had time to snatch a lungful of air before the fluid rock closed over his head. Once he was submerged, the rock solidified once again, encasing him in a pitch-dark tomb of stone. He couldn't scream. He couldn't even breathe. Brendan felt the icy rock pressing in all around him and prepared for the end.

PART 4

Proving

Yet Another Note
from the Narrator

Oh my! Brendan is trapped inside a stone. That wouldn't be fun, would it? I went through a similar experience once. I was trapped in a closet at my parents' house. My sister, the one who is now in prison, locked me in after telling me to search for hidden Christmas presents. She locked me in there for three days, feeding me only pita bread, a food which can be easily slid under a door. When I was thirsty, she trickled water through the keyhole. Not very pleasant. The water tasted of keys. So, Brendan is trapped in a stone and his friends and his sister are trapped in a tent. I'd prefer the tent, as I'm sure you would, too. I don't like camping, though. I have bathroom issues. Another thing I don't like about camping is that bears have easy access to you. Whereas bears would never trouble you in your thirtieth-floor condo suite, they tend to find tents quite irresistible. The canvas of a tent, in my opinion, is like a giant tortilla wrapper with the human inhabitants as the delicious filling. If I go camping, I usually suspend myself from a high tree branch to sleep. As a result I rarely sleep, and therefore I try not to go camping.

Why not never camp at all? I'd love it if that were possible, but camps have campfires and I'm often called on to tell tales around them. It's a part of my job I don't enjoy. Still, one takes the good with the bad.

I suppose you'd like to get back to the story now. I understand. There's a lot going on. I just thought you'd like to spend some time with me. I get lonely, you know.

Where were we. Oh yes! Brendan has found a way to pass all the tests and looks to be in the clear. He's had a little psychic powwow with his father and earned Dawn Cleaver, a very awesome sword. Just when everything seems to be smooth sailing, up crops Merddyn with a final test. Brendan is trapped in a stone! Will he escape? And what about the little party of spies captured by Pûkh's minions? What of them? We have quite a few unravelled threads to wind up. Let's not waste any time! Onward!

THE ORDEAL OF STONE

Brendan's first instinct was to panic. He wanted to thrash and scream, but he couldn't move. He couldn't even open his mouth to make a sound because the stone had sealed around him like the plastic wrap his mother used to vacuum-seal leftovers.

The darkness was complete. He was physically trapped. The only part of him that could move was his mind. He had to get his thoughts under control, quash the animal terror at being buried alive, and find a way out of his tomb.

Think! Think! Think! This is the test. You have to figure it out or you're finished!

He pushed aside the urgency that was building in his lungs as the breath he'd taken was leached of oxygen. Merddyn wouldn't have done this to him if he couldn't survive. There had to be a way.

He tried to remember their conversation in the dough-nut shop.

"The universe is full of energy. It's alive with it," Merddyn had said. *"We could tap into it readily and manipulate it to do anything we wished."*

Energy? Brendan's mind grasped at that straw. It seemed to be important. *Is that it? Everything is energy. Every leaf and flower. Water and air? Stone?*

Brendan was really in need of a breath now. He had no idea how long he'd been encased in the stone. It could have been a second or a minute. He had to figure it out.

Calm. Calm. Think ... The stone. His mind snagged on the memory of the Snoring Rock. If a rock could speak, could he speak to a rock?

Worth a try. I haven't got any other options.

He focused his mind and shouted. *Hey!*

Nothing.

Hey! Hey! In his mind, he was screaming.

His lungs were burning now. He was seeing spots of colour in his eyes, though no light could exist in the centre of a solid rock. He knew he was failing.

HEY!

Something stirred. A heavy, leaden presence blearily prodded the edge of his mind.

Mmmmmm?

Brendan's heart skipped. Was he actually talking to a rock?

I'm stuck in here, he thought as loudly as he could. *I need to get out!*

There was no response save for a grinding rumble. If anything, the grip of the stone tightened. Brendan's ribs creaked. The threat of suffocation was compounded by the possibility of being physically crushed.

Now that he had the rock's attention, he was finding it hard to concentrate. The claustrophobia threatened to shred his will. The cold weight of the stone all around him was overwhelming.

You're crushing me! I need you to let me out!

Once again, there was no response, no words in his head, but he thought he sensed interest, the ponderous thought process of an infinitely slow and patient mind considering what he was saying. He imagined the mind of the stone, sitting for centuries in one place with only a dim awareness of the passage of time. Such a mind would take a long time to stir. Brendan had to waken the rock somehow.

His eyes were open within the stone but there was nothing to see. Coloured spots began to swim in his vision. He was being asphyxiated. He caught himself slipping into unconsciousness and willed himself to stay awake, to stay focused. Brendan thought about Merddyn and their conversation in the doughnut shop. *All things are connected. No. Not just connected, they are one.* An image blossomed in his brain: a doughnut shifting its shape, becoming a pebble, becoming feathers, becoming a flame.

He mustered his last shred of energy and refocused on the stone. He forced his thoughts to reach out and see it. The rough hardness of the rock filled his mind. He willed himself deeper, like flipping a magnifying lens in front of his thoughts, and saw the minute structures that made up the stone, the glittering crystals stacked and linked. He pushed deeper and saw the structure within those crystals, infinitely tiny bits of matter vibrating slowly as they hung in space, a universe of atoms. Brendan saw what he must do.

What is happening? The rock's voice suddenly filled his head like an avalanche, almost shattering his concentration.

Don't be afraid. Brendan sent the thought laden with soothing emotion. *I must do this to continue in my existence. You will not be harmed.*

It is … strange.

Satisfied that the stone wouldn't interfere, Brendan returned to his task. He saw the tiny particles of matter dangling in space. With a finger of thought, he reached out and tapped one. That particle collided with the next, and the next. A cascade of tiny collisions rippled out from a single atom, a wave of movement that changed the state of the stone.

This is disturbing, the stone's voice quavered. *I fear it.*

Brendan, on the other hand, was no longer afraid. The stone's grip was loosening. He pushed against the stone and it gave way before him.

What is happening? The stone's panic was evident in Brendan's mind. *I don't like it.*

Be calm, Brendan found himself saying. *All things change and all things stay the same, for all things are one.* He didn't know where that thought came from but it felt right.

The stone flowed around him like dense syrup, clinging to his limbs. He leaned into the resistance and forged ahead. Presently, a dim, golden light grew in his path. He pushed harder, throwing himself against his prison. Abruptly, all resistance was gone. He was falling forward onto his hands and knees in the cold mud of the Faerground.

His lungs heaved in air in great gasps. His ears were roaring. Gone was the peace he'd felt locked within the stone. Grey stone dust showered from his hair and clothing. He felt completely drained. Unable to hold himself up anymore, he fell onto his face in the mud.

He must have fainted for an instant because he opened his eyes and someone was cradling his head. A girl was speaking to him.

"Brendan? Can you hear me? Brendan?"

He couldn't focus on her face. "Charlie?"

His vision cleared and he saw it wasn't Charlie but Kim, her face full of concern and a little hurt.

"It's only me," she said. "Are you okay?"

"I don't know," Brendan said, looking up into her brown eyes. "I'm glad it's you."

Kim smiled her crooked smile. A shadow fell across them. Brendan looked up and saw the wrinkled, kindly face of Merddyn. The old Faerie raised his bushy eyebrows and gave a nod. "I am satisfied."

Brendan sat up as Ariel mounted the platform and cried, "It is Proven. Brendan is one of us! He must be assigned to a Clan."

The crowd erupted into hoots and cheers.

Kim helped Brendan to his feet. He was still feeling a little woozy. Suddenly, Og was there, crushing him in a bear hug.

"Och, didn't I just know ye'd do it? Didn't I just?"

"Og, you big lummox. Let him breathe." Deirdre smiled and kissed Brendan's cheek. "Well done."

Greenleaf was at her side, smiling placidly. "See? No need to worry at all. Very impressive! I see you managed to alter the stone. So many Talents."

Brendan suddenly remembered the rock, the fear in its voice. He reached out and laid a hand on the cold, wet surface. Closing his eyes, he thought, *Forgive me. I didn't mean to scare you.*

There was no answer. He only felt vague contentment from the stone and took that as acknowledgment of his apology.

"A drink! A drink is required!" Og shouted. "Follow me!"

Deirdre rolled her eyes. "What a surprise."

Even in the midst of the festivities, Brendan was troubled. Where was Charlie? He scanned the crowd for her, searching for a swatch of black in the riot of colour. He'd given up finding her when he spotted Pûkh standing in one of the alleyways between the tents at the far side of the Faerground. He was speaking with someone, his expression tense and a little angry. Brendan followed Pûkh's gaze and saw that he was speaking to Charlie. She had her hood pulled up, obscuring her face, but he was certain it was her.

What's she doing talking to him?

As Brendan watched, Charlie shook her head vigorously at something Pûkh said. Pûkh's face darkened. He grabbed Charlie's arm roughly and pulled her into the alleyway out of sight.

Brendan wanted to investigate but the crowd swept him on into the open doors of the Swan. He wondered what Charlie was doing talking to the Lord of Tír na nÓg and what she'd said that made him angry. He had to hope that she could take care of herself.

BLT flew in rapid spirals around Brendan's head. "You did it! You did it! You did it!"

"Have you been eating sugar?"

"So suspicious! Can't a person just be happy?" BLT cried. She beelined ahead and into the open door of the Swan. Brendan laughed.

The Swan of Liir was absolutely rammed. A DJ, accompanied by a clutch of more traditional musicians, had set up on the upper gallery. The centre of the room was a heavy mass of dancers gyrating to the music. Og forged a path through the patrons to a corner of the bar.

"Ye'll have a drink, Brendan?" Og ventured.

"Diet cola," Brendan laughed.

Og shook his head in disgust. "It'll kill ya, that stuff."

Saskia was a blur behind the bar, serving drinks at a breakneck pace. When she spied Brendan she stopped and smiled wolfishly. "I heard about the handstand. Well done!"

"He was magnificent, I tell you." Leonard's deep bass rolled over them. He was helping Saskia behind the bar, pulling pints of beer and grinning with his gold teeth all the while.

Kim was silent, standing with her back to the bar and her arms crossed. She sensed Brendan's gaze and gave him a little half smile.

"You were amazing," she said, barely audible over the din of the crowd. "Everybody's talking about you."

Brendan nodded. He leaned in and whispered into her ear, "Thanks."

"For what?" Kim asked.

"For the Dawn Flight. For showing me that there's a good side to all this weird stuff. For being here." He took her hand and squeezed it.

Kim blushed and shrugged, saying gruffly, "Yeah, well. That's cool."

Brendan looked into her brown eyes and smiled. Here in the middle of this hurricane of Faerie insanity, he was at peace.

Suddenly there was a cry from the doorway. The music staggered to a stop as Lugh pushed his way into the pub, scattering the dancers and opening a circle in their midst. He dragged two figures, one in each huge hand, and threw them to the ground. Close on his heels came little Mâya, giggling like a demented child, pushing a boy in front of her.

"Look what we found," she crowed.

"Interlopers," Lugh growled. "They were trespassing on the Gathering."

A fierce cry rose from the Faeries. Brendan was off his stool in a flash and pushing through the crowd, Kim hot on his heels.

Brendan's stomach dropped away when he saw who knelt on the floor at Lugh's feet. Harold, Dmitri, and Chester Dallaire blinked in terror at the sea of hostile faces. Their hands were tied behind their backs, but otherwise they seemed to be all right.

"What are you doing here?" Kim demanded before Brendan could find any words.

"We were worried about Brendan," Dmitri answered.

"You are in mucho trouble, you idiots," Kim groaned.

"We all know the penalty for trespassing on the Gathering." Pûkh's clear voice brought a hushed silence to the room.

"Oh brother," Kim moaned softly. "Here it comes."

"People of the Moon!" Pûkh cried theatrically. He stepped into the circle with his henchmen and addressed the crowd. "The Pact is clear. Our Gatherings are sacrosanct. Intruders are punished. Humans are not welcome here."

"These three meant no harm." Brendan stepped into the ring and faced Pûkh.

"Three?" Pûkh said with an ingenuous look of surprise. "You are mistaken. There are four prisoners." This last he called over his shoulder.

Lugh pushed through the crowd and returned, dragging a reluctant Delia by the elbow. His sister had been bound and gagged. She struggled like a wildcat, but the tall Faerie's grip was firm.

Brendan's face was a picture of shock and dismay. Lugh pushed Delia to the ground and took a place beside Pûkh, his cold eyes glittering in the firelight.

"We all know the penalty," Pûkh said with a savage smile. "They must die."

RESPONSIBILITY

"Whoa, whoa, whoa!" Harold squeaked. "Let's not jump right to 'They must die!' I mean, that's a little over the top, isn't it?"

Brendan couldn't believe his ears. "Are you kidding me? Die? Isn't that a bit extreme? And why are they bound? Untie them right now."

"Our Laws are strict," Ariel interjected. "The People of Metal are not permitted to attend our Gatherings."

"Well, your little Gathering will end on a down note. Killing people's a thing you just don't do at parties."

"This is not a joke, Brendan," Pûkh said. "These people must be dealt with according to our rules. They must be executed."

"That's barbaric! Can't we just Compel them to forget?" Brendan suggested. "I did it before."

"Is that what happened?" Harold demanded. "You made us forget that day? I knew it!"

Lugh lashed out with the toe of his boot, catching Harold in the ribs and knocking him to the floor. Brendan stepped between Lugh and the prisoners. He glared steadily into the pale, dead eyes of the tall Faerie and said with as much steadiness as he could muster, "You kick him again, I'll snap your foot off and feed it to you, you creep."

Lugh's eyes widened slightly, then a slow smile spread across his pale, cadaverous face. "I await your pleasure, young Princeling."

Kim stepped up, reaching for her stick. "We'll give you a two-for-one deal."

BLT fluttered down to Brendan's shoulder, her fists cocked. "With a little extra."

Ariel was about to shout for order, but Pûkh refused to yield the spotlight.

"Such solidarity! Touching." Pûkh raised a hand and Lugh, with great effort, forced himself to step back. The Lord of Tír na nÓg stepped into the centre of the room. Every eye followed him. "Fair Folk," he said, addressing the Faeries crowding in around the prisoners. "This is an important moment. Our sacred Laws have been breached. These intruders show us that Humans have no respect for the Pact. Indeed, they have forgotten all about the bargain they made in the distant past. They keep the Pact only by accident, out of ignorance of our existence. The truth is, only we keep the Pact. We live on the fringes of the Earth, in the cracks, and try desperately to avoid the heavy, clumsy tread of the People of Metal. They take more and more, squeezing the life out of the Earth, choking her without remorse. We have imprisoned ourselves within the Pact." There were murmurs of agreement from some of the gathered Faeries. Brendan looked to Merddyn and saw that the old man was merely watching Pûkh, silently gauging the crowd's reaction to his words.

Pûkh waved a graceful hand at the four Humans huddled together on the floor. "These Humans must be punished. We must send a message. We have to begin clawing back what is ours." The murmurs became more pronounced.

"They didn't know what they were doing," Brendan cried.

"Ignorance is nothing to be proud of," Pûkh scoffed. "But of course, you would take their side. You have a weakness for these creatures. You were raised by them, after all."

"What a total wad," Harold breathed.

"They aren't creatures," Brendan grated. "They are my friends and family."

"I've read stories of children raised by apes and wolves." Pûkh laughed. "Very amusing. I suppose your case is similar."

Brendan was furious. "If you dare to call my parents animals one more time I'll make you sorry."

"Will you, little man?" Pûkh's dark eyes were deadly calm. "Will you?"

Looking into that Ancient face, Brendan saw the dark, capricious, and cruel spirit that inhabited the space behind Pûkh's eyes. He saw the bitterness and the hatred that coiled there behind a facade of sardonic humour and elegance. He saw the power waiting to be unfurled, and his heart quailed.

"Humans!" Pûkh mercifully turned his dark face back to the Faeries in the room. "They cannot be trusted. They are killing the Earth! They will be the death of us all."

Some of the Faeries clapped and cheered, but many were silent, uneasy.

Brendan opened his mouth to speak, but Merddyn's voice intruded. "There is a greater question we are overlooking."

Everyone looked to Merddyn, who was sitting on a stool at the bar enjoying a small glass of wine. "How did they get here? The Wards and glamours surrounding the island discouraged all the other Humans, and yet these four are here. How is that possible?"

Brendan frowned. It was true. He looked at his friends and his sister huddled in a group on the floor. Delia was trying to work her mouth free of her cloth gag. Brendan went to her and pulled it from her mouth.

"I'LL KILL YOU, YOU FREAK!" Delia shouted. Mâya, the object of Delia's wrath, merely giggled and danced from foot to foot. "Cut me loose, Brendan, and I'll kick her ass."

"You're not helping my case," Brendan sighed. "How did you guys get here?"

Dmitri and Harold looked at Chester. Brendan's former nemesis sat quietly on the floor. He looked up at Brendan. "You did something to me on that day you came to the hospital. From that day on I could see … these people."

Brendan shook his head in disbelief. "But what about the others?"

Dmitri spoke up. "We were following you. We were worried that you were into something bad. Well, at least Harold and I were worried about you. Your sister's just a bit of a batch."

Brendan opened his mouth to correct Dmitri, but one look at his sister's angry face deterred him.

Dmitri continued. "We asked Chester to help us and he told us he could see things that we couldn't see. We followed you to the docks and somehow he gave that ability to us when he forced us to see the Ferryman."

"You took a ferry? With the dude with the creepy voice and the hat?"

"Yeah," Harold confirmed. "Total zomboid."

"Ah!" Pûkh sighed. "I see! Brendan is responsible for this breach. Of course, this stands to reason. His foolish insistence on trying to live in both worlds has backfired disastrously. He's not truly one of us despite his miraculous success at the Proving."

"Oh, give it a rest, will ya," Brendan groaned.

"This episode only proves that he is powerful," Merddyn interjected mildly. "Which probably upsets you more than the trespass of these humans."

Kitsune Kai chose that moment to walk into the Swan. "Dear Kitsune," Merddyn said, rising to his feet. "I'm glad you're here. We seem to have a dilemma. These four Human children have managed to trespass upon our Gathering."

Kitsune's dark, almond-shaped eyes narrowed. "Oh. That's not good."

"Pûkh, in his predictably dramatic style, has suggested we execute these Humans out of hand. I believe that's a little extreme. I have another idea that may satisfy all involved. I suggest we retire to a suitable table and discuss my idea."

"Okay, good," Kitsune agreed with a flick of her tail. Deirdre nodded and Pûkh reluctantly shrugged. Together with Ariel, the four judges went to a table in the corner of the room to deliberate, leaving Brendan with his friends under the baleful gaze of Lugh and Mâya.

"Why did you guys do this?" Kim demanded of the prisoners. "You have no idea how much trouble this is gonna cause."

"Back off. Who are these people?" Delia hissed, her eyes darting from Faerie to Faerie. "What *are* you?"

Something about the way she asked the question and the fear in her eyes made Brendan pause. How could he explain this to her? He looked at Dmitri and Harold and saw the same fear there. Chester just gazed back at him evenly. Brendan decided he had to explain who he was, as much for himself as for them. He made a decision about his future.

"I never wanted to lie to anyone," Brendan told them. "And I didn't want anyone to get hurt. I thought that the only way I could keep you all safe, Mum and Dad, too, was by keeping it to myself. Dealing with it myself. But by doing that, I've cut myself off from the support I needed the most. I'm not going to do that anymore ... "

"Brendan, you can't ... " Kim interrupted.

"No," Brendan said. "This is the way it has to be from now on. I want to be honest. I owe it to them."

As quickly as he could, he told them about being a Faerie. He told them about the day when he first knew who he really was. He told them about Orcadia and the lost day he'd stolen from them all. He told them of the world within their world, of Faeries and Trolls and the Quest and his other family and how he tried to balance the two. They sat listening and didn't interrupt. As each detail unfolded, he saw flashes of recognition in their faces as the memories he had suppressed were allowed to surface again.

Kim stood by, arms folded, looking slightly pained. Obviously, she didn't agree with Brendan's choice, but he didn't care. He didn't want to live without his friends and family anymore.

At last, he reached the Gathering and his Proving and the point where they found themselves together again. He finished and waited for their reaction.

Delia was the first to speak. "Mum and Dad are gonna freak."

Brendan actually laughed. "Yeah, I think they are. But you know what, I should have told them right away, ignored the rules. I've really missed their advice."

"I know we're kinda totally screwed here," Harold said. "But this is all pretty awesome. I mean, Faeries? Trolls? It's totally amazing! I wish I had my sketchbook."

Dmitri nodded. "Yes. This is very sweet. I wish I'd listened to my babka more. I always thought she was just crazy. Well, she *is* crazy but she obviously sees things that I can't. The idea that there's a world we can't see, right under our noses … it's really bombed!"

"It's *the* bomb! Not bombed," Chester laughed.

Brendan laid a hand on Chester's shoulder and looked him in the eye. "'I feel worst about what I did to you. I didn't mean to cause you all that pain. I hope you can forgive me."

Chester shrugged and smiled. "I should thank you. I was a total ass before you did what you did. My dad died and I lost it for a while. The only way I could deal with his death was by punishing people. You opened my eyes. I'm glad."

"So," Delia said. "We're all BFFs now. Forgive me if I don't dance around but I'm tied up and someone's promised to kill me. So, if we can move on here, what's going to happen?"

Brendan straightened up. "I'll get you out of this. It's up to me."

Kim touched his elbow. "They're coming back."

The judges filed into the room and stood in the empty patch of floor facing the little group of prisoners. Ariel addressed the crowd.

"After much debate, we have come to a decision. The prisoners shall not be punished for what they have done." Brendan breathed a sigh of relief, but his heart fell when Ariel continued. "The true guilt lies with Brendan Morn. Through his reckless use of powers that he did not understand or control, these Humans were able to intrude upon our Gathering. He is now one of us, subject to our Laws and penalties. He must stand in their stead and face the consequences."

"No!" Kim tried to speak in Brendan's defence, but Ariel cut her off sharply.

"Silence!" The room was utterly quiet. No one breathed. "Brendan must face a trial to pay the penalty for this crime. We have debated the form this trial should take. In the end, we have decided that Brendan must enter the Circle and undergo a trial of combat."

"Are you kidding me?" Harold cried. "Are you people for real?"

"SILENCE!" Ariel's voice was a force of nature, rattling the entire building. Harold quailed. "You have no voice in this, Human! Be grateful that you are still alive. There were those who argued for your execution. Be thankful that more moderate voices spoke in your defence." Ariel's voice softened as he nodded to Merddyn. "Brendan will face an opponent of the judges' choosing and enter the ring. The fight will continue until one or the other is unable to continue. It is our custom and our creed to respect life. We never use the death penalty on our own people. When one combatant cannot continue, the fight is ended.

"According to the Ancient Law of Trial by Combat, should Brendan prevail, he will have paid his dues. If Brendan fails, he will be Exiled. Either way, his friends may go, under a Compulsion of Forgetfulness."

The Swan erupted into chatter and cries of outrage or delight. Brendan let the noise wash over him. He tried to settle his mind for the ordeal ahead.

BREAKING THE CIRCLE

"The judges have chosen their champion," Pûkh announced. The room became hushed once more. "Lugh Silverhair of the Long Arm shall have the task."

The tall Faerie bowed his head and stepped forward. He looked at Brendan, his grey eyes emotionless, and Brendan felt his heart flutter. He steeled himself to hide any outward sign of fear.

"I'm ready," Brendan said. "Let's do this."

Merddyn had been standing back, content to watch events unfold. Now he stepped forward with a piece of vermillion chalk held high. "I will draw the circle." He looked at Brendan pointedly. "Only I can release you from it."

As he bent to begin, Brendan was distracted by Chester's voice. "Brendan!"

Brendan squatted beside his former enemy. "What is it, Chester? I'm a little busy."

"Just be careful," Chester said quietly. "This guy is big and strong with a long reach. Stay outside until you know you have a clear shot, then duck in under and hammer him in close."

Brendan laughed. "I'll try to remember that when he's wiping the floor with me."

"Seriously," Chester insisted. "I do mixed martial arts. I know what I'm talking about. And Brendan?"

327

"Yeah?"

"Thanks. I mean it. I'm glad you helped me out, even if you didn't mean to."

A lump formed in Brendan's throat. He looked at Dmitri and Harold and they both smiled. They were plainly worried, but they trusted him. It meant a lot. Finally, he looked at his sister.

Delia frowned. "You are a total jerk wad, but don't worry about that right now. Whatever you do, don't lose. Mum and Dad won't be happy about it." The look in her eyes hinted that she might not be happy about losing him either. He smiled at her and bent down to kiss her forehead. "You're gonna make me puke," she said and smiled. Brendan laughed and stood up.

Kim was waiting to say something, but instead she threw her arms around his neck and hugged him fiercely. He hugged her back. She broke her grip and said, "Do your best." Then she stepped away.

Merddyn had drawn three-quarters of the circle on the polished floor of the pub. The crowd backed away, forming a ring outside the circle of chalk. Lugh stepped through the open section and entered the circle. Brendan took a deep breath before following. BLT distracted him by fluttering down onto his shoulder.

"I'll come with you," she said, her tiny mouth set grimly in a line.

"No. It isn't allowed."

"But I would if I could."

"I know."

"Be careful."

"I will." Brendan dug in his pocket and pulled out a caramel wrapped in cellophane. He handed the sweet to the Lesser Faerie. It was the size of a cinderblock in her tiny hands. "I was saving it for Christmas but ... "

BLT's eyes filled with tiny tears. "I'll save it for later and celebrate your victory."

She fluttered away, struggling with her burden. Brendan scanned the room for Greenleaf and Deirdre. They waved to him. Deirdre's forehead was creased by a frown and her long, elegant fingers worried at the cloth of her gown. Greenleaf merely smiled and nodded.

Brendan was distracted by Charlie's arrival. She pushed her way through to join Merddyn at the edge of the crowd. Merddyn whispered something in her ear and she shook her head. Brendan was surprised when he saw her look across to where Pûkh was standing and lock eyes with the Lord of Tír na nÓg. Pûkh's eyes narrowed and then he smiled.

Sensing Brendan watching her, Charlie looked up. As soon as she met his gaze, she slid her eyes away, as if she were ashamed to look at him. Brendan wondered again what Charlie's heated conversation with Lugh had been about. Nevertheless, he was glad she was here.

Finally, Brendan looked to Merddyn. The old man's face was serene, his ancient eyes as deep as the sea. When that gaze met his, Brendan felt calmness settle over him as he stepped in to meet his fate, a confidence that he had no business feeling. He wondered if Merddyn had subtly worked some glamour on him. Then Merddyn closed the circle. A sheet of energy flared around the combatants and then died, though both of them knew the barrier was in place.

Brendan faced his opponent. Lugh was easily half a metre taller than him. His long arms hung loosely at his sides in lazy readiness. The long face held no emotion, no clue as to his intention, so when his first blow raked out, Brendan had to react quickly and duck under the massive hand that clawed at him.

The fight was on.

The high stakes and the danger to his friends and sister all helped Brendan slip naturally into a warp state, but it wasn't easy to maintain it. He was distracted by the noise of the crowd shouting around him. He had thought he was home free after the Proving, and he'd let his guard down. Now he was fighting for his life. He had to focus.

Chester's advice to stay outside Lugh's reach was easier said than done. His opponent was so tall that when he swung an arm at him, Brendan had to dance dangerously close to the edge of the circle. He inadvertently bumped the barrier twice, scorching his left shoulder and his ankle. Lugh kept up a constant barrage of attacks that kept Brendan on the defensive.

Brendan's training with Saskia had given him a basic understanding of hand-to-hand combat. But nothing could have prepared him for the ferocity of a true fight. Lugh was intent on hurting him, drawing blood. He wanted to cripple him and finish the fight. Brendan had to want to do the same. He had his hands full just keeping out of the reach of the tall Faerie's hatchet-like hands. Lugh didn't even break a sweat. Brendan had a vague strategy in mind: let the big guy wear himself out early and then look for an opening. Lugh didn't seem to be tiring at all. Instead, Brendan found that he himself was breathing hard. He tried to keep his feet moving and prayed for Lugh to make some mistake he could take advantage of.

At last, he saw a chance. Lugh overbalanced after a massive swing that Brendan managed to avoid by a hair's breadth. Brendan stepped inside the arc of the swing and cocked his fist for a blow to Lugh's face. For a fraction of an instant, Brendan hesitated. He'd never hurt anyone on purpose in his life. After landing a blow on Saskia, which had been more accidental than premeditated, he'd been guilt-ridden, though she'd laughed it off. Now, faced with the prospect of hurting another person intentionally, he balked.

Lugh took advantage of his scruples, cracking Brendan in the cheekbone with a sharp elbow on his backswing. Brendan felt like a train had hit him. Pain exploded in his head and he staggered against the barrier of the circle. Purple lightning stung his back and flung him to his knees.

He was dimly aware of the crowd shouting, some in delight, most with dismay. He had trouble clearing his vision. He tried to stand, but his limbs seemed to be hung with lead. Something warm dripped from his chin. Raising his face, he saw something looming over him. A building? It was a tree, and the tree had a face. The tree was grinning.

"Brendan!" a voice was shouting. "Get up, Brendan!" He knew that voice. He blinked. Some of the fuzziness left his vision, but his head still buzzed. He saw the tree wasn't a tree at all but a man. The man was rearing back with his arm raised. That didn't seem good to Brendan. It seemed very bad. The arm, a giant fist attached, raced toward his skull like the head of a sledgehammer. Brendan frowned.

I don't think so, he said to himself. He saw the air in front of the fist. He saw the tiny particles of matter that formed the air he breathed and the vastly larger motes of dust that ploughed through them. He sent a thought out to the particles, suggesting they gather in the path of the fist. They did so, reluctantly at first, but then quicker and quicker until they formed a dense, gluey soup, slowing the fist in its advance. Brendan praised the tiny particles, thanking them for their help. They responded by calling more of their fellows, and soon the fist was completely arrested.

Lugh's fist halted a centimetre from Brendan's forehead. The silver-haired Faerie's face was a parody of shock. He looked at his fist in disbelief. He leaned with all his weight on the invisible barrier but to no avail.

The crowd watched in awed silence. They couldn't understand what was happening. Only Merddyn and Pûkh, standing side by side, were not shocked. There was an eager gleam in Pûkh's eye and Merddyn smiled benignly.

"He sees," Pûkh whispers.

"Indeed," Merddyn agreed. "He has the gift."

Brendan, in the meantime, was finding it difficult to keep his little army of particles motivated. This was not their normal state and they longed to be free.

Just one more thing and you are free, Brendan assured them. He asked them for one last burst of cohesion. The particles responded. They collapsed inward around Lugh's fist in a sudden spasm. A loud crack resounded in the hushed silence.

Lugh howled in pain. Brendan thanked the particles and allowed them to disperse. While Lugh staggered back, cradling the wrist of his now fractured hand, Brendan stood and wiped the blood from his cheek. The pain had dwindled slightly to a dull throb. He watched his opponent take deep breaths, trying to calm the agony in his broken hand.

"Do you give up?" Brendan asked. He didn't see how Lugh could continue the fight.

Lugh raised his grey eyes in an icy glare. Those eyes were so full of hatred that Brendan almost took a step backwards. Lugh let his useless hand drop to his side. "I do not yield to you, Princeling. I will not yield while I still breathe."

"This is a fight until someone can't fight anymore. You're badly hurt. Don't you think you should give up? Save us any more pain?"

Lugh grinned, showing sharp incisors. "You believe what you will, little boy. We're in the circle now. None may interfere." Reaching inside his tunic, he drew out a long, glittering dagger, its blade an opaque sliver of crystal. The edge flashed in the light, hungry for blood. The crowd erupted in shouting and jeering.

Brendan looked to Merddyn, but the old Faerie didn't move to intervene.

"You must stop them," Deirdre begged him.

"Have a little faith in your nephew, Deirdre," Merddyn said.

A roar washed over the crowd and the people parted to reveal a lion with gnashing golden teeth. It launched itself against the barrier. The barrier erupted in purple energy, flinging the magnificent creature back, its pelt smoking. Immediately, the beast sprung to its feet and launched itself against the circle again with the same result. Saskia was instantly at the lion's side.

"Stop, Leonard," she cried, burying her face in the lion's mane. "You're only hurting yourself."

The creature's fur rippled and flowed until Leonard lay there in her arms, his skin scorched and his hair smoking. His eyes were wild with fury.

"This isn't what we agreed!" Deirdre cried. She lunged forward but Greenleaf caught her arm.

"The circle is closed. It cannot be broken," Greenleaf said.

"This must stop," Ariel demanded.

"There's nothing that can be done," Pûkh said, his face a mask of regret. "The circle is sacred."

"Merddyn," Deirdre begged. "You must break it."

Merddyn shook his head. "I will not interfere. This, more than any other trial, is Brendan's true Proving."

In frustration, Deirdre spun away, her fists clenched.

Kim stepped up to the barrier behind Brendan and whispered urgently, "Break the circle, Brendan. You've done it once. You can do it again."

Brendan shook his head, never taking his eyes from Lugh's. "I don't cheat."

"Wake up. Lugh's already broken the rules. He and Pûkh want to kill you. They're afraid of you."

Brendan spared her a glance and a wry smile. "You think so? Wait until I beat this creep. They'll really have something to be scared of."

"Brendan … " she pleaded, but he cut her off.

"No, Kim. I've got to show them that no matter what they do, they won't beat me. If I lose, it doesn't matter anymore."

He saw Mâya's eyes widen with hungry delight and stepped aside instinctively as Lugh lunged at him. The blade skittered with a flash of sparks across the barrier where Brendan had been standing the instant before. Lugh checked his momentum, spinning and crouching with the knife extended, his broken hand hanging limp at his side.

Brendan sidestepped lightly around the outer edge of the circle, keeping his opponent as far away as he could.

"You can't run forever, Brendan Morn."

"Come over and get me, Lugh. I'll break your other hand for you," Brendan said with a bravado he didn't really feel. Lugh was still plenty dangerous, and the knife was an unwelcome addition.

Without warning, Lugh lunged at him. Feinting high, he came in with a sweeping slash that Brendan almost managed to avoid, willing himself to become as thin as possible. Despite his best efforts, the tip of the blade opened a long wound down the ribs of his left side. White fire sizzled in the wound. Lugh didn't give him a respite, slashing back and forth swiftly. Brendan, his T-shirt quickly soaking through with his own blood, wove back and forth, finally leaping up, stepping onto Lugh's shoulder, and pitching himself into a somersault. He landed easily on the floor in a crouch. Lugh spun to see Brendan waiting for him and sneered before renewing his assault.

Dmitri, Harold, Chester, and Delia huddled together and tried to watch the contest. It was impossible to follow. The movements of the combatants were blindingly fast, blurs of speed punctuated by moments of relative stillness as Brendan and Lugh sized each other up between attacks.

"I had no idea Brendan could do this stuff," Dmitri said in awe.

"I wish I had my sketchbook," Harold said wistfully.

"You guys!" Delia sneered. "This isn't some school field trip. This creep is trying to kill Brendan!"

"What do you care?" Dmitri said quietly. "He isn't really your brother."

Delia glared at Dmitri. "That's not fair."

Chester shrugged. "Don't worry. He'll beat this dude."

"How can you be sure?" Delia asked.

"He's made the guy mad and anger makes you sloppy," Chester explained. "Wait and see."

Inside the circle, Brendan and Lugh were partners in an intricate dance. They improvised the steps as they went along. It was a strange sort of dance with the partners never touching, avoiding each other by the narrowest of margins. Lugh's face was a mask of anger and frustration while Brendan's held a blank calm, though the sweat was streaming down his face. The battle went on and on with neither gaining the upper hand. Both were suffering from their injuries but they didn't let up. Brendan had lost his aversion to harming Lugh after the knife became part of the equation. Now it was a matter of survival.

In the end, Brendan's injuries caught up with him. Blood from the wound on his ribs dripped down his side and onto the floor, making the footing slippery. The floor was one massive sheet of polished oak, nurtured and crafted by generations of Masters of the Green Arts. The surface was slick at the best of times, but with his smooth-soled running shoes and the blood on the floor, Brendan lost his balance and fell with a crash onto his back. In an instant, Lugh was on him, slamming a massive foot onto his chest and pinning him to the floor. Brendan strained against the weight, but the tall Faerie held him fast. Brendan ceased struggling and looked up into the face of his assailant.

"Well fought," Lugh said with a leer. "Few could press me the way you have. You should be proud of yourself in the moment before I send you to the Far Lands."

"Stop this!" Deirdre begged from outside the circle. "This is pointless."

Pûkh shook his head in a show of great sorrow. "Alas, what can we do? The circle cannot be broken."

BLT raced around and around the circle. "Do it, Brendan! Break the circle!"

Kim shrieked at Brendan. "Break it! Break it, Brendan! Show him!"

Brendan turned his head to Kim. "Don't be afraid. It's all right!" He turned back and smiled up at Lugh. "Do your worst."

Lugh grinned savagely and raised the dagger above his head.

Brendan didn't move. The fear he had felt when he'd stepped into the circle with Lugh was gone. He felt only calm. During the frenzy of the fight, he had found a quiet place in the centre of his heart. He recalled the song that his aunt had drawn from him during the Proving and let it fill his being, guide his movements. He recalled the conversation with Merddyn in the doughnut shop and had a moment of wonderful clarity. He saw the blade glinting in the light and the strings of tiny crystals that made up its structure. The words he had heard while trapped inside the stone came to him with sudden urgency. *All things are one.* As the deadly point of the dagger quivered, ready to seek his heart, Brendan saw what he had to do. The thought of it made him laugh.

Lugh paused, a puzzled expression on his dour face. "Why do you laugh?"

"All things are one!" Brendan said. He grinned like a fool and focused his mind, seeing the change he wished to make and willing it to occur.

Lugh's weapon shimmered, quivered. Then the solid substance of the dagger began to flow into a new form.

The blade shortened and melted into an altogether new shape. Where there had once been a deadly blade in Lugh's hand, there was now a ring of pastry with multicoloured sprinkles on top. Lugh stared in utter disbelief.

"What is this?" he roared.

"A doughnut," Brendan replied placidly. "A Hawaiian doughnut, to be precise." Brendan shot a glance at Merddyn, who was grinning with delight.

Lugh, infuriated, crushed the doughnut and flung it away. He bunched his good fist and prepared to drive it into Brendan's skull. Suddenly, the wood beneath his feet changed state and became a sticky brown liquid. Lugh sank into the floor up to his ankles, and the wood became solid again. His eyes went wide with surprise. Brendan smiled grimly and swung his arm with all his strength, striking Lugh's shin just above the floor. There was a loud crack. Lugh howled in agony and fell backwards. The floor flowed open beneath him as he landed and then washed back over him, hardening so that his entire torso was trapped in the wood. Of his head, only his face was exposed. Terror filled his eyes.

Brendan, exhausted from the effort, pushed himself to his feet. He stood over Lugh, who strained futilely to free himself from his woody prison.

"This fight is over," Brendan said.

Lugh ceased to struggle. He glared up at his vanquisher, cold grey eyes filled with hatred. "It has only begun, Brendan Morn."

Brendan turned to the circle and looked for a weakness in the chalk line. Seeing a slightly narrow section, he reached out with his toe and wiped away the chalk. The circle flared and died.

Instantly, a streak of light shot into the circle, driving into Lugh's face. BLT kicked and punched his vulnerable, prominent nose with wild abandon. "That's fer cheatin', ya big wally!" she cried.

"Get off me, tiny demon!" Lugh protested.

Brendan laughed. She had obviously been unable to resist eating her caramel. For once, he didn't mind.

RULES

Now that the danger had passed, Brendan was overwhelmed by a wave of exhaustion. He tried to walk to the judges but staggered. Kim was instantly at his side to catch him. He leaned on her as he made his way to where the judges awaited him. The crowd parted, oddly hushed and watchful. He had done things that were thought to be impossible, and now they felt trepidation at being too close to this young boy.

He squeezed Kim's hand gratefully and nodded. She stepped back, within easy reach if he needed her support.

Pûkh rose to his feet and addressed Brendan with a warm smile. "Well done, Brendan. You have certainly Proven beyond a shadow of a doubt that you are your father's son and a Prince of Ancient Lineage. Congratulations. You may now be accepted into a Clan as a fully fledged Faerie. I extend my invitation to join the Clan of Tír na nÓg! We can use someone with your gifts.

"There is no Clan with more power and influence than mine," Pûkh continued. "You can be at my right hand. You have proven that you deserve the rank." He cast a scathing glare at the helpless Lugh.

Brendan couldn't tell if Pûkh's sincerity was just a show or he really meant what he said. Lugh was Pûkh's minion, and he'd tried to kill Brendan. The Lord of Tír na nÓg could not be trusted.

"I don't care about your Clans. I won," Brendan said brusquely. "Now let me and my friends and sister go."

"Of course," Ariel agreed. "They will be Compelled to silence and freed."

"No," Brendan said. "That isn't going to happen."

Ariel's pale face went even paler. "Those were the conditions of the bargain. They will be upheld."

"That bargain was finished when Lugh pulled the knife," Brendan said coldly. "The rules have changed. It's time for things to be different." Brendan looked at the faces of Og, Deirdre, and Greenleaf, full of pride and relief at his survival. Merddyn winked, and Kitsune Kai's dark eyes were watchful, expectant.

Brendan turned to address the silent throng.

"I've done all that's been asked of me. I've tried to follow the rules. I'm not going to do that anymore. These people …" He indicated the little group huddled on the floor. "They are as important to me as any Fair Folk will ever be. I love my new family. Aunt Deirdre, Greenleaf, Og: they have been as kind as they could be, but my Human parents were there in all the hardest parts of my life. They thought of me as their son. They took me in when my real father put me aside. I owe them everything." He smiled at Delia. "My sister has been … a sister. We've fought tooth and nail. We've shared our childhoods and grown up together." He turned to Harold and Dmitri. "My friends were there for me when I thought I was alone in the world. They risked their lives to help me, and I repaid them by not trusting them enough to tell them my secret. Well, that's going to change. There will be no secrets anymore."

Outraged voices cried out in protest. Brendan waited until the shouts ran their course. "I know many of you will disagree with me. Many of you will feel threatened. I want you to understand that I don't plan on going out into the world and revealing your existence. Humans aren't ready for that. Many of you feel they'll never be ready for that. I think you're wrong."

He looked to Merddyn. The old Faerie was watching him with bright eyes, eager to hear his words. He smiled encouragement.

"The truth is, the Human world needs us. The Pact was a mistake. It was born out of fear and mistrust. Our two tribes, the Humans and the Faeries, were never meant to be separated. We're two sides of the same coin. Faeries say Humans are destroying the world with their progress and their pollution, but then Faeries turn around and copy their technology, ape their ways. It doesn't make any sense. We sit back and despise the Humans when we should be helping them, guiding them.

"That's why the Pact must change. Faeries were never meant to be alone. Humans were never meant to be alone. We were meant to share the world, to complement each other. Instead, we've both been going our own ways, and now the Earth is suffering for it."

Brendan addressed Pûkh directly. "You, living alone in your fantasy world. You are the worst of all. You cut yourself off from what's real and cling to the Old Ways. That's absolutely the wrong thing to do. You can never return to the past."

Pûkh sneered, his normally handsome face distorted by disdain. "You have no idea what you're talking about. Humans can't be trusted."

"What? They're less trustworthy than you? I doubt it." Brendan laughed.

Mâya danced from foot to foot. "Let me kill him, my Lord! Let me!"

"Try," Brendan said evenly. He didn't want another fight, but he wasn't afraid of it either.

Mâya stilled herself but her eyes beamed hatred at him. Brendan ignored her.

"I'm going to leave now. I am taking these Humans, my friends and family, with me." He bent down and untied Delia as he spoke. When she was free, she worked on the others' bonds. "You can do whatever you want. I'm going to live my life as I see fit. No Pact is going to rule me. I will judge each moment as it comes and do what I have to to survive and to be the person I want to be. My mum and dad are probably wondering where I am. I'm going home. It's Christmastime and I'm going to celebrate with them. I don't need a Clan. I have a family and I have friends."

"Without a Clan," Pûkh said flatly, "you will die."

Brendan's voice was equally cold. "I'll take my chances."

He swept his eyes over the group. Deirdre's face was unreadable. Greenleaf's held a gentle smile. Ariel's face was cold and distant. Pûkh's lip was curled in disdain. Merddyn smiled openly. Brendan looked for Charlie but caught only a glimpse of her as she disappeared in the excited crush of Faeries.

His eyes fell on Kim last. She smiled at him, an exasperated, eye-rolling smile that made him laugh in spite of the pain that racked his ribs.

Brendan turned to leave.

"Brendan!" Merddyn's voice stopped him. The Ancient Faerie held the wrapped bundle that was his father's sword out to him. Brendan hesitated. Did he really want it?

Without it, he wondered if he'd ever be able to speak to his father again. Still, the sword scared him a little.

"Come," Merddyn said softly. "It is yours. No one else here may touch it."

What made him decide to take the sword was the annoyance on Pûkh's face. If taking it would upset the King of the Everlasting Lands, he had to do it. Brendan took the sword, sensing its power and energy through the wrapping. He nodded to Merddyn. Without a word, he joined his companions and walked out of the Swan of Liir. He wondered if it would be for the last time. Then he decided he didn't care. He was with those who mattered most to him. If others didn't understand, so be it.

They made it outside the door without incident and Brendan breathed a sigh of relief.

Later that night, safe at home, Brendan lay in his bed, content. He and his friends had split up and gone to their separate homes with the plan to meet up after Christmas to talk about what had happened. The boys promised Brendan that they wouldn't share their experience with anyone without discussing it with him first.

As he lay in the darkness thinking about what had happened at the Swan, he felt suddenly bereft. In the darkness, alone, doubts began to crowd in. He wondered, had he been too hasty? Had he burned his bridges? He had to believe he'd done the right thing. He knew he was right. All he'd seen since he'd become aware of the Faerie world convinced him that the Fair Folk and Humans could not continue living the way they were. The Earth was suffering because the two were not in tune.

The enormity of the problem suddenly pressed down on his chest. He felt completely alone. Sure, he had his friends Harold and Dmitri and now Chester. He had his sister, although he still wasn't sure where she stood. She'd been unnaturally quiet and subdued all the way back and had gone straight to her room. He hoped she would come around.

He heard his parents come home, giggling and a little tipsy. His father started singing and his mother shushed him. They came up the stairs to their room, trying to be quiet but laughing like children. Brendan smiled and a weight lifted. He loved them so much.

The road ahead was uncertain but he wasn't afraid. Well, not much. He had friends and he had family, and that would have to be enough.

He must have fallen asleep because the tapping on the window startled him awake.

He sat up and banged his head on the ceiling. Cursing, rubbing his head, he went to the window and raised the sash.

Charlie clung to the drainpipe outside the window. Her dark hair was once more in a mohawk and she was wearing a torn T-shirt, even though the temperature was well below freezing. Tweezers curled around her shoulders, his bright red eyes blinking at Brendan.

"Hi," Charlie said.

"Hi," Brendan answered. "Do you want to come in?"

"No thanks. I just came to say goodbye."

"Why? Where are you going?"

"Just away for a while. I need a little time to think."

Faced with the prospect of not seeing her, Brendan suddenly felt sad. He should have been glad to be rid of her after all her harassment. Now here she was going and he wished she wasn't. "Where will you go?"

Charlie shrugged. "No idea yet. Just away. Merddyn hasn't made any progress finding my parents."

"I'm sorry," Brendan said and meant it. "I wanted to thank you for your help. Without you, I don't think I could have made it through the Proving."

"You did very well."

"Where were you?"

"What?"

"Where were you, during the Proving?"

Charlie turned her face away.

Brendan pressed. "I really needed your support."

"I thought I'd done enough for you."

"Yeah." Brendan nodded. "I guess you did. I missed you, that's all."

Hair shadowed her features but Brendan could tell her mouth was set in a hard line. "I had to check on some things."

"What kind of things?"

"Personal things," Charlie snapped.

They were quiet for a moment. The drainpipe creaked gently under Charlie's weight. The wind gusted, a few flakes of snow clicking on the windowpane.

"I should be going," Charlie said.

"Wait," Brendan said. "I saw you talking to Pûkh. What did he want?"

"Oh." Charlie's eyes slid away. "Nothing in particular. He was just asking about you. I … didn't tell him anything. Nothing important."

"Be careful," Brendan said. "You can't trust him."

Anger flashed in Charlie's sapphire eyes. "Why don't you just mind your own business, Brendan? Go inside to your *family*. I'll take care of myself."

She turned to go but Brendan held her arm. She reluctantly looked into his face.

He thought of the moment in the basement. The sadness of her voice as she sang. "I'll miss you."

Tears stood in her eyes.

He felt his heart skip a beat at the sight of that beautiful face, glowing in the moonlight. He remembered running through the park under the stars.

"Be careful," he said.

She smiled. Gracefully, she slid down the pipe and landed lightly on the snowy ground. With a final wave, she set out across the backyard. Her body shifted and she became a stag that vaulted the back fence with ease and grace. In a flash, she was gone.

Brendan stared at the place where she'd disappeared for a long while. Just as he was about to close the window, a streak of light flashed out of the night sky and into the bedroom.

"Oh, boy!" BLT crowed. "You really stirred them up, I tell you!"

"Shhh!" Brendan hissed. "People are sleeping."

BLT looped the loop and lighted on the bed. "Ariel is totally furious with you, but Deirdre and Greenleaf are talking him down."

"What did Merddyn do?" Somehow, the enigmatic old Faerie's opinion mattered most to Brendan.

"He said he accepted your decision, which seemed to settle most people down. Then he up and left. He's gone!"

"What about Pûkh?"

"Old Puke was strange. He didn't seem all that angry. He actually seemed pretty mellow about the whole thing. Lugh is still stuck in the floor, though. Not a happy camper."

BLT started to laugh and it was infectious. Brendan found himself laughing along.

"Brendan?" His mother's voice from the hallway below interrupted the mirth. "Is someone up there with you?"

"No, Mum!" Brendan answered. He was going to tell them everything. Just not tonight.

"Why are you laughing all by yourself?" she asked. "That's a sign of insanity, you know. Should I be worried?"

"No!" Brendan called, smiling. "I'm just watching a video on my iPod. Sorry!"

"Time to sleep!" He heard her footfalls as she headed back to her room and closed the door.

"If you're going to sleep, I'm gonna go out," BLT announced. "I'll just have to celebrate for the both of us!"

BLT zipped across the room and waited at the window as Brendan opened it enough to let her escape. He then went and sat on the bed.

He thought about what his mother had asked him. *"Should I be worried?"*

He suddenly felt confident and optimistic. *I really did give the correct answer. No.*

He reached under his bed and slid out the cloth bundle that held his father's sword, now his sword. He peeled back the cloth and revealed the hilt. He clasped his fingers around the smooth crystal and it settled easily in his hand.

As soon as his skin touched the hilt of the weapon, he felt its contentment. It was like holding a cat that falls asleep in your arms. The sensation was so comforting that Brendan felt calmness wash through him. He closed his eyes and cast his mind out, searching for his father's presence, but there was only the soft purr of the sword. He lay back on his bed and let the hum lull him into sleep.

FAMILY

The next few days passed in happy preparation for Christmas. His mother was cooking and baking. His father spent a lot of time in the basement studio finishing his final Christmas projects for clients.

Brendan had to explain the bruise on his face from the fight with Lugh, but he claimed a clumsy fall on the ice as the culprit. His past history came in handy as an excuse. Luckily, he was now a quick healer thanks to his Faerie blood. He would have had a hard time settling his mother down if she'd seen the gaping, bloody gash the night before. The slash along his ribs had faded. By Christmas Eve it was just a red weal along his side. Fortunately, that was easily hidden beneath his shirt.

He was a bit worried that Delia would refute his story, but the next morning she didn't say a word. She didn't even make fun of him for being a clumsy jerk. She was in a pensive mood. If his parents hadn't been so busy, they might have wondered about the reason, but as it was, they didn't.

Brendan tried to have a conversation with Delia on a number of occasions, but she refused to talk about what had happened. She would simply walk away, hide in her room, or turn up the TV volume to a level that discouraged conversation. Finally, Brendan just left her alone. She needed to deal with the situation whatever way was best for her. He had to be patient.

He called his friends and checked up on them. He wanted to make sure they weren't harassed by any Fair Folk. They assured him that they were fine, and they made plans to get together after Christmas.

While his parents were busy preparing the house for the holidays, visiting friends, and taking care of their own business, Brendan spent a lot of time thinking about how he was going to break the news about his secret life to them. He imagined all the possible ways he might broach the subject, what to say and where to say it. He sat in his room, lying on his back and listening to music. He went for long, meandering walks through the city.

By the time Christmas Eve arrived, he still had no idea how he was going to tell his mum and dad what was going on. He was sitting in his bedroom in the dark, racking his brain. There was no obviously easy way. Every time he even imagined broaching the subject, his stomach tied itself in knots.

"Hey." Delia's voice was soft but he almost leapt out of his skin. Her head poked up through the trap door in the floor.

"Jeez, Dee. You scared me."

"Sorry. You could take it as payback for the other day." Delia smirked.

"Okay." Brendan smiled. "What do you want?"

"Just to talk," she said. "Can I come in?"

"Yeah."

Brendan couldn't remember the last time, if ever, Delia had been in his room. Sure, she'd stuck her head in and yelled plenty of times, but she'd never crossed the threshold completely. He watched as she climbed up and looked around.

"This is kind of cool."

"Thanks."

"It smells like teenage boy, though."

"That's what I am, so …"

"Yeah," she said. "About that … " She pulled the only chair over to the bed and sat down opposite Brendan. "It's dark."

"Yeah. I like it dark."

"People like … like you can see in the dark pretty well though, eh?"

Brendan laughed. "Yeah. People like me can."

Delia blushed and looked a little uncomfortable. She looked around. "Where's the little one … What's her name?"

"BLT?" Brendan offered. "She's out with some of her friends tonight."

"Good," Delia said firmly. "'Cause I wanted us to talk."

Brendan didn't answer beyond raising his eyebrows. He just waited.

After a few seconds, Delia seemed to make up her mind. "I'm sorry I haven't been talking to you lately."

"That's not unusual, really …"

"Just shut up, okay? I've been thinking a lot about all this and I needed some time to myself to work it out. It's a lot to take in. I thought you might be a criminal or a drug dealer or something. But it turns out …"

"It's worse?"

"Yeah. But it's also much better. It's incredibly amazing, in fact! I know you're probably worried about telling Mum and Dad."

"I'm crapping my pants, actually."

Delia shook her head. "You shouldn't be. You shouldn't be afraid of talking to them and telling them what you are."

"Wouldn't you be?"

"Probably. But then I'd remember that they've never once been angry about who I am. They get angry about what I've done but never at who I am. They've always supported us whatever we've wanted to do. If you think they'd be angry about what you are then you're selling them short."

Delia stood up and went to the stairs. She descended a couple of steps and looked back up at Brendan. "Just like you sold me short." She stepped down out of sight.

Brendan sat in the darkness thinking about what his sister had said. Every word of it was true. Imagine how much easier the last weeks would have been if he'd had his Human family's support. He should have told them right away. He made a decision. He picked up the phone and dialed Kim's number.

Two hours later Brendan sat in the living room watching his dad playing the guitar and singing "White Christmas." At the Clair household, Christmas Eve was a night for family. His mother laid out a delicious spread of cold food and baked treats for everyone to enjoy. There was the antique punch bowl full of eggnog, his mother's mother's recipe. His father brought out the guitar and forced everyone to endure a sing-a-long of Christmas carols. A fire burned in the fireplace. The Christmas tree was illuminated and all the decorations hung, each one a family memory of years past. Delia was rolling her eyes as Dad impersonated Bing Crosby. Everything was in place. Brendan felt a swell of happiness. He was making the right decision. He had no idea what would happen to him in the days and years to come, but at this moment everything was right in the world.

The doorbell rang. His father stopped playing and looked at his watch.

"It's kind of late," he said. "Are you expecting anyone?"

His mum, frozen in the act of lowering a plate of cookies to the coffee table, shook her head.

"It's for me, Dad."

His dad laid the guitar down. "Is it Charlie?"

Brendan felt a pang of sadness. "No. She's ... Her family's away."

"Who, then?" Brendan's mum headed for the door. Delia stood up and joined Brendan and his father as they moved into the cramped foyer. Delia caught Brendan's eye and winked. He smiled back.

Brendan reached the door first, and after a deep and steadying breath, he turned the knob and opened it wide.

Standing on the front porch were Aunt Deirdre, Uncle Greenleaf, Uncle Og, and Kim. They all wore subdued Human clothing and looked so awkward standing on the stoop, wrapped bundles in their hands, that Brendan almost burst out laughing.

"Brendan?" His mum said. "Who are these people?"

"This is Kim. Dad's met her. This is Og and Mr. Greenleaf. And this is—"

"Deirdre D'Anaan?" Brendan's father said incredulously.

"Hello," Deirdre said with a wry grin.

"What's going on here, Brendan?" Mrs. Clair demanded sternly.

"Mum ... Dad ..." Brendan began. "I have a lot to tell you ..." And for the first time, he found himself looking forward to it.

Epilogue

Pûkh watched impatiently as the stone was pried from the ground and dragged to the horses chosen to bear it. Straps were wrapped around its girth and secured with powerful Wards.

Pûkh sighed. He was content. He had seen the boy Brendan and tested him. The boy had the power. He had the gifts of the Ancients. He would be the key to Pûkh's plan. With Brendan's help, he would find the other Prisoning Stones and release the most powerful of the Dark Ones. They would be grateful to him. He would be rewarded for his patience and loyalty. Merddyn would be humbled. No one would stand in their way as they took this world back for the People of the Moon. The People of Metal would be crushed underfoot forever.

It galled him that he needed Brendan Morn, but the boy had the true gift. Pûkh was powerful, but there was something absent in his power, some flaw in his Art that crippled his attempts to find the stones on his own. Brendan was pure. He could sense the Wards on the stones that Merddyn had hidden so effectively for all these years.

Pûkh turned his head to gaze upon the slump-shouldered figure of Charles.

"You have been very useful, Charles."

"I told you I'd show you the stone," Charlie said sullenly. "I have shown you. Now, fulfill your part of the bargain."

"Not yet," Pûkh laughed.

"But you said you'd tell me who my parents were."

"And I will, as soon as I have assured myself that this really is a Prisoning Stone. I must return to Tír na nÓg to do that."

"That wasn't our agreement."

Pûkh laughed. "And you are such an honourable creature? Betraying Merddyn and Brendan both? What would they think of you, if they knew what you were doing?"

Charlie sneered. "Merddyn has made me wait for centuries. He keeps promising me he will find my parents but he never does. I can't wait any longer. Brendan ..." She stopped, biting her lip.

"Yes?" Pûkh prompted.

"I swore I'd never tell you anything about him. I told you about the stone, not him."

"Hairs are being split, dear. Hairs are being split."

The stone secured, the Wild Hunt prepared to rise again into the night sky.

"All right," Charlie said, ignoring Pûkh's laughter. She stood in silence for a moment before clambering up into the saddle of a fierce-looking horse. Its red eyes rolled back until she stroked it and whispered into its twitching ear. Instantly, the creature settled. "Let's go then."

Pûkh barked an order and the company mounted up. They rose into the sky, the Prisoning Stone in tow.

Acknowledgments

I would like to thank all of those who get books into the hands of readers: the printers, the proofreaders, the editors, the librarians, and the small book shops that have really been the link between the kids who want the stories and the writers who want to tell the stories. Thank you. And also, I want to thank squirrels ... because no one ever does.